Scott Mowbrey

ARLINGTON

Hope you enjoy my
first Novel.

Thank you for being a
positive influence to
Mark these past
few years.

Scott Mowbrey

Tellwell Talent
www.tellwell.ca

ISBN
978-1-77302-371-7 (Hardcover)
978-1-77302-370-0 (Paperback)
978-1-77302-372-4 (eBook)

Preface

Scott Mowbrey is a new author who brings a compassionate sensitivity to all of his characters and a brutal realism in both story and dialogue.

His book, *Arlington* is the first of a trilogy.

Arlington is a character-driven dramatic thriller with a tinge of horror, comedy and romance.

Scott is currently writing the sequel, *Jack Singer*, with an expected release date of December 2017 and the series conclusion, *The Ambassador*, with an expected release date of December 2018.

Acknowledgments

A very special thank you to all of my pre-readers.

My amazing wife and soulmate of 31 years, Kim.

My wonderful mother Angie and a very special young man, my son Mark.

To my inspiring Project Manager, Natasha. Thank you for your graciousness, diligence and support.

Thank you all for your time and encouragement throughout this challenging and truly rewarding experience.

This book is further dedicated to my sister Karen who passed away Oct 6, 2016. Karen's loving, tender soul enriched the lives of everyone fortunate enough to have encountered this truly remarkable and memorable woman.

"Never Forgotten, Always Loved."
Scott Mowbrey

ARLINGTON

A book written by Scott Mowbrey

For My Wife
Kim

Chapter One

IT STARTS

"Ouch, that hurt!"

"That's what she said."

"Jack, you're such an asshole, can you not take one day off of your misogynistic bullshit? Why did you even bring me here today, and why couldn't I bring Rose? No one likes you, you have no friends, you force a crew member here with you every day—why can't you understand that no one wants to come here with you?"

"Oh, and Jack, if you make one more joke about my chest, I'm going to break your fucking nose."

Debbie, now taking a pause from her diatribe against Jack, is examining the bite mark just under her left breast and is thinking that it really, really hurt!

"Relax Deb, it was probably just a sand ant. Just put some bug spray on it. And trust me, you did not want to bring 'what's-her-face' here today. She's better off on the Miranda."

"For the 100th time, her name is Rose, asshole. I'm done with this shit. I'm leaving now Jack."

"Were not done here yet, Deb. It's a long walk back to the Miranda and let's not forget who's got the keys to the Jeep."

"Something's not right, Jack. I'm really not feeling well."

"You probably didn't drink enough water. Did you eat this morning?"

"Yes, I ate, and I've had plenty of water. You're the one dressed head to toe in ninety degree weather. Come on, Jack, cut the shit, I'm really starting to get dizzy. Please take me back."

Jack, oblivious to Deb's verbal assault, continues the search for his quarry. It is what has brought him to this Argentinian sand dune in February every day for the last two weeks.

He is, however, extremely interested in what Debbie is physically experiencing and quizzes her about how she is feeling.

"Tell me exactly what you are feeling right now, Deb. Are you feeling any numbness around the bite mark? Is there an itchy burning feeling? How is your vision and depth perception?"

"Fuck you, Jack. I'm walking back to the boat."

"Listen to me, Deb. Just go sit in the Jeep or, better yet, find a nice tree to sit under. If you give me half an hour, I'll take you back."

Deb, now shaking and covered in sweat, ignores everything Jack is saying and makes her way out of the bunker and back onto the goat trail. She looks at where the hot sun is in the sky, then checks her watch and determines which direction will take her back to the boat. Deb has chartered herself a path back to the Miranda, more or less.

Looking behind him and realizing Debbie is nowhere in sight, Jack shouts out to deaf ears "It's a five kilometre walk, Deb."

Within twenty minutes, Jack has finished his final rigging and starts to pack up all of his gear. He takes notice that Deb didn't grab any of her gear.

He reaches back into his rut sack and pulls out his satellite phone then places a call.

"It's done. You have maybe an hour. Make sure everyone is alerted and everything is ready to go." Without waiting for a reply, Jack promptly disconnects the transmission.

Thirty minutes later, the Jeep loaded, Jack is ready to go find Debbie. He's hoping she at least went in the right direction, which is toward the sea and the salvaging boat that has been her home for the last two years.

The only thing left to do before he heads off is to finally get rid of the layers of clothing that have been clinging to him during the past two very hot weeks.

Starting at his feet, Jack begins to disrobe. Off come the thermal socks, long underwear, long-sleeved shirt, neck and head scarf and thick military camouflage gear that he'd been wearing overtop. He throws on a clean pair of shorts and a muscle shirt and discards his worn attire back into the pit of the sand catacomb.

Once in the Jeep, Jack slams it into first gear and starts ripping down the goat path. Jack is suddenly overtaken by a cold as ice, chilled to the bone trepidation, that he had better find Deb or all of this would have been for nothing.

Jack who is not normally attuned to such emotions as fear, regret or remorse, realizes that if he doesn't find Debbie soon, he's going to have to explain himself to the only man he respects more than himself, the Ambassador.

Thankfully, two turns down the goat path and about a half a click down the road, he spots Debbie. She is staggering forward across the sand. At least she is moving in the right direction, toward the sea. Actually, it is more incredible that she is moving at all.

Now only five metres behind Debbie, Jack slows the Jeep to a crawl and just sits watching her go forward, then sideways, then forward again. The first thing that catches Jacks attention is the way the sun is glistening off Debbie's toned and bronzed back, and the second is the fact that she is not wearing a top.

The tight black muscle shirt that Debbie had been wearing when Jack picked her up that morning, is now wrapped around her head, as Debbie is seeking any relief she can get from the hot Argentinian sun and the suffocating humidity.

Normally, Jack would be thrilled at the chance to view what he calls the best all-natural double Ds he has ever seen. But right now, his only concern is staying on mission. Which means getting Debbie back to his compound.

Jack continues following Debbie in the Jeep and is now only a few feet behind her. Debbie seems oblivious to the fact that a Jeep is behind her, let alone Jack himself. Debbie continues her slow methodical, disjointed shuffle of forward movement. She pauses briefly and raises her left breast. She examines her bite mark, which to Deb's bewilderment, is no longer emitting pain.

Jack removes his sunglasses, wipes his sweat-drenched face with a rag and continues to scrutinize Debbie's every movement. Growing weary and impatient under the hot sun, he glances down the goat path, just beyond Debbie, and spots a deep crevice in the road that is now only a few feet in front of his somnolent quarry.

He starts his countdown, "Three, two, one and down she goes." As if on cue, Debbie tumbles forward into the crevice and is now lying face down on the ground.

Jack turns off the Jeep and riffles through his rut pack for a clean shirt. He climbs out of the Jeep and with some trepidation starts walking toward Debbie. Debbie is not moving at all, and Jack starts to think, "Shit, she better not be dead."

"Deb? Deb? How you doing down there? Did you decide you were going to take a bit of a nap? How about we get you off this road and into the Jeep, okay?"

Debbie slowly rolls onto her back and raises an arm to block the blinding rays of the sun so she can see who is above her. With a big smile on her face, she finally grasps who is straddling her with a leg on each side of her waist, and says, "Oh hi, Jack. Is Rose with you?"

"No, Deb. Rose is back on the Miranda, remember? Why don't we get you outta that hole and into the Jeep, then we can both go see Rose together."

Jack reaches down and grasps Debbie's five-foot-four, 120 pound frame under each arm pit and hoists her back onto her feet.

"There we go. Doesn't that feel better?"

Deb is still gawking at Jack as he carries her back to the Jeep and plops her onto the front seat. "Damn your good looking, Jack. Too bad you're such an asshole."

"Yes, Deb, I am an asshole. Now why don't we wipe some of this dirt and gravel off of you so we can put this shirt on? You don't want to get a sunburn, do you Deb?"

Jack starts to put his shirt over a listless and now almost comatose Debbie and, while covering her topless form, Jack is thinking to himself, "Absolutely spectacular."

Reaching down, he puts a seat belt around Debbie. He grabs a towel from his rut pack and props it under Debbie's head to try and keep her comfortable.

Debbie is now sitting passively in the Jeep. Her facial expression contains a whisper of a smile and she appears to be relieved, now that she is under Jack's care.

Jack notices her eyes are flickering between open and closed, as if she is desperately trying to hang on to consciousness. She is white as a ghost and dripping with sweat. Jack reaches over and puts his hand on her forehead, which, contrarily, is cool to the touch.

Jack takes a quick glance around the jeep and is confident nothing has fallen out.

"Ok Deb, Let's go see Rose."

Barely cognizant, Debbie is still able to utter her calling card for dealing with Jack over the last two weeks, "Drop dead Jack," and with that final remark, she is out like a light.

Jack manages a smile but is masking a deep sadness as he looks over at Debbie and the condition she is in. He knows what the prognosis is for her and he is still wrestling with the fact, that of all the crew to pick from on the Miranda, why it had to be Debbie's turn to join him today.

Jack starts the Jeep and heads back down the goat path. As he glances at his watch, he calculates it has only been an hour since Deb's abrupt departure. He also estimates they are still only about half a click away from the Argentinian sand dune.

With dusk approaching, Jack picks up the pace and turns on the radio as loud as it can go.

Within five minutes, a loud distant rumbling explosion can be heard from the direction of the Argentinian sand dune. It is loud enough to startle Debbie awake. With her eyes closed and her body still, she manages to ask, "What was that noise Jack?"

"Just firecrackers, Deb. Go back to sleep, you'll be with Rose soon."

Debbie languor's back to a state of somnolent sleep.

Jack turns on the Jeep's headlights as the sun begins its decent against the backdrop of the Atlantic Ocean. Ten minutes down the path, he slows the vehicle and comes to a stop. Ahead of him is a fork in the road. The path to the left takes them back to the sea and the Miranda.

Debbie's boat, the Miranda, should be back from that day's salvaging run. Debbie's dog, Rose, and her ship crew family will be awaiting her arrival and their nightly trip into the local town of La Plata for a warm meal and plenty of drinks.

But with the previous day's discovery, Jack knows today's trip only has one path, and that is down the road to the right. Which takes them back to his compound, a farther seven kilometres into the barren mountainous region of Bahia Bianca.

Chapter Two

THE COMPOUND AND CREW

With the sun now setting, Jack spots lights off in the distance. As he reaches the lighted area, Jack approaches a man stationed at the side of the road. Spotting Jack, the man swiftly lifts up a rudimentary log-crafted barrier. Jack flashes his fist to the man and proceeds past the barrier and into the base camp that has been his home for the last two months.

The compound is about half the size of a football field and is tightly concealed inside a mountainous enclave, with only one way in and one way out.

It consists of a series of plywood-structured military-style buildings. There are communal sleeping quarters, a canteen, a bathroom and shower facilities. There is also an operational crisis room with satellite phones and Internet, as well as a manager's office with private sleeping quarters.

For security reasons, the mountain locale has been specifically chosen for its lack of cell phone coverage.

The compound is surrounded by ten-foot-high light towers with over seventy-five, 500 watt stadium bulbs. A dimmer switch has been rigged to lessen the current in the evenings.

In the farthest corner of the camp are a row of generators capable of providing enough juice to power a small town. Discretely placed behind this stack of generators is a large white hermetically sealed medical tent, equipped to handle any crisis.

Considering the size of the compound, it is operationally efficient and manned with a skeleton crew of seven.

Mr. Singh is the camp's cook. He also poses as the self-proclaimed group therapist, relationship counsellor and morale booster. Often at the chagrin of the rest of the group.

Mr. Singh was born into poverty in Mumbai, India. At the age of seven, Mr. Singh and several of his cohorts were caught stealing a can of petrol for his mother's small burner stove. The police brought him in and when they asked him his name, he proclaimed, "I'm Mr. Singh." From that day forward in the slums of Mumbai, a seven-year-old boy was known as Mr. Singh.

In his late teens, still living and working in the slums, Mr. Singh, worked on a crew that reclaimed scrap metal from the dumps of Mumbai.

When he was eighteen, Mr. Singh was miraculously able to leave the slums and join the Indian military. The local military outpost had received a call from a government official with instructions on where Mr. Singh could be located. With some prompting about his potential new career and a bit of negotiation on Mr. Singh's part, he was ultimately recruited.

The camp's I.T. geek and maintenance guy is Norwegian-born Sven.

Sven ended up in America where he studied Computer Science at Texas State A&E.

The thirty-four-year-old, six-foot-five handsome blond Norwegian joined the US Airforce because he wanted to fly choppers. With three tours in Iraq and Afghanistan where he flew Blackhawks, Sven achieved his goal.

Bored with the rules and regulations of the military, he got his honourable discharge and went back to coding for an I.T. company in Texas.

The doctor on site is the smarmy Dr. Skeane, an American doctor who had ran his own family practice until he was disbarred six months ago for running illegal OxyContin sales out of the back of his clinic.

He was able to avoid jail time when an unsolicited high-priced lawyer appeared on his behalf. The lawyer had arranged a back room deal with the D.A. that stipulated Dr. Skeane take the job his lawyer has lined up for him outside the country. Dr. Skeane knew he wouldn't do well in jail, so he took the deal.

During the disbarment proceedings, there was also a small class action developing involving improprieties between the doctor and several of his female patients. Criminal proceedings were suspiciously dropped after his disbarment and promise to leave the United States. Dr. Skeane can look forward to a huge civil case should he ever return to America.

Rick and Carl are the camp's security team. Both are Israelis and former members of Mossad. Their days consist of working out, cleaning their guns and fighting each other over who gets the midnight shift manning the front security gate.

Jack has had to step in more than once when their fisticuffs descended into broken-bone or neck-snapping ferocity. At least these two are smart enough to realize that when Jack steps in to stop them, the fighting ends, quickly and politely.

Victor Constantine is the compound's reigning manager of operations. Nothing happens in camp without his say-so. Except, of course, when Jack is in camp. Then Victor is relegated to the position of village idiot.

Victor was a major in the Greek army. He did not earn his position; Victor's military career was propelled ahead by his Colonel Father.

Victor is a large, round, stout man. Each morning he carefully flings his side hair over his bald head to give off the illusion that he still has hair. Victor spends his days looking at pornography on his laptop and sweating.

Jack is still out on the fact if Victor is officially retarded.

With the exception of Dr. Skeane, what all of the crew members have in common is that during the course of their military careers they all had a chance meeting with the Ambassador, or one of his recruiters.

Some of their careers continued and some were recruited on the spot. But once you were on the Ambassador's radar, joining his team was inevitable.

The rest, as they say, is history.

There are no local Argentines on site, and to date there have been no unexpected visits from the local police. The existence of the site is only known by a few select members of the Argentinian government.

Back on the road, Jack slowly maneuvers the Jeep through camp, and as he approaches the back of the medical tent he is met by Dr. Skeane and Victor.

Jack takes a long solemn look at Deb, cognizant of the fact that she has not moved a muscle or spoken since the explosion back on the goat path.

"Let's get her inside, and keep your slimy paws off her, Skinny,"

Jack says to Skeane.

Jack calls Dr. Skeane 'skinny'. His nickname for the toothpick size, pale white, hand shaking, clumsy, perverted Doctor.

Jack and Victor each grab an end of Deb while Dr. Skeane unzips the tent, opening and closing it tightly behind them.

Jack promptly undresses Deb and puts her in a hospital gown. She is placed on her back and into a bed you would find in any modern hospital.

Dr. Skeane is staring at Jack while trying to determine what type of a mood he is in. Skeane makes a timid facial and hand gesture that he has to slide Deb's gown down in order to inspect the bite mark.

Jack says, "Just do it, Skinny." The Doc moves Deb's gown down and lifts her left breast.

"It's starting to stream, Jack. We can still stop this," he says.

Jack moves his hand to the back of his waistband and pulls out a custom-made silver .45 with a cherrywood handle. He steps toward Skeane and sticks the muzzle hard into Skeane's forehead.

"I can do it now, Skinny, or I can do it later. You choose."

"What do you mean 'later,' Jack? Jack … what do you mean 'later'?"

Jack smirks and puts the pistol back in his waistband.

Jack says to Skeane, "Get her intubated, gas her up, put in an IV, secure her to the bed and start a chart. I want her stats written down every thirty minutes."

Dr. Skeane starts setting Debbie up for what would appear to be an indeterminate stay.

Jack is now walking around inside the medical tent always keeping one eye on Dr. Skeane. He is opening drawers, looking at all of the various medical equipment and drug vials, checking and tapping gauges. After a very short period of time, Jack's patience with anything Skeane is doing—just the thought of being in the same room as him—starts to make his skin crawl. He draws it all to a quick end.

"Okay, enough, Skinny. Go get your kit. You're gonna be sleeping in here from now on. I want her watched twenty-four-seven. You keep me apprised of any changes and I mean any changes. If she as much as farts, I wanna know about it. If I come in here and find anyone here but you, Skinny, you will answer to me, and that includes you, Vic."

Victor knows when to pick his battles when dealing with Jack and he sets aside his embarrassment at being dressed down in front of Skeane. He strategically turns his anger to the Doc in hopes of getting on Jack's good side, if only for a moment.

"Doc, I will wait here for you while you get your gear, and hurry the fuck up. I got miss July waiting for me back in my room."

The doc quietly mutters, "Pig."

After having "dressed down" Skeane, Victor is now feeling his misguided courage come back to him and he says, "And Jack, stay the fuck out of my office."

As per usual, Jack does not acknowledge anything Victor has to say and he's looking around the tent with an amused, puzzled look on his face when he says, "Was someone talking to me?"

Jack and the Doc are now walking back to the living quarters, Jack thinking about how sweaty, dirty and tired he is. He needs a hot shower, a warm meal and a few hours' sleep, but Jack knows he has a couple of phone calls he must tend to, before he can seek any form of personal relief.

Dr. Skeane is still nervously ruminating over what Jack meant by "now or later."

Both men approach the front of the living quarters where Jack has made sure they are strategically bunked at opposite ends of the structure. About to go their separate ways, Dr. Skeane mutters, "Uh, Jack, can I speak with you for a moment?"

Jack stops, and with a blank look of indignation says, "What?"

Dr. Skeane starts off with, "You know, Jack, we are both in this together and I would appreciate if you wouldn't speak to me like that in front of the crew."

Jack moves forward and puts his hand on Skeane's shoulder. He leans in and quietly and assuredly whispers into his ear, "If you touch her, I will kill you. Good night, Doc."

Dr. Skeane shuffles into his bunk and closes the door.

Jack enters his bunk and takes a long look at his rack and sighs.

He throws his rut pack on his desk and reaches down and unlocks his foot locker. Pulling the .45 out of his waistband, he places it into his locker and grabs a snub nose .38 nestled in a shoulder holster and puts it on his desk.

Jack sits on his cot and reaches for his pack. He digs around and pulls out a seventy-year-old rusted metal cigar case. It is the first time he has been able to have a good look at his find since he recovered it earlier that morning with Debbie.

It is a cigar case that can hold up to six cigars—most notable is the German World War II swastika on both sides of the case. Jack briefly ponders whether to open it again but decides not to. He places it at the bottom of his foot locker, and locks it back up.

With the cool Argentinian air now permeating the night, Jack grabs his dirty camo gear from the floor and gets dressed. He leaves his bunk and heads to Vic's office. He still has a couple of calls he has to make, both of which he's not looking forward to.

On his way to Vic's office, Jack spots Mr. Singh and Carl sitting outside the canteen on a couple of lawn chairs.

Mr. Singh shouts to Jack, "Is it true Jack? Are we 'status go'?'

"That's right, Cookie. We are green-light operational."

Jack is aware that outside of Skeane, Vic and himself, the rest of the crew really don't know what that means. But Jack thinks Singh is a good man and treats him as such.

Jack is now standing in front of Vic's office and he shouts back to the men, "Mr. Singh, is it too late to order a steak?"

Mr. Singh shouts back to Jack, "You going into Victor's office, Jack?"

"Yes, I am Mr. Singh."

"In that case, Jack, I will make you a beautiful ten-ounce porterhouse with all of the trimmings."

"Thanks, Cookie. About an hour, all right?"

"You got it, boss."

As much as Jack has grown to like Mr. Singh over the course of the last several months, he has always chosen to call him Cookie.

Upon their first meeting, Jack said, "Hey pal, no offence, but I'm not going to call you Mr. Singh. I hear you're the cook, among other things. How does Cookie work for you?"

"Anything you want, Mr. Jack," Cookie replied. "Mr. Singh can get tiring for me, as well."

A smiling Jack said, "just call me Jack, Mr. Singh."

Both men concluded to themselves, "This guy might be okay."

Jack reaches Victor's office and grabs the door handle, only to find the door locked, as usual. He reaches down about three inches below the lock, makes a striking blow with a palmed fist and the door pops open. Jack steps in, turns on the lights and locks the door.

Pulling a ten-inch bowie knife from his waistband, he walks over to Vic's filing cabinet. He bends down to the floor and jimmies open a precut piece of plywood. Hidden inside are several of Victor's favourite twenty-year-old bottles of Scotch.

Jack grabs a glass and sits down at Victor's desk. He helps himself to a cigar and pours himself a triple. Jack lights his cigar and, while leaning back in the comfortable chair, he plops his dirty boots up on Vic's desk.

Jack decides he is going to take a few minutes and enjoy his cigar and Scotch before he makes his calls.

He notices Vic's pile of porn magazines on his desk and grabs one. After a brief moment of rustling through the pictures, he throws it back on the pile and thinks to himself, "None of these chicks come close to Deb."

Jack's thoughts turn to the Ambassador. With no family of his own since he was seventeen, the Ambassador has been the closest thing to a family member that Jack can remember.

Since Jack sees the Ambassador as a father figure, he wonders to himself why he is so apprehensive about placing the call?

Is it the nature of the mission? The end game?

Or is it Deb?

After a few minutes, Jack realizes he has to face the inevitable and he reaches for the phone. He places the call and the Ambassador quickly answers.

"Hello, Jack."

Jack responds, "It's done."

There is a long pause at the other end of the line. Frustrated, Jack grabs one of Vic's porn magazines and starts reading an article.

The Ambassador finally responds. "Did you retrieve the package, Jack?"

"Yes, Mr. Ambassador, but we have a casualty, sir."

"Jack, I need to let you know that Victor called me after you called the compound about your retrieval of the package. I have decided to send you some help. You remember Ivanna, don't you Jack?"

"We don't need any help, Mr. Ambassador, and I'm not working with that psycho bitch again. We talked about this, sir."

"Language please, Jack. I thought I taught you better than that."

"My apologies, sir."

"Now listen closely, Jack. We need more security, so whatever issues you and Ivanna have, you will both have to put them aside for me. Is this true, Jack?"

Jack responds with a begrudging, "Yes, Mr. Ambassador."

"By the way, Jack, good news. They should be there in a few hours. I placed the call when you breached the target yesterday."

Jack thinks to himself dispassionately, "Yeah, great news."

The Ambassador further states, "I am really sorry about the casualty."

Jack interjects, "What about the Miranda?"

"You have not phoned them yet, Jack?" The Ambassador says. "This should have been your first call! Call them as soon as you hang up, and you already know what to say."

Before Jack could ask his final question, the Ambassador hangs up.

The words "Why Deb?" die on Jack's tongue.

Jack takes one last swig of Scotch, butts and pockets his cigar and chuckles as he leaves the office. He leaves the almost empty bottle of Scotch on the desk, the lights on and the door fully open.

Still pissed off at the news of his arriving guests, Jack decides his call to the crew of the Miranda can wait until after dinner. Instead, he'll take a shower and then hit the canteen for one of Cookie's fabulous steaks.

Showered and dressed in a clean set of clothes, Jack makes his way across the compound and into the canteen.

Sitting on the eight-foot-long picnic table used as the camp's dinner table is a solitary place setting. Mr. Singh has laid out a steak knife, a bright shiny fork, a glowing candle and an actual white cloth napkin.

The rest of the crew are standing and smiling and have been awaiting Jack's arrival. Jack takes his seat of honour and then Sven and Carl, and a pissed-off-looking Vic, start a chant:

'Cookie, Cookie, Cookie.'

Appearing from out behind the grill area, Mr. Singh approaches Jack and places in front of him a medium rare twelve-inch porterhouse steak, a basket of mollejas—a local sweetbread—potatoes, carrots and for dessert, a bowl of blood red cherries from the Argentinian region of Patagonia.

"Thanks, Cookie, it looks like you really outdid yourself this time."

Mr. Singh responds, "Anything for you, Jack. But, uh, Jack, rumour around camp is you won't be going back to the job site anymore. Did you find what it was you've been searching for? Will we be going home soon, Jack?"

Victor quickly chimes in before Jack can respond. "All right boys, it's been a long day. Let's hit the rack so Jack can eat in piece."

Jack responds, "It's okay, Vic. I could use the company tonight."

Just as the men are taking their seats around Jack, Carl gets a call on his security headset. "Hang on guys, it's Rick." He jumps up from the table. "We got lights approaching."

Jack, aware of who it is and why they are here, stares down at his absolutely delicious cornucopia of food. The only food he's had in front of him since his 5:30 a.m. breakfast.

Jack says to Mr. Singh, "Cookie, can you keep this warm for me?"

"You got it, Mr. Jack."

Carl asks, "Are we expecting company, Jack?"

"I just found out myself not more than an hour ago. Tell Rick to hold them at the gate and that I'm on my way. Carl, you come with me, the rest of you go grab some sleep. I have a feeling it's going to be a long day tomorrow."

Jack and Carl head off to meet the new arrivals. As Jack approaches the gate, he does a double take when he sees what's parked behind the barrier.

"Carl, I know I'm tired, but are you seeing what I'm seeing?"

"If it's an Argentinian ambulance, then yes, we are seeing the same thing, Jack."

Even having known the Ambassador since he was twenty-one, Jack still finds himself impressed by the things the Ambassador is able to pull off.

"A fucking ambulance, Carl." Jack shakes his head and throws a wave toward the vehicle.

As Jack approaches the driver's side door he is not surprised to see the man-hating, ultra-feminist bitch, Ivanna, behind the wheel.

Completely ignoring Ivanna, Jack spots the most competent member of his former unit sitting in the passenger seat and says, "Bricks, you mean bastard, what brings you out here?"

"Good to see you, Sarge. The Ambassador said you needed the best."

"Then why did he send you lot?"

Jack peers back into the ambulance and says in a mocking tone, "Hello, Ivanna. I thought you would have just flown here on your broom."

"Good to see you too, asshole."

"Who do you got in the back, Bricks?"

"We got Stryker and Stevens."

"Good stuff. Rick, you can lift the gate and let these bums and the witch in."

Jack says to Ivanna, "Park in front of the bunks. It's thirty feet ahead of you. You can store your broom wherever you like." He then turns to Carl and says, "I'll take care of it from here Carl, you can go get some sleep."

"Sounds good," Carl replies, "*Sergeant.*" He says this last word in a mocking tone.

Up until now, the rest of the crew has only known Jack as Jack.

Ivanna parks the ambulance, and the crew of four disembark and begin removing all of their gear from the back. All four are fully equipped in non-descript military attire and are strapped with Russian-made Kalashnikovs and various sidearms.

Jack approaches the group and gives each of the men a hard, solid embrace. Jack opens the door to an empty bunk and says, "Ivanna, this one is yours. Why don't you get some sleep and let the men talk?"

Ivanna, tired from the trip and in no mood to spar with Jack, grabs her gear, heads on in and closes the door. She quickly reopens the door and says to Jack, "Where's the shitter?" Jack points and Ivanna closes the door again.

Bricks says to Jack, "Why do you have to ride her like that, Sarge? She's not that bad."

Jack just smiles back at Bricks and says, "What do you know about the mission?"

Stryker jumps in and says, "we weren't told anything and don't know shit, Sarge. I'm just happier than fuck to see you running this shit show."

Stevens interrupts the discussion and chimes in, "How's the local pussy situation, Sarge?"

Jack, beleaguered by the day's events, momentarily envisions himself sitting at Cookie's table and eating his twelve-ounce porterhouse steak.

Bricks, with a look of unfamiliar concern, peers over at Jack and says, "Sarge, you all right?"

Jack slowly returns to reality and with a conspicuous glare, he peers into the eyes of each member of his new team, still getting used to the fact of them being here at all.

"We are a closed site, men. No one comes in and no one leaves."

"Great, just fucking great, no pussy," Stevens says.

Bricks reaches down into his pile of gear and pulls out a large hard- covered case. He hoists it up and hands it to Jack. "What have you got us into, Jack?"

With the case in hand, Jack walks over to an outdoor bench and opens it up. In it he finds half a dozen individually sealed paper- thin hazmat suits. He thinks to himself, "What are the other six unlucky bastards going to do?"

"Okay, it's late, guys. We got food and hot showers if you want. Then find yourself an empty bunk and we'll look at this with new eyes tomorrow."

Bricks, sensing Jack has reached his "do not cross the yellow line" limit, chimes in, "We'll see you in the morning, Sarge."

The four men embrace again and Jack helps them load their gear into their rooms.

"We'll have a sit rep and a tour of the compound at 0600, men. Get a good night's sleep."

Jack has only one more thing to do before he sits down to Cookie's porterhouse, and that's to call the Miranda and let them know Debbie won't be coming home tonight.

Jack, knowing another late night Scotch and cigar raid are out of the question, makes his way toward the conference room and the only other satellite phone in the camp.

Out of the corner of his eye he notices a light still on in Victor's office, so he starts to head that way.

As Jack gets closer, he can see a figure sitting in a chair and a sporadic amber light flashing. It's Victor, sitting outside his office, drinking a glass of Scotch and smoking a cigar.

Not wanting to deal with Victor tonight, Jack bows his head and hastens his pace toward the conference room.

In a loud, drunken pitch Victor says, "Jaaaack, there's something I need to tell you."

"Not tonight, asshole. I got a call to make and a steak waiting."

"Uh, Jaaack, it's about your call," Victor says, then mutters to himself, "You're the asshole, Jack."

Jack reaches Victor and says, "This better be fucking good, Vic."

"First off, Jack, my name is Victor. Not Vic, not asshole and not retard."

"Fuck you, Vic, I don't have time for this. Why don't you drag your fat, pathetic, drunken self to your bed. We all have a big day tomorrow."

Jack starts to walk away and Victor replies, "I guess you don't want to know that Mr. Ambassador called."

Jack stops in his tracks and turns back to Victor. "Jesus Christ, Vic. You better not be fucking around!"

"No, no, no, Jack. Mr. Ambassador phoned maaany hours ago and you know what else, dick brain? He was calling to speak to me, not you."

"Just spit it out Vic, before I seriously consider giving you a smack."

Victor, now sensing he has reached his limit with Jack's patience, replies, "Mr. Ambassador knew you wouldn't phone the Miranda so he told me to tell you that it is all taken care of."

Jack steps closer to Victor and says menacingly, "Start talking, Vic, or you'll pass out where you're sitting."

"The Ambassador told ME to tell YOU, that the Ambassador personally phoned the captain of the Miranda. He told the captain that he personally got a call from Debbie's sister in Texas. That Debbie's father was in a car accident and was gravely injured. He ended by telling the captain that they were able to secure an afternoon flight for Deb, and she is on her way back to Texas. Th-th-th-that's all ... Jackmeister."

"The captain knows Deb would never leave her dog, you fucking retard."

"Ah, Jack ... once again the Ambassador is one step ahead of you. He told El Capitan that due to quarantine laws, Deb agreed to let Rose stay on the Miranda and that she would be back with them as soon as she can.

"Anyway, Jack, the Miranda is not going to be an issue. I was also instructed to contact the Ambassador's government man here in Argentina and have their docking and salvage permits revoked. They were to be given six hours to leave or have their boat seized. I told the port master to just make something up, and according to my watch, they only have a couple more hours to be out of port."

Victor keeps on chirping, "Remember, Jack, if it wasn't for the Ambassador funding the Miranda's little 'pretend' treasure hunt, none of them would be here at all. And we would not have that innocent young girl dying in that tent right now, would we, Jack?"

Jack's first thought is to break Victor in half for not telling him hours ago about the call. But he can't deny that there is some truth to Victor's last statement. He acquiesces, thanks Victor for the information and says goodnight.

Victor, forever being the dick that he is, has one final comment, "Oh and, Jack, I forgot one little detail. The Ambassador will be here himself tomorrow at 4:00 p.m. He says he doesn't need to be picked up—apparently he's coming with a new crew or something? I hope they have sleeping bags and a tent, cause I'm not sharing my fucking office. Goooood night, Jacko."

Simply too tired and hungry to smack Victor, Jack continues his walk toward the canteen. He is hoping that the part about the Ambassador coming here personally is just Victor being his usual, delusional, drunkard asshole self. He has often suspected his own mother regretted ever popping him out.

Jack finally arrives back at the canteen and finds Mr. Singh hunched over and asleep at the picnic table. Jack gently wakes him and after what seems like an eternity, is finally able to convince Cookie that he can get his own meal from the oven, and that he does not have to come wake Cookie up when it is time to put the dirty dishes away.

Jack grabs his dinner from the oven and eats it standing over the canteen counter. He makes a commitment to himself to try to enjoy Mr. Singh's labour as he pushes the day's events out of his mind.

Then, having finished his delicious meal, he takes the time to wash the dishes and writes on the daily menu white board:

Thanks Cookie

Jack

With one final task to do before he gets some much needed rest, Jack decides he'd better check on Debbie and Dr. Skeane.

As he's walking through camp, Jack is starting to feel a bit better. He has accomplished his mission for the Ambassador, which means no more trips to the hot, dirty sand dunes. He has just had a delicious, filling meal and tomorrow he will start making plans for an exit strategy. The Ambassador took care of the dreaded phone call to the Miranda, and aside from waking to Ivanna tomorrow, maybe things won't be so bad after all.

Jack arrives at the medical tent and walks around back to the entrance and unzips the tent. Just as he is entering, he sees Dr. Skeane wiping something off Debbie's now fully bare chest.

As Dr. Skeane spots Jack, he quickly covers Debbie back up with her hospital gown.

"Uh, oh, hi, Jack, I was just …" Skeane is now shivering in panic and at a total loss as how to finish his sentence. He starts backing up and is trying to prepare himself for the inevitable.

Jack slowly and purposely walks over to the Doc. He grabs his wrist and while twisting it behind the Doc's back he maneuvers his body behind him and performs a standing rear naked choke. All while not saying a word. Jack systematically chokes Dr. Skeane into unconsciousness.

Jack guesses that at two o'clock in the morning while thinking the rest of the camp was sound asleep, Dr. Skeane thought jerking off over Debbie's comatose body onto her bare breasts was a good idea.

Jack pulls up a chair and places it right next to the doc's head. He is now leaning forward and glaring down at the unconscious Doctor Skeane. The doc's been out about ten minutes, and with Jack growing more and more impatient, he grabs a water bottle and pours the entire bottle onto Skeane's crotch.

Dr. Skeane regains consciousness and immediately recognizes the situation he has put himself in. Still on his ass, he starts crawling backward away from Jack while at the same time wiping his crotch and trying to assemble his hair and regain his wits.

Jack now stands up and continues to watch the doc's backward descent.

"Jack, listen, I'm sorry, I didn't think anyone would be by this late."

Jack continues to watch Dr. Skeane, still not saying a word.

Still slowly crawling backward, Dr. Skeane backs himself against his bunk and slithers into a sitting position. He starts pawing for something in his backpack.

Jack finally speaks. "I only have one question for you, Doc. Did you touch her?"

"No, no, Jack, I didn't touch her. I'm sick, Jack. I'm sick, you know that. The Ambassador knew that when he hired me. I'll get help Jack, I promise I will. I'm sick, Jack, and I'll get help."

Dr. Skeane now finds what he was looking for in his pack and his entire demeanor quickly changes. With a sly, knowing grin on his face, he slowly and methodically pulls out his own .45 and is aims it at Jack's head.

Jack, unmoved by the turn of events says, "I will ask you one more time, Skinny. Did you touch her?"

Dr. Skeane does a double take, looks at his gun and looks at Jack. Then, with a bewildered look on his face, he says, "Do you not see this gun, Jack? What are you, fucking crazy? Do you think I won't shoot you dead, you arrogant asshole?"

Jack, now about ten feet away, slowly starts to walk toward the doc.

Skeane raises the gun higher and more pointedly aims it at Jack.

"Okay, Jack, you want to play games? The only reason I didn't tap that sweet ass is because whatever she has in her, I didn't want in me. But, did I play with those large, round, beautiful titties? You're fucking right I did, Jack."

"That's all I needed to hear, Doc." Jack reaches down and pulls out his sidearm and before he can raise his gun to the doc, Skeane lets out a loud "Fuck you, Jack" and pulls the trigger. Only to hear click and then again click, and finally four more hollow clicks.

Dr. Skeane turns white as a ghost and again his face is enveloped with pathetic, sweaty panic. His eyes are searching the room and pleading for any kind of respite.

Jack reaches into his pocket and pulls out a handful of bullets. He slowly drops each bullet, one after the other, until all six are powerlessly dispensed to the ground.

Jack points his .38 at Dr. Skeane's head and within a split second of blowing a huge hole in his snivelling face, he quickly formulates an alternative plan. With a wry smile on his face, Jack lowers his gun and shoots Skeane in the middle of his kneecap.

Chapter 3

DEBBIE

Debbie's grandfather, Friedrich Zurich, was a pilot and an officer for the German Army in World War II.

It is reported that on his last mission near the end of the war, his plane was shot down and his body never recovered. He was survived by his wife and Debbie's dad, Karl.

Debbie's father, Karl, emigrated from Germany shortly after the end of World War II with his mother, Zelma, and a baby brother in tow.

Karl's first job in America was as a young rigger on a small oil rig just south of Arlington, Texas. Through hard work and dogged determination, Karl turned his role as a rigger into a role as the owner and operator of one of the largest oil drilling companies in Texas.

Karl is inherently a blue-collar man with white-collar friends. Everyone loves Debbie's dad, especially the political elite and the endless stream of charities that won't leave him alone.

This lifestyle has afforded Deb and her two older sisters the many luxuries life has to offer and a level of freedom none of the girls has taken for granted.

Always the keystone of their upbringing, their mother Emma was a fierce woman in her own right. She raised and mentored the girls with the mindset of family first and the community an extremely close second.

Taking her mother's mentoring to heart was not an altruistic placation for Deb. She's always really felt her best when helping others and, at the age of fifteen, won the Arlington, Texas, volunteer–of-the-year award. She was the youngest recipient in the award's seventy-year history.

To some, Debbie does have one egregious flaw.

Debbie is a curvaceous, vivacious, sensual beauty. A slim, extremely fit brunette who, at the young age of fifteen, already had her first *D* on her ever-expanding natural chest size.

Her breasts have been a constant talking point for men and woman alike—and an ever-growing issue not lost on her father, Karl. It was at an Arlington Texans baseball game two years ago that Karl came to the realization that Debbie was going to have to alter her attire from here on out. Obviously something no father wants to discuss with his thirteen-year-old daughter, so Karl had Emma speak with her.

The pivotal event took place on a Sunday afternoon in late spring. The Texans were playing their archrivals, the Los Angeles Angels. Emma and the older girls had no interest in baseball, so Karl and Debbie went to the game alone. Karl had an issue earlier that morning at a drill site, so the pair didn't arrive at the ball park until the start of the third inning.

As the two of them were walking to their seats, the stares and the cat calls soon started. Being as popular as he was, Karl first thought it was just friends and associates saying hi. Perplexed, when he didn't recognize anyone familiar, Karl happened to glance up at the ballpark's jumbo replay screen.

What was happening was an over-excited television cameraman was shooting from up top. He was following the pair to their seats and the image on the big screen displayed for the whole ballpark to see was that of young Debbie's ample chest tucked into a skimpy halter top.

Karl, temporarily losing his bearings, started shouting back at the crowd—and apparently the giant screen itself.

"She's thirteen, you disgusting pigs," Karl cried a number of times. He quickly put his coat over Deb to a chorus of boos from the crowd.

Unfortunately for the boys of Arlington, Deb's interests growing up did not mirror those of any pubescent boy. She did, however, have an endless list of adolescent male volunteers to help with whatever charitable cause she happened to be supporting at the time.

Irrespective of her mother's talk after the Arlington Texans incident, it wasn't until her mid teenage years that Deb really understood what all the fuss was about with regard to her remarkable God-given beauty.

That awakening could be attributed to a lifelong friend of her father's—a seemingly happily married man with two girls of his own, that finally forced the issue to the forefront when Debbie was only fifteen years old.

The incident took place at the annual Zurich summer barbecue where friends, family, employees, local and federal politicians—as well as any member of the community who shows up—are always welcome.

The popular event has been known to attract up to 500 people.

Karl's friend, Clifford, had been inconspicuously hanging around Debbie all afternoon. She had gone into the house to get something for her mother, and Cliff had followed her. With a house full of people, Cliff was hanging around, biding his time. When Deb slipped into an empty hallway, Cliff approached her and said, "You know what, Deb? I never did see that community service award you won this spring."

"Oh, would you like to see it."

"That would be great, where is it?"

"It's up in my room. I'll go get it and bring it down."

"That's okay, hon. I have to use the bathroom upstairs, anyway—private, if you know what I mean. I'll walk up with you."

Clifford followed Debbie into her bedroom and pushed the door closed behind them. Debbie saw the door closing and stopped and looked at Cliff.

Cliff walked up to Debbie and, without saying a word, put one arm around her shoulder to the back of her neck.

His other hand went under her bathing suit top and started massaging her breast. Cliff pulled Debbie's head closer and kissed her on the mouth.

Debbie didn't move. Her lips stayed perched in the same position, and after about ten seconds, she pulled away and said, "Are you done, Uncle Cliff?"

As if he'd been woken up after being hit with a heavy barbell, Clifford pulled away. "I'm so sorry, Debbie. I don't know what came over me. Please, please, Deb, can we just pretend this never happened. "Please don't tell your father, he will kill me."

Without missing a beat, Debbie said, "The award is on the shelf there. Let yourself out when you're done looking at it. And Uncle Cliff, I suggest you wait a few minutes."

Debbie pointed at Uncle Cliff's erection under his pants as she headed back outside to join the party.

In the backyard, she approached her father who was manning one of the half dozen fully loaded barbecues.

"Dad, Uncle Clifford followed me to my room and groped my breasts and kissed me. Don't worry, though, I took care of it. He won't bother me again."

With that, Debbie dived into the pool and started playing with the younger children there.

Left alone standing at the barbecue, Karl, now white as a ghost, was seething with the type of anger only a father under similar circumstances would understand.

Karl motioned to a couple of hired cooking hands to take over the grilling duties and spotted Cliff sitting with his lovely wife, Nancy.

He walked over to the pair. "Hi, Nancy. Looks like we are gonna have another beautiful day. Can I get you anything, dear?"

"Oh, Karl. You and Emma outdo yourselves every year. Everything is absolutely spectacular, and will you look at Debbie? Cliff was just saying earlier that she's growing into such a beautiful young lady."

"Thank you, Nancy. We are all very proud of her. Nancy, can I borrow the big mug for a minute? Cliff, do you mind?"

"Sure, Karl," Cliff said, his face reddening. "I'll be right back, hon. Keep an eye on the girls, will ya?"

"They're playing with Debbie Cliff, they couldn't be safer."

Karl walked Cliff to the front of the estate, shaking hands and promising everyone he'd be right back. Finally, once he'd made it to the front of the house, with Cliff about to start explaining, Karl calmly spoke.

"If you say one word, 'Uncle Cliff,' I'll knock your fucking teeth in. Come up with an excuse and be out of here in ten minutes. I'll have your final cheque couriered to you in the morning. If you're still in Texas in a month, your daughters will be without a daddy."

Karl promptly turned and walked to the backyard, pausing to greet and talk to people along the way. Forever the consummate host.

There was unequivocally no excuse or justification for Clifford's actions toward Debbie.

Aside from her physical appearance, Debbie also has an incredibly inviting personality. When she engages with people one-on-one, her piercing eyes give off the impression that no one else in the world exists. Men and women alike are invariably drawn into her realm.

The summer before her freshman year at the University of Texas, where she was going to study Geology, Debbie worked as a rigger for her father at one of his well sites. This is where she first met her best friend, Rafael.

He was a newly hired rigger with absolutely no experience. Karl liked the kid, but was worried that his incompetency would get someone killed.

The safety of his employees was always Karl's number one concern.

Deb had asked if she could have a couple of weeks to work with Rafael. Karl agreed that if anyone could train him properly, it would be his daughter.

Prior to their becoming friends, Deb was familiar with the over- muscled bear of a man. They had crossed paths several times on the work site and briefly talked at lunch one day.

What Deb liked about Rafael was that his eyes never once wandered to her chest, and he had never asked her that most hated question, "Do you know how beautiful you are?"

Rafael was in his mid-thirties, single, and somewhat of a man of the world compared to Debbie, who had yet to venture outside the state of Texas at the time. Rafael had even spent a couple of years as a crewman aboard a deep sea salvaging vessel that was on the hunt for treasure off the dangerous horn of Africa.

He had returned to his family home in Arlington when his younger brother was killed in an unsolved drive-by shooting. Being the only remaining son, he vowed to stay with his single mother, at least for a few years. He often regaled Debbie with his tales of the sea.

The two quickly became close and Rafael would accompany Deb to each successive rig site.

Karl was thrilled to see the two of them hit it off so well, and Debbie's mentoring of Rafael had the added result of turning the young man into one of his most competent and reliable employees.

The bonus is their working relationship has now extended into their personal lives and pair have become virtually inseparable.

Karl liked to refer to Rafael as Debbie's personal bodyguard. Not that she had ever needed any help in her own right.

On a late, warm summer Arlington evening, Debbie was driving home after a long day at the well site. She was now only one ranch over, but still twenty minutes away from a soothing bath and a hot meal.

It was part of Debbie's nightly drive-home ritual, to slow down as she drove past the shambolic, redneck-infested farmhouse owned by the Clement brood. The decrepitude of the property fascinated her. There were a half a dozen vehicles scattered across the front lawn, all in various states of rusted disarray.

On this particular night, with clouds covering the glow of the moon. Debbie could still make out the litany of empty whiskey bottles and beer cans littering the yard. The property was always lit with high-powered security lights, giving the illusion that it was forever daytime in Arlington.

There were always some vagabond characters out drinking on the porch. Currently, there were a couple of drunken assholes trying to fit an old carburetor wire into a battery cable.

Occasionally, Debbie would catch a glimpse of that night's brawl. Men, women, dogs, it didn't matter—they were all eager to go.

The four or five dogs tied to trees closer to the street only enhanced the insanity with their incessant barking, as if they were cheering on the roundabouts thirty feet back at the thunder dome-style fights.

On this particular night, Debbie had noticed a beautiful black Lab puppy that was not enjoying the nights show. It looked abhorrently skinny and emaciated.

Deb's first thought was of the obvious discomfort the Lab was in, but also that the little girl was not the usual mixed-mutt breed like the rest of the dogs on the property. "Probably stolen," she murmured aloud.

Then Deb's benevolent frustration and anger got the better of her.

It was 9:30 p.m. Deb was still wearing her work coveralls and reeking of oil and dirt. Her hot bath, nice meal and four or five hours of sleep before her 5:00 a.m. wake-up would have to wait.

Deb pulled off the street and drove about twenty feet up the Clements' long driveway.

She paused for a moment and raised her eyes to the roof of the truck in a solemn but resolute gesture. Maybe searching for some sign from above that would direct her to turn the truck around and head back home.

But that wasn't going to happen. Deb came to a magnanimous decision and she bemoaned aloud, "Shit, here we go."

Deb hopped out of her truck and walked over to the languishing black Lab puppy. The pup didn't stand, whimper or bark. She merely raised her nose ever so slightly, if only to let Debbie know that, yeah, she was still alive.

Deb reached into her pocket and unwrapped a partially eaten roast beef sandwich. She put it under the puppy's nose, saying, "Here you go, girl."

The emaciated pup smelled Deb's hand and looked up at her with sullen watery eyes. But the little gal passed on taking even the smallest of bites.

Deb petted the dog for a brief moment, cursorily looking for any indication of trauma or wounds.

Satisfied the pup was not going to die right then and there, Deb reached over to grab an empty bug-laden water dish that had been placed just out of the pup's reach.

Grabbing a water bottle from her coveralls, she rinsed the bowl and filled it with fresh water. She placed it by the pup's nose and the little girl drank it dry. After a brief hesitation, the pup lapped up a small piece of roast beef and slowly finished it.

This got Debbie even more enraged. She now figured the pup was literally dying of thirst.

Deb was suffused with overwhelming relief that she had gone against her instincts to just keep driving. She made a vow to herself that she would stop by each night to feed and water her new friend.

"Bye, little gal. I'll see you tomorrow," she said as she started to walk back to her truck.

Only a moment away from being safely ensconced back in her truck, on the road to her warm soapy bath and promised late meal of Texas beef ribs and slaw made by her mother Emma, Debbie heard the pathetic bellowing of one of the Clement boys.

"What the fuck you all doing with my dog, bitch?"

Deb froze on the spot. Her relief at having been able to help the pup was replaced by a steely internal acquiescence that some shit was about to go down.

Deb turned around and saw that two of the evening's earlier combatants were now drunkenly sauntering toward her. As they drew nearer, Deb could make out that they were the Clement brothers, Jeffrey and Stu.

Both were experienced "gun for hire" riggers. Several years prior, they were actually employed by her father. But come every payday, both men would disappear for a few days.

After numerous unkept promises that they would at the very least, show up to work, Karl was left with no choice but to add them to his "do not hire" list. A decision he did not take lightly, as he had known their late mother and father for thirty years and he'd always had a very amiable relationship with them.

With so many smaller drilling companies in Texas, the Clement boys still have a few drill sites left, to be irrevocably fired from. They had also inherited the once majestic expansive piece of property that had belonged to their parents, which they'd promptly turned into a dilapidated shit hole.

Having gone unchecked for the last ten years, the Clement property was now overrun with feral Russian razorback hogs, the scourge of the Texas plains that caused some 500 million dollars in damage every year. The common joke at the local watering hole was that there were 2.6 million feral hogs in Texas and half of them resided at the Clements'.

As the Clement boys descend on Debbie, their swearing and haranguing continued toward the stranger they admonished for even so much as daring to set foot on their blessed private property.

The surprisingly attractive but unofficially documented semi-retarded Jeffrey Clement was finally able to clear his booze-soaked vision long enough to say, "Oh, hey, Deb. Is that you?"

Jeffrey quickly spit on his hand in an attempt to straighten his hair and hurriedly worked at fixing his dishevelled clothing.

"Did you come by for a nightcap? Maybe a splash of shine, girl?"

Debbie was now standing next to the Lab pup and said, "Jeff, I'm taking this dog home with me."

"The fuck you are. That's Tammy's favourite mutt."

"Then why doesn't she feed it and give it some water? Just look at it, you idiot. She looks like she could die any minute."

Jeff replied, "You knows times are tough. Deb. We ain't livin' up in no mansion like your rich daddy with all your hired help tending to all your finer personal stuff and all, like cleaning your undergarments and stuff like that there, Deb."

Jeffrey quickly lost his train of thought and asked, "Hey, Deb? Your Daddy hiring again?"

Stu Clement finally caught up and reached the pair. On his way over he had to stop to talk to one of the mutts and accuse him of stealing a beer earlier.

Stu now had his arm over the shoulder of his brother Jeff. The same brother he'd hit in the back of the head with a 2x4 causing a deep bleeding gash, not more than ten minutes ago.

Like the rape scene right out of *Deliverance*, they were both unwittingly rubbing their crotches, and their bloodshot eyes were suggestively scanning up and down every inch of Debbie's body.

Licking his blood-and-chewing-tobacco-stained lips, Stu asked Debbie if she wanted to party.

Jeffrey interjected and said, "She thinks she's gonna take Tammy's favourite mutt, Stu."

"Well, I tell you what, Jeffrey. Maybe we gonna take a little something of our own tonight. What do you think of that, Deb?"

Deb had had enough. Reaching into her pocket, she palmed a three-inch metal compressor piece she'd replaced earlier in the day at the site.

She looked at Jeffrey then pointed to the ground and yelled, "Snake!" As Jeffrey was looking down in a panicked fright, she leaned back and punched Stu Clement right in the face, knocking him on his ass and breaking his nose.

Once assured that there was no snake, Jeffrey fell down to his brother's side and started crying and blubbering as though Stu had just been shot with a double barrel.

Deb reached down and untied the still listless pup and gingerly cradled her in her arms. She gently placed the dog in the driver's seat and gave her a little nudge for her to move over.

Then, a quickly as possible, she started the truck and reversed back down to the street. With a loud shout, she cried, "Clement boys, I own this dog now."

Debbie decided to call her new dog Rose, named after her favourite rock group, Guns n' Roses.

Debbie was only twenty years old at the time.

Several more years passed, and at Rafael's urging, Debbie started going on dates with other guys.

At school she had met a young handsome dental student, who like Rafael, was not beguiled by Debbie's more obvious assets. His principal interest was examining her flawless teeth and jaw structure.

Soon afterwards, Rafael began dating a local nurse who worked with his mother, and the once über-attractive twosome became an über-attractive foursome.

It was a warm summer Arlington morning. Debbie was back working the rigs when her alarm woke her up at the all too early time of 5:00 a.m.

As per usual, Deb hopped right into the shower. Afterwards, she put on her housecoat and opened her bedroom door. She'd always loved the smell of her mother's big breakfast permeating her room while she was drying her hair. She recalled that this was Tuesday morning, so the aroma should be that of bacon and sausages.

There were always a dozen hands that stopped by for breakfast on their way to the site. Her dad and her two sisters normally didn't wake up until after seven.

Halfway into drying her hair, Deb couldn't distinguish anything other than the unpalatable smell of her hair blower. Once finished, she turned the thing off and headed down to the kitchen.

There she found a couple of hands drinking coffee at the massive kitchen table. They both confirmed there had been no sign of Emma yet. After pouring herself a cup of coffee, Deb headed upstairs to check on her mother.

Debbie knocked on her parents' door. She wasn't about to open it as she learned her lessen as a child that parents could sometimes be engaged in intimate activities in the morning. After several more knocks, she heard her father yell, "Come in."

Debbie opened the door and walked over to the drapes, sliding them open.

"Wake up, sleepy head," she said to her mother. "We got a hungry crew waiting downstairs."

Deb leaned in to kiss her mother on the cheek and recoiled back in fear and panic. Her mother was cold to the touch and completely listless.

Karl leaned over and tried to wake his wife.

Emma Zurich, at the young age of fifty-eight, was dead.

The autopsy later revealed that Emma had a blood clot in her brain. Sometime in the evening, the clot had collapsed and she died peacefully, albeit much too early, in her sleep.

The funeral was attended by no less than 3,000 people.

In attendance at the private mass was a long time recipient of Karl's political donations, a former US president.

With Debbie's mother's passing affecting her so deeply, she felt there was nothing more keeping her in the all too comfortable confines of Texas.

Like her father, Deb had always been fascinated with what the land held beneath it. So it was only natural—after listening to all of Rafael's tales of life on board the Miranda—that she decided she wanted to see what lay beneath the oceans.

Rafael contacted the captain, and he was more than willing to have the pair join his team.

Debbie had made the difficult decision to leave her beloved Texas, the Geosciences program at the University of Texas, her two older sisters, and her father Karl.

For his part, Karl, knowing that her best friend and pseudo bodyguard Rafael would be going with her, reluctantly gave Deb his blessing.

Within a week, Deb and Rafael had joined the group of deep water salvagers on board the Miranda. And with

her father's political connections, Rose was allowed to
join them without having to worry about international
quarantine laws

Chapter 4

JACK

Jack was born in Orange County, California. His mother was an Armenian beauty named Sirvat. Aptly named, as Sirvat means "Beautiful Rose" in Armenian. She immigrated to the US when she was a child as her parents fled the Armenian thirty-year cold war.

Sirvat stayed at home to raise young Jack. She was a gifted seamstress who wove blankets, pillows and authentic Armenian rugs. She would sell them on the beach boardwalk to supplement the family income.

Jack's mother, being an unparalleled beauty, was often the recipient of unwanted sexual advances. But she had a razor sharp wit that would stop all advances cold. It was from Sirvat that Jack inherited this trait during their many times together on the boardwalk.

Jack's father, Paul Singer, was born in the US. His parents emigrated from the England. Jack's mother, who was of the Hebrew faith, insisted he be given a traditional Armenian name, that being Armen. Jack's dad hated the name, but couldn't say no to his beautiful bride. To keep the peace, Paul ended up acquiescing to Sirvat's request.

The first time Paul saw his baby son he said, "How you doing Jack?" And it stuck. Paul was a high school teacher during the day and a Karate instructor in the evenings. Paul's own father was a martial arts instructor with the R.A.F., and like most martial arts families the love of self-defence training was inherently passed down generation through generation.

Jack took up Karate at age four. In Paul's dojo, he only had two rules: The boys in your class were now your family and that meant you always had their backs. And if you ever got caught bullying the weak, you were out.

Jack took his father's words to heart and his moral character combined with his skill as a fighter earned him the role of neighborhood justice administrator for the weak.

Jack lived a comfortable life with his parents. But growing up in Orange County, California, a two-minute walk from the local pier, the silly extravagance of wealth was evident on a daily basis. With Jack's physical attributes and model good looks he was popular with the rich kids, and their mothers, too.

Jack always remained grounded in spite of being surrounded by opulence. He loved his life, his home and his family. He did, however, love the sea and took advantage of every opportunity to join his rich friends on their parents' pleasure crafts.

During their many boating excursions, while his friends were getting obliterated with their toots and booze, Jack's interest was learning everything he could about how the craft he was on that day operated and functioned. Jack always ended up being the designated driver on these sea journeys.

On his seventeenth birthday, Jack's parents took him and two of his buddies from the dojo out for pizza. After dinner, one of Jack's friends whose parents had just bought him a brand new beamer was taking Jack to a small surprise birthday party. It was at a girl's house whom Jack had been too scared to ask out on a date.

As it turned out, the young lady also liked Jack, but what wasn't to like? Jack was already six feet tall and chiselled like a piece of stone. His apparent shyness with the ladies was derived from the deep respect and reverence he held for his own mother. He was much more mature for his age than most of his peers and he saw backseat teenage fumbling as disrespectful.

After dinner that night, Jack gave each of his parents a goodbye hug and kiss and thanked them for his birthday dinner.

Ten minutes later, Paul and Sirvat, only blocks away from their home, were struck by a middle-aged man who had run a red light. The Singers drove a Volvo that was T-boned so horrifically and at such a high rate of speed that both were pronounced dead upon impact.

It took the fire department three hours to retrieve Paul and Sirvat's bodies from the mangled vehicle.

Jack's birthday was on a school night and even at age seventeen, he had to adhere to a strict early curfew. Defying his father on any occasion was never an option for Jack.

On his way home, Jack and his friends came across the scene of the accident and were witness to Jack's parents' bodies being painstakingly removed from the mangled wreck. All efforts by the police to remove Jack from the scene were fruitless.

One of Paul's Karate coaching assistants was eventually contacted, and he took Jack home.

The driver of the other vehicle was also killed on impact. It was later revealed he had a blood alcohol content of .36, six times the legal limit.

Jack never did ask the girl from the party out, but to this day he still remembers her name.

Jack ended up living with Paul's coaching assistant, Edgar, for the next year, and on his eighteenth birthday, Jack joined the United States Navy.

Paul's life insurance was not enough to pay off the mortgage on the family home and with no other living relatives, the state sold the home. When he turned eighteen, he received a cheque for $18,000.

Jack ended up buying a shitty dilapidated home outright with the $18,000, but at least it was his shitty dilapidated home. He purchased the property a few blocks away from his childhood home in Orange County.

Over the course of the next several years, Jack committed his furlough time to renovating it on his own and he ended up turning it into a pretty decent home. All that was left was for him to fill it with the family he so coveted.

Jack was never a big talker when he was younger and since the death of his parents, he spoke even less. He was a voracious reader, though, and would read anything military or involving combat sports. He occasionally took some ribbing when he would be caught reading the odd romance novel.

Since Jack was seventeen, his life has been a nomadic type of existence. Jack discovered as a young man that it was often more expedient to reflect his persona based on how he felt others had already predetermined him to be. He had become a chameleon of sorts.

With Jack having grown up next to the ocean his whole life, his decision to join the navy was a no-brainer.

Jack enlisted just as the first Gulf War had concluded. After basic training Jack was assigned to a war ship in the Persian Gulf to enforce the NATO and US no-fly zone.

Because of Jack's impressive physical fitness, mental acuity and maturity, his commanders had Jack on the fast track for advancement up the ranks.

The top brass were pushing for Jack to go to school to become an officer, but Jack had already deemed himself "in the game." Jack had no interest in attending military school or any school for that matter.

Although Jack always respected and held a thoughtful sentiment of command, it was the spontaneous reverence he received from his fellow soldiers that ultimately would fill the vacuum he had been experiencing since the loss of his family.

Whatever unit Jack happened to be assigned to, the other men in the unit quickly realized that if they were ever in a bind somewhere, they wanted Jack to be the guy standing next to them.

As his reputation grew, Jack had his detractors but that is where his competence and his mother's wit would come in, and very shortly, those same people would be exalting his virtues and rallying together under Team Jack.

Jack was ostensibly being monitored by a first sergeant who was the operational leader of reconnaissance missions in post-Gulf War Iraq. The sergeant became one of Jack's converted detractors and within short measure, he had Jack reassigned from a landing sweep-and-clear team, to his elite unit.

Jack quickly rose to the rank of sergeant and was soon operational leader of his own reconnaissance team.

Jack's feelings about his career in the navy were about to be changed by a life-altering metamorphosis when his elite unit was deployed to Bosnia. It was the second year of the Bosnian War.

NATO and the US initially decided they were going to sit this one out but still wanted US reconnaissance teams to infiltrate and document the rumours of war crimes being committed. The horrors and atrocities that Jack observed would ultimately change him for ever.

After his experience observing the all too surrealistic modern-day Serb genocide of the Muslim people, Jack was forced to confront his naïveté. The young California native vowed to dedicate his remaining time in the military to mitigate the loss of civilian casualties.

However, Jack did not leave the Bosnian War strictly as a documenter or observer, as mandated and dictated by the US military.

Other NATO and even US reconnaissance teams were finding small groups of dead Serb soldiers. These men were believed to be a part of systemic rape units. Upon their discoveries, the teams found the dead soldiers all had one thing in common: they had all been relieved of their own penises.

After a US-led internal investigation, Jack's unit was determined to be the only one that did not report finding any of these emasculated dead soldiers.

The unit responsible for the attacks was calculated enough to commandeer the weaponry and mags off the "first" group of dead Serbian soldiers. Any ballistics on future discoveries were found to have not been committed using US rounds. As for the blade curvature of the flayed penises, the review never got that far.

All Command knew was that there was now a rogue US recon team that was no longer just documenting and observing... they were hunting.

With a strong suspicion but no quantifiable evidence, Command was left with no alternative but to disband Jack's unit. Jack got his papers and was set to leave for an extended six-week furlough.

On the day Jack was headed home, he received a call to join the ship's second-in-command, the chief officer, for a private cup of coffee.

Meeting in the chief's office later that day, the chief gave Jack a folder containing an application form for Jack to join the Navy SEAL training at Naval Base Coronado in San Diego.

Jack thanked the chief for his consideration and told him he would definitely consider it. The Chief advised him to "Consider it hard, Jack."

With that, Jack was off to California and home.

Jack slept like the dead during the fourteen-hour flight back to the Los Alamitos Army Airfield.

After an extended tour in Serbia, Jack was back home in beautiful sunny Orange County California in July.

He kept himself busy during the first several weeks of his furlough. He had his neighbor cop and wife over for a thank you barbecue. They were a young couple who were living there when Jack first bought the house and were always happy to watch Jack's place when he was deployed.

Jack liked having a cop as a neighbor. He was always invited to his neighbor's parties and the odd poker game. Many of the officers he met through his neighbor were former military, so Jack always had a sympathetic ear if he needed one, plus the boys in blue knew how to party.

Jack spent a lot of time that July working on a back deck he started before his last tour and many an afternoon napping on the beach.

It wasn't until Jack resumed his morning running regimen that the horrors of what he witnessed started to come back to him.

No stranger to hardship, Jack was eventually able to compartmentalize the tragic loss of life to which he was forced to bear witness. He was able to assimilate a modicum of relief in the knowledge that a few of the most barbaric men had met their fate by his own hands.

After a month of fun and frivolity, Jack started pondering his future. Although Jack had been on a few dates on his furlough, he was still searching for the right woman to make his house a home.

He was still hanging out with some of his high school buddies though most of them were now working for or running their daddies companies. At least he still had access to a plethora of pleasure crafts.

Jack was at the end of his third year on his four-year contract with the navy. He knew he would most likely be redeployed to the Gulf off the coast of Iraq. He was pretty certain he would not be returning to Bosnia, even though NATO and US forces finally stepped up to the plate and had commenced with bombing raids in Bosnia. It infuriated Jack that it had taken the genocidal slaughter of 100,000 or so people, and tens of thousands of rapes, before the higher-ups became convinced that, yeah, maybe it was time to intervene.

Jack went into his kitchen and grabbed a cold beer. Then he picked up the chief's file folder containing his application to join the SEALs.

Jack headed outside to sit on his newly finished deck and decided to read what all the fuss was about.

Jack had a vague familiarity with the SEALs and their training protocol. Sometimes it was the only thing they talked about in Iraq.

What Jack was not interested in was the degradation you had to endure to make it into the special operations force. His thoughts were, "What the fuck? You water board your own men?"

Just then, Jack's neighbor Tom was meandering by their common fence looking as if he had nothing to do. Jack figured he must have heard the sound of a beer being opened from his kitchen.

"Hey, Tom, you want to join me for a beer?" Jack asked.

"Sure, Jack. Let me tell the wife and I'll be right over."

Tom was back in three minutes and Jack passed him a beer and his Navy SEAL application,

"You do paperwork all day, Tom. Can you help me out with this?"

Tom quickly browsed the document and said, "SEALs, sweet. Okay, Jack, I'll read it and we'll see if you'd fit in."

Tom started to read the application. "Extreme physical and mental fitness…yeah, that's you. Mature and resilient… well, you do own your own house and you just got back from Bosnia and you didn't eat a bullet, so yeah, I'd say that's you, too.

"Okay, here we go, twenty-four weeks training…is that you, Jack? Weren't you thinking about starting a family after the navy? You know I could get you on the force in a New York minute, Jack."

Jack was smiling the whole time as Tom was carrying on. Every time Jack was going to say something, Tom would put up his hand for Jack to not talk, just listen. Finally, Jack interrupted him. "You already had a couple of beer today, huh, Tom."

"I'm just fucking with you, kid. Hey, why don't you come over for a barbecue tonight? My sergeant's coming over and I told him to bring his daughter. She's twenty-three and fucking hot, Jack."

"Is that the same sergeant you told me had his daughter's ex- boyfriend's car towed every time he saw it? No thanks, Tom."

"All right, Jack, next time maybe. I gotta get going, but on a serious note, I think you would make an outstanding SEAL and they would be lucky to have you."

"Thanks Tom, say hi to Sarah for me."

Tom handed the application back to Jack and when Tom was out of sight, Jack crushed it into a ball and tossed it into his fire pit.

The next week Jack received a notice in the mail that he would be returning to his ship in the Gulf for the remainder of his term.

Jack spent his final week at home hanging out with friends, eating all of his favourite foods and doubling the intensity of his morning workouts to compensate for his increased caloric intake.

Jack arrived in the Gulf to a promotion to first sergeant. He was given a new team and was back running reconnaissance missions, only in Iraq, this time.

During Jack's six-week furlough, he'd hoped against all hope that what had happened in Bosnia would stay in Bosnia. It was not too often that you had a twenty-one-year-old team leader who was rumoured to have administered some good old US of A justice and got away with it.

Needless to say, when Command was forming Jack's new recon team, the ship had a record amount of applicants to join the elite group.

What Jack didn't know was that he was also still under Command's radar—and that an upcoming assignment would forever alter the course of his life.

The pervasiveness of the Bosnia rumours on board the ship continued. And with the top command's unwillingness to fully pursue the incidents at the time they occurred, they were left with no other option but to, once again, reassign Jack.

Unaware to Jack, his future with the United States Navy itself was now up for review.

Had Jack accepted the chief's transfer to the Coronado Naval SEALs training program in San Diego, it would have at least put him back in the US—the assumption being that talk of the rogue unit would eventually wane with Jack being on another continent and 10,000 kilometres away.

In a closed meeting with all of the ship's top brass, the consensus was Jack just had to go. He would be offered the chance for an honourable discharge and could claim it was due to unspecified health reasons.

Just then a lieutenant spoke up. "I'll take him," the lieutenant said. The lieutenant had just arrived from a ninety-minute flight by a Chinook helicopter from his permanent post in Israel. He was waiting to meet with the chief himself and was familiar with Jack and his predicament. He decided earlier he would join the meeting.

"What do you mean you will take him, Lieutenant?" the chief of the boat asked.

"We all know the Ambassador is always asking for a bigger detail. We'll make a submission for a larger compliment and I'll have Jack stand a post and run errands for the last year of his term."

Judging by the look on everyone's faces they were less than convinced, but the lieutenant continued on nonetheless. "Jesus Christ, gentlemen. This guy is what, twenty-one? We all know what happened in Bosnia was 'misguided,' but I don't think I would be too out of line in saying that everyone in this room believes there was some level of justice meted out by this exceptional young man."

The lieutenant continued. "Can anyone in this room say the incident has irrevocably altered Jack?"

The men looked around at one another for any dissenting viewpoints.

The ship's captain, who was standing by the door and listening in on the conversation had finally heard enough and exclaimed, "Chief of the boat...get it done."

"Yes, Sir, Captain."

"Lieutenant, find Jack and get him back here. I want him on that Chinook with you tomorrow morning. And Lieutenant, we both know who's going to greet him so I don't care how you do it, just make sure his personnel file is there before he is."

"Tell Jack to clean and press his dress blues and then have him do it again. Also, tell him to watch his fucking language or the Ambassador will have him back on the next chopper and then he's back to being our problem."

"Yes, Sir, Chief."

Jack was on the chopper to Tel Aviv the next day and arrived to a beautiful September summer morning.

While a far cry from war-torn Bosnia or Iraq, Israel still had its own share of violence. A week before Jack's arrival, Israel had recorded its third suicide bombing of the year.

The US Navy was also in the midst of an air and naval blockade protecting the border in the Israeli-Lebanon conflict. And most important to the country's quality of life, the Palestinians temporarily suspended their every-other-day rocket and mortar attacks. This was after Prime Minister Rabin announced a territorial compromise on the Golan Heights in exchange for a peace solution.

Jack, of course, had no concerns. Compared to his last deployments, he viewed this assignment as heaven on earth. And Jack was going to take full advantage of what he considered his 'down time' at one of Israel's many spectacular beaches.

Jack and his new command leader, Lieutenant David Ferguson, arrived at the US embassy in Tel Aviv and were met at security by a very mousy-looking young lady.

Jack started looking around for someone who looked a little more authoritative and at the same time was thinking to himself, "Are you lost, dear? Would you like me to help you find your parents?"

The mousy-looking lady said with a commanding tone, "Thank you, Lieutenant. I'll take it from here. I suspect Sergeant Singer will be with us for a few hours."

"Thanks, Margaret. Give me a shout when he's done."

Jack was swiftly escorted to the outer office of the American ambassador to Israel. As they were walking, Jack was thinking that Margaret must be some top guy's daughter because everyone was going out of their way to say hi to her.

Once Jack and Margaret reached the office, Jack about to take a seat when Margaret said, "You may want to just stand there, Sergeant. The Ambassador is big on first impressions and with your blues still looking fairly pressed, it may make for a better appearance. Don't you think?"

"Okay, then. Thank you, Margaret."

With Jack standing at semi attention, he glanced over at the mouse's name plate on her desk,

"Excuse me, Miss Aarons? Aarons … are you related to Mr. Aarons, the consulate general out of Jerusalem?"

"Yes, Sergeant. That is my father."

"You can just call me Jack if you want."

"It says here in your file your name is Armen."

"It's a long story, Miss Aarons."

"Well, we have time, Jack. The Ambassador is away at a meeting with my father right now. And you can call me Margaret."

Jack was thinking to himself, "Then why am I standing here?" He focused his attention on the diminutive little mouse whose attention had already moved on from the story of Jack's name and who was now rapidly typing away at her desk.

Three long silent hours later, Margaret got a call from security that the Ambassador had arrived and was on his way.

Margaret promptly hopped up and grabbed a stack of files and took them into the Ambassador's office. She quickly returned and stood at attention just as Jack had been doing for the past three hours.

The Ambassador arrived in the outer office followed by an assistant and two naval security officers.

"Good Morning, Margaret," he said with a warm smile.

Noticing Jack, he extended his hand for a handshake,

"And this young man must be Sergeant Armen Singer. My name is Wilhelm Oster, Armen."

"Pleased to meet you, Mr. Ambassador."

The Ambassador turned back to Margaret. "Margaret dear, don't you ever get tired of making these young men stand to attention? Armen, did she tell you to just stand there so as not to crease your pants?"

"No, Sir, she did not. I chose to stand."

Margaret was now smiling wryly at Jack.

Jack thought, "You sneaky little bitch."

"Has Margaret at least offered you something to drink, Armen?"

Jack replied, "Yes, Sir, she did," even though Margaret hadn't offered Jack a single thing.

"Please come in, Armen. We have a lot to talk about."

Jack followed the Ambassador into his office. As he closed the door behind him he saw Margaret trying to stifle her laughter and he gave her a steely look.

The Ambassador went to his desk and picked up Jack's file then motioned to him to take a seat in one of the upholstered armchairs flanking a coffee table.

"Please, let's sit over here, Armen. It will be much more comfortable."

While the Ambassador was flipping through Jack's file, Jack took measure of the man he had been repeatedly warned to heed.

The Ambassador was short and ethnic-looking in appearance. He seemed to be very fit and was just showing a hint of distinguished grey in his dark hair. He was dressed in a modest grey suit.

So far Jack's impression was of a very warm and pleasant older gentleman. But there was something in the Ambassador's gaze that Jack had seen before. A look he normally saw in the eyes of those who had been through tremendous hardships in their lives. A look that Jack himself saw reflected in the mirror every morning.

"Armen, it is dreadful what happened to your parents and you have my deepest sympathies. I see here you have no other family."

"No, Sir, I don't."

"I have another meeting in ten minutes, Armen, so we will have to cut our meeting short. I would like to welcome you to Israel more formally. I am having a small dinner party this evening and would like you and Lieutenant Ferguson to join us. He knows where I live and he will arrange for your transportation. Is this okay with you, Armen?"

"Yes. Thank you, Sir. I look forward to it."

"On your way out can you please tell Margaret I do not want to be disturbed for a few moments?"

"Yes, Sir. Thank you again, Sir."

Jack left the office and closed the door. Immediately, he started making faces and frantic gestures towards Margaret, implying that something serious had just happened.

"I'm not sure how to say this, but the Ambassador must have eaten something really bad. He said he pooped himself and he needs you in there right away."

"Oh my God. Thank you, Jack."

"Here, take these paper towels and this pitcher of water," Jack said, grabbing the items from a shelf. "And wait—take this can of air freshener, too."

"Thanks again, Jack. Oh dear, how embarrassing for him."

"Yes. I'm so sorry, Margaret. This is really horrible."

Jack removed himself from the office and then hurried down to the street to catch his ride.

Later that evening, Jack and Lieutenant Ferguson arrived at the residence of the US ambassador.

The duo made their way to the bar, and within minutes of their arrival, the lieutenant told Jack he spotted a girl he knew and asked Jack to wish him luck, leaving Jack on his own.

Jack is now standing alone at the bar in a banquet-size room full of people he does not know, and more importantly does not want to know. Standing alone in a room full of people may be an uncomfortable situation for some, but for Jack all it means is he doesn't have to fake small talk with anyone.

He then makes eye contact with the diminutive little mouse, and she appears to be on a direct path over to him with the distinct look of having an objective.

Ten feet before she reached him, she stopped and grabbed the arm of a middle-aged man, and then they both proceeded to approach Jack.

"Jack, I would like you to meet my father, Consulate General Aarons," Margaret said.

"Hey, kid. Like these digs? Pretty swanky, huh? Not as nice as our official residence but at least the price is right, know what I mean," the consulate general said, elbowing Jack. "Hey I thought you told me his name was Armen, hon… Oh, there's Bob he owes me ten bucks. Gotta go kids. Uh nice to meet you, uh, Jack or, er, Armen."

Once her father was out of sight, Margaret turned to Jack and said, "Sorry about that. My dad can be a little weird."

"No worries, Margaret. Do you want to go sit down?"

"Why not?"

Jack and Margaret ended up spending the rest of the night together, talking as if there was no one else in the room.

At around midnight, the Ambassador approached and apologized for interrupting the pair. He mentioned that he would like to speak to Jack in private before he left.

Margaret located her intoxicated father and Jack walked them both out to their car before going to speak with the Ambassador. Jack was very delicate in the manner in which he made sure Margaret was the one behind the wheel.

When he returned, the Ambassador was at the door saying goodnight to each one of his guests. He then left the front entrance and walked into another room. One of his assistants approached Jack as he was standing by the bar with Lieutenant Ferguson and said, "Would you come with me please, Sergeant Singer?"

Jack was brought into the Ambassador's parlour. The Ambassador was sitting behind his desk with his reading glasses perched at the end of his noise. Once again, he was going through Jack's military file.

Jack noticed two files open on the Ambo's desk. The standard military file and a second file, which also contained a picture of Jack stapled to the inside.

There were two men sitting quietly at the other end of the room on a couch. Jack didn't recognize them from the party nor did he think they were service men. Their hair was slightly too long and they were wearing very expensive suits.

"Have a seat please, Armen."

Jack took a seat across from the Ambassador at his desk.

"Tell me about your mother, Armen … she must have been a spectacular woman."

"Yes, Sir, she certainly was."

Jack had started to tell the Ambassador about his mother's incomparable beauty, wit and intelligence, when the Ambassador politely interjected.

"No, I'm sorry, Armen. I would like you to tell me everything. Please start from your earliest memories."

Jack proceeded to relay the story of his life to this man he had just met. Surprisingly, Jack felt very comfortable speaking to him.

When he reached the point of having to explaining his parents' untimely deaths, the Ambassador interjected again. His expression had changed a bit and, while looking at his two security men seated at the back of the room, he politely asked Jack, "It is my understanding the man who murdered your parents also succumbed to his injuries. Is that correct?"

"Yes, Sir"

The Ambassador, while still looking at his security guys, muttered an almost inaudible, "That's too bad."

Jack continued with the story of his life. It was not something he would normally discuss in such detail with anyone. But talking to this man was oddly calming … therapeutic, even.

The Ambassador thanked Jack for sharing his memories with him and, as he closed the files on his desk, he reached into his top drawer and pulled out a document. He handed it to Jack.

Jack looked at the document and realized it was a Navy SEAL application and, furthermore, it was completely filled out in type. All that was missing was Jack's signature.

"I'm sorry, but I'm not sure I understand, Sir," Jack said.

The Ambassador gestured to his security men, who promptly rose from their seats and left the office.

"Armen, after having accomplished what I had set out to do here, I am retiring from public service next year. I am going to remain in Israel and am currently having a home built in Saviorey Ramat Aviv. It is a wonderful gated community from where I will continue my work."

Jack was dying to ask, "And what work would that be?" but remained silent, waiting for the other shoe to drop.

"Yes, Sir."

"Armen, for a number of years now, I have sought out men and women with extraordinary backgrounds and capabilities. Armen, I think you are one of those individuals."

He continued, "I am a man who has been blessed with incredible wealth and, with God's blessing, my life's mission is to liberate the world of its worst inhabitants.

"I would like you to complete your training with your navy's SEALs. After a couple of years, you will come work for me."

"Is it not *our* US Navy, Sir?"

The Ambassador ignored Jack's comment and added, "Your commander is already aware of your decision to join the SEALs. I have secured you a two-week leave and you will stay in Israel. Your leave begins now, Armen. You have also been accepted into the SEAL program, and once you arrive back in California you will have another two days before you are to report."

Jack was wondering to himself how it was possible that he had never heard of this man sitting before him prior to now. Of course he knew that he was the US ambassador to Israel, but a man with this type of clout? There had to be more to the guy. What Jack really wanted to ask him was, "Are you serious?" The guy wanted to change the course of his life and, apparently, he wasn't used to asking first.

"The ever patient lieutenant waiting outside will drive you to an apartment of mine where you will stay. You will find all of your belongings there from the ship. Armen, I want you to spend every day of your leave enjoying our beautiful city and its people."

The Ambassador handed Jack an envelope and continued, "This is a little something for you to make sure you have a pleasant stay in our country. When you return to California, you will receive a cheque every month to help with your bills. Do you have any questions for me, Armen?"

Surprisingly, Jack did not feel he had to ask any questions and only said, "Thank you for your faith in me, Sir. If I may ask … would you mind calling me Jack?"

The Ambassador chuckled and Jack signed the SEAL application.

Then Jack stood up to excuse himself. He shook the Ambassador's hand and began to head for the door.

"Jack, when you take Margaret out, take her someplace nice. The Royal Beach Hotel has an amazing array of fresh local seafood. And one more thing—" the Ambassador reached down underneath his desk and picked up the can of air freshener Jack sent Margaret in with that morning. "Can you drop this off on Margaret's desk, please?"

With that Jack was set to begin his lifelong odyssey with the Ambassador at the helm.

Jack spent the next two weeks with Margaret, who was also given a two-week holiday by the Ambassador. Jack rented a car and the two of them spent their time getting to know each other and exploring the country.

By the start of the second week, Margaret was staying at Jack's place, overnight.

On the morning of Jack's last day in Israel, he told Margaret he had been summoned to a meeting with the Ambassador in the late afternoon.

He reaches into his still bulging envelope of money and gave Margaret a handful of bills. He told her to go out and buy the nicest dress she could find in Israel, as he was going to take her out to the newly opened, ridiculously expensive, Mul Yam restaurant next to the Tel Aviv Bay.

Jack apologized to Margaret, saying that he had no idea how long the Ambassador would keep him, and to be on the safe side she should just take a cab and meet him there for their reservations at eight.

When Margaret finally got the chance to speak, she was adamant that she didn't want to go to any restaurant, let alone the most expensive restaurant in Israel. She said she would prefer to spend the entire day and night with Jack alone.

Jack asked her to please just do this for him. The pair spent the morning together at the beach and walking among the local shops, as Margaret looked for her dress.

Back at the apartment later that afternoon, Jack put on his dress blues and headed off to meet with the Ambassador.

At 7:45, Jack was waiting outside the restaurant for Margaret to arrive. Margaret arrived five minutes early by cab and Jack watched her from across the street. His little mouse looked absolutely stunning in a floor-length blue chiffon dress, a sash around her waist, long white satin evening gloves, and matching high heels and a clutch purse.

Margaret peered through the large front windows of the restaurant and didn't spot Jack. Jack knew Margaret wouldn't go into the restaurant if he was not there. He spent a very brief moment wistfully watching her and his thoughts quickly turn to how this must have been how his Father felt with his Mother.

Jack starts out from across the street to greet Margaret. Jack was no longer in his dress blues. He was wearing a pair of khaki shorts, a tight white sleeveless T-shirt and casual white Bermuda shoes with no socks. Slung over his right arm was one of Margaret's light sweaters.

It was a beautiful, warm, humid evening in the mid-twenties. The cobblestone streets were full of couples and families taking in Tel Aviv's many authentic restaurants and stores.

Margaret spotted Jack and had to do a double take to make sure it was actually him. She immediately started to wonder if something bad had happened.

Jack approached her and remarked how gorgeous she looked. He gave her a big hug and kissed her passionately on the lips.

"Is everything okay, Jack? Did you get called back early?"

Jack offered the sweater to Margaret and gently placed it over her shoulders.

"Everything is great, Mouse. Just a change of plans. Let's go for a walk."

Jack proceeded to walk with Margaret the short distance to the Tel Aviv Marina. The entire walk Jack and Margaret were characteristically quiet. Margaret was tightly holding on to Jack's waist and trying to keep her mind off the fact that Jack was shipping out tomorrow morning. She couldn't help wondering if she would ever see him again.

Over the course of the last two weeks, they really hadn't discussed what would happen when Jack left for his SEAL training. They both understood that they came from two different worlds. Like any two young people in love, they were just living for the moment.

They arrived at the marina and Jack walked Margaret down the boardwalk until they come upon an isolated, dilapidated long wooden boat. They walked down the shaky pier to the front of boat.

At the entrance was a hanging sign with one drooping end. The sign was in English and merely said, "Restaurant."

The pair were met at the entrance by an American man dressed in casual clothing with a stained white apron.

"Welcome aboard, mateys. I'll be your captain for tonight's adventure. If you will follow me please, Ma'am and Sir, your table awaits you."

Margaret held Jack a little tighter, thinking, "What the frick have you gotten me into."

The captain walked them to the back of the boat where there was a table for two set with a white linen table cloth, a number of burning candles, and a vase of roses, irises and local anemones.

The table overlooked the bay, with underwater lights illuminating the marine life swimming below.

At the front of the restaurant, a new sign was being put up, "Sorry, closed for the evening."

Jack helped Margaret into her chair.

"Okay, Jack, this is all very impressive. Now would you like to tell me what's going on? And why are you wearing those ridiculous clothes?"

"Here it comes, Marg."

The restaurant owner returned with a huge metal bowl filled with fresh steamed lobster, shrimp, calamari and milbar. He hands Jack a big paper bib for him to wrap around Margaret.

"Okay, hon, we can eat now."

"I'm going to kill you, Jack ... but after dinner."

Margaret thanked the chef, asked him his name and told him everything looked delicious.

Margaret and Jack spent the next hour eating the elegant meal made with organic and local ingredients.

When they were finished, the chef removed all of the dinner items and handed Jack a wet rag to wipe his shirt. Jack decided to forgo the oversized bib.

"Jack, that was amazing. Thank you," Margaret said, patting her mouth with her napkin. "That is the fourth time you've looked at your watch—are you expecting someone? And why are you so flush? Are you allergic to seafood?"

Jack got out of his chair, walked over to Margaret and lifted her chair around to face him while she was still sitting in it. Margaret looked around the room, as if asking, "What the hell is going on?" Then Jack dropped to one knee, pulled out a ring from his pocket and said, "Margaret Aarons, will you marry me?"

Without missing a beat, Margaret replied, "Armen Singer, *yes.*"

As Jack was placing the ring on Margaret's finger, her mother and father, the Ambassador and a dozen close family friends appear from behind a large hanging carpet that Margaret had taken for being part of the eclectic decorum.

And just so Margaret wouldn't feel out of place, everyone else had also dressed to the nines.

The Ambassador's two security men carried in the chuppah—the canopy the bride and groom stand under in a traditional Jewish wedding ceremony.

Margaret, who was still in a blur of disbelief and shock, leaned into Jack and whispered, "We're getting married *now*?"

Jack reached back into his pocket and handed Margaret an airline ticket with a seat right next to his for the flight home the next day.

"Jack Singer, what if I said no?"

"I would have jumped off the boat and swam back to California."

The Ambassador performed a truncated traditional Jewish ceremony.

Time and location prevented the couple from completing the full seven blessings for a Jewish wedding ceremony. The newlywed couple were able to sign their marriage ketubah and break the cloth-wrapped glass at their feet.

The Ambassador concluded the ceremony with, "Peace, blessing and all good to you. *Mazel Tov*."

The party went well into the night. Jack found a moment to pull the Ambassador aside to thank him for all of his assistance.

Most important to Jack was that this kind, gentle man, whom he had only known for the briefest amount of time had given Jack his full blessing.

The Ambassador had also facilitated bringing Margaret's parents together earlier in the week so that Jack could ask for their permission to marry their daughter, and he'd booked his favourite seafood restaurant for the night and had his personal staff make all of the necessary arrangements.

Jack also thanks the American Chef Martin for his incredible meal and hospitality and promises he will stop by whenever he is back in Israel.

The next morning, Jack and Margaret—now husband and wife—were on the morning flight back to California.

Jack spent all of his remaining two days at home showing Margaret around the Orange County area and helping her acclimate to her new home.

As promised, Jack's first monthly cheque from the Ambassador was waiting for them when they arrived.

Then, Jack was off to begin his twenty-four-week Navy SEAL training at the Coronado Island Naval Amphibious Base, just outside of the San Diego Bay.

Jack completed his SEAL training near the top of his class. It was his incredible physical conditioning and mental strength that carried him through. He never once considered ringing the bell, but he was witness to a number of extraordinary men who ultimately rang out.

Two things would remain with Jack for the rest of his life from his SEAL training: the experience of being water boarded and that of meeting his lifelong friend and fellow SEAL trainee, Roger.

After graduating their SEAL training, Jack and Roger ended up being assigned to the same unit, but after only one year as a SEAL, Roger resigned and got a job in the private security sector.

Jack was only expecting to do a two-year stint in the SEALs as per the terms he'd discussed with the Ambassador, but at the Ambassador's insistence he ended up staying the full four years.

It was at the end of his second year with the SEALs that Margaret gave birth to a healthy baby girl.

Jack's SEAL deployments included missions in Kosovo, Lebanon and Afghanistan, along with numerous clandestine operations throughout the world.

Jack resigned from the SEALs as a sergeant. Just as in his early military career, Jack refused any promotions above the rank of first sergeant.

When Jack resigned from the SEALs, he was flown to Israel to meet with the Ambassador, who was now also working in the private sector.

The Ambassador now had his first "Six Million Dollar Man" in Jack, the estimated amount the US military spent on training this most elite group of men.

Jack spent the next sixteen years working directly for the Ambassador. His primary missions were high-level extractions of certain individuals the Ambassador wanted captured or eliminated. Some missions would be completed in a weekend while others that were more complicated and required Jack's full reconnaissance skills could take over a year.

It was the fall of 2013 and Jack was given a thirty-day cessation period of all activities, imposed by the Ambassador. The now reclusive billionaire had promised Jack upon his return a mission that would form his legacy.

Thirty days later, Jack was met at the Israeli airport by the Ambassador's limousine with a security car both front and aft.

As the limo approached the Ambassador's private mansion, he couldn't help but notice the increased compliment of men walking the estate.

Jack was escorted to the Ambassador's office and, for the first time in the last ten years, it would appear that Jack was the last to arrive. The Ambassador had his usual dead-eyed security staff sitting listlessly at the back of the room. Only this time, they were joined by several rough-looking individuals whom Jack had never met.

The Ambassador stood behind his desk. "Welcome back, Jack. How was your flight?"

Jack was eyeing the four new characters who had somehow supplanted Jack's OCD ritual of self-affirming one-on-one time with the Ambassador.

Pissed off at being the last to arrive, Jack addressed the Ambassador by his first name for the first time ever. "It was long, Wilhelm."

The Ambassador then made his way over to Jack and gave him a deep embrace.

Jack was temporarily placated but he could feel his stomach starting to tighten. An inherent fight or flight instinct was starting to take over.

The Ambassador returned to his seat behind his desk, nodded to his legal man, Harvey, and then turned away from the group while staring out the window overlooking the rear of his vast estate.

"Jack, this will be a one-time extended operation," he said. "The people before you are Bricks, Stryker, Stevens and Ivanna.

"Gentlemen … and lady, as we discussed, this is Jack Singer. Jack will be in command of this operation and you will refer to him as Sergeant.

"In front of you, you will find a package with your name on it. It outlines your responsibilities on this mission and is based on your specific skill sets.

"People, this is a highly sensitive extraction from Akron, Ohio, USA. The target is a Nazi war criminal who has avoided detection for over seventy years. Let's get this bastard before Father Time does."

The Ambassador, who was now facing the group, had noticed Jack had made the slightest, almost imperceptible facial expression when Harvey mentioned the target.

"Would you like to add anything, Jack?" he asked.

"No, Ambassador. Nothing we can't discuss in private after."

"No, Armen, we will discuss it here now with your new team. If you have any reservations, please speak up, otherwise I have made dinner reservations for all of you for this evening."

"It's the target, Sir. Are we sure the information is reliable? What is he now, ninety-five?"

The Ambassador and Jack locked gazes and no one spoke until Harvey finally interjected, "All right, everyone, grab your package. We have a limo leaving in twenty minutes. Jack, can you hold up for a minute?"

The foursome left the room and Harvey took a seat at the back.

"What are your concerns, Armen?"

"Excuse me, Mr. Ambassador, but this whole thing stinks. Something isn't ringing true for me, and who are these four thugs?"

"They are your new team, Armen, and they are yours to train and mold as you see fit.

"I have reserved the restaurant where you and Margaret got married. It is yours for the evening and I expect you to welcome your new team to our country. My jet leaves in the morning and it will fly you all to a safe house in Cleveland."

Harvey piped up from the back of the room. "If there's nothing else, Jack, your limo is waiting."

Jack ignored Harvey, looked at the Ambassador and replied directly to him, "I'm good. Thank you, Sir."

As Jack was leaving the room, the Ambassador had one more comment. "I want the extraction done on Sunday, December the sixth. Our target married a Jewish woman and I will be damned if he lives to celebrate one more Hanukkah. I want him taken alive and returned to me. Do you understand me, Armen?"

"Yes, Sir."

Just as Jack is about to close the door behind him, he heard the Ambassador mumble, "*Sie wahlen immer die waffe.*" Jack had heard that phrase spoken numerous times over the years by the Ambassador and decided that one of these days, he was going to have to look it up.

Having worked for the Ambassador for so many years on so many jobs with elite, highly trained disciplined soldiers, Jack couldn't help but think this group should be called 'Team Expendable." It was frustrating him deeply, as he was also a member of the Ambassador's latest gathering of men—and a lone woman.

By the time December sixth rolled around, Jack had spent a month getting to know his new motley crew and had come to realize that they were indeed mercenaries for hire—and if only a portion of their stories were true, they were also all stone-cold killers. Which was in direct conflict with Jack's mantra, 'No Civilian Casualties.' Jack repeatedly attempted to convey this message to his team over the course of the last month but he feared it had fallen on deaf ears.

Bricks, the sanest of the group, was a former US Army Ranger and had grown on Jack due to his competence and reliability. Jack trusted him and, for the most part, he thought Bricks could keep the other three in line.

Stryker relished in the telling of his shocking war stories, and when Jack had had enough of his tall tales one afternoon, he came to realize the guy packed one hell of a punch. The altercation concluded with Jack putting Stryker to sleep for a few minutes.

Stevens has similar tales to Stryker, only the majority of his included underage conquests in war-ravaged countries.

Ivanna was a Russian nationalist and the team's medic. According to Bricks, she was an impatient assassin with a quick trigger finger.

The group had spent the last month surveying the home of their target. They had the target and his wife's daily routine down to the second. The couple retired for the evening at 8:00 p.m. every night.

The team was planning to breach the home at 9:00 p.m.

The home has a long circular driveway and was nestled in the rear of their lot. It was surrounded by a thick tree line that provided the coverage they needed.

The plan was to silently enter the home within thirty seconds. All four team members would be equipped with nines and silencers. Ivanna insisted on having a pair of shoulder-strapped Uzi's, one for each hand.

Ivanna would be driving the van. It had been detailed to precisely resemble that of the local natural gas company and the team were all clothed with replicas of the company's coveralls.

It was now 8:55 p.m. Ivanna did a slow drive-by as they monitored the front of the house. The lights were all still on and there were two cars in the driveway.

Bricks checked his notes from their month-long surveillance and confirmed that they were the son's and daughter's vehicles.

Ivanna pulled over for a moment.

"Well, Sergeant, what now?"

"Ambo said we do it today, so we will proceed as planned. Instead of breaching silently, we will go right through the front door and move everyone into the back room. Absolute priority, get everyone's cell phones straight off."

Jack, confident that the mission could still proceed said, "Let's get moving, Ivanna."

Ivanna turned around and entered the driveway.

Jack quickly formulated a new entry plan for the team.

"Bricks and Ivanna, you enter through the front. Stryker, you're with me. We'll breach the rear. Stevens you stay in the van and monitor any chatter by the cops."

Jack wanted Ivanna at the front door. Putting aside the fact that she was a merciless killer, she was also a very attractive woman and should draw the least attention when she rang the bell. Jack wanted Stryker with him for no other reason than to try to maintain some measure of control.

All five were equipped with wireless communication devices with individual combat identification markers.

The team exited the van. Ivanna and Bricks strolled to the front door having a loud discussion about how cold it was.

Jack and Stryker made their way to the back. Stryker raced ahead of Jack and was the first to reach the back door. Stryker was about to ignore the command protocol and kick the door in alone. Jack whispered into the mic, "Wait, you fucking asshole."

Jack picked up his pace and, while watching Stryker and not the ground, he stepped onto a three-foot-wide flimsy piece of plywood and could feel it give way.

"Oh, fuck."

Jack collapsed into a waste storage cistern and was enveloped up to his shoulders in raw sewage. Stryker ran back to Jack and helped pull him out.

With Ivanna and Bricks standing at the front door for almost two minutes, Jack said over the mic, "Go, go, go."

Ivanna and Bricks gained peaceful entry to the home while Stryker shot out the back door locks. All four were simultaneously in the living room within fifteen seconds.

Bricks shouted, "Everyone remain seated and no one will be hurt. Let's see those cell phones."

Jack grabbed a couple of linen napkins from the table and began wiping off the shit and piss from his coveralls.

Their target was sitting at the head of the table with his wife next to him. His two children and their spouses—now seniors in their own right—were also present, as well as what appeared to be two teenage grandchildren. A total of eight people were at the table.

Jack, the only member of the team familiar with the Jewish faith, quickly realized what was going on.

There was a menorah on the table, and the first of eight candles was lit.

Jack was thinking, "This Nazi scum is celebrating the first day of Hanukkah, complete with the wearing of the Jewish yarmulke cap."

Knowing that in the Jewish faith they did not use cell phones during Hanukkah, Jack asked, "Where's the bowl of cell phones?"

The target's son replied, "On the kitchen counter."

Jack looked around the small room and, deciding on a change of plans, said, "All right everyone, we're going down to the basement. Keep calm and I promise you, no one will be hurt."

The team escorted everyone into the basement and had them sit in a corner on their knees facing the wall. Jack grabbed two chairs for the target and his wife, who were also forced to face the wall.

Jack asked the son, "Is there a shower down here?"

"Yes, at the end of the hallway."

"We are all secure down here," Jack said into his mic. "Any chatter?"

"We're good here, Sarge," Stevens replied. "How long is E.T.A.?"

"We have a minor issue. Fifteen minutes tops."

"Hey, Sarge, any good-looking pussy with you?"

Jack ignored the last comment and moved to a bedroom. He grabbed a pair of pants and a shirt and returned to the team, who were standing in a huddle away from the group.

"I'm not continuing covered in these people's shit and piss. I'm hopping into the shower. I'll be two minutes max. Bricks, you keep everyone in check."

"You got it, Sarge."

Jack hopped into the shower fully clothed, then dropped the overalls and did a quick soapy rinse.

Just as he was stepping out of the shower, he heard the distinct sound of continuous rapid fire from a silenced Uzi.

He grabbed a towel, his 9 mm, and ran back to the group.

He got there only to see that Ivanna, and Ivanna alone, had just sprayed the entire group. They were all dead.

Jack was in a momentary state of shock and disbelief as he surveyed the carnage. He quickly regained his senses and looked over at Ivanna, only to find that she now had one of her Uzis pointed directly at his head.

"Are we good, Jack?"

Jack, whose towel had slipped off, made a motion toward his own 9 mm.

Stryker jumped in. "Uh-uh, Sarge. That's not a good move." Stryker moved forward and took Jack's gun from him.

"Are we good Jack?" Ivanna asked, running her eyes up and down Jack's naked body. "I guess you are good."

"Last time, Jack—I not fuck with you. Are we good?" she asked again.

"Were good, you crazy bitch."

As Jack changed into some clean clothes he had pilfered from the target's closet, he began relaying instructions.

"Check the area for fuel. We have a shitload of ordinance in the van. I want this entire house engulfed in five minutes and nobody take a fucking thing."

Within ten minutes the team was back on the road to Cleveland, with the Ambassador's private jet waiting solely for Jack to take him back to Israel.

The rest of the group had separate airline tickets to various locations throughout the country.

Jack was able to shower and shave on the flight and put on some of his own clean clothes. He wanted to speak directly to the Ambassador on the jet's phone, but as usual he couldn't get past Harvey, so he reluctantly debriefed him on the mission.

At the end of the debrief Harvey asked Jack, "Are you okay?"

"I'm fine, Harvey."

"It's the second day of Hanukkah, Jack. You should have known the Ambassador wouldn't have spoken to you, even if he wanted to."

"Right Harv… long flight. Maybe I'll just take a nap."

Once they'd landed, Jack once again found himself back in the Ambassador's office.

The usual security detail and Harvey were sitting at the back of the room. Jack was sitting on the couch alone as the Ambassador walked in, only this time he walked in with his arm around Margaret.

Jack hopped out of his seat and gave Margaret a heart-felt hug.

"Is our daughter here?"

"I'm sorry, dear, she's staying at a friend's house for the next ten days. The length of our surprise holiday together, Jack."

"When did you get here, Mouse?"

"I flew in two days ago and spent some time with my parents."

Jack and Margaret sat down on the couch and, uncharacteristic of Jack, he couldn't stop hugging and kissing Margaret. Maybe because he knew that soon the Ambassador would ask her to leave the room and Jack would have to explain the Akron massacre.

"Margaret, our chefs are making a spectacular feast for this evening's Hanukkah celebration. Would you mind checking on the kitchen staff to make sure they're doing all right, dear?"

Margaret understood that the Ambassador wanted to speak with Jack alone. "Okay, Wilhelm, but don't keep him too long."

Jack gave Margaret one last hug and kiss then walked her to the door and closed it behind her.

Harvey stood and started walking toward Jack.

"Sit down, Harvey. This is between me and the Ambassador."

"You know the Ambassador doesn't discuss business during Hanukkah, Jack."

"It's okay, Harvey," the Ambassador assured him. "Will all of you please leave Jack and me alone for a minute?"

Harvey and the Ambassador's two security men left the room.

"What the fuck happened, Wilhelm?"

"Language please, Jack. I understand you're upset with the loss of life, as am I. Let me assure you I will get a full report of what happened from the others."

"What's to report, Sir? I was away for two minutes cleaning shit off myself and that crazy psycho bitch murdered eight people."

"Well, if it's any consolation, you won't have to work with them again, Jack. This was a one-time operation."

Jack, having known the Ambassador long enough, could tell by his demeanor that this discussion was invariably going to end up going nowhere.

He presumably got his man, and the cost of lives were totally irrelevant to him. Jack changed the subject, just so he could get back to Margaret.

"So, I guess I'm on a ten-day vacation."

"Yes, Jack. My limo will take you to any hotel you choose and, of course, it is on me. Would I be correct in assuming you would prefer to be alone with Margaret this evening and forgo our festivities?"

"If you don't mind, Sir. I just want to eat and then sleep for a couple of days."

"Well, we will certainly miss you and Margaret this evening Jack. After your vacation I will get you back with a crew that you are more familiar with. Is this o.k. Jack?"

"Yes, Sir."

Just as Jack started to head for the door, the Ambassador asked him, "Jack, how did the target behave? Did he beg and plead for his life? Did he deny his involvement in the Holocaust?"

"I wouldn't know, Sir. We never got a chance to ask him anything before the bitch sprayed the room." Now at the doorway, Jack motioned for the Ambassador's minions to head back in.

When everyone was back in their places, Jack decided he was also going to leave a final remark of his own. He stared straight at the Ambassador as he said, "Well, I sure hope we got the right guy."

Heading off to meet Margaret and feeling a sliver of trepidation over what he'd just said, Jack was now thinking to himself, "I hope that wasn't a mistake."

With a dumbfounded look on his face, Harvey said to the Ambassador, "Do you still think he's our guy for next year?"

"Armen is a good boy, he will do as he is asked."

Chapter 5

PRIOR TWO DAYS

Back in Argentina, and two days prior to Debbie's bug bite...

Jack, being a creature of habit and a slave to his own routine promptly wakes up every morning at 5:00 a.m. He begins his day with a light stretch, then hammers out fifty push-ups on his fists, followed by ten to twenty minutes of sit-ups or crunches. Jack then puts on his morning running gear and is off for his daily one-hour run. At a six-mile-per-hour pace, Jack can get his ten miles done in an hour.

Like every other day, Jack plans his running route so that it takes him toward the sand dune bunker he has been excavating for the last two weeks.

Today is a strikingly monumental day for Jack. The day that he finally penetrates the sand-covered tomb that no eyes have seen in over seventy years.

His expectations are high, his anticipation rampant. As for his fear level? The plan is to get in and find what he needs and get the fuck out of there as quick as possible.

Back from his run, Jacks stops in at the canteen and see's that Cookie is working hard at getting the camp's breakfast ready. Jack eats at 7:00 a.m. The crew knows that if you want a fresh, warm breakfast that is when Cookie serves it up. Not wanting to bother Cookie, Jack heads off for his morning constitution and a shower.

After showering, Jack gets dressed in light camo gear, knowing it's going to be another hot day. He straps on his .38 and bowie knife and is off to eat breakfast. When he's done, he loads the Jeep with the gear he's going to need today. Sitting in the Jeep and ready to go, Jack has a huge grin on his face. Being a creature of habit, he sets off to wake the late-sleeping crew aboard the Miranda.

The Miranda is a ninety-foot, thirty-year-year old crabbing vessel that spent her summers in Seattle pulling salmon and her winters hauling crab from the Bering Sea.

The ship was purchased by the captain ten years ago on a vacation trip to Alaska. After falling in love with the boat, he ditched his old forty-footer and converted the Miranda into a deep-water salvager.

The captain named his boat after his mother, Miranda.

Jack approaches the dock where the Miranda moors every night and proceeds to walk up the gangway. As usual, he spots Debbie sipping a coffee on deck, and Rose lying at her feet.

Jack is standing at the top of the gangway and says to Deb, "Permission to come aboard, Captain?"

Without so much as a glance toward Jack, Deb says, "Permission denied, Jack."

"Oh, come on, Deb. I haven't even mentioned your tits yet."

"I'm hungover, Jack. It's too early for this shit."

"You're absolutely right, Deb. We can talk about the twins later. Does four o'clock work for you?"

Deb lowers her mirrored sunglasses and looks over at Jack who is now standing right in front of her as she gives him the finger.

Rose makes a beeline to Jack and is all over him. Jack bends down and Rose licks his face with her tail wagging up quite a storm.

Jack pets her all over, rubbing behind her ears, scratching her belly. Then he stands up and says, "Rose, sit." Rose promptly obeys and Jack gives her a slice of Cookie's bacon he had stashed in his pocket.

Deb says, "Rose, you're a traitor."

"Can you blame her, Deb? She's a female."

"You're right, Jack. Do you give your dates bacon slices, too?"

Jack sighs. "I'm going to wake the captain. Would I be correct in assuming he's hungover, too?"

"Yes, Jack. Unlike you, we are people who have a life and know how to enjoy it."

Hoping Debbie is watching through her mirrored glasses, Jack puts his hand over his heart as if he has just been wounded and, with a fake comical limp, he starts walking down the deck toward the captain's cabin. Just before he opens the bilge door, he glances back at Deb to find that she is watching him and has a cute smile on her face. "She likes me," Jack thinks to himself.

When he reaches the captain's door, he says in a loud panicked voice, "Captain, Captain, the Miranda is on fire! We have to abandon ship."

Jack can hear some stirring through the paper thin door and eventually the dishevelled captain opens it.

"Don't you ever get tired of that shit, Jack? Go wake up whoever the fuck you're taking today and let me get back to sleep."

Jack responds, "I'm taking Bear again today, Captain."

"Good, then go wake *him* up. Now if you don't mind I'm going to go puke and then try to get some more sleep, asshole."

"Thanks, Captain. Hope you feel better soon."

"Fuck you, Jack."

This will be the fifth time Jack has taken Rafael with him to the dig site. He is a hard worker, and working with him also gives Jack a chance to practise his Spanish.

Rafael is a not your stereotypical diminutive Mexican but a bear of a man at five-feet-eleven-inches and 250 pounds of solid muscle.

Jack knows he is Debbie's pseudo bodyguard and he respects him for that. Jack nicknamed him "Bear" the first time he met him. It's a nickname the crew of the Miranda does not use, probably because Jack came up with it.

Jack walks up to Bear's bunk and politely knocks on the door,

"You up, Bear?"

Rafael quickly opens the door and says good morning in Spanish. "*Buenos Dias.*"

Jack replies the same. "*Buenos Dias.*"

"Are you ready for another exciting day? We'll be cracking the seal today, Bear."

Rafael responds in a less than enthusiastic tone, "Sure Jack, whatever you say."

"Oh, come on, Bear, are you saying coming with me isn't better than pushing air down a hose looking for something that isn't there? At least with me, you know we're right on the precipice, big guy."

"Whatever you say, Jack."

"All right then, grab yourself a coffee to go. I got a plate of Mr. Singh's breakfast for you in the Jeep. I want be Oscar Mike in five."

"Oh, Jack, my friend, why are you always in such a rush? Have you not yet discovered how precious and ever so short life is? You really need to take the time and just relax. Smell the flowers once in a while."

"You know my favourite saying, Bear. 'Why do tomorrow what you could have done yesterday.' We're Oscar Mike in three, now."

Jack goes back to the deck and says goodbye to Debbie. "See you later, gorgeous."

"Goodbye, Jack. You better look after Rafael today."

"Always, hon."

Eager to get the show on the road, Jack walks down to the Jeep and starts it up. Just then he catches a glimpse of Bear walking onto the deck. He starts chatting with Deb and she points to a stack of folded lawn chairs. Rafael walks over, grabs one, opens it and sits down next to Deb, sipping his coffee.

Jack thinks to himself, "Tits is doing this on purpose." Refusing to let Debbie prevail, Jack turns off the Jeep, pops the hood and starts making like he needs to check the fluid levels.

After an interminably long twenty minutes, Bear finally arrives at the Jeep,

"I'm sorry, Jack. I hope I didn't keep you waiting."

Ignoring Bear, Jack stands on the Jeep's running board and makes a final exaggerated wave to Deb. She replies with a nice smile but ends up flipping Jack the bird.

"Now where's that breakfast, Jack?"

"Oh gee… I'm sorry, Bear. A seagull shit on it, so I had to throw it out. I guess you'll just have to wait until lunch there, big guy."

When Jack and Rafael approach the worksite, they see the sand dune is about a metre off the ground and surrounded by a field of solid rock.

Over the course of the last two weeks, Jack and his daily helpers from the Miranda have managed to dig out a pathway that is four metres long and two metres deep. The base and sides have been shored up using two-by-fours.

The only indicator that something was buried beneath the sand dune surrounded by stone is a small, almost undistinguishable, tip of an airplane wing. Unless you knew exactly what it was you were looking for, it would have gone undiscovered for another seventy years.

Jack backs up the Jeep to the entrance of their manmade culvert. Both men quickly unload their gear and once again, commence digging.

Rafael mumbles while he is digging, "Bird shit on my breakfast, my ass."

Seven long, arduous hours later, Rafael is planted under a tree eating Cookie's delicious lunch while Jack is still hard at it.

One last swipe of his shovel and Jack hears what he has been waiting to hear for the last two weeks... a scraping clank. That is the sound of a metal shovel scraping the side of a metal plane.

Jack quickly looks up to see where Rafael is. He drops the shovel and starts wiping away the sand on the side of the plane.

"Fuck," Jack is thinking... no door. Jack has dug his way into the top back of the plane with no doorway in site.

Jack grabs some two-by-fours and covers any exposed sections of plane's fuselage. Then he starts gathering his tools and loading up the Jeep.

Bear approaches him with a full stomach and a content look on his face. "Good to go again, Jack?"

"I think we're done for today, Bear."

"You won't get an argument from me."

"Good to hear. The Miranda won't be back at port for another hour. Do you want to grab a drink in town?"

"If you're buying, I'm drinking."

"Sure, Bear. You've earned it today."

Within a few minutes the men are off to the town of La Plata and their favourite locale watering hole, the Santo Pecado Bar.

After Rafael chugs his usual six pints to Jack's two double Scotch with no ice, Jack pays the tab, leaves a nice tip. Then he takes Rafael back to the Miranda.

At the pier, Rafael asks, "Do you think you will be needing me tomorrow?"

"No, Bear, but thanks for asking. I'll be working alone from here on out."

"You're never going to tell me what it is we were looking for, are you, Jack?"

"I could, Bear, but then I would have to kill you."

Bear lets out a loud chuckle and says, "All right, Jack. It was nice working with you." He says goodbye in Spanish, "*Buenos tardes*" and Jack replies with "*Buenos noches, mi amigo.*"

On his drive back to the compound, Jack's mind wanders to his last meeting with the Ambassador. Prior to the Ambassador funding the construction of the compound and additionally hiring the Miranda and crew as, for the lack of a better term, a decoy, Jack was in Israel at the Ambassador's palatial home.

Jack spent several days with the Ambassador. It was during that trip that the Ambassador relayed his rudimentary proposal to Jack. Jack having never said no to the Ambassador for anything, agreed to lead the team.

Over the course of next several days, the two men carefully and meticulously concocted Operation Stasis.

If Jack was to take anything away from his two-day meeting, it was this—once the plane was breached, Jack was to enter it *alone*.

Back at camp, Jack parks the Jeep over by the equipment shed and heads off to look for Sven. Jack finds Sven in the canteen and asks him to load an acetylene torch in the Jeep for tomorrow's trip. He also inquires as to Vic's whereabouts and is told he's taking his usual late-afternoon nap in his office.

Jack will have to go without his Scotch and cigar for now and heads off to the conference room. He has to phone the Ambassador on the satellite phone to let him know they finally touched metal.

In the conference room, Jack calls the Ambassador.

"Hello, Jack."

"Good afternoon, Ambassador."

"We're five hours ahead of you here, Jack. It's eleven o'clock here."

"Sorry if I have woken you, Sir. I knew you would want to know immediately that I struck plane, Sir."

"That is great news, Jack. Have you breached yet?"

"No, Sir. I had Rafael with me today. I was, however, able to keep him from knowing the reason behind our mission."

"That is very good, Jack. Very good."

"One thing, Sir. I will need to torch an opening tomorrow. There is no doorway in sight. Are we sure the plane is not carrying any ordinance?"

"There was no indication of that, Jack. You do what you need to do. So you say you will you be entering tomorrow?"

"Yes, Sir."

"One final thing. Tomorrow I want you to take Debbie."

"Debbie, Sir? Why on earth would I take Debbie?"

"Listen to me, Armen. Tomorrow you are to go to the Miranda, you will go directly to the captain and you will tell him that you are taking Debbie with you. If you have any problem, you have him phone me. Goodnight, Armen."

The Ambassador promptly hangs up before Jack can say anything.

For the last twenty years, the only time the Ambassador ever calls Jack by his Hebrew name is when he is extremely angry with him, or, as in this case, demanding unquestioning loyalty.

Jack's relationship with the Ambassador may have started out as professional, but over time it has evolved into one of friendship. Close enough that Jack considers him his surrogate father.

All things considered, if Jack has learned anything about the Ambassador it is that you do not want to be on his bad side. Over the years, he has seen the fallout with people who have betrayed him, retribution often meted out by Jack's own hand.

The rest of the evening is quiet and uneventful. All too repetitive and redundant for Jack. With his inability to escape his sole thought, that being tomorrow's breach, Jack decides to just hit the rack at nine.

Jack wakes up to find his internal alarm has failed him. Upon awakening, he feels there is something wrong right away and he glances at his watch. It is not 5:00 a.m.; it is in fact 6:20. Jack places his hand on his forehead checking for any temperature variance, then checks his pulse, but everything appears to be normal.

Then, out of the blue, as if being shocked by a cattle prod, his heart skips a beat and he recalls the Ambassador's final words to him, "Take Debbie."

Feeling too anxious about today's mission, Jack decides to skip his morning workout. But the one part of his daily regimen that he is not willing to forgo is his morning breakfast and talk with Mr. Singh.

On this morning, Jack and Cookie are alone... kind of.

Apparently, when Jack went to bed early last night, the rest of the crew decided to have their own little 'New year's Eve' in July party.

The evidence is there for all too see. Carl is passed out under the pool table with his jeans down to his waist and a pool cue sticking out of his ass.

"Looks like I missed a helluva party last night, huh, Cook?"

"You didn't miss anything, Jack. Just a bunch of grown men acting like teenagers. I spent an hour this morning cleaning up their puke just so you would not have to smell it with your breakfast."

"Thank you for that, Cookie. By the way, the pool cue... was that you?"

"Yes, that was me, boss." Cookie gives Jack a concerned look. "Are you okay, Jack? I didn't see you leave for your run this morning."

"I'm actually not sure, Cookie. I'm just not sure."

Jack finishes his meal with Cookie then heads outside to make sure Sven loaded the torch last night. With everything in order, Jack leaves to pick up Deb from the Miranda.

He parks at the marina and glances over to check the deck but sees no sign of Deb or Rose.

Not knowing where Debbie's cabin is and thinking he'd better run it by the captain first, Jack knocks on the captain's door. No pretend fire today, just a couple of heavy knocks loud enough to wake him up.

The captain can easily be heard bellowing from his bunk, "What the fuck is it today, Jack?"

"I need to speak with you, Cap."

"Rafael said you were done with the crew, Jack, and the door is unlocked, asshole."

Jack enters the captain's chambers.

"How did you know it was me outside the door, Cap?"

"Cause no one on this boat is stupid enough to wake their captain at 7:30 a.m. So, who the fuck else could it be? Spit it out, Jack, what!"

"I'm taking Debbie with me today, so just point me in the direction of her cabin. I'll wake her up myself, and you can get back to whatever it is you do in here alone in the morning, Cap."

The captain brushes the sleep from his eyes and starts feeling around on the floor for his glasses. He finds them and puts them on.

"You...uh...wanna turn around for a sec, Jack? I sleep in what God gave me."

"Shy, Captain?"

"No, asshole, I just don't like you. As a matter of fact, just go to the galley and I'll be there when I'm there."

Jack gives the captain a half-hearted, flimsy military salute and heads for the galley.

The captain quickly gets dressed and the whole time he's thinking only one thing. 'There is no way on God's green earth that Jack is taking Debbie today! Or any other goddamn day, for that matter!'

Jack decides to make some coffee in the galley and is looking at the pictures on the wall. He guesses the captain hung them up as they are all of the Miranda when it was a crabbing vessel in the Bering Sea.

There are pictures of the numerous crab crews from over the years. Just shots of overloaded pots of crab, a few pictures of smashed-in fingers and a close-up shot of some poor dude's busted up nose.

The Captain finally stumbles his way into the galley. "Okay, Jack. What is this nonsense about taking Debbie today? Rafael is probably gonna be useless to me today. Seven hours of digging, Jack? Are you serious?"

Jack interrupts him long enough to say, "He's a big boy, Captain."

"Enough, Jack. I'm not done talking. On this ship I am the fucking captain, so when I say you can talk, then you will talk. Seven hours of digging… Did you ever think, uh, maybe we should rent a scoop truck from town? Now you can talk, Jack."

"First off, Captain, the nature of my work does not concern you. The crew members that I require do not concern you, and the condition that I return them in does not concern you.

"The only thing that need concern you right now is not pissing me off. One call by me and your little Argentinian vacation is over."

"Fuck you, Jack. That fat piece of shit you call a boss isn't going to do shit and if I say Deb is not going then she is not going with you today, Jack, end of story."

"If you're referring to Victor, Cap—" Jack pauses long enough to force a chuckle for the benefit of the Captain. "You got me there, Cap, that fat piece of wasted skin is not going to do anything.

"Unfortunately for you, Cap, I do not work for Victor. I take my marching orders from a man you have never met, and for your own sake, just be happy you are not on his radar. On this you will have to just take my word for it.

"If you still feel you need to call someone, go ahead. I'll give you ten minutes and I'm being gracious giving you that, Sig.

"But, before you go ahead with your call, may I suggest to help expedite the process you start by looking at the signature on the contract you signed? I believe you will find that nowhere in the contract is there a guy named Victor.

"However, if you were, in fact, to flip over to page four, you would see my name and the all-inclusive authority that has been granted to, you guessed it, me.

"I understand your reservations, Sig, I truly do. I happened to be at the Ambassador's home in Israel when he was signing your massive retainer cheque.

"And I'm sure when Harvey presented you with that fat cheque, I probably would have glossed over the contract myself and got the fuck outta there while the getting was good. Sound about right, Sig?

"So, enough of this bullshit. I want Deb in my fucking Jeep and ready to go in twenty minutes, and if you say one word to her about our conversation I will be back, and we will be having a totally different conversation.

"Now then, permission to leave the boat, Sir?"

The captain leaves the galley and Jack without saying another word.

As Jack is making his way out of the ship's holding, he overhears the captain knocking on Deb's door and yelling for Deb to get up.

Nineteen and a half minutes later, Debbie is walking down the gangway. She's got a scone lodged in her mouth, one hand on her coffee and the other hand trying to assemble some form of style into her hair. She climbs into the Jeep with a simple, "Jack."

Jack responds with an uncharacteristically solemn, "Good morning."

Jack should be feeling great this morning with the breach of his long sought-after quarry imminent. But on this warm Argentinian morning, Jack is just not feeling like himself. He missed his morning run and workout. He was forced into a battle of words with the captain, who happens to be a man he actually likes and admires.

The Captain was a decorated soldier and ran a gun boat in the Vietnam War.

Jack can't help but feel as though he has a hostage in his Jeep this morning and, frankly, his preeminent nervous thought is what he might find in that plane.

Jack is still at a loss and is trying to reconcile with himself as to why the Ambassador insisted on Debbie being here today.

Debbie finishes her scone and finally looks over at Jack and gives him the once-over. She does a double take and then looks down at herself. She is wearing a pair of shorts and a tank top—it's eighty degrees already and it's still only 8:30 in the morning. She's thinking to herself, "Am I missing something?" Jack is covered head to toe in not just one layer of clothing, but several. Deb is still pissed at her abrupt awakening so the trip to the job site is quiet.

"Okay, Deb, we're here," Jack says, when they pull up to the sand dune. "As you haven't been here before, just let me get everything setup first then I'll find something for you to do."

Debbie is not used to just sitting around doing nothing so she ignores Jack and helps him unload the Jeep. Together they set up the generator and the acetylene torch. Jack removes all the two-by-fours he laid out to obscure Bear's view the other day and starts to cut out an opening into the plane.

Within an hour, Jack has made an opening big enough to crawl into and he peels open the plane's metal covering like an orange.

Jack grabs a large flashlight and tells Deb to hang back for a few minutes while he makes sure everything inside is safe and secure.

Jack climbs through the opening and notices that the front half of the plane is completely covered by a wall of sand. The plane must have broken in half upon impact some seventy years ago. As Jack is looking around, he is now concerned whether the object he is looking for was supposed to be in the front of the plane or the back.

Through its markings, Jack discerns this is indeed the plane they have been searching for. A four-man Focke-Wulf Ta 152 high-altitude German fighter plane.

Spotting no human remains, Jack can only assume the crew must have all been in the front portion of the plane.

As Deb is clamouring at the opening, wanting to come in and see for herself, Jack rebukes her and hastens his search.

Years of searching for the plane's whereabouts and incredible amounts of money spent all rely on Jack finding one single item.

A cigar box.

Jack spots a machine gun bullet nest case that appears to have been badly damaged in the crash. Lying next to it is an undamaged metal cigar box with Nazi emblems on either side.

Jack opens the box and finds three undamaged cigars inside. There is one cigar that is broken in half and partially crushed. Surrounding the damaged cigar are small fragments of broken glass and the remaining half of a small hollow glass cylinder.

Jack grabs one of the undamaged cigars and, using his bowie knife, makes a lengthwise slit down the middle, gently peeling it open. Inside is the same small glass cylinder, only this one is fully intact. Jack shines his flashlight on the glass cylinder and notices there is a small item in it.

Jack quickly searches the area nearby and is able to uncover a file folder sitting under a pile of debris. The outer cover of the file folder is emblazoned with Nazi swastikas and has only two words on it, "*Betieb Stase*" which translates to Operation Stasis.

So intrigued and frankly terrified by his find, Jack has been temporarily pre-occupied and oblivious to his surroundings. Once he gets his bearings he shouts out to Deb, "Deb, I'm coming out."

Deb responds, "I'm right here, you moron."

Carrying a flashlight of her own, Deb had slipped into the plane without Jack noticing. She further says to Jack, "I wasn't going to sit out there all day, Jack. My God, how old is this plane and where the hell is the front of it? Did you find what you're looking for?"

Jack quickly closes up the cigar box, grabs the file and stuffs them both into his jacket.

"Deb, get the fuck out of here. I told you to wait outside, it's not safe in here."

The next thing out of Debbie's mouth is, "Ouch that hurt!"

Chapter 6

PLANS CHANGE

Dr. Skeane, having just been shot in the kneecap, lets out a bellowing wail of anguished pain.

"You know you had that coming, Skinny. Be grateful I didn't end your miserable life, you pathetic rapist."

"You're fucking crazy, Jack. You hit me in the kneecap. You have to take me into town or I'm gonna bleed out. Please, Jack."

"You got more problems than that knee, Skinny."

Jack walks over to Deb and gently lifts the sheet covering her. He points to the three tracking marks on her stomach that are heading off in three different directions just under her skin. He gently covers her up and walks over to the caterwauling, bellowing Dr. Skeane.

Jack reaches down and after slapping Skeane's hands away several times, he lifts up the man's scrub shirt. He then points to Deb and pats Skeane on his stomach, "Do you get it now, Doc?"

"You're crazy, Jack. Do you really think you're gonna get away with this?"

"Quit your whining, you little bastard. Lucky for you we have guests that just arrived. There is someone who can fix that knee right up for you. You'll no doubt have a limp the rest of your life, but you did this to yourself, Skinny."

"You're dead, Jack. When the Ambassador finds out what you've done…you're dead. Who's going to look after the bitch now? The others would have heard the shot, Jack. They'll be coming soon."

"With the noise coming off of those generators, Skinny, I don't think so."

Jack looks at the pile of medical supplies and throws Dr. Skeane a roll of gauze. "Here, Skinny. Wrap your knee in that."

"Jack, in that cupboard is a vile of morphine. Please hand it to me, the pain is unbearable. Please, Jack."

"How do I know you won't go into shock, Skinny? I can't risk anything happening to you. And by the way, you can file your grievance with the Ambassador in person. He arrives tomorrow afternoon."

With the news of the Ambassador coming in person, Skeane turns white as a ghost. The seething, blinding pain from his knee is now secondary. "You're not going to tell him what happened, are you Jack? Please Jack, don't tell him anything…and get me my fucking morphine, you sadistic fuck."

"I told you, Doc, no drugs. I gotta make a call, Skinny, so you just sit there and bleed. Help will be here when it's here."

Dr. Skeane continues to whine and berate Jack, switching back and forth between calling Jack every name in the book and pleading for some medicinal relief.

Completely ignoring Skeane, Jack walks over to Deb and slides her sheet down to her waist. He takes note of the progressive movement of the three markings just under her skin. Looking around, he grabs a thermal blanket and gently folds the blanket around her body, trying to make her as comfortable as she can be under the circumstances.

Unfortunately, Jack knows comfort is not anywhere in Deb's future. Even though Deb is in a fully comatose state, Jack still leans forward and whispers into her ear, "You will see Rose again, Deb. I promise." He is thinking to himself that Deb can't be more than twenty-five. He is thinking about her family back in Texas, about Rafael and the crew of the Miranda. If only she would have just listened to him and stayed outside of the plane.

Jack is also pondering the first time they met onboard the Miranda. He was saying hello to her and his eyes just happened to drop down to read the logo on her T-shirt. It had an arrow pointed upwards with the words, 'My eyes are up here.' Debbie noticed his eyes drop and said, "Getting a good look, are ya?"

Well, Jack couldn't help but be Jack. So if this was how Debbie saw him, he was going to play it up for her benefit.

Which was contrary to his true character. He had learned from his mother as a child that women should always be treated with the utmost respect and that is how he had always lived his life.

Jack made a conscious exception with Debbie. He could see right away that she was an exceptional young lady with a wit that matched his mother's. He truly believed Deb enjoyed their verbal jousting just as much as he did.

Now all he feels is sickening heartbreak.

Jack takes a final glance around the medical tent. He notices Dr. Skeane is crawling his way toward the morphine stash, which is atop a six-foot-high shelf. "Good luck with that," he thinks to himself.

He leaves the tent, seals it up and heads to the conference room to make his call.

All is quiet as Jack walks across the compound to the conference room. He spots the gate where he usually waves to either Rick or Carl, but he's so tired he can't remember who is on tonight. Rick waves back and shouts, "Hoo-hah, Sarge."

When Jack reaches the conference room, he notes it is now 3:00 a.m. Argentinian time. He does some quick math and figures it's 8:00 a.m. in Orange County, California.

Jack places his call home.

Margaret answers the phone. "Well, you're not dead," she says.

"You're still getting the Ambassador's cheques every month, aren't you?" Jack asks her.

"Yes, but you told me many times, Armen, that I will get Wilhelm's cheques every month whether you're alive or not."

"Can't you call me Jack, Margaret?"

"Why, Armen? Does my calling you by your Hebrew name remind you of your Ambassador being displeased with you?"

Jack mutters to himself, "You have no idea."

"What was that, Armen?"

"Nothing, dear. Is Debra home?"

"She's just getting ready. I'm driving her to that degenerate high school in ten minutes."

"What's the problem this time, Marg?"

"It's the same problem, Armen. The bullying, the teasing and that goddamn Facebook. We live in a county of beautiful genetically enhanced Barbie dolls. What do you expect? Your daughter inherited your chest and my looks, Armen, not yours."

"Stop that, Margaret. You will always be beautiful to me, and there is nothing wrong with our daughter."

"Okay, Armen, I'll call her—just prepare yourself to listen to all of her demands."

Margaret yells through the house, "Debra, your father's on the phone."

Debra answers the phone, "Hi, Jack."

"Good morning, dear. Why can't you call me Dad, honey?"

"Because a dad is not away for years at a time, Jack."

"You know Daddy has a very important job, honey."

"Give it a rest, Jack. I haven't seen you in over a year and you can stop calling me 'honey.' I'm not eight years old anymore."

"Fine, Debra. I was just thinking about you and I wanted to talk to you. How is everything going? How's school?"

"You already know what I want, Jack—the same thing I've been asking for since I was fourteen. You told me we would discuss it when I turned sixteen, I'm eighteen now... *Dad.*"

"Okay, hon. Dad may not be getting Uncle Wilhelm's cheques anymore, but I have some money put aside. When I'm back in the States we'll have a serious talk about it."

Margaret, who is listening in on the conversation on the other line, jumps in,

"What the hell are you saying, Armen? Is Wilhelm dead? Are you in trouble?"

"Let me finish with Debra, please, Margaret, then we'll talk."

"Listen, Deb, your father is going to be fine. I will try to make it back as soon as I can, then we'll go to the doctor together."

"Thank you, Dad. I love you. Are you sure you're okay?"

"Yes, hon. You know your father—nothing will keep me from seeing you again and soon. Now hang up please so your mom and I can talk."

"Okay. Bye, Dad. I love you."

"Love you, too, hon. Have a good day at school."

"Listen, Margaret," Jack says as Debra hang up. "Give me one minute without saying anything. I am fine—I have a minor hiccup I have to deal with and then I will be coming home."

"What home are you talking about, Armen? You left me, remember? You didn't even have the guts to just grant me a divorce. You know I'm seeing someone now, Armen. He's a banker, and he knows how to treat a lady."

"That's fine, Margaret. I'm happy for you. Now I need you to listen to me. Do you still have the key I gave you?"

Margaret's face pales and she tries to hide her panic with Debra standing right next to her ready to be driven to school.

"Oh, Armen, what have you done? Are you telling me the one man on earth you didn't ever want to be upset with you, now is?"

"No, no, Margaret. I mean, I'm just not sure yet. Something has happened, I will know more within the next twenty-four hours. I just need to know that you still have the key."

"Yes, Armen. I have the bloody key."

"If anything does happen, Roger will contact you. You listen to Roger and nobody else, especially if the Ambassador calls. If it comes to the point where you and Deb may need to leave for a while, Roger will be there and he will handle everything. You must do whatever he says, okay? I really have to go now. Goodbye, dear."

Jack hangs up the phone.

Margaret hangs up the phone and is now feeling horrible about lying to Jack about seeing someone else. She just wanted to try and get a rise out of him to gauge if he still cared about her.

Sitting alone in the conference room, Jack is thinking back to his SEAL training days, when he first met Roger.

Both started out in the navy and were in different units. They excelled at every level and had the respect of grunts and officers alike. They were both in the military for their fellow soldiers, not the government.

Roger stayed with the SEALs for only one year, as he took a lucrative position with a private security firm operating primarily in Iraq and Afghanistan, but he and Jack remained close friends.

With the nature of their ever-changing field of work and the omnipresent risk of corporate betrayal, years ago Jack and Roger devised run-and-hide strategies that also included Jack's family and Roger's mother.

Over the last couple of years, Roger has spent more time with Margaret and Debra, than Jack has.

The fact that Roger has never met the Ambassador and Jack has instinctively never revealed his employer or the nature of his work to Roger, makes Jack feel secure in the fact that Roger is the most reliable and dependable safety net for Jack and his family.

Whether the outcome for either men is death or a forced retreat. Jack is confident with the safeguarded efforts they have in place.

Having hung up the phone, Jack is now forced back to reality. He can't help but start to second-guess the Ambassador's most recent decision.

The original plan was for Jack to retrieve the package and deliver it in person via private jet to the Ambassador's mansion in Israel. The sealed medical tent was all set up for him, and him alone, should anything bad have happened.

Jack is racking his brain trying to figure out what could have possibly been the cause for the change in plans. His unbridled commitment to the Ambassador over the course of the last twenty years has been unquestionable. The only hiccup in their relationship was the Ohio extraction fifteen months ago, when Ivanna lost her shit.

Could it be as simple as that? Jack had insisted on being released from the group. The Ambassador wasn't pleased at the time, but he had assured Jack that all was good.

Jack had made himself clear with the Ambassador on many occasions that any civilian casualties were unacceptable. Was his insistence on this issue the beginning of the end?

As Jack sees it, he is now faced with three options.

The first is to leave Debbie and Skeane to their own devices and try to get a few hours' sleep before the new arrivals awaken.

The second is to go wake up Ivanna, hope she has kept up with her medical training and have her try to get the bugs out of Debbie. If he goes this route, it would mean trying to make it to the Miranda with Debbie, as the Ambassador would not want her alive to talk about what happened. He would then let Ivanna fix up Skeane, or he could just blow his worthless brains out.

The third is to have Ivanna fix up the doc and just let Debbie succumb to her fate.

Based on his conversation with his own daughter moments ago, Jack feels his only viable option is to think about his family first. If bigger tits and a nose job are going to give his daughter some peace, then he is going to make it happen.

Jack ends up choosing option four.

With the Ambassador having had Jack's back for over twenty years, it is his fervent hope that if he can get him alone for a few minutes tomorrow afternoon, he may be able to persuade him to have Ivanna do everything she can to free Debbie of her unwanted guests and quell her imminent demise.

Based on what the Ambassador detailed to Jack in Israel two months ago, Debbie has, give or take, another eighteen hours.

As for Skeane, Jack's still not ruling out a bullet to the head before the Ambassador arrives tomorrow. Back in Israel, both men reached an unspoken understanding that that would ultimately be the doc's fate anyway.

Jack shuts off the conference room light, closes the door and is looking forward to a couple hours' sleep.

As he is walking to his bunk, he looks over and notices the canteen lights are still on. Standing outside the doorway is a very tall figure. Jack figures it must be Stevens, as the depraved asshole is six-foot-six.

Stevens, seeing Jack, shouts for Jack to come over.

Jack yells back, "What the fuck are you guys doing up?"

"We heard the gunshot, Sarge. All the boys are inside having a drink. Why don't you come join us and tell us what's going on?"

"All right, I'll be there in a minute. Just let me grab something from my room."

Stevens quickly pops his head into the room and tells Bricks that Jack is going to his room first. Bricks yells at Stevens, "Don't let him go to his room, you idiot. Get him here now."

Stevens yells, "Hold up, Sarge. We already got a bottle here."

"Okay, shithead. I just wanted to check on Rick."

Jack quickly jaunts over to the gate, whispers something in Rick's ear and hightails it back to the cafeteria.

Once there, he says, "I told you this is a closed site, pervert."

"You said that about pussy, Jack. You never mentioned no booze," Stevens replies.

"With all due respect, Sarge, get your ass in here! It's freezing out there. Close the fucking door, Stevens," yells Bricks.

Jack quickly scans the room. Bricks, Stryker and Stevens are the only ones there. No sign of the witch. He looks to see if they are carrying any weapons. No visible Kalashnikovs, but it is a cool Argentinian evening and they are all in their military gear, so he's pretty sure they're all packing.

Jack wonders, if they heard the shot, where is the rest of the camp? Jack can only conclude that someone has been on 'Jack detail' ever since they arrived.

Jack takes a seat while Stryker pours him a shot of dark rum.

Bricks starts off. "What the fuck, Jack? You shoot some asshole in the knee?"

"He had it coming. Where's the witch?"

"We all walked over there, Jack. She's working on the doc as we speak. You can't expect the Ambassador to be pleased with this latest event, can you? Did you think about the ramifications before pulling the trigger?"

Jack can start to feel his blood boiling over and is becoming ever more impatient and really starting to get pissed off. The men are referring to him as Jack now, and he knows some shit is about to go down.

"Skinny was jerking off over the casualty, boys. He had it coming."

"That is the sweetest piece of tail I have ever seen in my life, Jack. I don't blame him," Stevens chimes in.

Bricks quickly admonishes Stevens. "Shut the fuck up, you fucking pervert. If Jack felt that is what needed to be done, then who the fuck are we to question him, right? We just got here a few hours ago for fuck's sake. Jack's been here for two months."

"We have to discuss the next step, Jack," Bricks continued. "The Ambo is here tomorrow—how do we explain to him you fucked up the doc?"

Jack now realizes Bricks is obviously the group's new leader, which is probably for the best since he is the sanest of the four. It's been 15 months since the bungled Ohio extraction and Jack's last mission with them.

"Fuck the doc, Bricks. Ivanna probably has more skills then that piece of shit anyway. Look guys, I see our bottle is running low, I know where I can get some more primo Scotch. I'll be back in five, and we can talk this through."

"You're not keeping booze in your room, are you Jack? I thought this was a closed site," Stevens says.

"No, moron, I got a stash in the manager's office. You'll meet that piece of work tomorrow."

Jack knows returning to his room without the situation turning into a gun battle is now out of the question. He suspects his room is all torn up anyhow.

Jack makes his way to Vic's office. Bricks makes a hand motion to Stevens to keep his eyes on Jack and goes back to standing in front of the canteen.

Jack uses his usual method to get into Vic's office. On this particular raid, Jack reaches under a second board he had loosened himself and that is unknown to Vic. He retrieves half a bottle of Scotch and the package he moved earlier in the evening.

Jack stuffs the package in his coat pocket and heads back to the canteen. Victor was so pissed drunk when he passed out in his bed, he didn't hear a thing.

Jack notices Stevens back out on the deck having a smoke and watching his every move. Jack thinks to himself, you die first tonight.

Jack is back inside and pours everyone a double. The three unwanted guests all slam back their drinks and feign like they are relishing the flavour and vintage. Frankly, home-made hooch usually placates their palates.

Stevens looks over at Bricks with a smug grin on his face, then says to Jack, "You know what would be great with this Scotch, Jack? A nice cigar."

If Bricks had anything in his stomach he would have shit himself on the spot. He just smiles and sips his Scotch, keeping one eye on Jack at all times.

"Okay, men," Jack says. "As I see it, nothing has changed. The doc fucked up and I delivered the appropriate level of justice. The witch is now fixing him up, so why don't we finish our drinks, hit the rack and we'll move the tour-and-sit rep to 0900?"

"The Ambassador won't be here till 1600 hours, so I think in the morning we can come up with a plan to placate the man. Do I have your backs, gentlemen?" Jack asks.

The men all look at each other and, judging by their faces, the general consensus is, what happened to the old Jack they remember? Why has Jack not already pulled his revolver? All are taken aback by Jack's attitude and proposal. The entire time, Stryker is sitting quietly, gun in his pocket, finger on the trigger pointed right at Jack.

Bricks is the first to speak. "We got your back, Sarge. Right, boys? Let's get some sleep and we'll look at the situation with clear eyes in the morning. Thanks for the extra sleep time, Sarge."

The others all acknowledge and agree to the plan, as well.

"All right then, you men hit the racks. I'm going to check on the witch and the doc and then I'll be heading straight for bed."

Bricks gives Stevens a look and Stevens pipes up, "Uh, Sarge, I'm all wired up from all this excitement. Do you mind if I join you?"

Jack finishes his Scotch. "Not at all brother. Let's go."

"Can you put the glasses away, Bricks?" he asks. "Cookie will be in here in a couple of hours and I don't want him to have to clean up our mess."

"You got it, Sarge."

Stevens politely gestures for Jack to leave the canteen first. "Age before beauty, Sarge."

"Have you looked at yourself in the mirror lately, asshole?" Jack replies, but Jack he leads the way out anyhow.

Stevens quickly glances back at Bricks and receives a nod.

The three men know that the inevitable has arrived. They can't let Jack return to see his upturned room and they can't kill him without getting the package. Doing so could cost them all their lives, most likely at the hands of the Ambo's imminently arriving, new crew.

The plan running through Bricks' mind is to let Jack do his thing, and before he enters his bunk do whatever is necessary to contain and detain him until the Ambo arrives. Much easier said than done.

Bricks surmises that Jack is not stupid enough to have the package on him.

Both men make their way toward the medical tent. As Stevens insisted on Jack leaving the canteen first, he is walking behind him the whole way.

As they approach the running generators with the medical tent strategically hidden behind, Jack takes a quick glance back and sees it is still only Stevens behind him.

Now out of view of the canteen, Jack turns back to Stevens and without saying a word, pops two into his chest from his .38 that is still in his jacket pocket. Jack pulls out his silenced gun and pops one more into Stevens' temple.

When he unzips the tent what he immediately sees catapults him into an unbridled, indignant rage.

The doc is comfortably laid out on the medical bed. He is knocked out and has air and intravenous lines all hooked up to him. Ivanna is wearing a hazmat suit under her scrubs. She has already removed the bullet and is just finishing sewing the wound around the shattered knee fragments. A quick job at best, most likely enough to stabilize the doc and keep him alive.

Debbie, on the other hand, has been unceremoniously dumped onto the cold cement floor, completely naked and with one leg twisted under her back in a position no leg should be in.

Jack now has his .38 centred directly at Ivanna's head.

Jack gestures to Ivanna to lower her mask,

"Put the needle down, Ivanna. We're all going on a little road trip."

"Uh, uh," he says as Ivanna goes to reach for her handgun. Jack walks over and grabs Ivanna's gun from where it is sitting on top of the medical tray.

"I'm not going anywhere with you, Jack. Actually I'm quite surprised you're still drawing breath."

Jack walks over to Ivanna and says, "That's what I was hoping you would say." Just then he lays down a thunderous right to Ivanna's chin and helps her down as she crumples, unconscious, to the ground.

Jack pulls out all of Skeane's medical lines and shoves him off the table on to the cold concrete floor. Then he quickly and very gently picks up Debbie. He wraps her in a blanket and rushes her to the back of his waiting Jeep.

He returns to the medical tent and straps Ivanna's hands behind her back, then ties her feet together and gags her mouth. Once he is certain she won't be able to move when she wakes up, he carries her to the front seat of the Jeep. He makes sure to strap his belligerent, unconscious passenger in with the seat belt.

Back at the tent again, Jack grabs as many cases of medical supplies as he can. With one final look around the tent, he is ready to bolt. He looks over at Skeane and decides to just leave him as is.

Knowing the generators should mask the sound of him starting the Jeep, Jack starts it up and begins backing out. He quickly stops the Jeep and notices the air has been let out of all four tires.

Jack has to make a quick decision: start a firefight with the two remaining men, both of whom he has no desire to kill? Or set out on a forty-five-minute drive on a goat path with no tires? The only viable option is to try to make it to the Miranda in the Jeep and pray to God she is still in port.

Jack proceeds slowly, and as he approaches mid camp, he guns it for the gates. As he reaches the front of the barracks,

Bricks and Stryker are standing outside. Stryker goes to raise his gun and Bricks pushes it back down. Bricks lets Jack drive on through. As Jack passes the men, Bricks shouts out, "See you soon, Jack."

Jack slows down just long enough to put a couple of bullets into the front and rear ambulance tires.

As he approaches the gate, Rick quickly opens the gate for him and shouts out, "Good luck, Jack!"

Jack isn't worried about the safety of his crew back at the compound when the Ambassador arrives. As he sees it, they have always been loyal hand-picked men and he's certain the Ambassador will be smart enough to realize that Jack is the only defector.

With the package now retrieved, the camp will be promptly liquidated as if it was never there. Where, theoretically, it never was.

After a jostling sixty-minute trip, Jack approaches the outskirts of the town of La Plata. He again has to remind the now-awake Ivanna to keep from bouncing around or he'll happily administer another blow. With the time approaching 4:30 a.m., the town is quiet with no one on the streets.

After another ten minutes—and leaving a wake of crumpled cement and sparks from the Jeep's now bare rims—the unlikely trio arrive at the water inlet of Rio de la Plata.

With Jack unable to come up with a Plan B on his way to the pier, he is overwhelmed with relief when he sees the Miranda is still docked.

Parking in his usual spot, he can see the Miranda has all of its running lights on and the engine going. Rafael is out on the deck. Five more minutes and Jack would have missed them.

Rafael won't be able to hear the Jeep's horn with the Miranda's engine running, so Jack makes the decision to grab Ivanna first. He throws her over his shoulders and runs her as fast as he can up the gangway.

With a look of total shock, Rafael is only able to muster a completely dumfounded, '*Buenos dias*' to Jack.

With no time for morning pleasantries or even a truncated explanation, Jack orders Rafael to grab a few men and go grab Deb and the gear from the Jeep.

Jack turns his attention back to Ivanna who is still tied up and lying on the damp deck. He once again hoists her over his shoulder and carries her down to a crab hold in the bottom of the boat that has a locking door.

Jack races back up to the deck. Rafael has Debbie in his arms and a look on his face that he is going to kill Jack as soon as he puts her down.

"Bear, put her in the captain's bunk for now and put all of the medical equipment in the galley."

Finally, Jack rushes to the wheelhouse to convince the captain they need to leave, and leave now.

Chapter 7

THE MIRANDA

The captain is sitting at the controls, sipping his morning coffee,

"Oh, good morning, Jack. Did you come to say goodbye or have you not heard we're now sitting at this dock illegally? Oh, of course you heard. Victor said the orders came from you."

"I don't have time to explain, Captain, but I need you to get us out of Argentinian waters now, or we will all be dead before breakfast."

"We will leave, Jack, when I'm ready to leave. I'm just waiting for those pissant government dicks to come by and kick us out. I expect them to show up any moment, and be sure I will be registering an official complaint with the Argentinian minister. Even Argentina has laws, Jack."

"Listen to me, Cap. The men that are coming may or may not be government men, but they are not coming to seize your boat. They are coming to liquidate everyone on this boat."

"What crap are you talking about, Jack? Have you been drinking all night at the Santo Pecado?"

"You need to listen to me for a change. Bear just carried Deb to your cabin. Call him up on the radio if you need to."

"Deb's back in Texas, Jack. Nice try."

"Jesus Christ, you fucking moron." Jack grabs the boat's mic and yells for Bear to get to the wheelhouse, now.

Bear, who was already on his way up, reaches the wheelhouse and tries to grab Jack, screaming, "What the fuck did you do to her?"

Jack quickly stifles Rafael's attempt to grab him and places him in a very uncomfortable wrist lock.

"Bear, I'm sorry. I will let you go if you promise to calm down. Captain, we have to get this boat out of port, now… please!"

Rafael finally gestures that he will relent and Jack lets him go.

Furious, the captain demands an explanation from Rafael. "Is Debbie downstairs or not?" he asks.

"Yes, Captain, and she's a fucking mess. I don't know what this guy did to her but …"

"Enough, Rafael." The captain grabs the mic. "All hands on deck, prepare to cast off. Prepare for full speed, gentlemen. We're getting out of dodge and we're doing it quickly."

The crew quickly scrambles and casts the ropes onto the pier, and within moments the Miranda is on her way.

Jack reiterates to the captain, "We need to get out of Argentinian waters as fast as this boat will take us, Captain."

"Rafael, when we're out of port, you take the wheel. I'm going to go check in on Debbie."

"Call someone else up to do it, Captain. I'm coming with you. You know we can't trust this guy, and if he tries that slick karate shit again, I'll be ready this time."

The captain, now at his wits end and nursing another major hangover, goes back on the mic. "First mate to the wheelhouse. If I don't like what I see down there, Jack. I'm going to let Rafael break you in two."

The Miranda is now out of port and operating at full speed. She's charted for the open ocean and the quickest route out of Argentinian waters.

Jack knows with the Ambassador's reach, it will only be a matter of time before all government coast guard vessels in the region will be looking for them.

The captain, Rafael and Jack make their way to the captain's cabin.

The captain enters his room and sits down next to Deb. He brushes her hair back and gently pats her on her face, trying to revive her somehow.

He then says, "What the fuck is this on her face? It looks like someone spit on her fucking face, Jack."

Jack looks closer and exclaims, "Oh shit, I was moving so fast I never noticed it. That would probably be the bitch I have locked up in the crab hold."

Rafael hurries to the galley and returns with a wet cloth to wipe Debbie's face.

"As ugly as this all is gentleman," Jack says. "We just don't have a lot of time. The bitch in the basement is medically trained and may be Deb's only chance for survival."

Having been in the military, the captain is familiar with all types of injuries. He slides down Debbie's blanket and starts checking her body for further wounds. As he lowers her blanket, his years of training and seeing some of the ugliest things men can do to one another are what keep him from jumping back and recoiling in fear. He takes his glasses out of his pocket and painstakingly examines the three streaming lines on Debbie's stomach.

"What is this, Jack? It's something I've never seen before."

"The simplest and quickest way to explain it to you both is she has a type of bug in her that has left her paralyzed. When she was bitten under her breast, the mother released two babies. They are now feasting and growing, and they will soon make their way out of Debbie's skin and assume their mother's role and look for a new host. The mother is going for the heart, where she will continue to feast until Debbie and then her, both die."

As Jack was talking, the captain and Rafael slowly rose from their seats and maneuvered themselves to the farthest open corner of the very small room.

"I know this is some unbelievable science fiction shit. The reality is, it is here. It is in this room and it is inside of Debbie right now. We need to turn the galley table into an operating table and we gotta get Ivanna from downstairs.

She's Debbie's only hope for getting these little bastards out of her and I'm sorry, gentleman, but we need to do it now!"

The captain, still in shock and disbelief, orders Rafael to set up the kitchen galley table for the operation. He instructs Jack to go get Ivanna. The captain plans on calling all the men to the wheelhouse and is trying to formulate something to tell them. His final comment is for Jack.

"When this is done, Jack, if you don't explain yourself better as to how and why this occurred, there is going to be a burial at sea today. Do you understand me?"

The captain's words barely register as Jack's mind is focused on how to convince Ivanna to help Debbie without having to kill her to do it.

As Jack unlocks and enters the crab bay, he is punched hard on the side of his face. He quickly recovers, backs up and pulls out his .38. He gives Ivanna the option to die on the spot or help him get the bugs out.

Having spent a month with Jack in Cleveland prior to the Akron Eight massacre, Ivanna instinctively knows that he is not fucking around. She quickly acquiesces while Jack follows her to the galley with his gun nestled squarely at the back of her neck.

As they're walking Jack asks, "Was the spit really necessary?"

"Her looks pissed me off."

"That's low, even for you Ivanna."

"Maybe I slip with the scalpel, Jack."

Jack stops Ivanna in her tracks and pulls her close to him. "Let there be no false illusions here, Ivanna. The girl dies, you die on the spot. She lives, then you put on the performance of your life as to why I shouldn't just kill you, anyway. Now keep walking."

Back in the galley, it's just Rafael, Ivanna and Jack. They all put on the hazmat suits Jack managed to grab, and Rafael calls up to the wheelhouse and asks the captain to keep the boat as steady as possible.

Lucky for Debbie, the seas are unseasonably glasslike this morning.

As Ivanna is prepping Debbie for surgery, the captain is back at the galley opening. It has been an hour since their abrupt departure and the Argentinian coast guard is trying to make contact with the Miranda.

Jack tells the captain to ignore all calls and asks how long before they are out of Argentinian waters. The captain tells him as of ten minutes ago.

Jack removes the silencer from his .38, making it easier to hold in the tight confines. He hands the gun to Rafael and tells him that if that scalpel moves one inch away from Deb's chest, to blow the bitch's head off.

Ivanna, aside from thinking her jaw may have been broken by Jack's punch, is conspicuously calm, and she doesn't seem to be bothered by any of this in the slightest.

Three painstaking hours later, Ivanna has removed the two top-feeding bugs. They were unceremoniously stomped on the galley floor and flushed into the ocean. Ivanna finishes stitching Debbie up, and the concern is now that she has lost so much blood. She is going to need a donor prior to tackling the bug making its way toward her heart.

Jack packed all the medical supplies to do a transfusion and calls the captain to check if Deb's blood type is listed in her record of employment. It is a mandatory requirement for all captains to know the blood types of their crew.

The captain quickly finds the information and, as it happens, Jack and Deb have the same blood type. Ivanna sets up a direct line from Debbie to Jack's arm, and she proceeds to dig for the last bug.

Several more hours pass, and with the skill of a board certified surgeon, Ivanna has made Debbie bug free.

After her final stitch, Ivanna looks over at Jack and asks him one simple question, "Why, Jack?"

"Something you would never understand, Ivanna. Let's clean up this mess and get you back into your hold until I figure out what I'm going to do with you."

The captain walks in and, upon hearing Jack's last comment, says, "Do we really need to lock her up again, Jack? This woman you call a bitch just saved Debbie's life."

"Let me stop you right there, Cap. Ivanna, if we keep you untied and give you your own bunk, will you play nice?"

Ivanna steps over and peers into the captain's eyes and, with a cold calculated grin, says, "You will be my first kill, Captain."

The captain laughs at Ivanna's death threat and says, "I saw psychos like you in the Nam, Ivanna, but they were all fuckin dudes. Take this lost soul to the hold, Rafael."

"Okay, then," Jack says. "There we have it. Bear, make sure you have my gun pointed at her back the whole way, please. She can be a bit tricky.

"Oh, and Bear? Can you also bring Ivanna something to eat? Ivanna you go to the back wall when he returns with your chow."

"Jack, how can little me take on such a big strong man like your Bear? You better make it soup, too. I think Jack broke my jaw."

With Ivanna on her way, the captain sets his sights on Jack.

"Jack, I think we need to have that talk now."

"Thank you for everything, Captain, but I think we should discuss this with the whole crew. Unfortunately, you are all involved now and you need to know exactly what it is we can expect.

"If it's okay with you, I'll clean up this mess first and then I'll need the use of your computer. I brought a lot of drugs with me and I want to see if we have something that may revive Deb while not killing her in the process."

The captain replies, "Fine. I'll call a meeting in the wheel-house in an hour. But why can't Ivanna help revive Deb?"

"Ivanna is a trained field medic. She stabilizes people, removes bullets and stitches them back up. I just don't trust her when it comes to giving Deb anything right now. We will have to do this on our own."

"The computer is in my bunk—it's on and ready to go. Rafael and I will clean the galley but, before we do anything, let's move Deb back to my bunk. It's the biggest room and has the best bed."

"Sounds good. One more question, Cap. Aside from my thirty-eight, are there any more weapons on board?"

"Does the pope shit in the woods?"

Jack and the captain carefully move Debbie into the captain's bunk, then the captain leaves to help Rafael clean up the galley and Jack sits down at the computer.

Before Jack can look up the drugs for Debbie he has to send a couple of quick e-mails. The first one is to Roger. Jack sends the following message:

Christmas cruise is a go, but you must book today.

While Jack is waiting for a reply he wipes down Deb's forehead with a damp cloth and keeps an eye on her bandaged stitches to ensure none of them start to leak.

Within three minutes Jack gets his reply from Roger.

Will book trip immediately, will be packed in four hours.

Jack is overwhelmed with relief that Roger was able to reply. It can only mean that he is back in the States and relatively close to Orange County.

Jacks next e-mail is to Margaret.

Uncle Roger is on his way to pick up the key.

Like Roger, Margaret also has a smartphone, so she should see the message immediately.

Jack checks his watch. It's now noon in Argentina, so Margaret should just be making dinner back in Orange County. Jack quickly gets his reply.

How long this time?

Jack is not happy. That is not the agreed-upon response, and he starts to wonder if Margaret has already been compromised or if she is still just pissed off. Before Jack has time to start freaking out, the correct response arrives.

I'll make him something to eat.

Jack reassures himself that there is no way the Ambassador could have moved so swiftly. With his mind at ease, he begins searching the Net for a drug to revive Debbie.

Earlier, back at the compound...

With no word from the Ambassador, and with Bricks not knowing what to do, he wakes up all of the crew as soon as Jack has fled the gates, and gathers them in the canteen. The majority of the men end up just falling back to sleep, either on one of the pool tables, a bench or the floor.

Bricks sends Stryker out to man the gate.

The crew wakes up at their usual time and aren't acting as if they're in any real jeopardy.

Although Bricks' Kalashnikov is sitting out in the open on the picnic table, nobody seems to be bothered by it.

Mr. Singh makes breakfast for everyone and finishes washing the dishes. He then takes a walk around the room, trying to get a consensus from everyone on what to make for lunch.

Rick and Carl are in the middle of an arm wrestling competition. With their parity, they are now at the best of forty.

Sven is sitting at the table with Bricks and is hopelessly trying to explain to him what the cloud is on Bricks' new Apple phone.

Victor is sitting out on the deck with his shirt off and is napping off Cookie's big breakfast. The butt of his cigar has gone out and is wrested from between his small, fat fingers seconds before burning a hole in his pants.

Bricks tells the bored group that he is going to check on the doc and that he's putting Victor in charge. He picks up his gun, opens the cafeteria door and drops his weapon from chin level onto the still sleeping Victor's lap.

"Whoa, what the fuck? Christ, that hurt … oh, Bricks, it's you. What's going on?"

"You're in charge, Victor. I'm going to check on the doc."

Mr. Singh comes to the door. "We all agreed on barbecue steak for lunch. Is that okay with you guys?"

Bricks says, "Sure thing, Mr. Singh. That sounds good."

Victor stumbles to his feet as he puts his shirt back on and tries to smooth out the wrinkles. He picks up the gun and says, "Don't worry, Bricks. I'll keep these guys in order."

"Just don't shoot anyone, Victor."

As Bricks is making his way to the medical tent, he can't help but think back to the Ohio extraction. Jack falling into the cistern in the backyard and insisting on taking a shower right in the middle of a fucking mission.

Bricks chuckles to himself, but abruptly stops when he remembers how Ivanna pulled her usual shit and ended the situation. He thinks to himself, "You're right, Jack. The dame is a witch, bitch, whatever."

Upon entering the medical tent, Bricks sees Skeane resting comfortably on the bed with his leg raised under a pillow.

"You all right, Doc?"

"Yes, Bricks. I'm fine, considering."

"Considering what, Doc?"

"Well, uh, considering that fucking psycho shot me in the knee for no reason."

"I've known Jack for a lot of years, Doc, and you'll just have to take my word for it—Jack does not shoot civilians unless he's got a damn good reason."

"Do you need anything? We're expecting the Ambassador shortly and then you'll have your chance to explain your case to him."

"No, I'm fine. Uh...what exactly did Jack tell you about what happened?"

"As I said, Doc, the Ambo will be here soon and he'll sure as shit sort out this fucking mess."

The Doc mutters quietly, "That's what I'm afraid of."

"What's that, Doc?"

"Nothing, Bricks. I'll be fine...maybe some more water please."

Bricks hands the doc a bottle of water and heads back to the canteen.

Back at the canteen, Victor has moved his patio chair in front of the doorway with his back facing the outside, thus blocking anyone's chance of escape. He is holding the Kalashnikov with both hands with the gun in the firing position and he is slowly moving it back and forth, pointed toward the men inside.

Seeing this, Bricks approaches quickly and grabs the gun from Victor. "Thanks Vic," he says. "I think I can handle it from here." Bricks places the gun back on the picnic table.

Back on the Miranda…

Now that Jack feels some modicum of relief that his family will be taken care of by Roger, he begins to plan his strategy for the day.

His plan, in no specific order, is to somehow get Ivanna off the boat, try to revive Deb from her continuous state of unconsciousness and attempt to contact the Ambassador to arrange the delivery of the cigar box. Hopefully, all before the Ambo's men can get to it first.

Most important is ensuring his own safety, and that of Debbie and the crew of the Miranda.

From his Google search, the only thing Jack came up with that could possibly help Debbie was to try an insulin shot on her. Jack checks his stock of stolen drugs from the compound and there is no insulin. He then heads up to the wheelhouse to speak with the captain.

Jack is hoping against all hope and is praying that his lucky streak will continue—that is that one of the crew members is diabetic.

He finds the captain sitting in the side chair and his first mate, driving the boat.

The captain has the radio off and he is peering through his binoculars. Normally he would be standing, but he's sweating profusely and his legs are shaking so badly he can barely stand. The last time he felt this way was forty years ago when, as a young man of twenty, he was maneuvering the rivers of Cambodia.

Jack approaches the two men and asks the first mate if he could speak to the captain in private. With the captain's blessing, the first mate is told to gather the crew for a meeting in the galley.

"Listen, Sig, I thinking maybe a meeting at this time is not such a good idea after all."

"It's Cap or Captain on this boat for you, Jack. And why is that?"

"First off, I need your help to revive Deb and then we've gotta drop the bitch off somewhere. I think we can both agree that she is a liability as long as she remains on this boat. Second, and you're just going to have to take my word for it, the less your crew knows about what really happened, the better off they're gonna be."

Jack continues, "If you insist on having a meeting, I strongly suggest that we tell the crew that Deb got into some trouble in town and she somehow made her way back to the Miranda, and now the authorities are after her."

"That's the stupidest idea I've ever heard, Jack. We're talking about Debbie here. Did you forget we all thought she was back in Texas?"

"Do you at least agree that the truth is just too fucking unbelievable?"

"Okay, forget about the crew for now. What did you come up with for Deb, and how exactly do you propose we lose Ivanna in the middle of the fucking Atlantic?"

"Is anyone on this boat diabetic?"

"As a matter of fact, Jack, I am. A little side effect of Agent Orange, compliments of the US government. With all this shit going on, I'm actually a couple hours past my regular shot."

"Oh, that's fucking great. I mean, sorry to hear that, Cap, but an insulin shot may just be the thing to get Deb out of her comatose state."

"How long has she been out?"

"About twenty-four hours, Sig... sorry, Captain."

Jack continued, "As for Ivanna, you got a T.E.L.B. lifeboat on board and she could last a week in one of those. We toss her in and call the Argentinian coast guard and they'll come and pick her up. If anything, it may just buy us some more time."

"I would lose my licence forever if I cast Ivanna into that boat, Jack. Something I am not prepared to do. Did you forget she just saved Debbie's life? What is wrong with you, man?"

"You heard it for yourself what she would do if she managed to free herself. This lady is a highly trained assassin. Does the life of your crew mean that little to you, Captain?"

"Do not fucking put that on me, Jack. You, Ivanna and your precious Ambassador, you're all a new breed of depraved."

Just then, Jack and Sig's conversation is interrupted by the sound of an incredible roar that can be heard throughout the entire ship. Rafael is shouting, "Captain!"

The captain quickly puts the boat into autopilot and reaches under his chair and for the revolver that is taped underneath it.

Jack instinctively reaches for his .38 but then remembers he left it with Rafael to bring Ivanna back to the hold, as both he and the captain race down to the galley.

Jack and Sig reach the galley to find no one there. Then they hear quiet rustling and they move toward the sleeping quarters.

Standing in the hallway is the entire small crew of the Miranda, including the first mate and two divers. In the captain's cabin is Bear, and he is sitting next to a now-awakened Debbie. Next to Debbie is a half vile of the captain's insulin and a spent needle.

Bear had been listening in on Jack and Sig's conversation from the bottom of the wheelhouse stairs, and he ultimately took it upon himself to go ahead and give Deb the insulin injection.

Working with a captain who views water as something that goes with Scotch, Bear has had plenty of experience administering insulin shots to his usually too-inebriated captain.

Standing at the back of the group of men, Jack turns around and walks out onto the deck. He quickly returns and makes his way past the solemn group. He has Rose in his arms and he places her on the floor next to Debbie's head.

Rose has been kept away from Debbie until now for both of their safety.

Debbie's eyes are open and tears are trickling down her cheek. She has yet to move or speak. She is covered by a light sheet that masks the grotesque litany of over forty rudimentary stitches on her body.

Rafael is talking to her in a soft voice. He tells her where she is and that Rose is right next to her, and that she is going to be fine.

After a few minutes, Debbie loses consciousness again.

The crew all gather in the galley while Rafael remains seated next to Deb. Worried about Rose possibly upsetting her stitches, Jack places her just outside the closed door.

The captain—while angrily staring at Jack—relays Jack's earlier bullshit excuse to the crew about Debbie getting into trouble in town.

He sternly brushes off any questions and, against Jack's objections, he instructs the first mate to plot a course for the next port away from Argentina and toward Brazil. Sig has had enough and is determined to get Debbie some proper medical attention.

With no further calls from the coast guard and Ivanna safely tucked away, Jack knows the benefit of a few hours' sleep. He hopes he will awaken refreshed so he can start formulating his next plan. He asks the captain for an empty bunk and then he hits the rack.

Back at the compound…

The men in the canteen are all jostled back to attention as the ground begins to shake and reverberate. Whatever is rolling down the goat path is big, and it sounds as if there are a lot of them.

Bricks tells all the men to gather outside of the canteen to wait for the Ambassador's arrival. With Mr. Singh prepping for dinner, he stays inside.

Bricks does a quick head count, then pops his head inside and yells, "Mr. Singh, your presence is requested outside."

Mr. Singh makes his way outside and, none too pleased with Bricks' interruption, begins to chastise Bricks.

"I'm making beef brisket for the Ambassador. Do you know how much work is involved in making it just right for the boss? Do you want to explain to the Ambassador why his brisket is tough?"

Bricks thinks about it for a second, then tells Mr. Singh to head back inside and do his thing.

The other men overhear that Mr. Singh gets to do what he wants, so Rick and Carl chime in about how they want to finish their arm wrestling competition. They try to explain to Bricks that they are still tied and you have to win by two.

Bricks looks at them and says, "Are you two complete idiots? Take a look at your arms. You've got popped blood vessels all over them."

Just then, a Jeep comes around the bend and stops at the gate Stryker is manning.

The Ambassador has arrived and, judging by the number of vehicles in tow, he has brought the entire Argentinian army with him.

The lead Jeep has four men in it. Two soldiers are in the front and seated in the back is the Ambassador, and what would appear to be an Argentinian general, with a grossly exaggerated chest full of ribbons and metal trinkets.

One soldier jumps out and assumes the position of gatekeeper. Stryker climbs into his seat and the Jeep proceeds forward toward the group of men standing outside the canteen.

The Jeep is followed by six large army-type moving trucks, with two soldiers aboard each.

The six trucks park at various locations around the compound, then the soldiers all run back and immediately stand in military formation in front of the general, who is now standing on the deck of the canteen.

The Ambassador begins greeting each member of his compound crew with a warm smile and hearty handshake. The Ambassador doesn't call the men by their nicknames, and addresses Bricks first.

"Mr. Walker, are we not missing a couple of the crew?"

"Yes, sorry, Sir. Mr. Singh is inside making dinner and Dr. Skeane is resting in the medical tent."

The Ambassador looks at Bricks, and looks, and looks.

"Oh, right, sorry again, Sir." Bricks pokes his head inside the canteen and shouts, "Mr. Singh, can you please come out here for a moment?"

Mr. Singh comes out wearing his apron and a dish rag slung over his shoulder. The Ambassador shakes Mr. Singh's hand and gives him a warm, earnest hug.

"How are you today, Mr. Singh? Have you been treated well?"

"Very well, thank you, Sir. I'm making you a beef brisket, but I have to tell you, this is a larger group than I was prepared for, Mr. Ambassador."

"That's quite all right, Mr. Singh. Why don't you go back inside and make preparations to leave? You can make me a portion of your brisket to go if that is all right with you?"

"Yes, Sir. I will get on it right now."

"The rest of you, go to your rooms and pack. And make it quick, gentlemen," Bricks orders.

With sunset approaching, Bricks asks Sven to crank up the lights and then go ahead and pack, as well.

The general draws his men to attention and, with a few instructions, the men all scatter back to their trucks to begin dismantling the camp.

The Ambassador has definitely had an exit strategy in place for some time, as one of the trucks is equipped with a forklift.

At the Ambassador's prompting, Bricks asks Victor to lead the way to his office. The Ambassador, the general, Bricks and Victor all make their way to Victor's office.

The Ambassador takes his seat behind Victor's desk. The general and Bricks sit down in the two chairs in front of the desk, leaving Victor without a chair. Not sure what to do with himself, Victor asks the men if they would like a drink.

The Ambassador replies, "I'm sure the general could use a drink. And a cigar for everyone, if you please, Victor."

Victor passes each man a cigar and quickly tries to clean four glasses. The men are all now curiously watching Victor as they're waiting for their drinks. Red-faced, Victor fumbles his way into his hiding spot, where he retrieves his last bottle of Scotch.

Victor proceeds to pour everyone a drink.

The Ambassador then starts the discussion.

"Mr. Walker, the package?"

"It wasn't in his room, Sir. We now have enough men—you give me the order and we will tear this place apart. We'll find it, Sir."

"No, Mr. Walker. Jack has it with him."

"Are you sure, Mr. Ambassador? Jack left here kind of quick."

The Ambassador ignores Brick's comment and turns his attention to the general.

"General, this is Mr. Victor Constantine. Maybe you have met his father, he is a colonel in the Greek army."

The General mutters, "Uh, no, I don't believe I have." He then motions for Victor to refill his glass.

The Ambassador then turns his attention to Victor.

"Victor, the general here has graciously agreed to accept all the equipment he can carry back with him and will donate it to the local community. I have made him aware that they must have everything they need stowed on the trucks by morning. His men will be working throughout the night."

"That is very gracious of the general and, of course, yourself, Mr. Ambassador. I am here to help in any way I can," Victor replies.

"For now, if you could stay here with the general, and both of you please enjoy your Scotch and cigar. I have a minor personal matter to attend to at the other end of the camp."

As Bricks, Stryker and the Ambassador head off toward the medical tent, Bricks asks the Ambassador, "So, what about Jack, Sir?"

"When Jack is ready, he will come to me, Mr. Walker."

"And his family?"

The Ambassador does not answer Bricks' second question and with a tone of impatience he says, "Mr. Walker, I am giving you twelve hours to have this camp packed and the general's men gone. Once they have left, I want this camp burned to the ground. Do you understand me?"

"Yes, Sir."

"Then you and Mr. Palmer get yourself to Buenos Aires where you will rent a hotel room and wait for a call."

They enter the medical tent. The Ambassador gives Dr. Skeane a quick glance and smiles. He then starts pointing to items in the medical tent while giving Bricks instructions on how to dismantle the room.

Dr. Skeane appears at a loss as to what is going on. He starts sputtering, "Mr. Ambassador, I'm sorry for all that has happened, but that boy of yours, well, he just went crazy, I don't know what I did, but just look at me, he shot me in the knee."

The Ambassador glances back at Skeane and, with a kind, warm smile on his face, looks down at the doc's knee. Then, ignoring the Doc's comments, he continues his conversation with Bricks.

Skeane is completely dumbfounded. For the moment, he chooses to just sit and wait for his turn to tell his side of the story.

After about ten minutes, Bricks closes his notepad and says, "We will take care of it all, Sir."

Skeane has been quietly watching Bricks and the Ambassador and, seeing his opening, props himself up into a sitting position and starts to prepare for what he is going to say.

At the same time, the Ambassador starts to make his way toward the exit and, when he reaches Stryker standing at the doorway, he says, "Mr. Palmer... if you please."

Stryker walks over to Dr. Skeane and double taps the doc's chest then finishes him off with a shot to the forehead. The men all vacate the tent.

With the Ambassador and the general now back in the Jeep and ready to leave, Mr. Singh comes out with a large metal foil container with the Ambassador's beef brisket.

The Ambassador thanks him kindly and asks him to make as many sandwiches as he can for the crew and troops. He then tells Mr. Singh to do it as quickly as possible, and that when he is finished, he, too, should go and pack his belongings.

Bricks approaches the Jeep and hands the Ambassador Ivanna's and Jack's passports. He also hands him a briefcase he took from Victor's office. In the briefcase is the Nazi "Operation Stasis" file they recovered from Jack's footlocker.

Bricks asks, "What about the rest of their stuff, Sir?"

Again, the Ambassador just smiles and motions for the driver to get going.

The men drive off with the Ambassador telling the general to take him back to his private jet, as he has immediate business back in Israel.

Back on the Miranda...

Jack abruptly awakens to what he perceives to be a screaming, pounding headache—only to find Bear on top of him raining his fists down on his head. Jack ends up on the floor with Bear now putting the boots to him. Regaining a small amount of his mental acuity, Jack is able to notice that the entire crew of the Miranda has been crammed into his cabin and they are all carrying weapons of some sort.

Jack gives one final look up at Bear. As he sees his boot coming down hard toward his head, he's just able to make out Bear saying, "She's dead asshole."

With that final blow, Jack is knocked unconscious.

Chapter 8

RUN

Jack awakens to the reality that he is now locked in the crab hold with Ivanna.

He immediately does a self-examination of his injuries. Possible broken nose, a cracked rib or two and a cut over his eyebrow that has at least stopped bleeding.

He makes a mental note to never, ever, give up his .38 again, as he admonishes himself for doing such a ridiculousness thing.

Then he sits up and—with a slight tinge of embarrassment—figures he'd better address the elephant in the room.

Ivanna is sitting a foot away from him silently smirking.

"What the hell happened with Deb, Ivanna? Is she dead?"

Ivanna makes an uncaring noise "pfft" sound. "You tell me take out bugs, I take out. Pretty bitch was dead when bit, she just don't know it. I think you break my jaw, mean man who punches helpless woman".

Jack makes his own "pfft."

"One question for you, Jack? Why did you take pretty dead girl with you to excavation of plane?"

Jack doesn't answer Ivanna out loud but thinks to himself, 'I don't know, you crazy bitch, but I am sure as fuck going to find out.'

"How long have I been out?" he asks her.

"I don't know, but a long time I think. I fall asleep, as well. If you haven't noticed, smart man, boat is no longer moving."

She continued, "I want you to know, Jack, I will have to end you. Captain tells me you wanted to drop me in sea."

"The best thing for a possible broken jaw, witch, is to shut the fuck up."

"Why you call me witch, Jack? I am very pretty Russian woman."

"Right, sorry bitch."

At that moment, the captain, Rafael and the two divers arrive and unlock the crab bay. They enter the room and Jack sees they are all still armed.

Rafael is brandishing Jack's .38.

Jack looks at Rafael. "I'm sorry, Bear."

The captain responds, "We all loved her, Jack, everyone on this boat. She was your best friend as soon as you met her."

Rafael jumps in, "Why did you take Debbie to the plane, Jack? It just doesn't make any sense. Why, Jack?"

The honest answer is that Jack doesn't know why, so he chooses to ignore Bear's question.

The captain adds, "It doesn't matter now, anyway, she's gone. The quicker we get you two off the boat, the better we will all be.

"Get yourselves ready. Oh yeah, not much you can do all tied up, is there? Well, just sit tight then and we'll be back for you shortly, and uh, Jack, welcome to Uruguay."

Ivanna speaks up, "Captain, I must use washroom."

"Don't worry, Ivanna, we're gonna scrub this room really good when you're gone." The men leave and lock the door behind them.

Jack is now trying to recall if he is wanted in Uruguay. "Shit, I think I am." Jack arrives at the stark realization that he is wanted in most countries and, in the past, he has always had the security of the Ambassador and his various government connections.

Over the years, Jack has taken many beatings at the hands of soldiers, local police and even private security members like himself. But the one thing he could always rely on was someone eventually coming to the door of his cell, apologizing to him and letting him go.

That was always after they got around to calling the phone number Jack would give them. And, on a few occasions, his reprieve had not come a moment too soon.

With their having docked in Uruguay, Jack realizes the search for the Miranda must have been called off.

If the Ambassador had really wanted the boat, he would now be in an Argentinian jail cell hanging by his feet in chains with a hot poker up his ass, not tied up in a stinking crab tank.

Many hours earlier, the captain had plotted a path down the Rio de le Plata seaway to escape from Argentinian waters. When the boat was outside of Argentina's maritime delimitation of twenty-two kilometres, according to his first mate's charts, the captain stopped fleeing and sat idle in the open Atlantic Ocean.

With no calls from the Argentinian coast guard for hours, the captain sent his crew to their bunks for some sleep. Rafael and Rose were lying on the floor in the captain's cabin next to Debbie.

The Captain then had some peace and quiet to figure out his next move.

The closest port that was not in Argentina, was the Campichuelo Port of Uruguay. Sig would have to return through the Rio de le Plata seaway as it borders the two countries. His main concern was being spotted by any searching Argentinian coast guard vessels.

His other concern was getting into the Uruguayan port unnoticed, unloading the "cargo" and getting back to the safety of the Atlantic.

Sig took measure of his liabilities: dead girl on board; two, no-doubt, globally wanted felons; and a shitload of illegal firearms.

In a random sea search, Sig's hiding spot for his own weapons always went undetected. Should the boat be seized and they brought in a dog and some form of detector, they would invariably find them, though.

Sig decided to take his chances on Uruguay and, at twelve knots from where he was currently located, he figured he could make it there in about six hours. Sig plotted the course and put the boat on auto pilot so he could catch a few hours' sleep in the wheelhouse.

Just before daybreak, the captain awakened and woke the crew for a meeting in the galley. He let the crew know that during the night he plotted a course for Uruguay and they were now sitting just outside the country's maritime boundary, ninety minutes from port.

With the crew of four all awake and sipping their coffees in the galley, the Captain laid out their options: Toss Jack and Ivanna into the sea and make their way toward more familiar salvaging territory, that being Brazil, or return through the Rio de le Plata seaway and do a quick dump-and-run in Uruguay.

The vote was three to one to toss them into the sea. The captain was the lone dissenting vote and with some much needed comic relief, he instituted his legal right as captain to do the dump-and-run instead.

What Jack had already figured out, unknown to Sig, was that once the Ambassador realized Jack almost certainly had the package on him, he had the general put a stop to the Argentinian coast guard pursuit. All local governments had also been contacted that the Miranda was to remain untouched.

The Ambassador never took or made these calls himself. He simply placed a call to a gentleman Jack called "the Ambassador's boy."

"The Ambassador's boy" is Harvey Blumberg, and he is not exactly a boy. Harvey is a sixty-two-year-old man and one of the most exclusive, decorated lawyers in the world.

Harvey was a young immigration lawyer in Israel. Like all of the others, he had a chance meeting with the Ambassador and the rest is history. Harvey was given one directive, to get as many law degrees in as many areas as he could. All paid for by one of the Ambassador's foundations.

Harvey travelled with the Ambassador to Argentina and was dropped off at the local government office. Harvey was working with the local officials on locating and seizing the Miranda and, just as quickly, initiated the stoppage of all activities once he got word from the Ambassador.

Currently situated in the La Plata Port in Argentina, Harvey has been tracking the Miranda's every movement, including her docking at the Campichuelo Port of Uruguay.

Jack now has a new concern. He is sure the Ambassador's boy is around and pulling the strings, but who is waiting for them in Uruguay?

Jack tries to reassure himself that "Hairy," as Jack so aptly calls the man he fears might be waiting for him, is presently working somewhere else in the world.

"Hairy" has only been with the Ambassador for about five years. Even though Jack has only met the man a couple of times and hasn't exchanged more than a few words with him, he considers him to be one of the fiercest, most impressive people he has ever met.

He has never been able to quite place what it is about "Hairy," and he has spent more than a healthy amount of time trying to analyze it.

Jack doesn't impress easily and has worked with some of the most powerful men in the world. But, frankly, the thought of having "Hairy" on his path made the hairs on the back of his neck stand up. Hence, the nickname Jack had given the man who was rightly named Ian Malcomson.

After their meeting, the captain, crew and a growling Rose re-enter the crab bay.

The captain says, "Get up, and, Jack, if you want to leave this boat alive, all I ask is that you keep your fucking mouth shut. No one here is interested in hearing anything you might have to say. It's time to go."

With three guns pointed at their backs, Jack and Ivanna are led out of the crab hold and climb their way up to the cabin hallway.

As they make their way past the captain's bunk, Jack can see that the door is closed. Jack says to the captain, "Come on Captain, please, just let me see her."

Rafael makes a motion that he is about to cold cock Jack, but the captain yells at him. "Rafael, enough. We're two minutes from being free of these parasites. Everybody just keep moving."

Jack starts to struggle and make his way closer to the cabin door. He asks the captain, "How do I know if she is really fucking dead or not?"

The captain simply says, "Rafael."

Bear punches the still tied-up Jack in the back of the head so hard he knocks him to the ground.

"I told you, Jack, all you had to do was keep your fucking mouth shut. Pick him up and get him moving, Rafael."

The group of six make it to the Deck, where Jack and Ivanna's ropes are cut and Rafael, at the insistence of the captain, hands Jack his .38.

"Don't bother checking it, asshole. It's empty."

Of course, Jack has to check it anyway.

Jack and Ivanna, now on deck, take notice that the sun is just rising so they must have been asleep all night.

They are led down the gangway and are now on Uruguayan soil.

They are both covered in blood and bruises and, in Ivanna's case, piss.

Back on the deck of the Miranda, the captain is shouting loudly, "Prepare to cast off, men!"

Jack looks over at Ivanna and says, "You got any money?"

Back in Orange County, California…

Roger is in his vehicle and is nearing Jack and Margaret's street.

As he approaches the house, he spots a vehicle with three men sitting in it. He makes a point of not looking at the men as he passes and continues past Jack's house and parks around the corner.

Roger riffles through his trunk and pulls out his US Postal Service jacket, hat and mailbag. He grabs some flyers, a wrapped package and starts delivering a flyer to each house leading up to Jack's.

Each time he hits the street, he glances toward the parked vehicle. The men are definitely watching him and the house, but do not seem to have taken any interest in the "mailman."

Roger reaches Jack and Margaret's house, and as he rings the doorbell, Margaret is quick to answer and opens the door only half an inch. With a glance over to the street, Roger notices one of the men is now climbing out of the car.

Within five seconds, Roger is leaving Jack's with the package still in hand. When he reaches the public sidewalk, he stops and puts it back in his mailbag. The presumption being for the men watching that no one was home.

Roger continues delivering the flyers down the rest of the street and, when out of view of the suspicious vehicle, makes his way back to his car.

Within five minutes, Margaret and Debra, both wearing backpacks are climbing into Roger's car.

The five seconds Roger spoke to Margaret at the door, he simply said, "Hop the neighbor's fence behind you. The car is around the corner on your left. I'll watch for the bandits.

Back in the car, Margaret tells Roger that the men have been ringing the door all morning and that she and Debra were hiding in the bathroom.

Years earlier, Jack had put alarm signs all over the house and property. He'd also had the house fully equipped with front and rear security cameras, and made sure the house was on a main street with lots of foot traffic.

Having put his mailman gear away, Roger is now ready to battle the LA traffic and proclaims a hearty, "So, who wants to go to Vegas?"

Margaret leans over and gives Roger a big hug then sits back in her seat and says, "We do, Uncle Roger." Debra is in the backseat listening to music on her headset.

Only a block away from Marg's house, Roger points and says, "Hey look, mailman."

A couple of hours later, the trio passes the LA county line and now headed northwest on the I-15 to Roger's bungalow in South Vegas.

Roger pops back to attention as he remembers one final detail. "Cell phones, ladies." After a few minutes of negotiation, he checks his mirrors and out the window they go.

After an hour or so of silence, and with Roger getting more bored by the minute, he asks, "So Debra, how is school going?"

Debra doesn't hear him as she is listening to her music in the back.

"Don't worry about her, Roger. She's glad to get out of that school."

"Same problems, Marg?"

"Yes, I'm afraid so."

"Kids are assholes. Anyway, I got some good news. You haven't been to my place in a couple of years but I got air conditioning this spring."

From the backseat, Debra mutters, "Thank God." Clearly she was taking selective interest in the conversation up front.

Roger looks back at Debra through the rear view mirror. "That's right, Deb. And when we get there, you can go to Walmart and get yourself a new burner phone."

He turns back to Margaret and says, "I hate to ask, Marg, but Jack will be contacting me soon and he's going to be asking me if you brought the key with you."

"Yes, Roger, I have the key."

"All right then, how about we stop and grab something to eat in Yermo? There's that Peggy Sue's diner there, if you remember. Feel like a burger, Deb?"

Again, Debra doesn't answer.

Roger's eyes meet Debra's in the rear view mirror and she gives him a warm smile.

"So Marg, when was the last time Jack was home?"

"Over a year ago, Roger. You know he won't tell me anything about his job, but something happened out there and when he finally did come home, he was different. He packed his usual stuff to go off on another job and we haven't seen him since." She paused. "Do you know what happened, Roger?"

"He doesn't tell you to protect you, Margaret. He tried to reach out to me last year, but I was on a four-month job in Europe. When we finally hooked up for dinner in Buenos Aires, he wouldn't talk about it. He said it was over and done with and he wasn't looking back.

"What I can definitively guarantee you, Margaret, is that Jack loves you and Debra very much. Jack will be fine, and he will come around. He always ends up on top that much I can promise you.

"The other thing, Marg, is you are absolutely safe with your Uncle Roger. That Ambassador fella doesn't even know I exist."

Sensing that the car needs a change of mood, Roger says, "So what is it about Jack's nicknames for everybody?"

Margaret starts chuckling. "Oh, I know, it's crazy. He's been doing that since he was a boy. He claims he's dyslexic when it comes to remembering names. Ask him anyone's actual last name and he wouldn't be able to tell you."

About halfway between LA and Vegas, Roger, Margaret and Debra stop for lunch. Roger's favourite spot is Peggy Sue's 1950s diner.

After a tasty lunch, the ladies take a nap the rest of the trip. Roger wakes them up just as they are approaching the "Welcome to Las Vegas" sign.

"Deb, quick, look—the sign area is not busy. I got a camera in the back. Why don't we stop and take a picture for your dad?"

To Roger's total shock, Debra replies, "Sure, why not? We're on a holiday, right?"

"You're an amazing young woman, Debra Singer. Your father would be very proud of you."

"Don't push it, Uncle Rog,"

"Got it hon."

After snapping a bunch of fun family photos, they continue the drive east toward his bungalow. Like Jack, Roger picked a home on a busy street. As Roger drives past his bungalow, Margaret says, "Didn't we just pass your place, Roger?"

"I don't know how, Marg, but they're here. Older brown sedan across the street with two shady-looking characters inside. Why don't we pop into Walmart and get you those phones I promised."

"Don't you need a new phone, too, Roger?"

"Nah, mine is a company phone. I have half a dozen SIM cards. The one I have in here now is Jack's only way to contact us."

"And after the phones, Roger?"

"No worries, Marg. I used to date the day manager at the Hard Rock, and amazingly we're still friends. We'll stay there until we can get a hold of Jack."

Roger, Margaret and Debra wander around Walmart. They get their burner phones and end up spending an hour shopping for extra clothes, bathing suits, snacks for the room, Corona for Roger and wine coolers for Margaret.

Roger also buys a cheap Styrofoam cooler. Using the ice at the hotel, he likes to load the cooler with cold beverages. Roger can be a bit of a miser and spending nine bucks for a non-comped beer at the hotel bar is too much for him.

While in Walmart, Roger places a call to his friend and ends up securing a two-bedroom suite. According to his friend it's all going to be comped with no check-out date.

When the group pulls up to the Hard Rock valet, Roger's friend, Pat, is outside waiting.

Pat gives Roger a big hug, hands him his room key and gets his staff to unload their stuff onto a cart.

"Marg, Debra, this is my friend, Pat."

They exchange the usual pleasantries and Pat says, "So Margaret, I hear you've been in a car all day with Roger. Would you like to follow Mr. Parker here up to your room? You can have some time to freshen up and relax so I can get caught up with my old friend."

"Thank you very much Pat that is a wonderful idea."

"I've also arranged for you to dine at the Pink Taco restaurant this evening. Do you like Mexican food, Debra?"

"Yes, I do, Pat. Thank you. I've eaten here before with Uncle Roger and it was delicious."

"Very good, Debra. I've also arranged for a tablet to be delivered to your room, so you should be getting a knock on the door in the next thirty minutes."

"Thank you, Pat, that's great. I really appreciate what you're doing for us."

"No worries, dear. Any friend of Roger's is a friend of mine." Pat looked to the bellhop. "Okay, then, Mr. Parker, please take the ladies and their luggage to their room. Roger, shall we go have that drink?"

"Sounds good, Pat, just give me a moment with Margaret."

Roger pulls Margaret aside and gives her a big hug and whispers into her ear, "I told you, Marg, everything is going to be okay. We will be safe here. I won't be too long with Pat."

Margaret gives Roger a firm hug and whispers rhetorically, "And Jack?"

While the ladies and the bellhop head to their room, Roger and Pat head to the Hard Rock's main bar.

Pat orders a coke and Roger asks for a cold Corona.

"I saw you're still lugging your own cooler around, Roger,"

"I'm not paying ten bucks or whatever you charge for a dollar-fifty beer, Pat."

"It's good to see some things never change. Anyway, these are on the house. Margaret and Debra seem like lovely people."

"They're the best and so is Jack."

"Is that the delicious blond Adonis you told me about?"

"The one and only."

"And as usual, you won't tell me anything about what's going on, right? More specifically, why you are here, and why you are here with Jack's family in tow?"

"I just can't, Pat. But I really want you to know how much I appreciate this. You have no idea how grateful I am for all of your help."

"Enough for another date sometime?"

"Absolutely. When this is all over we'll head to the strip and have a proper date."

"I would love to kiss you right now, Roger."

"Pat, we talked about that."

"Oh, that's right … Roger still hasn't come out of the closet. Heaven forbid you show me some affection after everything I'm doing for you and your friends."

"We've been through this too many times, Pat. Do you remember why we broke up? In my line of work, 'coming out' could get me killed, by my own crew no less. How many times do we have to go over this?"

Pat leans closer to Roger and starts talking in a school-girl's voice. "I'm sorry, Rogee. I'm just so glad to see you and you just look so scrumptious."

"Okay, Pat. Just let me get through this and we'll go on that date."

"Promise, Rogee?"

"Yes, Pat. Thanks for everything."

Back in Uruguay…

Ivanna and Jack have been unceremoniously dumped on a Uruguayan port with no money, food or water and, more important, no bullets for Jack's .38.

They both look like a couple victims of violent assault. An attention-drawing spectacle that they don't need right now. Any passing soldier or police officer and Jack's ass would be back in a jail cell, again.

Ivanna says, "I have no pesos, you?"

"No, Ivanna. Everything I had was left back in my room at the compound."

"Same as me, no thanks to you, asshole. What do we do now, Jack?"

"We go sit on that bench right there, and then we wait."

"Why would we do that, Jack? We must come up with plan."

"Just sit down, Ivanna. We're not going to be here long."

Just then a couple of local fishermen walk past them on the pier to start their day's fishing.

"*Buenos dias,*" Jack says heartily.

Their boat is moored only a foot from Jack's bench. The men climb aboard and are talking back and forth to each other. One of the men finally points at Jack, then at Ivanna. They seem to be concerned that, because of Ivanna's face, she may be in need of assistance.

One of the fishermen says something to Ivanna in Spanish. She replies back to him, "*Metete en tus asuntos, o lo hare yo cortar sus gargantas putos, con ese cuchillo en la mano.*"

The men nervously chuckle and hurry up getting their boat to sea.

Jack, still not up on his own Spanish, is wondering how many languages this bitch knows. Reluctantly, he asks Ivanna what she said and why the men suddenly looked so uncomfortable.

"All I tell them is have nice day fishing on their nice boat."

What Ivanna actually said was, "Mind your own business or I will cut your fucking throats with that knife in your hand."

Ivanna then says, "You know, Jack, I'm in same boat as you. Ambassador can't be happy with me right now."

"That's right, Ivanna. How do you say in Russian, 'We're both fucked'?"

After about ten minutes of sitting on the bench in dejected silence, Ivanna says, "*Oba byli trakhal.*"

Jack says, "What?"

"We're both fucked, in Russian."

"Right, thanks."

"So now that we're talking Ivanna, what exactly was the plan back at the compound? I'm assuming it was to get the package and then what? You stick a knife in the back of my neck?"

"Sorry, Jack. Mr. Ambassador instruct to secure package, nothing more." She paused, then asked, "Now that you mention it, Jack, package on you, no?"

"See that boat waaaay off in the distance, Ivanna?"

"You mean the Miranda?"

"Yep, after Bear knocked me out, I never got the chance to retrieve it."

"Oh, Jack, now you really are '*trakhal'*...fucked."

After several more minutes, Jack notices a man coming toward them on the pier.

"What did I tell you, Ivanna? Help has arrived."

"It's Ian, Jack. Now we're both dead."

"Good morning, Ian. What brings you out this fine morning?"

"Good morning, Jack ... Ivanna. Jack, do we have the package on us today?"

"Sorry, Hairy, it just caught the last ship out."

"I'm in no mood for riddles this morning, Jack."

"It's hidden on the Miranda, and the Miranda just left, Hairy."

"Can I assume you're armed, Jack?"

Jack pulls out his .38 and hands it handle-first to Ian. Jack is again impressed that Ian did not as much as bat an eye as he pulled out his gun.

"Are you both ready to leave or are you waiting for a fishing charter?"

"Can I grab your luggage, Jack?"

"You're in a good mood this morning, Hairy. What? Did you run over a couple of kittens on your way here?"

Ian leads the way to a waiting Hummer. The Hummer's window tint makes it impossible to see how many men are inside.

A young man unfamiliar to Jack pops out of the backseat and starts to frisk him. Ian intervenes and says, "Get back inside, Owen. They're both clean."

Ian opens the back gate and grabs a clean shirt for Jack. He hands Ivanna a men's blazer to put on. Ian requests that Jack take the front seat while Ivanna gets in the back with Owen.

Ian locks the doors and turns the air conditioning down,

"Jack, Ivanna, I beg your forgiveness, but I just have to make a quick call."

Ian places a call to the Ambassador's boy, Harvey Bloomberg.

"Good morning, Harvey…They are both in the car… A little worse for wear, I guess …The package sailed out on the Miranda …Yes, I believe him…Goodbye, Harvey." Ian hangs up the phone and centers himself facing Jack.

"Now, Jack, if I heard you correctly the package is aboard the Miranda, which as best as we can figure is on its way to Brazil. You have hidden the package somewhere on board, assuring it will not be detected by the crew or any customs agent. You are now unarmed and have no money or documentation. Am I correct?"

"That's right, Hairy."

"Now, Ivanna, please correct me if I am mistaken. You also are without money or documentation and your circumstance is that you were forcibly kidnapped by Jack here, held against your will, transported to the Miranda where you were forced to operate on the young Debbie, who presumptively succumbed to her injuries. By the looks of you, Jack took physical measures back at the compound to gain your acquiescence. Is that correct?"

"Yes, Ian."

Ian looks in the rear-view mirror and simply says, "Owen."

Immediately, Jack shouts, "Ivanna!" In a split second Ivanna has Owen's hand in an extremely painful hand bar and her other hand is about to pop his Adam's apple.

Jack and Ian make no moves toward each other, they are just waiting to see what culminates in the back seat.

Finally, Ian says, "Ivanna, if you would let Owen continue with what he had in mind you might be pleasantly surprised."

Jack says, "Okay, Ivanna, let him go. If he pulls a gun, kill him."

Ivanna replies, "I don't take orders from you, asshole." She feels around Owen's upper jacket pockets and finally lets him go.

Owen rubs his wrist and his throat and mutters, "Fucking bitch."

Jack laughs. "Owen, you've met Ivanna before, too?"

With everyone appearing to have calmed down for the moment, Owen reaches into his inside jacket pocket and pulls out two envelopes. He hands one to Ivanna and tosses one up front to Jack.

Jack and Ivanna open their envelopes to find the passports they were forced to abandon back at the compound and $10,000 each in US funds.

Ian states, "We have booked a room for each of you at the Regency Park Hotel. Jack, you look like a forty-two long and Ivanna, what, a size six?"

"I'm a size four, asshole."

Jack actually wears a forty-two long, but Ian's ostentatiousness is beginning to piss him off so he replies, "Sorry, Hairy. Forty long."

"After we drop you off at the hotel, Owen will go get a change of clothes for each of you. And Jack, after you order room service, the hotel has an excellent exercise facility for you to use. Judging by the way you look, though, maybe we'll just leave that for another time."

He continued, "Ivanna, we have arranged a masseuse to come to your room once you have eaten and had a chance to cleanup. We could order one for you, as well, Jack in light of you missing your morning workout."

As impressed as he is with Ian's acuity, Jack has only one pressing concern.

"And my family, Ian?"

"No worries there, Jack. They are safe and on the run with your homosexual best friend, Roger."

Owen chuckles in the back seat.

Jack thinks to himself, "Okay, this guy doesn't know shit. Roger's not gay. The guy's a fucking chick magnet—he's got a different girl every week, going shopping and for lunch."

Ian puts the Hummer in gear and starts the drive to the Regency.

Within twenty minutes, the group arrives at the Regency Park Hotel and Spa. It is one of Uruguay's finer hotels and has an outdoor pool and health spa. It's a three-story hotel that appears to be made of authentic Uruguayan stone and marble.

Ian parks the Hummer in the back and motions to Jack towards the direction of the glove box. Jack opens it and removes two room keys.

Ian's demeanor suddenly gets serious and he reaches over and grabs Jack's hand holding the room keys, "And Jack … take it easy on the mini bar."

He then makes a noise and gesture that one could only assume meant he was joking. "Just kidding, kid, the Ambassador says you're welcome to anything you want. Owen here can even arrange for some of the local talent to come to your room later."

"Ivanna, a young lady for you, as well?"

With Ian looking in the rear-view mirror, Ivanna flips him the bird.

Jack is wondering who this happy-go-lucky jokester is sitting next to him and, says, "Jesus Christ, Ian. What is with you today?"

Ivanna, who has been quiet through most of this morning's ordeal, has finally had enough.

"Enough of this shit, Ian. Everyone in car knows Jack and I could end you and your little goon, if it pleased us. So cut to the chase and speak of what you want."

"No, you're right, Ivanna. And allow me to say, your English is really improving. I don't know, I guess it's one of those days where you're just glad to be alive, you know." Ian stops speaking as his cell is ringing. "My apologies again," he says.

"Hello, Harvey… You're kidding… He actually took your call…I will be on my way within the hour… Goodbye, Harvey."

"Well, Jack, when this is all over, and if you find yourself looking for another career, you could always be a crabber. The Ambassador just bought the Miranda."

"You're a smart guy, Jack. How long to get the Miranda from Brazil to the Ambassador's port in Israel?"

Jack quickly calculates it in his head and thinks to himself that it would take about a month. "No idea, Hairy."

"Again, I am very sorry for how long this has been taking and for my less than appropriate jocularity. Ivanna is right. We all have other things we would rather be doing, so let's get down to the brass tacks. If you don't mind, I only have a few more questions for Jack." He paused. "I will take your silence as indication that you would like me to proceed."

He continued, "Jack, does any member of the compound crew know about the package, with the exception of Victor?"

"No."

"Does any member of the Miranda's crew know about the package?"

"They were witness to Ivanna's operation and other than that they have no clue as to what actually took place."

"Does Roger or your family know anything about the package?"

"Nothing, and they never will, Ian."

"Thank you for your honesty, Jack. I will relay to the Ambassador that I explicitly believe you. I think you have both figured out by now that if we wanted you dead, you would not have left the bench on the pier. Frankly, there is nowhere for you to hide, Jack, where we would not find you.

"You, more than anyone, can appreciate the staggering magnitude of time and expense the Ambassador has incurred to procure the package.

"Aside from securing the package, Jack, I was given direct unequivocal instructions. That being to find you, make you as comfortable as possible under the circumstances, give you your passport and some travelling money and most importantly to let you know that the Ambassador relishes the day when you will again be in his company.

"Needless to say Jack, without the package being in the Ambassadors possession, and soon, everything changes."

"As for you, Ivanna, the Ambassador said to take a couple of days off. Then you can rejoin your team or not, it's up to you.

"You can now go to your rooms and enjoy the rest of your day. And so that no one bothers you, your room phones have been removed."

Jack and Ivanna get out of the Hummer and start walking to the front of the Hotel.

Ian pulls up the Hummer next to Jack and says, "One final thing. Seeing as how I have a flight to catch, Owen will be back with a change of clothes and he's been instructed to get you whatever else you need during your stay."

Jack starts to walk away again, and once again Ian calls him back, "And Jack, I'm sure Roger being gay is just an ugly rumour."

Ian and Owen drive away.

Jack and Ivanna agree to meet in the bar after Owen arrives with the change of clothes. For now they retreat to their rooms for a warm bath and to tend to their wounds.

Chapter 9

HIDE

Back in Las Vegas at the Hard Rock Hotel...

Roger, Marg and Debra are sitting down to dinner at the Pink Taco restaurant.

Pat, sensing they have all had one hell of a day, decided he didn't want to be intrusive and bowed out of joining them for dinner. He also told Roger that the entire meal had been comped and the cheap bastard better at least leave the waitress a good tip.

"Did you ladies manage to get some rest?"

"Yes, Roger, we both dozed off for a bit," Margaret says. "And you?"

"Nah, I had a few beers with Pat, then I made a few calls in Pat's office about Jack. Let me assure you that I have some very good people shaking some big bushes. Everyone loves your boy. I could have a dozen guys here in the morning if I wanted to, but knowing Jack, he wouldn't want me to do anything until I hear from him first."

"I know, Roger, and thank you again. The question is how long do we wait?"

"Oh, here comes the waitress. Who wants a taco?"

The threesome finish their meal and are deciding on ordering dessert when Roger's cell phone rings. Roger recognizes the number on his phone and starts to get up. "It's not Jack—it's my crew. I have to step out to take this, hon. Go ahead and order, I'll have whatever you do."

Roger steps out into the hallway and makes a beeline for the closest exit.

Once in the lobby, Roger answers his phone. "This is Roger. Hang on, I'll be outside in twenty seconds."

"Okay, go," he says. After several minutes of listening, Roger replies, "I thought we weren't doing Syrian extractions." After several more minutes, "Okay… if the military is involved, I can be at Nellis in two hours." Another brief pause. "Private hanger at McCarran? I still need two hours. I have something I need to wrap up first. Over and out."

Roger returns to the restaurant and finishes his dessert with the ladies before deciding to say anything.

"Marg, I got a call and I'm sorry but I'm being deployed. If I turn it down, I'm out of a job. They tell me it's a five-day job, so I'll be back before we have to leave the Hard Rock. Let's grab the bill and I'll call Pat then we can all meet while I grab a cab. I have all of my gear in the trunk and I'll leave you my car."

"I understand, Roger, but what about Jack?"

"I got your number, hon. As soon as I hear from him, I will call you. I'm going to give you a number and if you don't hear from me in five days, call it, and you will be picked up and moved."

The waitress drops off the bill and tells Roger the meal has been comped and all he needs to do is sign it.

Roger looks at the bill. Eighty-nine dollars. He reaches into his pocket and drops down a five dollar bill. "Okay, let's go ladies."

As they get to the restaurant's lobby, Marg says that she left her phone at the table. Back at the table, Marg reaches into her purse and drops down a further twenty.

Within half an hour, Pat and the girls are at the back car park watching Roger load his gear into a cab. They all embrace and Roger says one final thing to Pat before leaving, "Take care of my girls, Pat."

As the trio watch Roger's cab depart, Pat looks at the ladies and with a pissy, snobbish tone, says, "I'll give you until 3:00 p.m. tomorrow to find somewhere else to stay. This hotel is for paying guests. And Debra, make sure that tablet remains in the room." Pat promptly walks back into the hotel leaving the ladies standing there dumbfounded.

Back in Uruguay…

Several hours have passed and Jack can hear a knocking next door at Ivanna's room. He opens his door to find it is Owen standing there with half a dozen bags.

Owen says to Jack, "I got the bags all mixed up."

Ivanna opens her door and the trio go into her room to sort the bags.

Owen peers into each bag before handing it to either Jack or Ivanna, then puts two bags aside for himself. Jack quickly reaches for Owen's two bags.

"No, Jack, those two bags are mine. What? If the Ambo's buying, what the fuck?"

Ivanna opens her bags. Owen has bought her a pair of pyjamas, a tracksuit, some T-shirts and a summer dress. A bag inside the bag is from a pharmacy. It includes several kinds of makeup and lipstick.

Jack and Ivanna both give Owen a conspicuous look.

"What? I bought it so you could cover up the bruise on your chin that Jack gave you."

"Thank you, little man. It will do."

Jack opens his bags. He also has a pair of pyjamas, a tracksuit, a couple of shirts and pairs of slacks. Jack also has a smaller bag inside his bag, which contains several first-aid items.

"I thought you might want to wrap those ribs of yours, Jack. You've been doing a pretty good job trying to hide the fact that you probably got a few broken."

"Thanks, Owen, I appreciate it. Seeing as how it feels like it's Christmas morning in here, why don't we all take a look at what you got in there for yourself, Owen?"

"No, that's okay. I was told to drop off your stuff and then leave you both alone. I'll just grab my bags and be on my way."

Holding the side of his ribs gingerly, Jack quickly reaches forward and grabs the bags from Owen's feet. He tosses one to Ivanna while proceeding to search the other one.

"You go first, Ivanna,"

Ivanna pulls out a snazzy waist-length brown suede jacket.

"Okay, then. Looks good, Owen. Now let's see what's in this other bag."

Jack pulls out a pair of matching brown suede shoes and a belt. Owen also has another smaller bag inside his bag. Jack opens it up to find a very nice Cartier watch.

"Holy shit, Owen. What? They don't pay you enough?"

"Okay, I'll just take them back then fer fek's sakes," Owen decries.

Ivanna jumps in. "Don't be silly, boy. We will not tell boss man."

"Were gonna change and go eat," Jack says, stifling a smile. "Would you like to join Ivanna and me for a late lunch?"

"I've already been up here too long. You know the Ambassador better than anyone, Jack, and you should also know that I'm not alone here."

"I expected as much. Thank you for being decent, Owen."

"The Ambassador just needs his package, Jack."

"One more question, how long have you known Hairy?"

"If you're talking about Mr. Malcomson, I fought the Brits with him back in Ireland. He was a living legend till the Ambassador dragged him away from the fight."

"Ian's lucky he did, kid. If he didn't, Ian would either be dead or in a British jail cell now. You don't look old enough to have fought with Ian."

"Well, maybe I didn't fight right next to him, but I certainly followed the path he paved for all of us."

"How long have you been working for him?"

"Six months."

"All right then, young Owen. Your shopping spree is okay with us and if they ever ask, we'll say we ordered the extra stuff. But listen to me carefully, if you want to stay alive in this business or to ever see Ireland again, you better understand who you're dealing with."

Jack continues, "Back to Ian, Owen. Have you seen him act this way before?"

"Oh right, his wife had a baby late last night. It's their first and he is pretty excited, I think he was just having a craic with you."

"Okay…that makes sense now. So is he on a flight back to Israel?"

"Nope, charter to meet the Miranda in Brazil."

Owen, sensing the mantle of power may have turned against him and realizing he has said way more than he should have, says, "I'm just going to take my stuff back, or did you want it, Jack?

"Well, Owen, let's take a look at ya…bit of a height difference, but the weight is pretty close, so yeah, thanks, I'll give them a tryout."

Jack asks Ivanna for her money bag and hands Owen a handful of hundreds.

Owen leaves the room and Jack and Ivanna try as hard as they can to hold off their laughter until the kid is out of hearing range.

"Holy shit, Ivanna. How does the Ambassador go from hiring a stone cold killer like you to a naïve young man like that?"

"Don't fool yourself, Jack. I see in eyes, boy may be naïve but is stone cold killer."

"Well, I don't know about you, Ivanna, but I am going to go put on my new threads and try out the restaurant downstairs. What are you going to do? Are you still going to end me? Are you going to rejoin your team? Do you still think you're safe? Would you like to hold off on killing me for now and join me for a late lunch? I hate eating alone."

"I will join for lunch. Everything else … fuck off."

"Alrighty then, knock on my door whenever you're ready."

Jack goes back to his room and quickly pulls out his first-aid supplies. He pokes his fingers around his ribs and with his breathing feeling fairly normal, he doesn't think he has an actual break, most likely just a crack or two. Jack wraps the area with gauze as tight as he can get it.

Jack had checked his nose earlier, when he first got in the room, and ended up just popping it back into place.

He's hoping the restaurant has better Scotch than what he found in the mini bar as he has every intention of tying one on the Ambo's dime.

Within twenty minutes, Ivanna knocks at Jack's door. Jack opens the door and does a very visible double take. He is reminded for a moment that Ivanna really is a very beautiful Russian woman. It is her propensity for slaughtering families because she's bored that makes him forget that fact.

Ivanna's wearing a classy knee-length red dress that Owen picked out for her. She used the makeup to cover her bruised jaw and is wearing matching bright red lipstick. The only thing grossly out of place are her military boots that she's been wearing since they were back at the compound.

"Jack, say anything, I go back to room."

"Ivanna, step into my room for a minute. I'll be right back, I promise, just give me five minutes. Open a bottle of wine from the mini bar if you want."

Ivanna steps into the room and sits on the end of the bed.

Jack skips the elevator and, in spite of cringing in pain, he takes the three flights of stairs down to the lobby.

Five minutes later, he arrives back at his room and respectfully knocks on the door. Ivanna opens the door, and Jack pulls out from behind his back a pair of sandals from the gift store.

Ivanna, who had a corkscrew gripped in her fist behind her back, sheepishly places it back on the mini bar.

Ivanna puts on her matching pair of red sandals and they head down to the restaurant, both taking the elevator this time.

Earlier, back on the Miranda …

The captain is now sitting quietly with Rafael in the wheelhouse. The first mate and divers are playing chess in the galley and Rose is asleep on the floor next to Debbie.

They are charted on a course for Brazil. They are three-and-a-half days into a four-day trip when the Miranda's phone line rings, breaking the calm.

Sig and Rafael are jolted out of their daydreaming to a shocking jolt of still subjective reality.

Both men are nervously eyeing each other, neither one giving any indication to the other as to what it is either should do.

With the phone on continuous ring mode, Sig, for the first time in his life as a captain, just doesn't know what to do. He asks Rafael,

"What should we do?"

"Let's just pick it up and see who the hell it is."

Sig answers the phone. The call is very brief and Sig's only words at the end of the call are, "Okay, sure. Brazil port at fifteen knots will take about two-and-a-half days. And my crew? Shit, the bastard hung up."

"Who was it, Cap?"

"I just sold the Miranda for 2.5 million to the Ambassador. That was the guy we got this gig from, the Ambassador's lawyer Harvey Bloomburg. Oh and get this, after we get it to Brazil, we are then tasked with delivering it to Israel. Harvey says they want the boat, the crew and the girl."

"What the fuck, Sig? Who are these people?"

Sig picks up the boats mic. "All crew to the wheel-house, immediately."

He brings the Miranda down to a three-knot crawl and puts her on autopilot.

With the crew of four now huddled in the wheelhouse, Sig starts to lay down the reality that awaits the Miranda.

"Okay, men, we all saw what happened to Deb. I just got a call and I now know the Miranda has been tracked from the moment we left the dock in Argentina. The man who hired the boat has now offered to purchase it outright in Santos. After what we were witness to, I think it's a fair bet none of us are safe.

"I was also told there will be some men joining us in Santos, Brazil. Their final destination for the Miranda is the Port of Ashad, Israel. About a month-long trip, gentlemen, and my inclination is that none of us are intended to make it to our final destination alive.

"I don't know about the rest of you, but I don't plan on being there to collect my money. I do have a plan, but as this includes everyone including Debbie, I'm open to any and all suggestions."

Arden, the first mate suggests, "Fuck their tracking. Let's fuel up at the Rio Grande Port and then head for open seas. I mean, Jesus Christ, did you see what they did to Deb? This is like some creepy fucking science fiction horror show. Those bugs? What the fuck is that?"

Earl, one of the divers speaks up. "It's not as strange as you think. Before I switched my major from Entomology to Marine Biology, it was amazing the shit they were pulling out of the Amazon. The question is what the fuck was it doing in Argentina?"

The second diver, Franky, asks, "You worked with bugs?"

"Yeah, fucking hated it …yech."

"Enough, we will go with my plan," Sig says. "Arden has it partly right—we are going to make a quick stop in Rio

Grande and when they notice we've stopped early, I'll tell them that we had to make a pit stop for more fuel. That is when everyone gets off. I'll take the Miranda alone the rest of the way to Santos."

"I'm not leaving you alone, Sig."

"Sorry, Rafael. I need the 'Bear' to stay with Debbie. Someone has to get her and Rose back to her father, and it should be someone he knows."

"I'm not going to let you drive to your own death, Captain."

"I have no intention of pulling right up and docking, Rafael. I'm going to anchor it around the bend and take the TELB to the closest dock. I got friends in Santos, I'll be fine.

"I want the rest of you to pack one knapsack each and leave everything else. If you're stopped by anyone, you're just a bunch of hikers carrying a girl who's had too much tequila.

"We have two options where you can go. The Rio Grande Airport is about eleven clicks away but is only for regional flights. At Pelotas, you can catch an international flight, but it is seventy-seven clicks away and if anyone is out there looking for us, it's obviously more risky."

"And what do we do for money, Captain? You're the only one with a big credit card. It's not like we're all sitting out here flush in cash."

"I got that covered, too, Rafael. While you're packing, I'm going to call Debbie's dad, Karl. Seeing as how it's his daughter we're talking about, I can probably arrange for him to get us a charter plane."

"And what are you going to tell him about Deb?"

"I'm going to tell him she has been badly injured, she was treated and we need to get her out of the country as there are men coming to kill us all. Which is, almost, the whole truth.

"Okay, everyone, go pack. We'll be at the Grande in about six hours. Rafael, you pack any of Debbie's valuables. I got that call to make and I want to be alone when I'm making it."

Back in Uruguay…

Jack and Ivanna arrive at the hotel's lobby restaurant. Jack insists on a booth at the back with his back to the wall. Ivanna wants that seat, too, but with Jack giving her a last-second strategic shove, he snags it himself. "You can sit next to me, Ivanna," he says. Not impressed, Ivanna takes the seat across from Jack rather than having to sit right beside him.

Jack goes on to remind Ivanna that he had called the seat first back in the lobby.

The waitress arrives promptly, which is a good thing as both Jack and Ivanna are starving.

One of Jack's many little idiosyncrasies, having been a world traveller since he was eighteen years old, is that he's under a false illusion that he is fluent in half a dozen languages.

He was learning Spanish from Bear, but if saying hello, goodbye and being able to painfully order off a menu constitutes fluency, then Jack's false illusion would be dead on.

Jack tries to order off the menu in Spanish, but the menu also has pictures, so he ends up just pointing to what he wants.

Jack orders the *asado* which is barbecue grilled beef and a *chivito*, which is a sandwich with steak, ham, cheese, lettuce, tomato and mayo. He also orders a double Scotch and reminds the waitress to top it up whenever it gets low.

"Are you hungry, Jack?"

"Yes, Ivanna. I'm ready to drop any minute."

Ivanna orders a chowder soup and a big bun she can soak it in the soup.

"Is that all you're having Ivanna?"

"Maybe I break your jaw, then you try to eat sandwich."

"I would say I'm sorry, Ivanna, but the way you treated Debbie back at the compound, you're lucky I didn't kill you on the spot."

"No, because you needed me, asshole. How quick you forget I try to save your pretty girlfriend."

"But you didn't, did you?"

"As I say, girl dead when bit, she just didn't know it yet."

"Yeah, you said that already."

As they are both starting to get angry with each other again, they sit quietly until lunch arrives, only occasionally moving their respective injured body part, trying to gain some measure of relief.

The restaurant is busy and Jack and Ivanna both think they may have spotted a couple of the Ambassador's men in the lobby earlier and now possibly another pair, who are eating, as well.

After they finish their self-proclaimed delicious meals, Jack motions to Ivanna that her makeup is coming off and suggests she goes to the bathroom to fix it up, lest they garnish some additional unwanted attention.

"Thank you, Jack. Did you want some tissue? Bear's punch has nose bleeding again."

As Ivanna is walking to the bathroom, Jack quickly checks his nose, and after finding no blood dripping, he shouts out louder than he'd probably intended, "Bitch!"

The other patrons in the restaurant all turn around and stare at him and Jack makes a "sorry about that folks" hand gesture. Of course, with Ivanna laughing out loud all the way to the washroom, it certainly doesn't help matters.

Jack is so out of sorts he is now talking to himself, aloud.

"Fuck … I have to eat, then I gotta kill a bunch of bad guys and then I'm getting the fuck outta this place.'

With Ivanna in the bathroom, Jack puts the ketchup bottle cap on the table and flicks it into the kitchen opening. As he stands up to go retrieve it, two men at the other end of the room start to stand up. Spotting them, Jack holds up the ketchup bottle for them to see, and he performs a "What a goof I am, the top rolled into the kitchen" skit for their behalf.

Both men sit back down but continue to watch Jack's every move.

Jack slips into the kitchen and, seeing a box of thin rubber sanitary gloves, he pockets a pair and picks up the ketchup top and returns to his seat.

Ivanna returns to the table and Jack immediately starts to laugh. The lighting must not have been good in the bathroom as Ivanna looks like a clown in a minstrel show. Ivanna, being so tired, starts to laugh as well not even knowing what they're both laughing at.

Jack dabs a napkin in his water and leans forward.

"Do you mind?" he asks before wiping off some of her overabundance of misdirected lipstick.

"Thank you, Jack."

"What the fuck are we doing here, Ivanna? Here we have one of the most highly trained, elite liquidators in all of the world and a family-killing psycho bitch both being watched by a couple of fat boys in flowered shirts."

"You're not a bitch, Jack, an asshole maybe. So, you spotted them?"

"Yes, we weren't even close with the two guys we thought at first, though."

"How do you know?"

"Well, one of them leaned over to kiss the other." He paused. "I'm gonna come out and just ask you straight, Ivanna. Why did you kill the whole family?"

"What are we? Comrades now, Jack? Is this when I tell you life story of Ivanna?"

"No, Ivanna, we're not. Frankly, I've come across people like you my whole life, on both sides of the fence. You're the first one I've left alive to ask that question to. Why, Ivanna? Why an entire non-combatant family? I really do want to know just ... why?"

"I not grow up in sunny California, Jack. Russia is very different culture, human life not as valued as in America. What we did in Chechnya make Ohio look like picnic."

Jack starts laughing again. "What are you, thirty-five at most? You were a kid when the shit hit the fan in Chechnya."

"Okay, Ivanna, if you really want to be a bitch your whole life then don't tell me. I'll pay the bill, you go on back to the Ambassador—if he doesn't kill you before then—and I will clean up these amateurs they have watching us, by myself. And if you get in my way, you'll be gone, too."

"You think you want truth, Jack, but I suspect you know already."

"And what would that be, Ivanna?"

"Your precious Ambassador give me one special order, Jack. As you called it, liquidate everyone in home, everyone."

"Why didn't you just shoot me back in Akron?"

"Ambassador said if I can prevent, no shoot Jack. I did enjoy the peep show, though, Jack."

"I guess I should thank you for not shooting me, then. So, what's your plan now?"

"I call young Owen to room to fuck and then he tell me everything. Then I go to airport and see mother in Stalingrad. And you?"

"I don't have a whole lot of choices, do I? I guess I'll just stick around and wait till they board the Miranda and they find the Ambo's trophy. I am thinking about ordering that masseuse, though. My whole body could use some kneading."

"It's not on boat, is it, Jack?"

"Well, if it's not, I guess I'm dead, aren't I?"

"You've been with Ambo long time. No, he not kill you?"

"What's your point?"

"You know a lot about him. He is changed man since you met, no?"

"Do you want any help getting down to your cab later?"

"No, silly, Jack. I'm going to have Owen drive me to airport."

Ivanna stands up and surprisingly gives Jack a kiss on the forehead. Neither say another word to the other as she walks off on her way to find Owen.

Jack orders another double Scotch from the waitress, and the bill.

Jack begins a stare down with the men in the flower shirts. Their first reaction is to menacingly stare back, but after a few minutes they become visibly flustered. To counter Jack's penetrating gaze, they begin pointing toward him and engage in some mock conversation, trying to hide their nervousness.

Without missing a beat, Jack polishes off his Scotch, drops $300 on the table and gesticulates to the men of his intention to leave through the back service door of the restaurant.

Jack stands up and heads out the back door with one of the men in pursuit and the other hastily trying to get the waitress's attention to pay the bill.

Jack makes his way into the alleyway and is leaning against a garbage bin when the first man comes charging out, frantically looking around for Jack until he spots him, just standing there by the garbage bin.

Jack can't help but laugh. Still without saying a word, he pantomimes to the man to wait for his buddy. After a minute or so Jack says, "Jesus fucking Christ. What is he waiting for? The receipt?"

The other man soon comes out and Jack says to them, "I need a phone and a gun. You can just walk them over or I will come over there and take them off of you."

Both men slip their hands into their jackets and one man mockingly indicates to Jack to come on over, if he dares.

Jack, with one hand firmly bracing his ribs, begins to walk toward the men. On his short walk over he does an ever-so-slight, too-much-Scotch stumble.

The men appear to be relieved, and with big grins they take their hands out of their jackets and are now laughing and pleading with Jack to come on over.

A couple of minutes pass and Jack is now searching the pockets of the unconscious, but still alive men.

Jack angrily ruminates, "Fuck you, Hairy." Both men have no guns or cell phones on them. Jack has to get a hold of Roger and he determines that he will do whatever it takes.

Jack takes a piss by the garbage can, then heads back to his room.

Back in his room, Jack takes the rubber gloves out of his pocket and heads for the bathroom. Twenty minutes later, he's rinsing the shit off of three intact glass tubes in the sink. He thanks God that Bear didn't break them when he was kicking him in the stomach back on the Miranda.

Back in Las Vegas…

Roger arrives at a private terminal at McCarron, spots his team leader, Robinson, and grabs his bag from the trunk. He hands the cabbie a dollar tip and sends him on his way.

"Robinson? Where's the team? Am I the first one here?"

"I'm really sorry, Roger, but the money was just too good."

Three men appear from behind a fuel carrier and are all brandishing Uzis with their site tracers all aimed right at Roger's heart.

"What the fuck, Chris? Is this about Jack?"

"Don't know any Jack, Roger. All I know is you're getting on that plane and they really insisted you be alive. So please drop the gun that's in your pocket, and let's get going."

"Where the fuck are we going, Chris?"

"Don't know that either, Rog, but I'm told the pilot does…let's move."

Roger is cuffed and walks peacefully into the plane with the three men. The plane is cleared for takeoff and departs, leaving Chris Robinson alone on the tarmac.

Back in Uruguay…

Jack has finished cleaning the vials and drops them in the toilet tank for safe keeping.

He sits down at the end of the bed and looks around the room at the furniture. He's hoping he can construct some semblance of a weapon from it. He figures that if he just tries to walk downstairs and hail a cab, one of the Ambo's men will get him. There's no way it could be that easy.

Suddenly, there is a knock at the door. Jack moves to the door and peers through the peephole. He can see the now conscious flowered-shirt thugs standing on the other side.

Jack quickly turns a room chair sideways and breaks off one of the legs. He answers the door while holding up the leg behind the door.

"Back for more, boys?"

One of the men hands Jack a hotel phone that he can plug into his room.

"Here, asshole. You're gonna be getting a call."

"Thanks, boys. Anything else?"

"Real tough guy when we have instructions not to hurt you."

"Step into my room and we'll go again, I won't tell Hairy."

The men both lift their jackets and Jack sees they are now strapped with shoulder-harnessed 9 mms. "Sure, asshole, let's do it."

"I got a call coming remember? Maybe later."

Jack closes the door and plugs in the phone. No sooner has he plugged it in than it starts to ring. Jack resumes his admiration for Hairy and thinks, "Fuck, that's good, Hairy."

"Hello, Hairy. Congratulations on the little one."

"Hi, Jack. I can't hear you very well. I'm on a charter flight right now, so if you could please just listen. First off, thanks for not killing my guys. Second, the Ambo wants you on the next flight to Israel. My guys will take you to the airport. I'll have the Ambo's limo waiting for you at the airport. Bye, Jack." Hairy hangs up the phone.

Jack hangs up and places a call to Roger.

The phone is answered on the first ring,

"Roger, boy, is that you? I can't hear you very well."

"Roger can't come to the phone right now, Jack. Just catch your flight to Israel." The line goes dead.

Jack slowly places the phone down. A sensation of dread overtakes him that he is not used to feeling. All he can think about now is Marg and Debra. The Ambassador couldn't possibly hurt his family, could he?

He's reflecting on Ivanna's comment about the Ambassador being a changed man. The Ohio extraction? Bringing his old team and that psycho bitch to the compound? Has she been in on it the whole time?

The one thing Jack decides is to not risk calling Marg or Debra's cells. In the event they are safe, he doesn't want to risk any possible attempt at a trace.

Jack starts going over options … go next door, kill Owen and Ivanna, kill the flowered shirts and anyone else who bats an eye at him. And then what?

Jack comes to the painful conclusion that the only option he has left is to take the Ambassador's jet to Israel.

The painful part? Swallowing the three glass vials again.

Back on the Miranda …

The crew are all packed and are helping load the captain's life raft with a few sentimental items that he's been carrying around since his army days.

They are now thirty minutes from their first stop at the Port of Rio Grande, Brazil.

Sig was successful in tracking down Debbie's dad, Karl and, as Sig had been praying for, Karl agreed to cover all of the costs.

Back in Texas, Karl had been on the phone all night, calling in favours from his Washington political friends. His friends came to his aid in spades and arranged for an aircraft to pick up the crew and bring them to Texas. They even had it classified as a US government charter with all of the diplomatic immunity exemptions one might expect.

Karl further insisted there be a team of armed soldiers to meet them at the Rio Grande Port with a military escort for the seventy-seven kilometre journey to the Pelotas International Airport.

Upon learning Sig's full plan, Karl was confident he had enough political leverage that he could get the whole Brazilian army, if necessary, to meet them at the Grande port, and to ensure the Miranda was secure, as well.

Sig had to put it as delicately as he could to Karl that he had not seen this level of government coercion since his illegal missions into Cambodia. And the first priority was to get Debbie and his crew secured upon docking at the port, and then out of the country as quietly as possible.

He went on to further suggest that a pissing war at the port between two different groups of soldiers with vastly different agendas was the last thing they needed right now.

Karl had agreed, and after Sig reassured him that he would be fine on his own in Santos, Brazil, Karl concluded with, "Just get my baby home, Captain."

Sig was so distraught after his conversation with Karl that he stepped out onto the upper deck and threw up into the Atlantic.

As Sig is outside puking, he can hear his phone ringing. Harvey is still monitoring the Miranda's progress at the Argentinian Port Authority, and he was just notified of the Miranda's change in course. That being that they are heading into the Port of Rio Grande.

Sig answers the phone. "This is Harvey, Captain. What are you doing?"

"We need to refuel, Harvey. I got clearance from the Port Authority to refuel and we will be in and out within an hour."

"That's fine. I will have men there to ensure no one leaves the vessel, Captain."

"Goodbye, Harvey." Sig hangs up the phone. As he is approaching the dock, Sig is hoping against hope that this group of reprobates can't possibly get a team down there that fast.

Sig moors the Miranda and, as promised by Karl, they are met by a small group of soldiers. The crew, Debbie and Rose are loaded onto a covered military vehicle and immediately begin the drive to the airport in Pelotas.

The Miranda is refueled and Sig is back in the wheel-house taking it alone on the remaining forty-hour journey to the Port of Santos. Sig jacks the Miranda to the boat's maximum speed of twelve knots. He figures he's about to lose his life's investment, so he's going to push the engine to the max for the remaining voyage. He's hoping it will ultimately die on the Ambassador and his crew on their way back to Israel.

Back in Las Vegas…

Margaret and Debra woke up early and are now packed and ready to leave the Hard Rock Hotel. All the staff have been wonderful to them with the obvious exception of the duplicitous Pat.

Margaret is standing at the door waiting for Deb,

"What are you doing, Debra?"

"Just leaving the tablet on the counter so Pat won't freak out."

Margaret walks over and, smiling at Debra, places the tablet in her own purse.

"This is the cost of him being a jerk, honey."

"You won't get a complaint from me, Mom. I just hope he doesn't have a security team manning all the doors to make sure the 'riff raff' don't steal anything on their way out."

Once they are inside Roger's car, Marg says, "Well, where to, hon?"

"Let's just go home, Mom."

"You got it, kid. I feel like Dairy Queen for lunch. We can stop in Yermo on the way home. Think we can put aside our diets for one day and get a couple of Blizzards?"

"We deserve it, don't we?"

"Yes, Debra, we certainly do."

Chapter 10

THE AMBASSADOR

The Ambassador was born in 1935 in the largely communist city of Düsseldorf, Germany. He was the only surviving child of Siegfried and Helena. He had a much older brother and sister who were both lost to consumption during World War I, both of whom he did have the chance to know.

The Ambassador's real name is Wilhelm Oster.

Wilhelm's father was of Jewish descent. He had fought on the losing side in the First World War.

Several years after the end of World War I, Siegfried and his childhood friend, Peter Osterman, retooled their government-mandated armament plant back to its original farm equipment operation.

They were equal partners in one of the largest farm equipment plant operations in all of Germany. Over the course of the next several years, their operation extended to a series of plants and other highly profitable business ventures.

Like many of Germany's Jewish elite, over the long and gradual course of time between 1933 and 1940, Siegfried had all but ignored Hitler's Anti-Semitic laws, decrees and edicts, invariably, until it was too late.

When Hitler was appointed Chancellor of Germany in January 1933, he and the 'Reichstag' (German legislature) slowly and methodically eroded the rights of German-born citizens of Jewish descent.

With the death of the more moderate German president, Paul von Hindenburg, in 1934, Hitler's anti-Jewish policies ran unopposed with no legal or moral barometer of human decency.

During this period of time, Siegfried and his wife Helena saw their everyday basic rights erode. They lost their right to vote in any German election, to fly a German flag or even to own a pet.

Hitler's 1933 campaign of *Kauf nicht bei Juden*—Don't buy from Jews—was supplanted by Herman Goering's 1938 campaign and eventual law decree. Jews could no longer work alongside Aryans. They were also forbidden from owning any part of a business or a company or any physical property.

Siegfried was ultimately forced to sell any and all interests in his joint ventures to his lifelong friend, the German-born "Aryan," Peter Osterman.

By 1940, the Jewish people could no longer own a car or even have a driver's licence. Their passports had a large

J stamped on them, and they could no longer own, or even use, a telephone. Yet still Siegfried and Helena stayed.

Through all the years of moral descent and insanity, Peter had maintained the highest level of character and loyalty to his friend and partner, Siegfried.

Peter on many, many occasions tried to get his friend to go to the United States before it was too late. But Siegfried loved Germany and more important, the German people. He always considered himself a proud patriotic German. It was because of Siegfried's proud faith in Germany and the German people, that he always maintained a futile conviction that the German people themselves would one day rise up and put a stop to Hitler and his henchmen.

A proud World War I veteran, Siegfried had been awarded the German Infantry Iron Cross. He had reasoned to himself that Hitler was a passing phase and the moral compass of his nation would once again return.

Peter himself had come under ever-increasing scrutiny by the SS and was under surveillance for many years. Once World War II started, Peter had to end all contact with Siegfried and paid an extraordinary amount of money in bribes to keep from ending up in Sobibor as a race traitor.

Siegfried and Helena's modest family home was finally impounded by the SS, and they were resettled into a Jewish ghetto.

Their relative wealth at the time afforded them the ability to bribe their way into getting their own bedroom in a 600-square-foot apartment that they were forced to share with fifteen other displaced Jews.

Sickness and hunger ran rampant in the small apartment. The constant coughing, a baby with colic and the smell of filth and death permeated the air.

It was on a warm and beautiful spring afternoon in Düsseldorf that the unthinkable occurred.

Siegfried, Helena and young Wilhelm were starving for some fresh air and sunshine. They had made an agreement with the group that they would go line up for stale bread and potatoes.

The crowded cobbled streets of their once majestic city were littered with waste water, human excrement and bodies of the dead or dying. Most had been unceremoniously shoved off the street and into the gutter.

Even with the family all wearing the mandated Star of David, because of their expensive clothing and with it still looking fairly new at this point, the Osters could not walk two metres down the street without being surrounded by their own fellow Jews, who were begging for food or money.

Wilhelm, like all Jewish children his age, was not sure what to make of his new reality and was busy playing the "don't step on a crack" game on the cobbled sidewalk, a difficult challenge no doubt.

Wilhelm was several metres behind his parents. When he had caught up to them, he looked up from the cracked cobbled streets to see three German soldiers had surrounded his parents.

"You Jews walk in the gutter now!"

"I'm sorry, *Oberführer*. We did not know."

"You need to keep apprised of the postings, you filthy Jewish pigs."

Helena, who was battling a bad case of dysentery, forgot herself for a moment and began to speak from her proud heart, "Why can't you just leave us alone? You strip us of our homes, our property, our dignity, and you herd us into these slums. Is it too much to ask to just leave us…"

A young German soldier pulled out his Luger and shot Helena in the head before she was able to finish her diatribe. As Siegfried was bending down to hold his wife, another soldier removed his rifle from his shoulder. He backed up half a metre and shot Siegfried in the back of the head.

The walking masses briefly paused to observe the murder scene but quickly continued on with their foraging and monotonous daily activities.

Young Wilhelm was grabbed by the arm by one of the soldiers and dragged toward a cattle truck at the end of the street. The truck was already full with other Jews who had been arrested in the daily street sweep.

When they were metres from the truck, an older Jewish man passed the three German soldiers and young Wilhelm. He did not remove his cap as the soldiers passed. One of the soldiers took exception to this and let go of Wilhelm's arm to confront the old man. Not pleased with his response, they also shot him in the head.

As soon as Wilhelm was released, he was grabbed by a teenage Jew and shuffled into an alleyway. Wilhelm's pockets were quickly searched and he was robbed of two

German pennies his father had given him. His coat was also stolen and he was left standing alone in the alley.

Left alone in a state of shock and disbelief, Wilhelm finally managed to make his way back to his apartment. When his fellow apartment dwellers realized Siegfried and Helena would not be returning, they split up their belongings and William was given a thin sheet and a new place to sleep on the cold wooden floor in the main room.

Over the next three months, Wilhelm learned the code of the streets. With the help of some older boys, he had become a master smuggler and was able to feed himself every day. He had earned the respect of his apartment dwellers and even got a small corner of his old bed back.

It was a freezing cold morning in the ghetto. There was a foot of fresh snow on the ground and the presence of German soldiers was unusually non-existent.

The night before, Wilhelm had been pushed out of his corner of the bed to make way for a badly beaten older Jewish lady. He had nestled on the ground against the bosom of a large Jewish woman to keep warm.

On this cold, quiet morning, an unknown man and woman had appeared in the doorway of the apartment.

They had walked right into the house and were searching all of the smaller children. The man bent down and looked at Wilhelm's face and continued on with his search. It was at that very moment that Wilhelm had recognized the man's distinct bowler hat, but before he had a chance to say anything, the couple had left the apartment.

Wilhelm slipped on his "new" winter jacket that he had stolen from a large dead man in the street. He tiptoed out into the hall, being very careful as to not step on anyone or wake those who had managed to find some temporary solace in sleep.

Just as the man with the bowler hat was opening the door at the foot of the stairway that lead out onto the street, Wilhelm called out, "Uncle Peter?"

Peter ran up the stairs and picked up Wilhelm. Holding him out at arm's length, he looked long and hard at the thin, soiled face before him. "Wilhelm is that really you?"

"Yes, Uncle Peter, it is me. Mom and Dad are gone."

"I know, Wilhelm. Let's go home."

Peter removed Wilhelm's coat, which had the Jewish Star of David sewn onto it, and replaced it with his own. Then he carried the boy down into the warm, waiting car on the street.

Peter, who years earlier had been forced to publically decry his former friend and partner, was no longer under constant SS scrutiny and was once again considered a good Aryan German. Peter had heard of his friend's fate and made it his mission to rescue Wilhelm and get him out of Germany.

At the age of eight, Wilhelm was quickly moved out of Germany and was now living a reasonably secure life at a ranch in the Ukraine. The German Army was on its last legs in the Ukraine, with the arrival of the Soviet Republic in the East and the Americans approaching from the West.

It was this period in Ukrainian history where common Ukrainian citizens along with the now weathered German troops committed some of the War's most barbaric atrocities.

On a quiet Saturday morning, Wilhelm left the ominous security of the ranch and went out alone to a nearby pond to shoot frogs. Wilhelm wanted to try out his new slingshot. He made it himself out of a piece of leather and a strap of military medical tubing he had found.

At the pond, Wilhelm had to make several adjustments to his new weapon, and after several attempts he was finally able to hit a frog. After making contact with the frog, Wilhelm experienced feelings of success and accomplishment. He was proud of his ability to have been able to make the slingshot in the first place.

Wilhelm went to retrieve his prize. He had shot the frog through the eye with a small pebble and, as he looked down upon it, he discovered it was still breathing. Wilhelm poked the frog with a small stick and was suddenly overcome by the senselessness of his actions. He could not leave the frog to suffer so he picked up a heavy flat granite rock and dropped it on the frog's body. At that very moment, Wilhelm heard a gunshot and what he understood as accompanying joyous laughter.

Going against every instinct in his young mind to run back to the safety of his ranch, Wilhelm was sufficiently intrigued with what he had heard that he stilled himself to see if he would hear the sounds again.

Within a few moments, there was another ringing gunshot and again the sound of joyous laughter and celebration. Against his own judgment, and after countless hours of being trained to run and hide, Wilhelm's intrigue got the better of him.

Being only eight years old and still full of curiosity and adventure, he determined that he needed to find out where this dichotomy of sounds were emanating from.

Forgetting the regrettable death of the frog and with a happy smile on his face and a warm feeling in his stomach, Wilhelm made a path for the unexpected but contrary celebration. That being gunfire and then jubilation.

With his survive or die instincts still intact. Wilhelm stealthily moves through the countryside taking advantage of every large tree he can manoeuver to and from. Ever closer, Wilhelm heard another single bullet shot followed by cheering and laughter. Only this time he thought he could also make out the sounds of muffled crying and anguish.

At that moment, Wilhelm felt a haunting knot growing inside of his stomach. At 8 years old and with a level of maturity well beyond his years. Adventure and curiosity would ultimately prevail, but Wilhelm decided he would carry onward with the utmost of caution.

After about five minutes of going from tree to tree, Wilhelm made a final turn and came upon a building. A few metres from the building was a large cart of hay that was blocking a gravel roadway. Wilhelm walked around the cart only to discover that he was now veritably exposed and vulnerable.

He is now standing alone and in open view for all too see.

Wilhelm, who looked like any other small Ukrainian child, was spotted by a German soldier. With a smile on his face, the soldier waved at Wilhelm and shouted in German, "*Kommen, kommen bei der party,*" which translated to "Come, come join the party."

Frozen in fear, Wilhelm shook his shoulders and made a look on his face as if he did not understand what the German soldier was saying to him.

As the soldier looked back to the action, Wilhelm slipped behind the cart and bent down to watch what was going on through the wheel of the hay cart. The soldier eventually looked back to see if Wilhelm was still there and displayed no sign of concern when he presumed that the young child had left. The soldier returned his attention to the action.

What Wilhelm was about to witness would go on to haunt him every day for the rest of his life. An incident that he had never told another living soul.

Wilhelm was ultimately adopted by Peter, and they spent the next thirteen years moving from country to country as Peter continued to expand his farm equipment operations around the globe.

Peter and Wilhelm ultimately settled in Arlington, Texas.

There, Wilhelm began working on the construction of their new plant in Arlington. He had an apartment of his own and many girlfriends to keep him company.

On Wilhelm's twenty-first birthday, Peter kept his promise to Siegfried that he had many years ago and authorized the release of Wilhelm's forty per cent shares in the company. The property and share value equated to exactly 200 million dollars.

His entire adult life, the Ambassador has been a silent donor to the Wiesenthal Centre. If an underground Nazi war criminal was identified and ultimately captured by the centre, chances were that the entire operation was covertly funded by Wilhelm Oster.

The Ambassador's unbridled hatred of America began at the end of World War II when the Americans were giving clemency and citizenship to many German scientists and people of wealth.

Many of these individuals were believed to have contributed to the German war machine and the atrocities against the Jewish people. In its zeal, it had become American government policy to combat the Russians and the advent of ever-spreading communism.

The Ambassador also set up numerous scholarships for underprivileged youths throughout the free world.

The Ambassador's initial endeavors were of the altruistic nature, but over time and circumstances, the loyalty of those lucky recipients were often put to the test for less than lawful endeavors.

Chapter 11

FALTERING PLANS?

Back in Argentina ...

Harvey who has been stuck in a Port Authority office for the last couple of days and sleeping on a couch for the most part, finally gets a call from the Ambassador, who is now back in Israel.

"Good afternoon, Harvey."

"Hello, Wilhelm. You're up late."

"Yes, yes ... I'm sorry for keeping you in that office, Harvey. Are you eating okay?"

"Yes, Sir, and so is the whole floor on your dime."

"Well, order in a big lunch for everyone and don't forget to hand out a few envelopes to the appropriate people. I want you to get yourself on a flight to Arlington, Texas."

"Are you sending the private plane, Sir?"

"No, it is on its way to get Jack in Uruguay."

"Is he coming home, Sir?"

"He will be, Harvey."

"And Texas, Sir"?

"It is time to bring this operation to an end, Harvey. I am not getting any younger."

"You are still a great man, Sir. Have you given more thought to just dispatching the target?"

"We've been through this more times than I care to recall, Harvey. If your allegiance is wavering, tell me now and I will have Ian step in."

"No, Sir, that's not it all, and I apologize for giving you that impression. It's just Texas, Sir? We're still hearing rumblings about what happened in Ohio."

"Was Akron's local crime reporter not made a very rich man?"

"Yes, Sir. He will never be a problem. It's the Wiesenthal Centre. One of our hackers has been monitoring some disturbing private e-mails. When eight Jews are blown up during Hanukkah…"

The Ambassador interrupts Harvey in mid-sentence and is now audibly upset.

"Yes, yes, Harvey. We already anticipated all of this, did we not?"

"Yes, Sir."

"And what did we conclude?"

"Sir?"

"Goddamn you if you don't answer me correctly."

"If there is any major concern from the centre, you would be the first person they contact."

"And have they?"

"No, Sir, they have not."

"Then please finish up there and get yourself to Arlington."

The Ambassador hangs up and just in time. Harvey has a few minutes to unpucker his ass and make it to be bathroom. He suddenly needs to take a very serious unanticipated crap.

With the Ambassador now sitting at his desk, his two security members approach. The Ambassador is staring off into the distance and, after a long pause, he looks at the two men and says,

"After Arlington, we will be making some personnel changes."

One of the men says, "We should start with Jack, Sir."

"Get Jack's room ready for me. He will be staying here for a few days."

As the men leave the room, they can hear the Ambassador muttering the phrase, "*Sie wahlen immer die waffe.*"

One thing the men have learned over the years is that whenever they hear that German phrase, it's best to leave the Ambassador alone for a while.

As the guards leave, closing the Ambassador's door behind them, Mohammed motions to Noa to take a walk with him.

Both men were born and raised in Israel, and at the age of eighteen they did their mandatory two-year army enlistment. They also both enlisted with Mossad for a number of years prior to being recruited by the Ambassador.

"The old man is losing it. Once Arlington is over, I think he plans to liquidate anyone who was in on it, and that could very well include us, Noa."

"I think you're losing it, Mo. Where is he going to get a couple of highly trained former Mossad agents he can trust? We're lucky enough just to be living in Israel, and have you forgotten what your pay stub reads every month? We will be fine, Mo, my brother."

Mohammed replies, "For our own sakes, I hope you're right, brother."

The Ambassador is now standing alone at his office window overlooking his expansive property.

He spots Mohammed and Noa engaged in conversation in what would appear to him as being an inconspicuous spot on his property. Which, in this particular case, would be behind a cluster of trees, presumptively out of their boss's line of sight.

The Ambassador is thinking, 'That does not look like they are getting Jack's room ready as they were charged with doing.'

The Ambassador returns to his chair and is feeling a little forsaken. He is thinking about Harvey's frustrating defiance and the fact that his two most trusted security men are hiding behind a cluster of trees involved in a private discussion.

He looks back out the window—yes, they are still standing there.

The Ambassador's thoughts unexpectedly take him back to Jack and Margaret's wedding at the boathouse restaurant. He had a discussion with Jack prior to the event and had insisted that Jack be properly attired for the holy Jewish occasion. But Jack being Jack was able to convince him that the gag on Margaret was just too apropos.

He further ruminates just how worldly and wise Jack was for his age at the time, that being only 22 years old.

The Ambassador is now trying to remember if Jack has ever referred to him as anything other than Mr. Ambassador or Sir. He can't recall a time…unless, maybe there was one time in his office after the Akron Eight debacle?

"Real old-school respect, that kid," he thinks to himself.

The Ambassador has an epiphany. He is feeling tired, his old bones are feeling their age. He knows those closest to him are looking at his home and calculating how they would redecorate if it was theirs.

The Ambassador has come to a decision. He grabs a gold pen holder off his desk and moves back to the window. His men are still standing and talking. He knocks the gold pen holder on the window loudly in order to get the security men's attention.

They both stop talking and, in the distance, they can make out a figure standing in the window watching them. They move closer and can see the Ambassador is waving for them to return to his office.

"Oh, fuck."

"You can say that again."

Both men return to the Ambassador's office.

"You gentleman got Mr. Singer's room done fast."

"We asked Miss Schuster to do it."

"Miss Schuster works for me, not for you."

"We'll get right on it, Sir."

"Yes, you will, but for now get me Mr. Malcomson on the phone and then leave."

Mohammed walks over and picks up the phone and, after a brief pause, says, "I forgot his number."

The Ambassador places his face down on the desk.

"Noa, do *you* have Ian's number?"

"No, Harvey always does that stuff. Don't you have it written down somewhere, Sir?"

The Ambassador says, "Go sit in your corner." He picks up his phone and whispers into the line then hangs up.

The Ambassador is now sitting quietly, staring at the two seated men. His face bears its usual warm, gentle expression.

Within a couple of minutes, five security men who work the security detail outside of the house, enter the room. They are all equipped with mini Uzis.

The Ambassador says, "These two gentlemen are no longer in the employ of our organization. Please escort them off the property. If either one of them speaks, take them both to the rear of the property and shoot them … over by the rocks would be fine."

As the large group of men begins silently filing out of the office, the Ambassador adds, "Before you leave, does anyone in this room have Mr. Malcomson's cell number?"

A young Irish fellow speaks up. "I do, Sir."

"Are you Mossad?"

"No, Sir, former I.R.A."

"Thank you, son. Leave me the number and return to your duties."

The Ambassador asks the group, "Anyone here Mossad…besides the two men leaving?"

Two men step forward, "We are, Sir."

"Good then. You men will now be working directly with me. The rest of you please proceed and kindly close the door on your way out. Names, please, gentlemen?"

"I am Joshua, Sir."

"Yes, Joshua. If I am correct your father was Shin Bet?"

"Yes, Sir, he passed two years ago."

"*Barukh attah Adonai Eloheinv Malekh ha-olam' dayan ha-emet.*" The Ambassador says a Jewish blessing translated as, "Blessed art Thou, Lord our God, Master of the Universe, the Judge of Truth."

"Amen, Sir."

The second man asked to stay proceeds, "My name is Peter, Mr. Ambassador."

"Ah, yes, Peter. Your father is running in the upcoming election."

"Yes, sir, we are all very proud of him."

"As well you should be."

"Passports, gentlemen?"

"We left them with Harvey when we signed on, Sir."

"Yes, yes…they must be in here somewhere. Have either of you been to the US?"

Both men say they have not.

"Well, we will be going to Arlington, Texas, in a few weeks. I am just waiting on a very dear friend, with a very special package. Then we will make plans to go.

"I have to make a quick call then I will be retiring for the evening. Miss Schuster will take you to your rooms after I am situated. You will be moving to the third floor, down from my room.

"Normally, Harvey would run you through your responsibilities but, alas, Harvey is away, so we will discuss it together in the morning. In a nutshell, gentlemen, where I am, you are."

The Ambassador directs the men to take a seat in the back of the room.

The Ambassador calls the number given to him by the young Irish lad.

"Hello, Ian. Congratulations again on the birth of your beautiful daughter. Have you given her a name yet?"

"My wife and I will name her together when I see her, Sir."

"My deepest apologies, Ian. As soon as this boat debacle is cleared up, please, with my blessing, return home to them."

"Thank you, Sir."

"Okay, Ian, where are you right now?"

"Santos Port Authority, Sir. Brazil."

"Did Harvey arrange an office for you?"

"Yes, Sir. I've got a captain following me wherever I go and half a dozen armed men at the ready."

"That is good. I want you to call off the men outside of Margaret's house and do it as soon as we conclude this call."

"Yes, Sir. Anything else?"

"How was Jack when you left him?"

"A little beat up, but it was the old Jack. He has something in the works, Sir."

"Ian, I had instructed our men that he wasn't to be touched."

"No, Sir. It happened on the Miranda. The girl died, so the crew gave Jack a pretty good beating."

"How could the crew have gotten to Jack?"

"I believe they jumped him when he was asleep, Sir."

"The girl, have we confirmed she is actually dead?"

"No, Sir, but I hope to in about an hour when the Miranda is due in port."

"Thank you, Ian. I want you to call me directly when the boat and crew are secured. Harvey is on his way to Arlington, so you deal with me exclusively from now on."

"Yes, Sir. One final question if I may."

"Yes, yes."

"What about Roger, Sir?"

"Roger will be taken care of Ian … goodbye."

The Ambassador hangs up the phone, leaving Ian with a few unanswered questions as he thinks to himself, "What the fuck? Roger is with my guys. Am I supposed to let him go or dispatch him?"

Ian suspects something must be up with the Ambo and Harvey, but he needs to know what to do with Roger so he places the call. "Harvey. How you doing, piker?"

"Hello, Hairy."

"Only Jack can get away with calling me that, you Shylock nose motherfucker."

"Yeah, yeah … what do you want Ian? I'm trying to get some sleep on this fucking plane."

"Sorry, Pikey, I just got off the phone with Ambo. He told me to call off the men from Marg's but didn't say anything about the queer. You know what I'm supposed to do?"

"Yes, Hairy, I do. He's on his way to Israel, right? Tell your men to take him to the Ambo's mansion and bring him directly to his office. And wake him if it's night time there. Fuck, I have no idea what time it is anywhere right now. I just want to try and get some fucking sleep. Goodbye, Hairy."

As he hangs up the phone, Ian is thinking to himself, "When was the last time I slept?"

There is a knock on Ian's office door.

"You better come look at this Mr. Malcomson. It's the Miranda."

"Let's go have a look, Captain."

The captain takes Ian to the port command centre and points to a blip on a radar screen.

"That is the vessel we have been tracking, Sir—the "Miranda," as you call it. It has been stationary at this location for the last fifteen minutes."

"How far is that from the port, Captain?"

"We could have a team there in five minutes, Sir."

"Okay, get a boat ready to go. I'll call her first and if there is no answer, I'll be joining you."

Ian phones the Miranda and lets it ring a good five minutes. No one answers.

"Let's go for a boat ride, Captain."

An alarm starts going off throughout the Port Authority.

"What is that, Captain?"

"Sorry, Mr. Malcomson. I don't yet know."

The captain starts shouting commands in Portuguese and a soldier with binoculars points to the sea and says, "*Temos um navio en chamas.*"

"We have a ship on fire, Mr. Malcomson."

"Jesus Christ, that better not be the fucking Miranda Captain, but I suspect it is."

"We cannot be having this in our ports, Sir. We will now have to get other agencies involved."

"Captain, you just get me to that boat and I'll make sure you get a bonus that you can retire on, but I need that goddamn fire out!"

The Captain shouts, "*Obter o barco de fogo La fora, e este homem esta se juntando a nos.*" He then turns to Ian and says, "I told the men to get the fireboat out and that you will be joining us."

Another port staff member bellows, "*Voce ja ouviu o capitao, deixa o movimento,*" which translates to, "You heard the captain—let's move."

Ian is now on his way to the fire with the captain and only minutes away from the burning Miranda, another loud crippling explosion occurs.

Ian's first thought is, "That doesn't sound like a fuel explosion but a planted ordinance." They obviously underestimated the old navy vet, Captain Sig.

He asks for a pair of binoculars and is now searching the banks. He calculates that Sig would not be willing to blow up a group of Brazilian nationals, so he most likely detonated from shore, just as their boat was approaching.

Unable to locate anything unusual in the immediate area or on shore, Ian tells the captain to take him back, the Miranda is lost.

Back in the port office, Ian calls the Ambassador.

"Sorry to wake you, Sir. The Miranda was anchored off shore and sunk, Sir. There were no signs of the crew. I believe the crew exited the boat prior to blowing it up, Sir."

"Thank you, Ian. Tell your captain to continue a search for survivors. I want you to stay one more day. If they do not find anything, then take a few days off and go see your daughter."

"Thank you, Sir, and after?"

"I want you to join Harvey in Arlington."

"Yes, Sir, thank you. And again, sorry for waking you."

Back in Uruguay…

Jack has spent the last two days healing at the Regency. He concluded that he should be at his best before he proceeds with his plan regarding his flight to Israel and his meeting with the Ambassador. All he has left to do is concoct an *actual* plan.

The Ambassador's men in Uruguay are also getting a few days off. It has been twenty-four hours since anyone has knocked on Jack's door, saying, "Let's go Jack, you got a flight to make."

The last obtrusive visitor was warned. "I will kill the next person who knocks on this door."

They must have believed him, as they then just started phoning his room. Jack finally had to unplug the damn phone.

Jack has not heard a peep from Ivanna's room. He assumes she caught her flight back to her Mother Russia.

Jack is personally torn on how he left things with Ivanna. The fact that she spit on Debbie's face when she was lying on the compound operating table and then shoved her off the table, incites a rage in him he hasn't felt since Bosnia.

He figures he meted out some level of justice when he broke the bitch's jaw. But, he's still torn as to whether he should have just taken her out like he did that rapist, Stevens, back at the compound. He did share some moments of brevity and humanity with her, but he can't help but not think about her next civilian victims.

Ultimately, his anger is redirected to the Ambassador for hiring a group of stone cold killers in the first place. And even worse, for making him the leader on the calculated, duplicitous assignment.

Jack comes to the stark realization that he knows what must be done when he gets to Israel, but he'll give the Ambassador the opportunity to explain his side of the story. At the very least, he has to know why, for the love of Christ, was he specifically instructed to take Debbie on the mission to breach the plane.

Jack is also fully aware that any plan he may concoct for his own benefit hinders on whether or not he will be immediately dispatched as soon as he hands over the vials.

With his ribs feeling much better, Jack is up early and planning his first run in almost a week.

He plugs the phone back in and within two minutes, it starts ringing.

Jack answers it and immediately starts speaking. "Tell whoever you have to tell to have the plane ready for takeoff at 1:00 p.m."

He does not wait for a reply and simply hangs up. Earlier, Jack had calculated that it would take fifteen hours to fly to Israel. With Israel being five hours ahead, Jack's plan is to be sitting in the Ambassador's office at 10:00 a.m. tomorrow.

Jack begins with thirty minutes of crunches before his run. Twenty minutes into his crunches, the phone rings again. Jack furiously picks it up. "What?" he bellows.

"Jack?"

"Marg, is that you?"

"Yes, Jack. We're home, we're safe, Debra is fine. Where are you?"

"I'm in Uruguay, honey. How did you get this number?"

"A man named Ian phoned me and said to call you right away."

Jack is silent for a moment. He is overwhelmed with relief and tries to compose himself before saying anything else.

"Jack, are you okay?"

"I'm fine, Marg. I'm just so relieved to hear from you."

Margaret can sense in Jack's voice that something is still very wrong.

"We're fine, Jack. Roger picked us up and took us to Vegas for a nice visit. Jack, are you safe?"

"Yes, Marg, I'm fine. I'm just so relieved that you and Debra are okay. Is she there? Can I speak to her?"

"What time is it there, Jack?"

"Oh, sorry, Marg, I wasn't thinking. I was just so happy to hear from you. It's 7:00 a.m. here. I guess that would make it the middle of the night for you. Sorry again, hon."

"It's 2:00 a.m. here, Jack, but I can wake her if you want. I know she would love to hear from you. I'm sorry, but I have to ask again. Are you really safe now?

Jack thinks for a second. He really doesn't know what is coming up for him, and if he misses the chance to talk to Debra for what could very well be the last time, he knows Debra would end up blaming Margaret.

"I am safe, hon, but I would like to talk to Debra if you think that's okay."

"Hang tight, I'll wake her… and Jack, I love you."

"I love you too, Marg, more than you could ever imagine. When all of this is over, I will be home to stay."

"I'll get her now."

"Hi, Daddy."

"Hi Deb, I love you. I heard you had a nice trip to Vegas. I don't have a lot of time, dear, but I am going to be home soon and you can tell me all about your trip with Uncle Roger."

"Okay, Dad, I love you, too. Roger was called back to work, so we decided to just come home. Roger's friend Pat is a real bitch. Oh, and Dad, I got a new tablet."

"That's great, honey. You go on back to bed. I love you and will see you soon. Please put your mother back on."

"Love you, too, good night."

As soon as Debra has hung up, Jack asks Margaret, "Roger left you alone in Vegas?"

"He got called away, Jack, you of all people should understand. Go or get fired. He thought we were good for a week's stay at the Hard Rock, but that's a long story. Just promise me when you get home, we can all go on a nice vacation to Vegas. There's someone there I want you to meet."

"That Pat gal?"

"Sure, Jack, that Pat gal. Have you heard from Roger?"

"No, hon, but I'm sure he's fine. Okay, Marg, I have some things to do before my flight. I'm going to Israel to meet with Wilhelm. His people keep assuring me everything is fine."

"I thought you were 'his people' Jack."

"I am, honey. Things just got real complicated over here and I am going to resolve it, for good. Goodbye, dear."

"You call me when you get there. Bye, Jack."

Jack finishes his crunches and with a new vigour, he is off on his run and to formulate a plan ...

Chapter 12

TRAVEL DAY

Jack arrives back at the Regency. He was able to complete a two-hour run and is actually feeling pretty good. His ribs were not as bad as he had first anticipated and he feels he could have run for another two hours.

His run had started with the two flowered-shirt gentlemen following him in a car. After a couple of clicks, he was in the Uruguayan countryside and he had quickly lost them.

Upon his return to the hotel, the two men are leaning against their car waiting for Jack. "Have a good run?" they ask him.

"Yeah, guys. You should have joined me."

"Maybe next time, Jack. I suggest you start getting ready for your flight Jack. The Ambassador can't wait to see you."

The two men begin to chuckle ominously.

"When I'm done my chat with the Ambo, I strongly suggest that you two, well, let's just say you probably don't want to be around."

"Oh, we're not coming with you, Jack. You'll be flying with a couple of guys you're very familiar with. We're going to pick them up from the airport right now."

"Well, that's good news. Let's hope they're better conversationalists than you two humps. Now if you don't mind, fuck off. I'm going to take a shower." He starts to go then stops. "Oh, wait. Hang on a second. You, the not as fat one that's dripping in sweat, give me your shoulder strap and gun."

"That's not going to happen, Jack."

"You can give it to me, or I can take it from you. Remember I got a flight to catch and the Ambo wouldn't be too pleased if I wasn't on that plane, so you need to decide now. Give it over or you can both catch another beating."

The two guys talk briefly and they both agree that Jack will be disarmed, anyway, before getting on the plane. They hand him the gun and strap.

"Thank you, guys. Maybe we'll meet again on a more equal setting."

"We're driving you to the airport, asshole."

Jack laughs and heads off for his shower with visions of a big breakfast before the flight as everything on the Ambo's jet is usually kosher.

After he finishes his meal, Jack, once again, painstakingly swallows the three vials.

He then heads downstairs to catch his ride, only to find Owen is alone in driver's seat of the Hummer.

"Where's the two goons, Owen?"

"I asked if I could drive you and, surprisingly, they didn't give a shit."

"Is there a reason you wanted to take me, kid?"

"I'm not a kid, Jack. I'm fekin twenty-three years old."

"All right then, just let me ask you something… are you deliberately aiming for every pothole?"

"They're not too hard to miss. Is that what you wanted to ask me, Jack?"

"No, kid, sorry. Now Owen, don't take offence to this, but you don't exactly fit the profile of the Ambassador's regular recruits. How did you come about joining our little group of jolly travelling exterminators?"

"I was I.R.A. for not even a year and my commander found out that I was on the Brits' list as a grasser. I ain't no grasser, Jack. I would never squeal to the peelers."

"I'm amazed your commander didn't just kill you right then. You I.R.A. boys must be getting soft."

"Mr. Malcomson knew my mother since they was kids. He got me out of Ireland without either side knowing."

"Trust me, kid, someone knew. So I take it you can't return to Ireland?"

"Mr. Malcomson said…

"Kid, stop. Jesus Christ, just call him Ian or Hairy. You're with me now, for fuck's sake."

"Ian assured me I am fine with Sinn Féin."

"Sure, Sinn Féin . They're loyal to family and Hairy's a pretty solid dude, but the reality is you know all too well that Sinn Féin and the Real I.R.A. are two different bodies, don't you? And you probably have first-hand experience what they do to grassers—"

Owen angrily interrupts Jack in mid-sentence. "I'm not a fekin grasser, Jack."

"I know, kid, but it just doesn't matter. That's how the Brits work. They out you as a rat, so you turn or run from both sides. I'd say Hairy saved your life."

"I know."

"So, why are you driving me today, Owen?"

"There's been no communication lately. Ian went home to see his kid and Harvey is not answering any calls."

"Then why not just hang out at the hotel? Eat, swim, meet a girl and consider it a nice paid holiday until you get the call."

Jack is watching Owen and his facial expression reveals he has no desire to return to the Regency.

"Okay, Jack."

"What is it, kid?"

"It's nothing, Jack. Don't worry about it."

"Owen, you're pissing me off now. What the fuck?"

"It's those two pigs back at the hotel…they think I'm a fucking Shirley."

Jack starts laughing uproariously and manages to squeeze in a "Maybe if you got a haircut," as he continues to laugh.

Owen is trying to watch the road and Jack is laughing so hard tears are leaking from his eyes. At first, Owen is despondent, but Jack's laugh is so contagious he can't help but start laughing, as well.

"Okay, kid, enough laughing, and keep your eye on the road or we're both gonna end up in the ditch. Pull over when you can and we'll turn around. I'll fly out in a couple of hours. We'll go back and I'll have a little talk with your friends."

"I can't, Jack. If you miss this flight the goons will kill me and probably fuck me after they do."

Both men begin chuckling again and then break into such a giant laughing fit that Owen has to pull over.

When Jack calms down he is thinking that the only other person that could make him laugh like that is Marg. He also puts his hand on his stomach and thinks, "These little bastards better not break in there."

"Start driving, kid. What do you want me to do, Owen? I can't help you if I'm on a plane."

"Take me with you, Jack."

"Do you even know where I'm going?"

"Yeah, you're going to meet the Ambassador in Israel."

"Kid, I don't even know what I'm walking into. If it goes bad, what? Do you think they're going to just let you walk out of there?"

"I'll take that risk, Jack, please."

Jack sits quietly for the remainder of the trip to the airport with Owen glancing over every couple of minutes looking for any indication from him as to what he's thinking.

They arrive just outside of the airport, which is about ten minutes from the city of Montevideo.

The Ambassador's private jet is waiting as promised. Jack immediately notices that there are no guards standing outside of the plane, as he reaches into his jacket and flicks his handgun safety switch to off.

Owen pulls the Hummer over beside the plane.

"Do you know who's on the plane, kid?"

"I only know what the pigs said—a Mr. Walker and a Mr. Palmer."

"Bricks and Stryker are no misters, kid. Jack reaches into his pocket and hands Owen his remaining wad of bills that he got from Ian several days ago. With Jack having handed out some big tips at the hotel, it works out to be about seven or eight grand.

"I want you to wait here, Owen. If anything happens, you get the fuck out of here. Don't go back to the Regency—just go and try to contact Ian."

Jack looks over at the plane and can now see a pilot walking down the jet's stairway. Jack hops out and meets him at the bottom.

"I take it you are, Jack," the pilot says.

"That's right, Sir."

"I will be flying you to Israel today, Jack. We will be flying with the jet stream so I expect our flight time to be about fourteen hours and thirty minutes."

"Sounds good, Captain."

"Uh, Jack, I don't normally do this, but I am supposed to search you for weapons."

"I got a question for ya, Cap. Can you twist your nose like on *Bewitched* and still fly the plane?"

"Excuse me, Sir?"

"You know, like on the TV show *Bewitched*. Can you twist your nose and fly the plane?"

"I don't understand, Sir."

"Well, if you put one hand on me, the only thing that will still work on your body will be your nose, so you better have the skills of the charming witch on *Bewitched*."

Just then, Bricks pops his head out the jet's door and shouts, "It's all right, Captain. Let him up and let's get going."

The captain heads up the stairs. Jack looks up at Bricks and says,

"How's my favourite black man doing this fine morning?"

"Good to see you, too, Sarge. Can we please get moving?"

Jack looks over at the Hummer and, with some reticence, waves Owen to come over.

Owen's face lights up. He quickly grabs his gear and runs over to Jack.

"Thank you, Jack."

"I hope you're still thanking me in about eighteen hours, kid. Now get up there."

When Owen is almost at the top of the jet's stairs, Jack shouts to him. "Kid? Where are the keys?"

Owen reaches into his pocket and holds them up. Jack motions to Owen to toss them down to him.

Jack looks around and sees a groundskeeper raking some leaves. He whistles for the man to come over. The man runs over and Jack hands him the keys and says, "It's yours, if you want it." The man graciously thanks Jack, takes the keys and drives away.

'I guess they're gonna need a new guy to rake leaves,' Jack thinks to himself.

He enters the plane and sees Bricks and Stryker sitting in the two front seats. Two very hot stewardesses are sitting in the row behind them.

"Morning, Sarge."

"Good morning, Stryker."

Bricks says, "We were instructed to give you the back of the plane, Jack, and to not converse with you in any way. And…" Bricks pauses.

Jack impatiently asks, "And what?"

"If you are in any way offended with us being here, we are to stand in the plane's bathroom for the duration of the flight."

"Well, now that you mention it, I do believe that is for the best, guys. Come on, get moving."

"Are you fucking serious, Sarge? This is a long fucking flight."

"Sorry Stryker, get going."

"Fuck you, Jack." Both men get up and go into the plane's bathroom and close the door.

The plane promptly takes off and once it reaches altitude, the stewardesses ask Jack and Owen if they would like anything,

"Can I get you a drink, magazine, pillow or blanket sir?"

"What's your name, dear?" Jack asks the pretty brunette.

"I'm Charlene, and that over there is Patty."

"Well, Charlene, do you have a cell phone?"

"Yes, Sir, but you have a satellite phone in front of you, Sir."

"Call me, Jack, Charlene. Can I borrow it, anyway? It will just be for a moment, dear."

Charlene walks up to the front and grabs her cell from her purse and promptly brings it back to Jack.

Jack fiddles with it for a moment and then instructs Owen to very quickly open the bathroom door when he says, "Now!"

Owen flips open the bathroom door and Jack snaps a picture of Bricks and Stryker standing in the bathroom.

"Come on out, guys. Fuck, are you stupid. What the hell happened to you, Bricks? Go take a fucking seat, you whipped fucking morons."

Surprisingly, Bricks and Stryker don't say much, but Bricks does whisper to Jack, "I'm gonna get that phone back." Both men return to their seats at the front.

Jack spends the next twenty minutes sending the picture to every person who is in their line of work. And with Jack's memory, that is a lot of people.

Charlene returns for her phone and Jack asks for some magazines.

Patty ends up bringing back a stack of magazines for Jack. Jack is flipping through them—a couple of Israeli mags, a *Time* and a *Newsweek* as well as *O* magazine.

Jack looks at the cover of *O* magazine and thinks, "Oprah's not looking too bad," and begins to flip through it.

Sitting in the row next to Jack, Owen looks over and sees what he is reading. Jack gives him a steely glance and Owen proceeds to look straight ahead.

About two hours into the flight, Jack starts to get bored. He had a full meal earlier but he is still not tired enough for a nap. Having just finished reading his *O* magazine, he decides to have Bricks and Stryker join him in the back of the plane.

"Owen, go to the lads up front and see if they want to join us for a drink."

Owen heads up front and promptly returns.

"They say they're not supposed to talk to you, Jack."

"Tell Bricks if he comes back, I'll delete the picture from Charlene's phone. And if they do decide to come, grab her cell and tell Charlene I only need it for another minute."

Owen heads back up to the front and, after a brief moment, the men turn and can see Jack waving for them to come on back.

Bricks and Stryker look at each other and decide to head on back while Owen grabs Charlene's cell.

Jack stands up to stretch his legs and Bricks and Stryker remain standing in the row at the back. Jack shows Bricks that he is deleting the picture and sends Owen back up with the cell and instructions to hang out with the ladies for a while.

Jack has a partial smile on his face and is starting to feel a little embarrassed about the bathroom joke. He looks at Stryker then over at Bricks. "Okay, the bathroom? What the fuck is going on?" he asks them

"You're an asshole, Jack."

"Yeah, Jack, a real fucking asshole."

"Yeah, yeah ... I've heard that before. So what's going on, Bricks?"

"We were stuck in Argentina for a week, Jack. You tell me."

"Hey, guys, I'm the one who's been on the run and, by the way, thanks for not shooting me at the compound. I would like to know however, who's got my shit."

"The fire got it, Jack."

"And you're telling me Victor wasn't in there cleaning out all my stuff first?"

"Come to think of it, Jack, he was in your room for a while."

"Thanks, Bricks. Who's the asshole now?"

"You just thanked us for not shooting you, asshole."

"So what are you doing here, Bricks? Why were you stuck in Argentina for a week?"

"Something going on with Harvey. He's not answering calls and when he does he couldn't sound more disinterested. We asked about you and he muttered something about you being the Second Coming. The Ambo must like assholes."

"Well, you two are here, so I guess you're right."

Stryker jumps in on the conversation. "There's something else, Jack."

Bricks looks at Stryker and shakes his head in mocking disgust, but then decides to take over the conversation from Stryker. "There's talk about Akron, Jack."

"What talk?"

"Someone's been talking … we made a few calls from Argentina to hook up with another crew. We were told to go hide, Jack, and that no one is going to hire us. That we're too hot."

"The Ambo doesn't leave holes, Bricks. Did they mention Akron, specifically?"

"All we heard is that we were involved in a messy sweep in the US and the attorney general is now involved. Why the fuck do you think we're sitting with you now on our way to Israel and standing in a fucking bathroom, for fuck's sakes?"

"Yeah, sorry about that, guys. I didn't think you would actually do it."

Bricks continues, "It could be the Ambo himself, Jack."

"You were in that bathroom too long, Bricks."

"Think about it, Jack. The Ambo knows he's politically protected. He ordered the sweep but he didn't just want that Nazi dead, he wanted him outed as a Nazi. There aren't too many of those fuckers left, am I right?"

For one of the few times in his life, Jack is at a loss for words. His mind is now racing, his thoughts taking him back to the basement in Ohio and the eight dead bodies on the floor with Ivanna pointing her Uzi at him.

"Where is Harvey now?"

"Best we can figure is he's in Arlington."

"Arlington, Texas?"

"Is there another Arlington, Jack?"

"Let's see, Bricks. There's Arlington, California, Arlington, Arizona, Arlington, Iowa, Arlington, Kansas... should I go on?"

"That's right, the asshole with the big brain. Yes, Texas, Jack."

Jack sits back down in his chair. He finally knows what the Ambo's plan is...he's going after Debbie's family.

"You guys sit wherever you want. I'm going to take a nap."

Stryker looks as if he's about to keep talking, but Bricks gives him a "Shut the fuck up" look and a forward nudge. They both return to their seats at the front and send Owen back.

Jack is becoming drowsy and his mind takes him back to one of the days he and Bear were excavating the plane site. They'd been digging all day and Bear told him the story of how Deb brought Rose into her life.

Jack imagines Deb being surrounded by a group of hulking, belligerent beasts and Deb pulling out a pipe from her oil rig coveralls and beating the living shit out of all of them as she rescues Rose from their evil clutches.

He falls asleep with a smile on his face.

The remainder of the flight is uneventful and quiet.

Jack arrives at the Ben Gurion Airport in Israel and again, as promised, is met by the Ambassador's limo.

"We were instructed to take a cab, Jack. I think we should take Owen with us, as well."

"Thank you, Bricks. I guess I'll see you guys later. Owen, you'll be okay with these two, they won't try to rape you."

In an unplanned unison chorus, the three men reply, "Fuck you, Jack."

Jack hops into the limo, checks his watch and figures he has some time. He instructs the driver to take him to his favourite beachfront restaurant. He wants to see if the owner is there yet, possibly prepping for lunch.

The driver asks, "Are you talking about the old boathouse restaurant, Sir?"

"Yes, I am. Why?"

"They did a bit of an upgrade since you were last here, Sir. It is quite remarkable now. They have changed the name to the Blue Porpoise, Sir."

"Okay, thanks for the update. Let's go check it out."

The limo pulls up to the Tel Aviv Marina, and Jack says he'll be back in twenty.

As Jack is walking down the pier he still has the dilapidated boat in his mind as he approaches the new Blue Porpoise restaurant.

It is shaped and configured like a large blue porpoise, but still somewhat resembles a boat.

The sign outside says Closed, but Jack proceeds to walk the plank and goes around the back of the restaurant. It still has the familiar romantic table settings overlooking the bay.

A man wearing a chef's apron appears. "We're closed, Sir. We open at 11:30."

"Yeah, sorry about that. I'm looking for Martin. Is he in yet?"

"I'm his son, Curtis. Did you know my father?"

"Did?"

"My dad died a year ago. I run the restaurant now."

"I'm very sorry to hear that, Curtis. My name's Jack. I knew your father and was actually married at this spot right here, God, 20 years ago now."

"Nice to meet you, Jack. My dad did mention you. Did you want to have a seat?"

"Thank you, Curtis. If you don't mind me asking, what happened to your dad?"

"Fifty years of smoking."

"That would do it. How about you? You smoke?"

Curtis stands up, walks over to the bar and grabs a bottle of Sabra, a couple of liqueur glasses and an ashtray. He sits down, pours each of them a shot and lights a smoke.

Jack smiles and grabs the glass. "To Martin," he says, raising it.

"Mazel tov."

Jack is scanning the restaurant while Curtis relays how his dad told him of the wedding he had there twenty years ago and how Jack always came by to see him whenever he was in Israel. He tells Jack his dad was always very pleased to see him and that Jack treated him like a true friend.

"Thank you, Curtis. That is very nice to hear. I really liked your dad. He was old school and a great guy to talk to."

"Can I make you something, Jack? I have a fresh Milbar that I can have ready in five minutes."

"No, thank you, Curtis. I just landed from a fifteen-hour flight. I loaded up on the plane. What I could really use is your washroom. The kosher food isn't sitting too well, so I could be a while."

Curtis laughs. "Have at it," he says. "Come see me in the kitchen on your way out."

Jack heads to the washroom. He quickly scans the room and notices it has a drop ceiling. Jack grabs a handful of paper towels, moistens them and heads into a stall to expel the three vials.

With the vials out, Jack cleans them and stashes them in the corner of the ceiling and heads back to the kitchen.

"Thank you, Curtis. Can I set up a tentative reservation for the table we were sitting at for tonight, around 8:00?"

"No, problem. I'll block it off after 7:00. Why tentative, Jack?"

"I'm going to a meeting and, frankly, I'm not sure of the outcome yet."

"I'm just a cook, Jack, but I hope it works out for you."

"Yeah, me, too, Curtis. Me, too. I'll be bringing a young Irish lad with me. It's his first time in Israel."

"I look forward to seeing you both."

Jack returns to the limo and says to the driver, "Well, let's go see the Ambassador."

Chapter 13

THE MEETING

Jack is brought into the Ambassador's office by security and the door is promptly closed. He looks around the room to find it is only him and the Ambassador.

The Ambassador is standing and looking out the large window onto his estate.

He turns toward Jack, and his expression is that of a father who has not seen his son in a very long time.

Jack is immediately enveloped with a sense of warmth and loss over how things have turned.

Both men greet each other in the middle of the room and embrace. The Ambassador kisses Jack on both cheeks and says, "You've had me very worried for you, Armen."

"I'd like to think I'm alive because of our bond and not the two vials you are coveting."

The Ambassador backs away from Jack, and his disposition changes.

"Only two, Armen?"

Jack is thinking, 'That was a quick reunion. I guess we're back to business.' He is also cognizant of the fact that the Ambo must have read the Nazi file taken from his room at the compound. The file documented that there were four vials being transported on the ill-fated plane.

"Sir, one of the vials was broken in the crash, and that was the bug that got to Debbie. I was able to retrieve the three remaining vials."

"But now you say there are only two, Armen?"

After Ivanna got the babies and mother out of Deb, I had to know what these things were. I slipped onto the deck of the Miranda and broke open one of the vials.

The Ambassador's demeanor instantly changes and he looks at Jack expectantly. "And what did you discover, Armen?"

"Within ten seconds of being exposed to fresh air, the bug started to show signs of life."

"And then?"

"It started to crawl directly toward me. I backed away and turned and walked a couple of feet in the other direction, and it changed its path and was still coming directly toward me."

"It was sensing your beating heart, Armen. It did not take flight, did it?"

"I don't think it could, Sir."

"And then what, Armen?"

"I stepped on it, Sir."

"Well, you did what you thought best at the time. I am sure it was very traumatic witnessing young Debbie having been penetrated by one of those nasty creatures."

"About Debbie, Sir. I have a question for you that has been bothering me ever since the compound."

"Yes, yes, Armen. All of your questions will be answered in time. You say you have two vials. I take it they are both intact."

"Yes, Sir."

"And you will give them to me now Armen?"

"Can we sit down, Sir? Sorry, I just had a long flight. Would the couch be okay?"

"Yes, of course Armen. Would you like me to order you a beverage first?"

"Thank you. Coffee would be fine."

The Ambassador goes to his phone and places an order for coffee and a tea and returns to a comfortable side chair next to Jack on the couch.

"Before we start, Armen, who is this young Owen?"

"He is one of Hairy's men, Sir. Is he here?"

"Oh, yes, yes. He is fine, Armen. He's outside with Bricks—they're getting a tour of the compound and he will work on my property security. Is that okay, Armen?"

"Frankly, I don't know yet, Sir. If I end up leaving today, I will leave it up to him to decide if he wants to come with me or not."

"And where are you going to go, Armen … If you leave here today?"

"Home to Margaret, Sir."

"And after?"

"I've been away from her for a long time, mentally and physically. She tells me we have a Vegas trip planned."

"And how are Margaret and Debra?"

With that single question, Jack becomes furious in the pit of his stomach and he is certain his anger is now evident on his face. He is trying very hard not to overtly express his disdain in front of the Ambassador.

Just then, there is a knock at the door. Jack slowly moves his hand closer to his sidearm inside his jacket.

The Ambassador says, "Come in."

Miss Schuster comes in, pushing a silver cart. It contains a carafe of coffee, a pot of tea, along with a variety of finger sandwiches, pastries and some raw salmon.

"Are you hungry, Armen?"

"I didn't get a chance to run yet this morning but I guess I could eat something, seeing as how Miss Schuster went to all this effort. Thank you, Miss Schuster," Jack says.

"Would you like to go for a run before we eat Armen?"

"No, Sir. I think we have some issues at hand to deal with, don't we?"

"Thank you, Miss Schuster," the Ambassador says, dismissing her. "Yes, we do, Armen."

Just as Miss Schuster is closing the door, a man appears in the doorway. The man spots Jack and walks in.

"Jackie, boy. Good to see you, buddy."

Jack is in a state of shock. He looks at the man, then looks at the Ambassador and gives him a cold, mean glare.

He promptly returns his attention to the other man and stands up to greet him.

"Roger, you old dog. I guess you already met the Ambassador."

"Good to see you, Jack. Isn't this place great? I know you guys are in a meeting. Wilhelm, I was just wondering if I could borrow the Jag—I got a hot lunch date today."

"Certainly, Roger. You know where the keys are. Say hi to Richard for me."

On his way out of the office, Roger turns back to Jack, "Hey Jack, did you hear we're going to be working together?"

"That's great, Rog. See you later, and have a good date."

Jack notices a thick brown envelope sticking out of the back of Roger's pants. He remembers when he got the same envelope twenty years ago.

Roger leaves and closes the office door. Jack stares at the Ambassador, who has a self-serving grin of contentment on his face.

"Are you enjoying your morning, Wilhelm?"

"Now that I have you back, Armen, yes, very much, thank you."

"Now, where were we?"

"You were asking me about my family, Wilhelm."

"Oh, yes, yes … terrible business that brief time. Margaret will find a very nice compensatory cheque this month for her worries."

Jack is elated to see Roger safe and, from the looks of his old pal, he appears to be quite happy. He is now has a growing concern as to when and how he will leave the

Ambassador's estate. Jack has to get himself and Owen out safely. And now Roger, as well. His thoughts of just pulling his revolver out and putting one in the Ambassador's forehead head have not left him since his arrival.

"I'm sorry, Sir. As I said it was a long flight. Can we just cut to the chase? What happens when I give you the vials? Then what, Sir?"

"Do you have them with you now, Armen? No, no, I think you were much too well trained to have them on you now."

Jack quietly smiles back.

"I will, as you say, 'cut to the chase,' Jack. I want you to command one more operation for me. And upon its successful conclusion, I would like you to return to Israel with your family and run my company. I will give you a starting salary of three million dollars per year and a small portion of stock. Just to start, of course.

"If you agree today, I will have my contractors begin designing a home for you and your wonderful family, all with Margaret's input of course."

Jacks face was completely expressionless during the Ambassadors opulent offer and the Ambassador took notice as well. Now the Ambassador is feeling slighted and is hiding his growing anger.

"Arlington, Texas, Sir?"

"I see Mr. Walker did not follow my instructions on the plane."

"Why Arlington, Sir? Are we going to have another Akron?"

"All right Armen, I can see the long flight has made you irritable and left you in a less-than-appreciative state of mind. I suggest we take a break. I have your room prepared upstairs. You will find your items from the compound there. I was able to have them retrieved from Victor for you."

"I'm fine with continuing our discussion now, Sir."

"I am going to have to insist, Jack. I suggest you go for a nice long run and when we resume this afternoon, for the sake of both of us, I expect you to return in a less cantankerous mood."

Jack is thinking to himself, "Armen, Jack, Armen, Jack … Jesus Christ, just figure out if you're mad at me or not, for fuck's sake."

He could sure use a run, though. It would give him a chance to clear his head, as he's now thinking that the unfortunate inevitable may have to occur this afternoon. Him taking over the company? How, why and when did this all unfold? Jack can't seem to come to grips with this sudden change in the Ambassador.

"Okay, Sir, I'll be back here in three hours."

The Ambassador stands up and is making his way to the phone.

"Yes, yes, Jack. That is fine. See yourself out, please."

He picks up the phone. "Get Mr. Walker and Mr. Palmer in here at once, please."

Jack goes up to his room and puts on his newly purchased workout gear that somebody bought for him. He drops down for fifteen minutes of crunches and then leaves on his run. He stops at the Ambassador's limo and talks to the driver, who is washing the vehicle.

"Can you pick me up at the Blue Porpoise in two hours?"

"Yes, Sir. So far, your pickup was my only booking for today."

Jack plots a course that will have him at the Blue Porpoise restaurant in one hour and fifty minutes, and he begins his run.

Just as he is leaving, he sees two security men walking Bricks and Stryker in to see the Ambassador.

Jack arrives at the Blue Porpoise. He heads into the kitchen to greet Curtis and asks to use the bathroom again. Jack grabs two of the vials and leaves the third in place. He reconfirms his reservation for that evening, and is on his way back in the limo.

Arriving back at the Ambassador's gated luxury estate, Jack briefly ponders if he could get used to this kind of life.

He takes a quick shower and dresses. He checks his newly retrieved .45. He makes sure it has a full mag and one in the chamber and he places it into his shoulder strap.

Jack walks back to the Ambassador's office and, with Wilhelm yet to return, Jack finds himself looking out the office window onto the vast estate. Out of the corner of his eye he can make out the pool area, where he spots Roger and an attractive young man sitting at a table drinking cocktails.

The Ambassador returns alone and takes his traditional seat of authority behind his desk.

"Have a seat, Jack. Did you enjoy your run?"

"Yes, Sir. Where are Bricks and Stryker?"

"I see your run did not change your disposition as I had so hoped it would, Armen. Mr. Walker and Mr. Palmer are no longer in my employ."

"And Owen?"

"I just left him in the kitchen. He's having a late lunch and then he is going to have a nap. He says he is feeling some jet lag from his flight this morning."

"Sir, before we begin, you're gonna give me a personality disorder. Can you please pick a name for me and just stick with it?"

"What would you prefer I call you?"

"My friends call me Jack, Sir."

"Agreed, but only if you call me Wilhelm when we are alone."

"Well, I'm glad we were able to settle everything, Wilhelm. See ya, I'm off to California."

The Ambassador begins to laugh and the nagging pain in his shoulders has suddenly diminished. "That's the Jack I had hoped to see today. Your parents did a wonderful job raising you."

"They were the best, Sir. Sorry, *Wilhelm*. Some habits are hard to break."

"You address me in the manner in which you are most comfortable Jack."

"Yes, Sir."

"I had some time to think while you were on your run, Jack, as I am sure you did as well. As I stated earlier, I want you to run the daily operations of my company when I step down.

"I think you've earned the right to ask me anything that is on your mind. My promise to you is that I will answer any questions you may have, and—as hard as it may be for me, considering the latest very unfortunate misunderstanding between us—I will answer them truthfully."

Jack is thinking to himself that Margaret and Roger appear to be safe for now. But he still wants to know why Debbie was chosen to accompany him to the excavation site that fateful day. He decides to start with an upbeat question before it has the potential to get ugly.

"Is Roger gay?"

"Is that a problem for you, Jack?"

"No, Sir, it's not. It's just that I've known him for such a long time that I find it hard to fathom. I was really unaware of it."

"In our line of work, you know what would happen to him if it ever got out, don't you, Jack?"

"You're okay with it, Sir?"

"It's the twenty-first century. I have a wonderful nephew who is gay. He is a very accomplished writer for the Haaretz newspaper and a real decent person whose company I enjoy very much."

"Is that the Lavignes' son?"

"Yes, that is correct."

"Well, I was reading that Israel's stance on homosexuality is the most advanced in the Middle East."

"Yes, this is true, and if we could ever find a way to cease the rocket fire from Northern Gaza, we would have a truly great, blessed country."

"I don't know how you live here year round, Sir. It's a real turkey shoot."

"Lately, Tel Aviv has been a big target. I would presume it is because the US embassy is there. The government is also warning of an imminent major terrorist attack."

"And so why would I want to move Marg and Debra here?"

"You know the odds of getting hit are the same as winning the lottery. Jack. And, as you know, this property is defended with ballistic counter measures. Something we would most certainly install for your new estate, as well.

"I know you have some troubling questions for me and, as I promised, I will answer them truthfully. I also know your reticence getting to them is because you are a deeply respectful man. Please put aside all of your reservations and proceed."

Jack is amused by the Ambassador's last comment. With his eyes firmly fixated on the Ambassador, Jack slowly reaches into his jacket pocket and pulls out his .45. He places it on the desk with the barrel pointed directly at the Ambassador's chest.

He then unbuttons his top shirt pocket and pulls out the two vials. He also places them on the desk between himself and the gun, just out of the Ambassador's reach.

The Ambassador can't help but stare at the vials he has been seeking for so long that are still just out of his grasp.

Within a few seconds the office door bursts open and two security guards burst into the room with their laser-pointed guns aimed directly at Jack's head.

The Ambassador waves them off and admonishes them for interrupting.

Jack looks around the room and spots several small camera lenses and asks, "When did you get those installed?"

"Two days ago. Do you like?"

"I'm not sure. As we just witnessed with your guards, it's kind of like arriving at the scene after the crime has been committed, isn't it?"

"Enough with this foolishness, Armen."

"Why Debbie, Wilhelm?"

"That's better, Jack. How well did you get to know Debbie?"

"Enough to know that what happened to that beautiful, funny, witty, intelligent, remarkable young lady was absolutely inexcusable and preventable."

"Well said, Jack. I would not have expected any other reaction from you. That being said, did you know she was of German descent?"

"No, Wilhelm, I don't believe it ever came up."

"Debbie's grandfather was a German pilot by the name of Friedrich Zurich. If you would have spent some time to look for the front of the plane in Argentina, you probably would have found him. Or, I imagine, what was left of him, still sitting in the pilot's seat. The ambulance that Ivanna arrived in at the Argentinian compound was there to take Debbie to a waiting plane and back to her father's loving arms.

"Time was critical, Armen. We needed Debbie on that plane and back in Texas within thirty-six hours of gestation for the timely release of the two spawn within the Zurich ranch."

"So your plan was to perpetuate a Nazi horror story from seventy years ago and reintroduce it in modern times."

"Yes, that is absolutely correct, Armen."

"On the basis of simple human compassion, Sir, how can you possibly justify going after the families of these long dead monsters?"

"I believe evil is inherent, Armen."

"You would not believe that if you had met Debbie."

"Then perhaps she was the exception."

"And Debbie's father, he is inherently evil, based on what?"

"Yes, yes, Karl Zurich. The son of Friedrich Zurich. Only one generation removed, Armen."

"Again, a man you have never met."

"That is where you are wrong, Armen. As you know, I owned and operated many companies as a young man in Texas. Karl was a budding oil man who had also achieved a great degree of wealth in his own right. With wealth come never-ending charity events and political functions."

"So I take it you met the man."

"Oh, yes, on several occasions. I was told Karl knew of my story of survival and my story of wealth derived from my Uncle Peter.

"Our first meeting was at a Governor's re-election campaign dinner.

When we were first introduced by a mutual acquaintance, Karl could not have been a more prejudiced bigot if he tried. But alas, I suspect he was trying."

"Maybe he's just a stuck-up asshole?"

"Armen, as I was walking away, I overheard him say, 'Looks like one got away.'"

"He was probably just drunk, Sir. I'm sorry you had to hear that."

"The top echelon of the Nazi party were also drunkards and drug addicts, Armen."

"True."

Jack and the Ambassador are now both taking a bit of a mental break. Jack realizes that he has brought the Ambassador back to his horrific past and feels uncomfortable continuing with his inquisition. After a few moments of introspective silence by both men, he asks, "Sir, what is that German phrase you have been repeating the last twenty years, '*Si wall imy da waf*?'"

"It is '*Sie wahlen immer die waffe*,' Jack. One minute please."

The Ambassador picks up the phone and tells whoever is at the other end of line, that for the next thirty minutes, he does not want to be disturbed under any circumstances.

"Jack, I am going to tell you a story from when I was an eight-year-old child. I have never told this story to anyone. Now I feel … maybe after all of these years, it is time.

"It was near the end of 1944. The Americans were on their way to liberate the Ukraine and it was the latest refuge my Uncle Peter had secured for me.

"I was relatively secure, living under the guise of a young Ukrainian farm boy residing in an isolated farm house deep in the Ukrainian countryside.

"It was sunny Saturday morning. It had been raining for several days and I had plans to go to a nearby pond to shoot frogs. I had made myself a slingshot and was waiting to try it out once the rain had ceased.

"Anyway, Jack, I had found a nearby pond and discovered my slingshot worked very well. It was not good for the frog I killed, but none the less it had worked and I was proud.

"It was just as I finished putting the frog out of its misery with a large stone that I heard a distant gunshot. It was the accompanying laughter that had me so intrigued.

"I admit, at the time I was so captivated by the dichotomy of sounds I heard that I stilled myself to see if I could hear them again.

"Within a few moments, there was another ringing gunshot and again the sound of joyous laughter and celebration.

"My curiosity had gotten the better of me, so I decided I would cautiously search for where the sound was coming from.

"I moved through the woods, taking advantage of every large tree I could hide behind. Popping in and out like a young boy playing soldier.

"As I was almost upon the scene, I heard another single shot followed again by cheering and laughter. Only this time, Jack, I could also make out the sounds of muffled crying and anguish."

The Ambassador pauses for a moment and takes a sip of his cold tea then wipes his brow with his napkin. Jack is sitting quietly and respectfully but can't help think, "Jesus Christ, just get on with it for fuck's sake." Instead, Jack solemnly asks, "Are you okay, Sir?"

"Yes, thank you, Jack. I will continue.

"At that moment, I could sense that something terrible was happening. A day does not go by where I wish I would have just run home to the farmhouse as quick as my feet could carry me."

"But being an inquisitive child of eight, curiosity and adventure ruled the day and I continued to proceed very carefully."

"I had come around the side of a barn, and there was a hay cart blocking my view of the festivities. The hay cart was much bigger than I was and as I walked around it, there I was, standing completely alone and out in the open for all too see.

"As I looked like any other young Ukrainian farm boy, I was quickly spotted by a German soldier and with a smile on his face he waved me over and said, '*Kommen, kommen bei der party*' which when translated is, 'Come, come, join the party.'

"Being a German, I knew what the soldier had said, but even at eight, I had enough sense to continue to play the role of the Ukrainian boy and I just shrugged my shoulders and made a look on my face as if I did not understand the German language.

"The soldier returned to observing the events, and I slipped behind the cart and continued to watch. He eventually did look back for me but must not have seen me hiding, as he did not come forward again.

"We were on the outskirts of a small farming village. There was a dilapidated barn and a narrow cart pathway. Beyond the hay cart, I could see a farmhouse 100 metres at the end of the road.

"To the left of me were half a dozen German soldiers and a lone SS soldier. He was clad in his long black leather coat. His coat was spotless and he had shiny black knee-high leather boots and the unforgettable SS insignia cross on his chest.

"Some of the soldiers were seated in chairs. There was a wooden table strewn with various bottles of alcohol and bowls of fresh fruit and plates of cheese. All of the men had glasses in their hands and were sipping from them and taking samples of the food items.

"The lone SS officer was standing a bit to the side of the others and was not partaking in any of the local delicacies.

"To his right were about a dozen local farm families, including men, women and children. I had carefully looked at all of their faces and I did not recognize any of them.

"To this day, I do not know why I did it, but I counted eleven naked Jewish men of all sizes and ages. They were all huddled together as close as they could possibly be.

"The men were all covered in filth and had been very badly beaten. They all had wide open gashes of flesh, and pools of blood were flowing from their wounds. The blood loss was so severe that they were trying to stay afoot in the slippery red pool of their own blood on the muddy ground.

"On the open pathway leading to the front door of the farmhouse, there were three long wooden dinner tables staggered at various distances.

"At a table closest to where I was hiding was a man who appeared to be the local blacksmith. He was standing next to a large metal cauldron of burning embers. He was wearing his blacksmith's apron and gloves, and he was incessantly stoking the fire with his forge.

"On his table was a pile of steel spikes about thirteen centimetres long and twenty millimetres thick.

"About twenty metres farther down the path was a second table, which held a single revolver.

"A farther twenty metres from that table stood a lone farmer holding a long pair of pliers.

"At the second table, I could see a large pool of blood with drag marks that extended over to the SS officer's Jeep. The bodies were apparently dragged away from the middle table and stacked in a pile next to the SS officer.

"I counted three dead bodies, which accounted for the three shots I had heard.

"An SS officer then pointed to a young girl in the Ukrainian farmers' group who were collected there to watch the event. He was smiling and he said to the girl, '*Junge schone Madchen, sie um das nachste zu holen'* which translates to 'Young beautiful girl, you get to pick the next one.'"

"There was another German soldier who knew the young girl did not speak any German. He walked over to her and roughly dragged her over to the standing group of beaten and naked Jewish men. He signalled for her to pick the next man.

"With a little trepidation and urging from her own father, she pointed and said '*Oh ton*,' which in Ukrainian means, 'That one.'

"The German officer grabbed the man she had picked and dragged him over, violently throwing him onto the ground at the first table in, front of the blacksmith.

"The blacksmith motioned to four other Ukrainian men in the crowd to come over. They immediately came over and—with each of the men clutching a limb—they held the Jewish man on the ground. The blacksmith, using his forging prongs, removed a burning, red steel rod from the embers. He bent over and inserted the rod into the opening of the Jewish man's penis."

"What the fuck, Sir?"

"Please, Jack, let me continue."

"The man was then released and he staggered to his feet, running as quickly as he possibly could to the next table twenty metres away. He grabbed the revolver, pointed it at his temple and pulled the trigger. The crowd was now laughing, clapping and celebrating what they had just witnessed.

"The only man who displayed no emotion whatsoever during the sickening show was the lone SS officer, who loudly shouted the one sentence that has haunted me my entire life: '*Sie wahlen immer die waffe,*' They always choose the gun."

"In some sick, twisted unfathomable act of cruelty, there was always the third table, a farther twenty metres from the table with the revolver, with another Ukrainian farmer holding a pair of pliers. I have always presumed the pliers were for removing the steel rod, thus allowing the victim to live. Hence, the Nazi pig's always concluding with, '*Sie wahlen immer die waffe.*'

"Thankfully, Jack, I was only transfixed long enough to have witnessed but one of these executions, with a further ten more to come."

The Ambassador pauses, and both men are lost in their own reflective thoughts.

"Shall we continue, Jack?"

"I could use a Scotch right about now. How about you, Sir?"

"Yes, Jack. I think a Scotch would be very appropriate."

"If you would kindly excuse me for a moment, Jack, I am going to wash up a bit. Feel free to pour us a couple of drinks while I'm gone."

The Ambassador reaches into his lower desk drawer and pulls out Jack's favourite brand of Scotch. He hands it to Jack and both men exchange weathered smiles.

As the Ambassador is getting up to leave, Jack stands and the two men quietly and firmly embrace. The Ambassador then leaves to go freshen up.

With the office door now left open, Jack spots Roger walking past and he calls him into the room.

"Rog?"

"Oh, hey, Jack. Where's Wilhelm?"

"Get the fuck in here, he's gonna be back soon. What the fuck, Roger?"

"Honestly, Jack, I thought I was a dead man. This Ambo fella has got some real fucking clout. He paid off my own fucking crew chief for Christ's sake, who does that? No, really, Jack. Who the fuck does that?"

"He does, Roger. Are you okay?"

"I'm fine. What are you going to do?"

"I don't know yet but he's gonna be back soon, so just keep playing along and I'll figure something out."

"I'm not sure I'm 'playing' Jack. I kind of like the guy. I'm actually kinda pissed you didn't get me on his crew years ago."

"Yeah, and I'm pissed you didn't tell your best friend you're a fucking pillow biter. Listen, trust me that you don't know what's going on here. I have to make a decision and I have to do it now. We may end up leaving here hot, do you fucking understand me, Roger?"

"Okay, okay, I get it."

"Then get the fuck outta here." "Wait, Roger... how did you just happen to walk by when our door was open?"

"Wilhelm told me to hang around here and come talk to you when he left the office."

Jack is now looking up at the lenses the Ambassador had just had installed and he figures they must have come with listening devices, as well.

"Okay, Roger, just go. I'll see you in a bit."

Jack pours a couple of Scotches and puts his gun back in his holster. As he takes his seat on the couch, he figures he will find out soon enough if the Ambassador was listening in on his conversation with Roger.

What Jack does know for certain is that if anyone else walks through that door in the next five minutes—anyone who is not the Ambassador, that is—that poor sap will be going down today, and he won't be getting back up.

"Oh, hey, Jack. Can I come in?"

Jack rolls his eyes,

"Sure, Owen, come on in. How you doing, kid? I thought you were taking a nap."

"Nah, couldn't sleep. I want to see this country, Jack, and honestly I was too worried about you to sleep."

"You're a good man, Owen. The Ambassador will be back soon. Trust me that I'm fine. Listen, I made dinner reservations for us tonight at eight, so why don't you try to sleep and we'll stay up late tonight exploring the city. Sound good?"

"Thanks, Jack. I truly am fekin asleep on my feet."

"See you later, and if you see a guy named Roger out there, tell him about our dinner plans as well, will you?"

"Yes, Sir."

"Just Jack … okay, kid?"

"Yes, Jack, I mean, Sir, no wait, Jack." Owen leaves the room issuing a completely sleep-deprived chuckle.

After another ten minutes the Ambassador returns, alone. He closes the door and walks over to the front of his desk then looks over at Jack and makes a gesture implying, "Can I pick them up?"

"Have at it, Sir. You paid for them."

The Ambassador carefully picks up the two glass vials. He looks at them very quickly and places them in the top middle drawer of his desk, which he promptly locks.

"Before we resume, Sir, I just want to say thank you for having enough trust in me to reveal your story. I know it couldn't have been easy. Now I know why that German saying has been stuck in your head your entire life."

"Sadly, Jack that was only one of the many atrocities I was witness to during the war. Not to mention what I was personally subjected to."

"That was a long time ago, Sir. I would like to think humanity has learned a little something since then."

"Like you operating your own revenge crew in Bosnia, Jack? You could not begin to imagine the powers of influence a US Ambassador has in the Middle East."

"You knew, Sir?"

"That was one of the reasons you were standing in my office that day. In front of your future bride, no less." The Ambassador smiled at him. "I employ the best and the brightest, Jack, and you exemplify both of these things. What you did in Bosnia just confirmed our shared commitment to justice and revenge."

"I was a twenty-year-old kid."

"Do you regret what you did?"

"No, I guess I don't."

"Very well, then. So maybe you now have some understanding of what my life's work has been."

"In some respect, yes. But if you are asking me if I would continue hunting Bosnian war criminals for the rest of my life, my answer would have to be no."

"You think the two are comparable, Armen?"

"I meant no disrespect, Sir. No, I do not believe they are comparable. But going after these monsters' families, seventy years later, I just don't see it."

"I know you have grown into a man of conscience over the years, Armen. Your reaction to the Akron affair and, more recently, what happened to Debbie … and now you have young Owen in tow? Why is Owen even here?

"So I can get him a decent haircut, Sir."

The Ambassador is not amused with Jack's response and the two stare at each other for an uncomfortable moment. After a brief pause, the Ambassador repeats his last question.

"Why is Owen here?"

"He showed me something in Uruguay, once he was out of Ian's grasp."

"That being?"

"Humanity."

"I immediately saw something in Owen, too, Armen. I think the best thing for Owen is that he be returned home to be with his family."

"He can't go home, Sir."

"Then it's settled, he is your new charge. You will take him to Arlington with you. Now, let's discuss your team."

"The cart before the horse, Sir. Should we not discuss the mission first? Again, I thank you for having the trust in me to tell me the story of what happened to you for the first time in your life…"

The Ambassador politely interrupts, "You are like a son to me, Jack. You are the only person on this very fragile planet that I would ever tell."

"When you went to freshen up, Sir, did you have a chance to pop into your little recording device room?"

"Yes, yes, Jack. I heard your conversation with Roger and Owen."

"And?"

"May I join you tonight at the Blue Porpoise? I have not been there for a few months."

"The more the merrier."

The Ambassador picks up the phone and tells whoever is on the other end of the line to make reservations at the Blue Porpoise for a private table for four, overlooking the bay, at 8:00 p.m.

"It was a crime what happened to Martin. His son Curtis has done a wonderful job renovating the restaurant and keeping his father's legacy going."

"I agree. Smoking is a crime."

"Smoking? Martin was killed by a mortar while picking fresh fruit. I secured a very low interest rate loan for Curtis to keep the restaurant going."

"Have you reached your decision about leaving here 'hot,' Armen?"

"Are you still planning on destroying an American family?"

"Yes. With or without you, Armen, it is going to happen. Harvey has all the instructions. Should anything happen to me, he will continue forward, but we both know Harvey will just facilitate a more conventional—and messier—ending."

"It was my understanding that Harvey was not totally on board with your plan either, Sir."

"Mr. Walker again."

"You put people on a flight for fifteen hours, they're gonna talk, Sir."

"You would not have 'talked', Armen. Just so you understand, Harvey will take two contracts with him to Arlington. If something happens, and Harvey has to arrange to have the mission completed on his own, he will then take over my position when I step down. On the other hand, should you accept to launch the mission, then the company will be yours. Either way, it the mission is going to be concluded, Armen."

"I take it Harvey can't be too pleased about any of this."

"Armen, I am growing tired. I would like to have a rest before our dinner tonight. Can I please have your decision?"

"If you could indulge me for a few more moments, Sir, I do have a couple more questions."

"Yes, yes."

"The Miranda?"

"Our captain unloaded the crew at a closer port in Brazil, then he continued on to his destination to meet Ian. Prior to the arranged destination, he scuttled the boat and disappeared."

"Do we know what happened to the crew and Debbie?"

"The captain was able to contact Karl, who arranged for a charter to pick them all up in Brazil and presumably get them back to Arlington."

"Are you searching for the captain?"

"No, Ian convinced me that they were all just pawns in this little adventure. Ian assured me from his conversation with you in Uruguay that they did not know what was truly happening. Is this true, Armen?"

"Yes, Sir. They know nothing of any relevance."

"Ian was very impressed with our captain's escape plan."

"Uh-huh. Is there any word on Debbie's condition?"

"No, I'm sorry, Armen. You must believe me when I say there is no way she could have survived. Again, I am sorry."

"With all due respect, Sir, what are you sorry about?"

"From what you described to me, she sounds like she was quite the remarkable young lady. I regret deeply what she had to go through."

"You always talk about employing the best and the brightest—well, you missed one in her."

"That I am sure of, Armen."

"We sent a very wealthy man's daughter back in a bizarre and grotesque fashion. Do we know if any security measures were subsequently implemented at the property?"

"The estate is too isolated to make an attempt to find out—there is one road in, one road out. This is where you and your team will come in."

"And our budget?"

"It costs what it costs."

"Finally, for my own selfish reasons, Sir, can you tell me how you came upon the discovery of those little bastards and the German flight itself? And do you know who the intended victims were?"

"As you well know, Armen, the Germans documented everything and I mean everything. At the conclusion of the war, the American's focus switched to Communist Russia. It was a race between both countries to bring over these sub-human German scientists to their respective countries. America had more to offer, and we made these monsters American citizens.

"My work with the Wiesenthal centre and becoming a US ambassador were all calculated decisions. We had discovered the flight manifest and its cargo. As for the intended victims, Sobibor was only one of the many identified test sites.

"If you have no further questions, when would you like to proceed?"

"Why do tomorrow what we could have done yesterday?"

"Who said that?"

"I just did."

"So we are in agreement, then."

"I will do it, Sir, but only if all of my conditions are met. I will allow no exceptions. If we can't come to an agreement, I would hope that you would still join me for our last dinner together as I will be returning to California first thing in the morning."

"Agreed, and I will even fly you home on our company jet, Armen."

During the course of his lengthy conversation with the Ambassador, Jack had been multitasking in his computer-like brain. Jack had been blessed with the mental acuity to assimilate the conversation at hand while simultaneously running through every possible scenario he could think of, both pro and con.

"Your conditions, Armen."

"First, Miss Schuster gives Owen a haircut before dinner."

"Agreed."

"Second, our single intended target will be Karl and Karl alone. I will work out the logistics on how this can be accomplished. It will most likely be an extraction and the implant will occur at another location."

"Agreed."

"Third, I pick the team. I want Mr. Singh, Sven, Rick, Carl and Bricks and Stryker back. I will utilize Ian on a need-to basis. We don't need Harvey there, so he can return to Israel and be our liaison. Owen will be with me. I would like you to get Roger rehired by his former employer. I suspect you'll need Ian's team to dispatch the fella who set him up. As of this moment, Roger is no longer in your employ."

"Agreed."

"Fourth, the Blue Porpoise no longer has a loan. You can take it out of my new salary, if you want."

"I will eat the cost myself, Armen."

"And finally, when Karl has succumbed to his fate. We destroy all remaining remnants of those little bastards. I will take them back now, Sir"

"Agreed."

The Ambassador unlocks his drawer, takes one last look and hands Jack the 2 glass vials.

"Would you like me to find a more protective carrying device, Armen?"

"No, thank you, Sir. These little bastards and I have become quite intimate."

"Okay, then. I will have Harvey work on getting your team to Arlington immediately."

"I have only one condition of my own, Jack."

"Go ahead, Sir."

"I want to be there in person when Karl is bitten."

"I wouldn't have it any other way, Sir."

With that said, Sir, I guess I have a couple more conditions."

"Yes, Armen."

"I and I alone will ultimately decide the fate of the operation. That being whether to proceed as planned, or to fold and go home."

"I am giving you full and ultimate control of the operation, Jack."

"Do not forget to sign your contract with Harvey when you get to Arlington. I will put my signatures on them when Harvey returns."

"Also, Sir, Owen and I will take the jet to Arlington tomorrow. I will stay for a day to check on Harvey's progress and then I'm going to take a charter home for a few days. Owen can stay with Harvey in Arlington until I get back."

"Yes, Jack. You should go see Margaret and Debra."

"See you at dinner tonight, Sir."

On his way out of the office, Jack says with perfect pronunciation, "*Sie wahlen immer die waffe.*"

Chapter 14

THE GANG'S ALL HERE

A week has passed and Harvey has been a busy guy in Arlington. He has secured hotel accommodations at the Arlington Hilton for some of the incoming group and has also rented a warehouse in an old abandoned section of Arlington's old commercial district with no local traffic or regularly scheduled police drive-bys.

Jack wanted his crew sleeping at the warehouse, so nine sleeping pod units were quickly constructed, similar to their rooms at the compound. All of the work was done by local day labourers who were generously paid for their discretion.

Harvey acquired physical maps of the entire Arlington area right down to the house. Harvey is a paper man and does not leave anything to chance should any technical issues arise.

Harvey made contact with all of Jack's requested team members and secured flights for their immediate arrival. Eventually, he returned to Israel as per Jack's instructions, but not before he concluded the contract-signing with Jack. Jack is now a three- million-dollar man with stock options.

Sven was the first to arrive in Arlington as he lives in Texas. He was the first one on site and installed all of the computer equipment and other gadgets.

The warehouse was equipped with kitchen facilities for Mr. Singh, who arrived several days ago. Mr. Singh took the company rental van and went shopping for a month's worth of staples to feed the crew of nine.

Rick and Carl, who had both returned to Israel after the compound mission, ended up flying to Arlington with Jack and Owen.

The only member from the compound group who will not be returning is Victor. He is back in Greece working under his father. Jack decided to forgo Victor's unintentional comic relief as he just doesn't trust him enough for this intricate American operation.

The only pair Harvey could not locate was Bricks and Stryker.

With the continuing underground chatter by the Wiesenthal centre regarding the 'Akron 8' still prevalent on their private network. The 2 men have seemingly disappeared.

The Ambassador has some very real private concerns, which he did not relay to Jack back in their meeting in Israel. One being, why did Jack request Bricks and Stryker to join the operation at all, considering his renouncement of the group following the Akron debacle?

Rick and Carl are assigned to twenty-four-hour on-site security again. Upon their arrival, they changed their method of resolving who gets the boring evening shift. They are no longer arm wrestling for the day shift. Now they take turns punching each other in the shoulder, first man to quit wins. For the first week, Carl is on the 8:00 p.m. to 8:00 a.m. watch.

Earlier in the week and back in Orange County...

After arriving home in the middle of the night, Jack places the three glass vials behind a basement heating vent. He looks in on Debra and crawls into bed with Margaret. They hold each other in their arms until Jack is awakened an hour later and nudges Margaret awake.

"Marg, what is that noise?"

"It's our new neighbors, Jack. Just try to fall asleep, hon."

Being as tired as he is, Jack quickly falls back to sleep and promptly gets up at 6:00 a.m. After a twenty-minute series of crunches, Jack plans out an eleven-mile run from Huntington to Newport Beach and back, and is on his way.

Completing his run in just over two hours, Jack allows himself to take in the beautiful beach scenery. He stops at Newport Beach and walks along the marina, looking at the various extravagant pleasure crafts.

He arrives back home and walks in through the back gate. He looks over at the property next to his that Tom, the cop, and his wife, Sarah, used to own.

Jack and Tom were the long lost vestiges of original neighbors. Tom was eventually promoted to captain and moved eighteen months ago. Before they moved Tom had left Margaret with their new address and phone number but the group has yet to get together.

The neighborhood has basically turned into a complex of time-share rentals because of its close proximity to the beach.

Tom and Sarah were proud homeowners who had a wonderful garden and kept their yard and home in immaculate condition.

That is not what Jack is seeing this morning. He shrugs off the state of disrepair of his new neighbor's yard and is looking forward to spending the day with Margaret and Debra.

He enters the house through the back door and is happy to see Marg and Debra sharing their morning coffee together. Marg is busy reading the Ambassador's contract that Jack left on the kitchen table the night before. Debra looks like she's doing some last-minute studying.

"Morning, ladies. Come here, hon," he says to Debra. "Come and give your dad a big hug."

"Sorry, Dad, not till you shower."

"I thought the three of us could spend the day together. What do you think, dear?"

"Sorry, Dad, I have an exam in forty minutes. Can you drive me to school?"

"Sure, just let me quickly jump in the shower so I can get that hug." He looks over at Margaret. "Enjoying your reading, honey?"

Margaret looks up at Jack and, frankly, she doesn't know what to think. A three-million-dollar yearly salary with stock options and the construction of a private estate in Israel... Did that mean they were moving back to Israel?

"We can talk about it when you're back from school, Jack."

It was not exactly the reaction Jack had envisioned on his run home. He had pictured Marg standing on the kitchen table, waving the contract in her hand and singing, "We're in the money, we're in the money."

Jacks finishes his shower, gets his hug and drops Debra off at school. With no other exams that day, Debra agrees to take the afternoon off to spend time with her dad.

Jack arrives home and Marg is all cleaned up and looks like she wants to go out. She asks Jack if he wants breakfast at home or to go out.

Jack has other plans right now, as he picks up Margaret and carries her into the bedroom.

An hour later...

Jack and Margaret are sitting at the local Big Boy's restaurant while Margaret is staring at the series of plates in front of Jack. Jack ordered a plate of pancakes, a plate of four slices of toast, a plate of eggs, ham, sausages and bacon, and a side plate of hash browns.

"You didn't want a grapefruit this morning, Jack?"

"No, thanks, hon. They bother my stomach sometime. How's your bagel?"

"Fine, thank you, Jack."

"So, what's the story on the neighbors, hon?"

"It's the same every night, Jack."

"No worries, I'll take care of it this afternoon before we go to the beach."

"Uh, okay, Jack."

"So how about that contract, Marg?"

"Don't you think it's missing something rather important?"

"The Ambassador's signatures … yes, I know. We will be getting them couriered before I head back to Arlington. The deal was that I had to show up in Arlington, which I did, so they will be coming. I won't go back to Texas until they arrive, hon."

"How long this time, Jack?"

"Long enough for you to start packing and get all of our affairs in order."

"When do we get to the point of you asking me if I want to move to Israel?"

"It's simple, Marg. You say you don't want to go, then we tear up the contract."

"It's just a copy, Jack."

"Oh, I forgot to tell you, Roger is back in Vegas. His last assignment went off without a hitch. Are you going to tell me about this Pat guy from Vegas?"

"Cripes, Jack, you are the smartest man I know. But really! How could you not have known that Roger is gay? Pat is a man, Jack, and Roger's former boyfriend."

"I know, crazy isn't it? That one really slipped by me, Marg. So, are you going to tell me what happened?"

"When we found Roger's house was also under surveillance, he contacted his old boyfriend, Pat, who graciously took us all in at the Hard Rock Hotel. He's the day manager there and said it would all be comped."

"I'd say he sounds like a pretty decent fella."

"Can I finish?"

"Sorry, hon, go ahead."

"Anyway, Roger had secured us a week's stay in a very nice two-bedroom suite."

"All comped? That's a pretty sweet deal, Marg."

Margaret is now staring at Jack. She is glad he's home and she knows he's just messing with her, but she's beginning to lose her patience with him.

"Interrupt me again, Jack, and you can run your breakfast off all the way home."

"Sorry, Marg, but Debra getting a tablet out of the deal, as well ... still sounds pretty sweet to me."

"On our first night after dinner, Roger got a call and he had to leave for the airport in an hour. We all met at the lobby and Roger jumped in a cab and left us his car. As soon as we waved goodbye to Roger, Pat waved goodbye to us. He let us stay that night but said we had to find other accommodations the next day. He then basically told Debra to not steal the tablet on her way out."

Jack's jovial mood is replaced with a few quiet moments of strategic planning.

"I got an idea, hon. It's Friday and I really don't need to be in Arlington until Sunday night. Let's catch a flight to Vegas and go see Roger's friend, Pat."

"What are you going to do, Jack? You know you can't do anything to him."

"With all due respect, Marg, you don't know what I can or can't do."

"Oh, the big former Navy SEAL assassin. What are you going to do, make him pee his pants?"

"That's why I love you, Marg. That's exactly what I had in mind."

"Well, Roger did promise Debra a night on the strip and it is only an hour flight on Southwest. This week's flyers said they're having a one-hundred-and-forty-nine-dollar special. You know what, Jack? Let's do it. Should we tell Roger we're coming?"

"Uh, no, Marg. Let's just get there and then maybe we can just surprise him."

"We still have his car, though."

"That's between Roger and me, and I'm still not too happy about him leaving you both there on your own. When I see him again I'm gonna deal with him, too.

"Right, then it's settled, Marg. Let's grab the bill and head home. I have an important call to make so if you wouldn't mind booking the flight and getting Debra from school, that would be great."

An hour later, Margaret has packed for the weekend and is off to pick up Deb from school.

Jack is watching from the front window and, as soon as Margaret pulls away, he slips next door to meet his new colourful neighbors.

Jack notices numerous cars and motorcycles on the street with several more on the front lawn. As he gets to the front door, he notices his neighbors have added some extra security features of their own, including a thick steel door with multiple deadbolts.

Jack knocks… and knocks and knocks. Getting no answer, he decides he'll try the back door. He hops over the locked side gate and starts knocking on the back door.

After a few more minutes of knocking, Jack notices the kitchen window is partially open, so he walks onto the deck and climbs his way in.

Jack now finds himself alone in an empty kitchen. He decides to check out the fridge and grabs himself the last cold Corona. Somebody is going to be pissed with Jack taking the last, 'morning wake up' bottle.

Jack saunters into the living room and finds a litany of bodies strewn about in various stages of undress. Scanning the room, he takes note of a sawed-off shotgun leaning up against the corner of the closed front door.

His neighbors are of a mix of races and appear to be surfer types, hence all of the surf boards scattered around the house.

Still completely unnoticed, Jack walks over to the front door. He unlocks the deadbolts and steps outside. Jack once again begins knocking, only this time he deliberately pushes the door open as he is doing so. Now with a foot inside the front door, Jack loudly says,

"Hello… anyone plan on answering the goddamn door?"

A couple of shirtless surfer dudes finally struggle to their feet. They appear to be in a hungover, panicked state of disarray and confusion.

"What the fuck? Who left the goddamn door open?"

Jack stands amusedly still and quiet while the two desperately try to regain some of their basic faculties.

They both start searching the empty bottles for a quick wakeup and while one manages to light a smoke, the other one pulls out a glass vile from his jeans and takes a snort off the back of his hand. Jack hands his Corona to the smoking dude and he quickly polishes it off. When he thinks they're finally ready to have a coherent discussion, Jack says, "Hi guys, I'm your new neighbor, Sam. I'm looking for the owner."

"How the fuck did you get in here man?"

"I'm sorry, guys. I just knocked on the door and it was open."

"What the fuck do you want, Grandpa?"

"As I said while you were, uh, waking up, I'm your neighbor, Sam, and I am looking for the owner."

"What kind of a stupid bitch would name her kid Sam?"

"Maybe his mom was on the pipe when she named him."

"No, I don't think my mother was 'on the pipe' when she named me."

"What, we got ourselves a fucking comedian? We both own this crib, cracker. Now why don't you fucking bounce before you get hurt?"

"When you call me a cracker, you two boys do realize you're white, too, don't you?"

"What the fuck are you doing here, cracker?"

"I came home late last night and I noticed your music was a little loud. I had some difficulties falling asleep. In the future, if you boys could just keep the volume down a little at night, it would be greatly appreciated. Anyway, thank you, and it was very nice to meet you, gentleman."

One of the men, now regaining some of his functions looks over to the other with a wink and a sly smile. They are about to have some fun, with the old man.

"Which house is yours, man?"

"Uh, right next door, the one with the fire pit on the deck."

"Oh yeah, I know that house. Here, I got something for you, old-timer."

The man grabs a large paper bag from the coffee table and dumps the contents. Dozens of baggies of dope drop onto the table. The man then hands Jack the empty bag.

"Here, Neighbor Sam, you really need to take this with you."

"What's that for, neighbor?"

"It's to put over your daughter's face when she goes outside, man. That bitch hurts my eyes, dude."

The other man laughingly chimes in. "Yeah, man, that bitch hurts my eyes, too."

The first man gets right in Jack's face and says, "We're a little short on dope this week, otherwise I would give you a second bag for that wife of yours."

"Okay, then, thank you, fellas. I should be on my way now."

"Fuck you, Grandpa."

"Yeah, fuck you, Grandpa."

Jack folds up the paper bag as he is walking back to his place.

Just then Margaret and Debra arrive home and the three of them meet in the kitchen.

"Good news, Marg. I went to speak with our neighbors and it seems they're moving out Sunday morning, so we won't have to worry about them anymore."

"Well, that is some good news."

"Yeah, Dad, those assholes were pigs."

"So, I never got a chance to make those calls. Give me twenty minutes and then we can head to the airport. You go pack, Deb. You can tell me how your test went later."

Jack goes into his office, closes the door and places a call to Harvey in Israel.

Back in Tel Aviv…

It is just past 11:00 p.m. in Israel. Harvey is sitting behind the Ambassador's desk with the Ambassador lying on the couch next to him. Both men are speaking with Salcom, one of the Ambassador's local computer experts, via the speaker phone.

"Okay, Salcom, the Ambassador would like to wrap this up. Once again, you are positive there were no texts originating at the Wiesenthal Center other than what we received from them this evening? Is there anything else that could be construed as being detrimental directly to us?"

"No, Sir. It would appear as if they are simply seeking the Ambassador's assistance, once again."

The Ambassador says loudly, "Thank you Salcom. Please continue monitoring the traffic for me. If anything unusual comes up, I would like you to contact Harvey immediately. Good night, Salcom."

The Ambassador motions for Harvey to hang up the phone.

"Well, Harvey, what do you think?"

"As Salcom said, we are fine. The center wants you to put your resources to work and look into the Akron Eight, simple as that."

"Yes, Harvey, really simple."

"We discussed this, Sir. We must give them Palmer, Walker and Ivanna. Obviously, with you making Jack your heir apparent, they must be dispatched. They are all witness to Jack being there."

"I would feel much more secure if Jack was handling this himself."

"I don't think Jack has the stomach for the wet work anymore. Is that not why you're bringing him back here?"

"Jack will be assuming a role I plotted out for him twenty years ago, Harvey. Over the course of the last twenty years, Jack has been the most honest loyal employee and friend I have."

"Right, the son you always wanted."

"Are we going to do this again, Harvey? I'm too tired for this right now."

Harvey stands up and walks over to help the Ambassador off the couch. He gives him a warm hug and, with a smile, he says, "No, Sir. We can go at it again tomorrow."

Just as the men are preparing to retire for the evening, the phone rings. The ambassador says, "Who is calling so late?"

"It's the secure line, Sir."

"You answer it, I'm going to bed."

"Good night, Sir."

"Good evening, Harvey, it's Jack."

"Well, well, the heir apparent. What can I do for you at this late hour, Jack?"

"Sorry about the late call, Harv. I'm surprised you're still up."

"Well, we have had a bit of drama here today, Jack. What line are you calling on?"

"I'm sitting in the backyard having a beer with my friend, Tom. He's a cop and I'm using his police cell. Do you want to say hi to Tom, Harv?"

"Still an asshole, Jack. It's late and I want to go to bed. What do you want?"

The Ambassador overhears that it is Jack on the line, and he walks back and takes a seat in the chair in front of his desk.

"What's happening, Harvey?"

"Nothing you need to worry about, Jack. As I said, it's late, what do you want?"

"Put him on the speaker phone, Harvey, and change your tone, please"

"Jack, I'm putting you on the speaker phone. The Ambassador is here."

"Hello, Jack. How is the family?"

"Very well, thank you, Sir, and that is the reason for this late call. We're all going to Vegas for the weekend—in fact, we're leaving shortly."

"That's a wonderful idea, Jack do you want me to get you a suite anywhere?"

Are you still going to be in Arlington by Sunday night?"

"Yes, I'll be there Sunday. So what is going on over there Sir, that has you both up so late?"

The Ambassador gestures to Harvey for him to give the reply.

"The Akron thing, Jack. It has finally reached the desk of the

Ambassador."

"Jesus Christ, why won't that fucker die already?"

"Language please, Armen."

"Sorry, Sir, I'm just excited about going to Vegas with the girls."

"All right, Armen."

"Harvey?"

"They got to go, Jack."

"Who has to 'go,' Harvey?"

"Walker, Palmer and Zikoski."

"Were going after a Russian Mafia family now, Harv?"

"Ivanna Zikoski, Jack. And before I continue, I will say the Ambassador and myself still have some real concerns as to why you wanted Walker and Palmer with you in Arlington. You made it very clear you didn't want to work with them again after Akron. Something just doesn't ring true, Jack."

"First off, asshole, that was a private conversation between me and the Ambassador, and who I chose for my team is none of your fucking business. Sorry, Sir, but this guy is really starting to piss me off. Do you share the same concerns, Sir?"

"I will admit to you, Armen, I did have some initial concerns about you choosing Bricks and Stryker. After some reflection and appreciating the quick timeline I had placed upon you, I have come to understand that these are men you know and at the very least they have maintained their discretion regarding our sensitive operations.

"If you would have wanted Ivanna, as well, then we would be having a completely different conversation. And once again, I have explained to Harvey several times now, that I have no further concerns.

"Now, Armen, what is this about the Russian Mafia?"

"The last name, Sir—former Russian Mob boss, Viktor Zikoski."

"Can we move on, Sir? There is no relation between Ivanna and the Russian Mafia," Harvey interjects.

"Do you want to bet your life on it, Harvey?"

"Ok, enough. I would like to retire for the evening gentleman. I'm sorry, Armen, but it is settled. Mr. Walker and Mr. Palmer will be located and 'retired.' Harvey, you check on the relationship between this Russian group and Ivanna."

"With all due respect, Sir, I think I should know what the plan is regarding our communication to the Wiesenthal Center."

"It was a simple robbery gone bad, Armen."

"And are you okay with this man not being outed as a Nazi, Sir?"

"He is dead, Armen, and along with his death shall his secret die with him."

"Please tell me that we are not going to have Hairy take care of the Akron crew. We need it done quietly and quickly. Hairy's methods tend to drag out the inevitable."

"He's in Arlington, Jack, and he will be there with you until the mission is complete."

"Enough again … rest assured, Jack, Harvey and I spoke with Ian not more than an hour ago. He has it covered with his best team and has promised it will be a quick ending. So, why was it you were calling, Armen?"

"It's nothing I can't discuss with Harvey, Sir, if you want to retire."

"I believe I will, gentlemen. Good night to you both."

Once again, as the Ambassador is leaving the office he suddenly has two more questions for Jack.

"Oh, Jack, did Margaret receive her compensatory check?"

"Yes, sir, thank you. It was very generous."

"And did you receive your copy of the signed contract?"

"No, Sir, we have not received anything yet."

"Harvey, look into this first thing in the morning. Good night."

"Okay, asshole, He's gone. What the fuck do you want?"

"Take me off the speaker phone, dick."

"Start talking, Jack."

"Do you remember a few years ago when we helped a close friend of the Ambassador's neighbor move?"

"That was in Tripoli, I believe."

"Exactly. Well, I need a quick move done here and I need it done on Sunday morning."

"With all that's going on here, Jack, do you honestly expect me to help you out on this? What happened to you, man? You can't take care of this yourself?"

"Harv, you have no idea how close I came to cleaning an entire house this morning. It's my fucking neighbor, man, and I can't risk the heat right now. It affects my family— even you should understand that."

"I'm sorry, Jack. I just don't have the time right now. Maybe next week."

"No, no, you're right, you're just too busy right now. I guess the safety and security of my family will have to wait, maybe next week. Good night, Harvey..."

"Let me guess, Jack...Thailand again."

"That's right, Harv."

"What's the address?"

"It's in the Ambassador's book. We're 201, they're 203."

"Permanent move?"

"Permanent move. Have the new occupants you instil reside for about a month, and then I'll probably just buy the property myself."

"The tenants…hospital or shovel?"

"Okay, this is where you need a pen. Caucasian male, upper left shoulder Swastika tattoo—he gets a week's stay in the hospital."

"Swastika. That's kind of ironic, eh, Jack?"

"Second fella, also a Caucasian male, smudged teardrop tattoo below left eye—he's not so lucky. A month's visit and, Harv, his tongue is the problem."

"Ah, that's really gross, Jack, but consider it done. Fuck, Jack. What did these guys do?"

"They stepped on Marg's rose bushes, Harv."

"Alrighty then. When do you want it done?"

"It's got to be Sunday morning around ten. They'll all still be asleep. Anyone else in the house gets a pass if they behave. Also, arrange a moving truck and some locals to get rid of their shit."

"What about police?"

"That's my next call. It'll be covered."

"Okay, Jack, consider it done. I expect this will make us even."

"You'll never be even on the Thailand thing, Harv, but this is certainly a start. On the Ivanna thing—don't fuck around, just let her be."

"Until Arlington is concluded, Jack, I take my orders from the Ambassador. Good night, Jack."

Just as Jack is hanging up the phone, Margaret and Debra walk into the office.

"Let's go, Jack. Our flight leaves in ninety minutes."

"Sorry, ladies, one more quick call then we'll be on our way. How was your test, hon?"

"I think I aced it, Dad. Please hurry up."

"Oh Marg, before you go, did you get the Ambo's last cheque?"

"It's on your desk. Please hurry, Jack."

"Last thing, Marg. The key?"

"Back in the safe, Jack."

Margaret closes the office door and Jack flips through the mail for the Ambassador's cheque. He finds it in the unopened pile. Jack sticks it in his pocket and hopes it will cover some of the costs of the Vegas trip. He places his next call.

"Tom, this is Jack Singer. How are you doing, Sir?"

"Jack, you old bastard. Good to hear from you. It's been too long. Are you in town for a change?"

"Just got in last night. But just leaving again for Vegas with the girls for the weekend. Congratulations on making captain, Tom. It was way overdue, if you want my opinion."

"Ah, fuck, Jack. It's like the navy, you know? It's all fucking politics. You still working private security?"

"Yeah, Tom, still protecting old rich men from their younger rich wives. You ever get tired of being a cop, I can get you on at four times what you're making now."

"You know, Jack, I'm reaching my twenty-five soon and I might just take you up on that. So what can I do for you today?"

"Have you been to the old neighborhood lately, Tom?"

"I know, Jack. Why the fuck do you think we moved? And I'm a fucking cop for Christ's sake. Do you need me to come by and shake some branches for you?"

"I appreciate that, Tom, but I got it covered. Just wondering if your guys can sit on their phones Sunday morning around ten. It's your old house."

"Consider it done, Jack, but only if you promise we all hook up after your Vegas trip."

"I'm sorry, Tom. I'm back Sunday night then off on another job for a couple of weeks. As soon as I get back, we'll do the barbecue thing."

"Sounds good, Jack. Good to hear from you again."

"You, too, Tom, and thanks again. I'll place a bet for you in Vegas and let you know how you did when I'm back."

"A big bet, Jack. Later, kid."

Jack grabs his stuff and he and Debra head outside to load the car. Margaret is locking up and making sure all the lights are turned off.

Once he and Debra are seated in the car, Jack anxiously honks the horn.

Margaret sets the alarm and is walking to the car when she spots the teardrop tattoo guy drinking a fresh forty alone on his front porch.

Jack notices Margaret stop to say something to Teardrop and he quickly jumps out of the car ready to step in. After a brief moment, Margaret is on her way back to the car and hops in the front seat.

"What did you say to him, hon?"

"I was being polite, Jack. I said I was sorry to hear that they're moving Sunday."

Jack laughs and the trio heads off to the airport.

Back in Arlington...

Harvey had initially arranged for the crew to stay in a hotel while in Arlington, but after Jack's meeting with the Ambassador in Israel, he had insisted that the crew be housed in the warehouse.

The entire hotel floor now consisted of Ian. When they eventually arrived, the Ambassador and his new security detail, Joshua and Peter, would be staying there, as well.

After working on logistics all day for the Akron disposal team, Ian decides to take a break and places a call to his wife, Patricia. She puts the phone next to his new baby girl Maggie's mouth and he can hear her loudly snoring.

Ian looks at his watch and figures Mr. Singh should be prepping for supper. He is bored to death so he decides to pop in on the group at the warehouse. He's hoping the group of misfits haven't burnt it down already.

Ian arrives at the warehouse and can see the new security shack has been installed. Owen comes out of the shack to unlock the padded front gate.

"I see they finally found something for you to do. Let me see your arm."

Owen lifts up his sleeve to show his upper arm completely covered in black, blue and yellow bruises and some severely popped blood vessels.

"They both outweigh me by fifty pounds, Ian."

"You can't keep playing their games, kid. You're gonna end up in the hospital and we don't need that right now, understand? I'm gonna park around back and bring you something to eat in a bit." Ian pauses and asks, "By the way, Owen, what shift did you get?"

"They said I'm out here until I pass out."

The warehouse is an 8,000 square-foot facility that was a specialized machinist shop for the cattle industry. It had become antiquated over the years and was eventually shuttered some ten years ago.

At its peak, it ran twenty-four hours a day and, as such, was equipped with a number of the amenities Harvey was looking for.

Located at the end of a three-block strip of abandoned commercial properties, the warehouse backs on to a private cattle farm that extends as far as the eye can see.

The warehouse is surrounded by the remnants of a chain-link fence, with the occasional piece of barbwire guarding the top. The day labourers did the best they could to shore it up and close any gaps.

A small shack was built at the front of the property with a small opening on each side. The intent is to keep whoever is manning security out of plain sight, should any random vehicle happen by.

Rick, Carl and now Owen have a series of extension cords lined up to power a radio, a fan and a heater for the occasional cool April Texas evening.

All of the crew's rental vehicles are hidden at the rear of the property. The warehouse has a rear entrance leading to the kitchen.

The main objective is to not draw any unwanted attention to the site. The site was stripped of its copper years ago, but there is an ever-revolving transient population in the area.

Most important, the warehouse now has a fully functional kitchen for Mr. Singh, with a large Texas barbecue grill just outside the rear door.

There is a large walk-in freezer unit that now stores all of the generators and technical equipment ordered by Sven. What would have taken an entire crew months to configure, Sven managed to set up in a week.

The only complaint from the crew so far is the sound of the running generators. They are a bit too close to the sleeping pods and too loud at night. Sven did ensure they were properly exhausted well away from the rear of the building.

Harvey leased the property under the guise of an exploratory purchase for putting in a meat processing plant. The site has no power other than the generators, again to avoid any unnecessary attention.

The warehouse has a small office for Jack. There are sleeping quarters for nine men, a single shower and a specially built containment room for a special soon-to-be-arriving guest.

There are two large picnic tables in the centre of the room for meals. Unlike the compound, there is no recreation equipment. The only diversion from the daily monotony is a deck of cards and a backgammon set.

Having parked the car, Ian approaches the rear entrance and can still see smoldering gristle on the barbecue. He's thinking he's just in time for one of Mr. Singh's amazing meals.

He walks down the hallway, past the kitchen entrance and the first room of sleeping pods and out into the main warehouse. The crew are all in their places at the dinner table.

Mr. Singh has made barbecue beef ribs, which have been slow cooking for the last eight hours. He has also prepared slaw, salad, potatoes, and an Indian curry dish that only he and Carl like.

Ian grabs a plate and works his way around the men. He figures it's easier than asking the men to stop their voracious shovelling and pass him everything. Meals are the only thing the crew looks forward to everyday and that Jack will be arriving soon.

Ian takes his seat and the men, who are all surprising quiet for some reason, continue working on their meals. He notices that Rick is constantly rubbing his right upper arm and using his left hand to eat with. Ian also notices the occasional smirking glance from Carl directed toward Rick.

Just as the men are finishing up, Mr. Singh spots a scraggly brown mutt gingerly making its way to the first picnic table.

Mr. Singh jumps up and tries to grab the mutt and says, "Ian, did you leave the back door open? You have to close it hard, man. I will get rid of this beast. Maybe for our lunch tomorrow, huh?"

Carl jumps up and says, "You don't eat dogs in India, do you, Mr. Singh? Anyone touches that dog and they'll have to deal with me."

Carl grabs a huge rib bone and tosses it to the mutt, who picks it up in his mouth and moves to a corner of the warehouse to eat it.

"We can't have a fucking dog in here in here, Carl."

"Why not, Ian?"

"Look at it—it's filthy. Do you want us all to get lice or ticks or whatever the fuck it is they have in these parts?"

"I'll spray it down after dinner and we can keep it in the shack at night. A dog would start barking long before we heard anything coming."

Ian gets up to go close the back door properly. When he returns he replies, "There's a pet shop next to Sven's coffee shop. Go now and get some type of cleaner and then you and Rick clean him up. Put him outside for now, but you're right, when you two idiots are taking your nightly naps, the dog will wake you if anything is happening out there. But Jack will be the one to ultimately decide if we keep him."

"Can we phone him now to ask him?"

"No, Rick. We are not going to phone Jack to ask him if we can have a dog."

Rick is despondently muttering, "I don't want to clean the dog if we don't even get to keep it."

Sven tells Carl he'll go with him, as he wants another coffee.

Sven, who has been at the site the longest, has been making daily trips to the local Starbucks for his morning double double espresso with extra froth. He noticed something interesting in the local paper one morning and has been accumulating them daily, as he presumes they will interest Jack greatly upon his arrival.

Ian tells the rest of the crew to help Mr. Singh put away all of the food and dishes. He wants to hold a quick meeting before he heads back to the hotel.

With the crew all settled and Owen eating in the security shack with the new team member watching him swallow his every bite, Ian starts the impromptu meeting.

The attendees are Mr. Singh, Rick, Carl and Sven.

"Jack is expected to be here sometime Sunday night. I have yet to be officially informed if he will be staying in one of the sleeping pods

or at the hotel."

"Why can't we stay at the hotel? It stinks in here and those generators are too fucking loud. No offence to you, Sven. I know you tried your best."

"Sorry, Rick. If I had more time to set up I could have ordered some sweet quiet ones. At least we're not dealing with the fumes."

"You two finished?"

"Sorry, Ian."

"Yeah, sorry, Ian. Go ahead."

"Upon Jack's arrival, we'll get our mission plan and you'll each find out exactly what will be expected of you. Again, no one is to go out to the target site. Jack has a plan in place for first contact. Sven, you make sure you get Jack those newspapers as soon as he gets here. Until that time, continue on with your sitting around doing nothing. If Sven needs any help with anything, I want you all to give him a hand. Sorry, Mr. Singh. Of course I didn't mean you."

Carl chimes in, "You got a nice TV in that room of yours, Ian."

"Yeah, Ian," Rick says. "H.B.O. and shit, I'm guessing."

"Can we get a TV, too, Ian? What do you do all day in that posh hotel room of yours but watch TV?"

Ian walks over to Carl and places his right hand on his shoulder and continues to talk.

"If Jack calls, I will ask him if we can get a TV. How you expect to get a signal in here is beyond me."

Rick adds, "Sven can hook anything up."

The group is starting to notice Carl's face is turning extremely red. Ian has been applying incremental pressure on Carl's shoulder in the hopes he would shut up. With the group starting to notice, he backs up and continues.

"I would like to finish my fucking point for this meeting, gentlemen, so, please no more fucking questions about dogs or a fucking TV. I will shoot the next person who interrupts me. Now, we all know what happened in Argentina with Jack's quick departure..."

At that moment, Owen pops in the front door, carrying the mutt.

"The fekin dog's choking on a bone."

Mr. Singh jumps up and puts his hand right into the dog's throat, dislodging the obstruction. The dog does a few coughs and a sneeze but appears to be no worse for wear.

After a minute of petting and preening over their new mutt, the group finally looks up to see that Ian has left.

Rick leans over to Carl and asks, "What was he doing to you, man?"

"I can see why Jack calls him 'Hairy.' That dude is fucking strong."

A few hours earlier in Orange County...

On their quick flight to Vegas, Jack and Margaret are sitting together in a two-seater row with Debra sitting in the row just in front of them.

"Now that I have you alone for an hour Jack ... Israel?"

"Do you have my magazines, hon?"

Margaret reaches into her bag and puts a *Woman's Day* on Jacks tray, then puts her hand firmly on top of it.

"Not until we discuss this, Jack. Now please, dear."

"You're right, Marg. It's a big move for you and Deb. Let's look on the bright side. Debra wants to get her cosmetic work done. She could have it done in LA and then present herself in Israel once she is all healed up. She can move to Israel as the young lady she's always wanted to be. You lived there for a number of years with your father, so you obviously know the city and how beautiful it is."

With Margaret about to reply, Jack takes out the envelope he got from the Ambassador and starts to open it.

"I love Israel, Jack, but I'm really concerned with the level of violence. Dad says the attacks on Tel Aviv are getting out of control. It's not just the air attacks anymore—there are mass shootings now, as well."

Without answering Margaret, Jack quietly stares at the check and passes it over to her.

"Oh my God, Jack. Is that real?"

Jack takes the check back and puts it in his pocket.

"I guess we can get Debra the best surgeon in LA now. And you could even get some new boobs if you want, Marg."

"I'm going to pretend you didn't just say that, Jack."

"Just kidding, Marg. Yours are fine."

"Oh, thank you very much, Jack. Maybe I will get them now."

"Whatever you want, hon."

"You would let me get big boobs, Jack?"

"No, hon, you just always talk about one being bigger than the other. You could just get them balanced and maybe add a cup size or two."

"Just read your magazine, Jack."

"I know Israel is a big move, so why don't we just try it for a year and if we don't like it, we can come back. You read the contract, hon. I'll be home most of the time. My office is only twenty minutes away. And how about you getting to design our estate—how cool is that?"

Jack is smiling now and wants to have a little fun with Margaret.

"Maybe we could look at having another kid once you get those big new bazookas."

"Okay, Jack, I'll think about Israel. Stop drooling and just read your magazine."

Jack leans over and kisses Marg on the lips and whispers into her ear, "I don't ever want you to change a thing about yourself, hon."

"Oh, no, Jack. Now I'm thinking about it … big honking double Ds."

Jack can't help himself as his thoughts and a solemn mood overtake him. He's thinking about Debbie. He leans forward and gives his Debra a shoulder squeeze. Then he leans back over to Marg and again whispers in her ear, "When Arlington is done with, Marg, I am going to tell you a story."

Margaret looks over at Jack and can see that something has changed in him. They clasp hands and both sit quietly for the remainder of the flight.

Although Jack is sitting quietly, his mind is anything but. Jack has come up with a change of plans regarding Arlington and he will have to make a call as soon as they get to the hotel.

The trio make their way to the Hard Rock in a rental car and check into a nice two-bedroom suite.

The ladies plan to do some shopping in the hotel's stores while Jack makes his call. Jack agrees to meet them at the Fuel Cafe for a light snack in an hour.

After seeing the Ambassador's check, Margaret decides they are going to splurge and she makes late dinner reservations at the opulent 35 Steaks + Martinis restaurant.

Margaret and Debra keep their eyes open for Pat, but can't find any trace of him anywhere.

Jack picks up the hotel's phone and places a call to Ian in Arlington. Ian is now back in his hotel room, watching TV.

"Hello Jack, how's Vegas?"

"Not too hot, not too cold, Hairy. How are you?"

"I need you back here, Jack. The guys need their leader."

"I was never their leader, Hairy. That was Victor's job. Until I get there, you're their guy."

"About that, Jack … when you get back I'd like to head home for another week. You know, see the little one."

"I'm sorry, Ian, I forgot. How is she doing? Did you and Patricia give her a name yet?"

"Thanks, Jack, they're both doing really well. Her name is Maggie."

"Great Irish name, Ian. I'm sorry, Ian, but I'll need you in Arlington. That said, I do have some good news. I originally anticipated the job to last four weeks. I have a plan where we could be outta there in less than one week once I arrive. That's why I'm calling."

"Okay, Jack, what do you need?"

"I want Owen on a flight to my house Sunday morning. We'll be back from Vegas by three and I'd like him there by 4:00 p.m. We will then be driving to Arlington in a friend's car. I'm going to leave early Monday morning, and with us taking turns driving, we should be there Tuesday for supper. Tell Cookie to make his beef ribs."

"We had that for dinner today. How long a drive is that?"

"About twenty hours."

"Why the fuck do you want to drive twenty hours with Owen, Jack?"

"Part of the big plan, Ian. Harvey's got my home info, and tell Cookie to give Owen a haircut—he refused to get one back in Israel. But I need it done. I'm not driving through New Mexico and Arizona with their highway patrol and a hippie sitting next to me."

"Uh, Jack? The guys want to know if they can get a TV."

"Why not, Ian? Gotta go. See you soon."

Jack hangs up and walks out into the hallway, looking for any room service trays yet to be picked up. He spots one and brings it into his room. He scatters some items around the room and places a call to the hotel's front desk.

In a feminine voice, Jack asks for the day manager. He says he is extremely frustrated and unhappy with the condition his room was in upon check-in. After Jack repeatedly insists it must be the day manager he speaks to, the front desk finally connects him.

"This is Pat. How may I help you?"

Jack continues in his feminine tone and explains to Pat that he is very nervous about the room being so messy and, further, that his sister and niece will be back shortly and he doesn't want them to see the room in the condition that it's in.

Pat assures Jack he will be right up.

"And Pat, can you please come alone? I just so embarrassed, and I don't want anyone else to see this. I just want to pee my pants because of all the clutter. You understand don't you, Pat? You sound like a real sweetheart who would also not like a messy room."

"I completely understand, Sir. That is totally unacceptable. I'm on my way up right now and, let me assure you, I will come alone."

Jack quickly strips down and grabs Margaret's way-too-small nightgown and ties one of her scarves around his neck.

Pat arrives at the room within minutes.

Just before Jack opens the door, he unties Marg's evening gown strap and loosens it at bit, exposing his broad chest and ripped abs.

Jack opens the door. Pat takes one look at Jack and his eyes can't take in the sight that is standing in front of him quickly enough. He emits an almost inaudible, lusty, "Oh, my."

Pat looks at Jack with a ministerial focus and storms into the room.

"You are absolutely right, Sir. This is completely unacceptable. I am going to fire whoever left your room in this condition. I'll get you another room immediately."

"No, please, Pat. Oh, I'm sorry, can I call you Pat? My sister hates having to change rooms, so if you could just have it tidied up a bit, that would be marvelous."

Pat charges his way to the phone and calls for a full crew of cleaners, immediately.

"You can call me Pat anytime, Jack. Can I call you Jack?"

"Well actually, Pat, my good friends call me Jackie."

Jack deliberately brushes against a chair, pulling open the bottom part of Margaret's gown and revealing his goods to Pat.

"Oopsie," he says.

"So, Jack," Pat says, trying to let his eyes wander to Jack's pelvic area. "While we wait for the crew…you say you're here with your sister and niece?"

"Yes, Pat, I just broke up with my boyfriend. I caught him cheating on me so the girls and I thought what better way to forget him than a trip to Vegas? The problem is, I'm just so distraught by the whole mess that I'm going to stay in tonight while the girls go out clubbing."

"Well, Jackie, I'm actually off soon. I could come back tonight if you wouldn't mind some company. Only if you'd like me to, of course."

"I'm not sure Pat…I just got hurt so bad…you wouldn't hurt me, would you, Pat?"

"Not in a million years, Jackie."

"Well, the girls are going out at ten. Maybe you could stop by at eleven? They gave me my own little room right there. I know I'll just end up crying on my bed when they leave, so maybe you could just let yourself in."

The room crew arrives and Pat gives the cleaners instructions as to every specific item that he wants cleaned.

"All right, Jackie. So, I'll see you tonight?"

"Thank you ever so much, Pat. And, please, it would break my already fragile heart if anyone gets in trouble for this. Do you promise me no one will get fired?"

"I promise, Jackie."

Pat leaves the room and as he enters the elevator alone, he starts dancing around joyfully, thinking of the evening to come.

With Pat gone, Jack takes a seat at the end of the bed. He is feeling a bit torn. Pat actually seemed like an okay guy. He thinks he can see a smidgen of the je-ne-sais-quoi Roger saw in him. There's no way Pat could've known the possible repercussions of eighty-sixing his family. But Jack decides that, at the very least, he needs to be taught a lesson, so he will see his plan through.

Jack's next thought is to get out of Margaret's gown ASAP, in case Margaret and Debra suddenly come back. Jack puts Margaret's stuff back and heads down to the restaurant while the cleaning crew finishes working on the room.

Back in Arlington...

With the lack of things to do around the compound, washing the dog has turned into a big event, much to the chagrin of Mr. Singh. The crew is right now washing Leon, newly named by Carl, in the large kitchen sink.

The office phone line starts to ring. It can be heard throughout the warehouse, as Sven has it hooked up to the speaker system.

Mr. Singh goes to answer it.

"Hello, Mr. Singh here. How may I help you?"

"Hi, Mr. Singh. What's going on?"

"They're washing that filthy dog in my kitchen sink, Mr. Malcomson, that's what's going on. I can assure you, Sir, Jack would not tolerate this type of behavior at all."

"I'm sorry, Mr. Singh, just hang in there. You tell them that when they're finished, they are to clean that sink to your exact specifications. Is that okay with you?"

"Yes, Mr. MalComson. I intend to do just that."

"All right, good then. Please tell Sven he can go ahead and buy a TV. Also, I just spoke to Jack, and he asked me personally if you would be so kind as to give young Owen a haircut, before tomorrow night, please?"

"I will do it after the dog is done."

"Good idea, Mr. Singh. See you tomorrow."

With Leon all cleaned up, Sven has him in a towel in the seating area while Rick and Carl are arguing over who gets to hold him next.

Mr. Singh comes out of the office and tells Carl to go fetch Owen for his haircut. Rick is laughing, as he just got out of his shoulder punching rematch with Carl, and he gets the next turn holding Leon.

The evening is now coming to a close for the Arlington crew.

Carl is working the night shift. Owen finally gets some sleep after getting his haircut. Sven is looking for a TV online at Best Buy, and Mr. Singh is just finishing up cleaning the kitchen sink by himself. The crew did offer to help but he shrugged them off, wanting to make sure it was done hygienically.

Back in Las Vegas…

Jack, Margaret and Debra have just come off of spending an incredible evening together. They took a cab to the Mandalay Bay and walked the strip, making it up to the

Paris Hotel and back. They made plans to hit the rest of the strip tomorrow night.

The evening concluded with a fantastic meal at the Hard Rock. It is now 10:00 p.m. and with Margaret saying she has had enough for the night, Jack suggests the ladies head back to the room. He tells them he's going to have a Scotch before bed and play a couple of hands of video poker at the lobby bar.

The ladies off to their rooms while Jack makes his way to talk to a security guard that he had spotted earlier in the evening. Jack had noticed he had a distinctive navy tattoo on his forearm.

Jack approaches the guard and, after a short conversation, he shakes his hand and heads off to the room.

It is now 10:50, and Margaret—after a full day and maybe a little too much wine at dinner—is already sound asleep in bed. Jack talks to Debra for a few minutes in her room and after saying good night, she puts her headset back on and Jack closes her door.

At 11:00 p.m. on the nose, the hotel door opens and, noticing all of the lights are off, Pat slips into the bathroom and removes all of his clothing. He then carries it into the sitting room and places the pile on the end of the couch.

He then walks naked into Debra's room. As soon as she sees Pat standing there, naked, in her doorway, she starts screaming at the top of her lungs. Jack flips on his own bedroom light and he and Margaret rush to Debra's aid.

Just as they're leaving their bedroom, three security guards burst through the front door, run over and tackle the naked Pat.

They wrestle him into the sitting area, handcuff him and throw a bedsheet over his waist.

During all of the scuffle and confusion, Jack manages to secretly slip Debra a thumbs-up sign for a job well done.

Needless to say, once Margaret clued in to whom their unexpected visitor was, she also played her role to a T.

The most ironic part of Jack's little mission was that Pat, in his state of shock and horror, did not initially recognize either Debra or Margaret.

Jack says good night to Debra again and, after a kiss and a hug, he closes her door. Jack takes Margaret into her room to talk, while the security guards allow Pat to put his clothes back on.

Jack and Margaret return to the sitting room and Jack walks the guards to the door, handing one of them a nice mound of cash.

The guards depart, leaving the still dumbfounded Pat alone with Jack and Margaret.

Margaret is the first to speak.

"Did you learn something about how to treat people tonight, Pat?"

Pat starts stumbling and fumbling for an explanation and once again feeds them his 'Everything is now comped for you' mantra.

Margaret jumps in. "Just leave, Pat. We pay our own way."

Debra who has been listening at the door, hands Pat her tablet. "We're not thieves either, Pat. Now please leave."

Pat leaves the room.

The ladies are now left staring at Jack.

What comes next is the longest round of hugs, kisses and a few laughing, happy tears from Margaret that Jack has ever experienced.

"Okay, ladies, we have a big day tomorrow. We'll head back to the strip, but not before we hit the outlet mall to get Deb a new tablet.

After more hugs and kisses, the trio head to their rooms.

Needless to say, once they're back in their bedroom, Margaret is not quite ready to go back to sleep.

Chapter 15

ROAD TRIP

Back from Vegas, Jack and Margaret are in the basement doing laundry for Jack's upcoming trip. Jack normally won't let Margaret touch his laundry, as he has a certain method for washing and drying his clothes that all but eliminates the need for ironing.

Margaret is clinging to Jack's every move. She is newly smitten with the man who restored her stolen dignity, back in Las Vegas.

Margaret's sixth sense is working overtime. She fears that there is more to the Arlington trip than what Jack has revealed. Which, as usual, is basically nothing.

Upon entering the front door after returning from Vegas, Jack instinctively flipped a switch in his mind—a caustic metamorphosis that has converted him from the amiable, happy-go-lucky family man into the virulent, mission-mode Sergeant Jack Singer.

Margaret has experienced the transformation many times in their lengthy marriage. Her biggest concern is always which Jack will return to her. She secretly prays it is not the Jack who returned after the Akron job was complete.

Jack is now restlessly awaiting Owen's imminent arrival.

The front doorbell rings. Jack wouldn't answer the front door if he was standing right in front of it. As Debra just happens to be walking by—even though Jack is only two feet away from the door—she answers it, knowing her dad won't.

Debra knows they are waiting on a friend of her father's. But she was not expecting the very handsome young man now standing before her.

Owen is a bit weathered-looking and his gaze belongs to a much older soul than his almost childlike features suggest. Owen has a sharp new haircut by Mr. Singh and, having spent the past month surrounded by a group of miscreants, Debra is truly a sight for sore eyes.

Debra's shiny reddish auburn hair immediately reminds him of an old girlfriend he left back in Ireland. Owen is impressed by what he sees and subconsciously exaggerates his Irish accent a bit. He wants to appear a little more foreign and exotic than he is.

"Good evening, Miss. I'm Owen. I take it you're the young lady that I heard so much about, then?"

"Dad, Owen's here," Debra calls over her shoulder. When she doesn't see him right away, she yells, "Daaaaaad!"

"Come on in, Owen. Sorry, he was just standing here a minute ago. I'll show you where you'll be sleeping tonight."

"So, what, your father said you're in grade nine now?"

"My dad didn't tell me you were so funny, Owen. Does that line actually work on the girls where you're from?"

"What makes you think it's a line, Miss? Where I'm from I'm old enough to be your da."

Debra starts to speak in her own mocking Irish accent.

"Oh, 9 year old girls are having babies in Ireland are they, piker?"

"Well, you certainly have inherited have your father's wit, Miss Debra."

"Can we cut the shit now, Owen? So, how long have you worked with my dad?"

"Long enough to know he's a very decent man, Debra."

"Well, that tells me absolutely nothing. Anyway, Owen, let me give you a bit of warning in advance. My dad's turned his little head switch on, so he's being a bit of an asshole."

"You call your da an asshole in America, do ya?"

"Yeah, we do. What do you call your dad in Ireland when he gets all weird?"

"I'd have to dig through the daisies and six feet of dirt to call him anything."

Just then Jack walks into the living room. He looks at the two of them standing there and says sharply, "Drop your shit, Owen. We're going out for an hour."

Jack leaves the room as quickly as he entered and goes to the kitchen to tell Margaret he can pick up some takeout for dinner, if she wants.

Owen and Debra enter the kitchen and Jack—in a friendlier tone for Margaret's benefit—asks his guest what his preference would be for dinner.

"Oh, no, Sir. Whatever the family wants is good enough for me."

"Nonsense, Owen. You're the guest in our house, Jack will stop and get whatever you want."

"Do you have a decent chippies place, ma'am?"

"Oh, Jack, doesn't that sound good? That's what they call fish and chips in Ireland. Right, Owen?"

"Yes, ma'am."

"The Cheesecake Factory is real good, Dad."

"Owen only likes his fish if it has an inch of batter on it, ladies."

"They have battered fish there, Jack. You guys go and I'll order dinner for pickup. Fish and chips for everyone?"

"That's fine, about ninety minutes, o.k. Marg?"

Jack and Owen leave through the back door and Jack walks over to fence adjacent to Tom's old place. He peers over it and notes that all is quiet except for the flickering of what would appear to be a TV, emanating from the kitchen.

"You want to see something sweet, Owen?"

Jack opens the garage door, revealing Roger's fully restored, mint condition, '68 Mustang GTO.

"We're taking that, Jack?"

"Yes, we are, kid. We'll fill her up, wash her and then we've got to pick up some stuff for Arlington."

Back in the kitchen, Debra is speaking with her mom.

"I said something stupid to, Owen, Mom. How was I to know his dad was dead?"

"Did you apologize?"

"Dad walked in before I had the chance to say anything."

"Well, just say sorry after dinner. Your dad told me a bit about him, hon. He has had quite the challenging life. He can't even go home again if he wants to."

"Then I'm glad he's with Dad now."

"He's kind of cute, wouldn't you say, Debra?"

"He's okay"

Back in Israel…

Harvey is back sitting behind the Ambassador's desk, the Ambassador is lying on the couch in front of him, and Joshua and Peter are sitting in their corner trying to stay awake.

"Are you sure you want to do this, Sir?"

"You're the one who put these thoughts in my head, Harvey."

"You pay me for my objecting opinion, Wilhelm."

"Place the call, Harvey, and put it on speaker phone."

"Hello?"

"Hi, Margaret, is that you?"

"Yes, Wilhelm, you're up late. Jack just left—can I have him call you back?"

Harvey, who is listening in on the conversation, looks at the Ambo and tugs on his collar, indicating that she could not sound any colder toward him right now.

The Ambassador waves him off.

"How's the weather down there, dear? Did you get my last cheque?"

The Ambassador is sporting an embarrassed grimace on his face. He's seriously pissed at having been talked into following Harvey's plan at all.

"The weather is fine here, Wilhelm, and yes, we got your cheque. I have to order our dinner, so if there is nothing else I will have Jack phone you as soon as he's back. He should be home in about an hour, if you want to stay up."

"Well, dear… actually, it was you I wanted to speak with."

"Is my father okay?"

"Yes, yes, dear, he's fine. I actually had dinner with him yesterday, everything is fine here. Anyway, dear, the reason I'm calling is that Harvey has called a meeting for tomorrow with our developer and I was wondering if you and Jack had had the opportunity to discuss when you will be relocating here."

"We have discussed it, Wilhelm, but we haven't made a decision yet. Getting your signed copy of the contract would be a good start."

"Hi, Margaret, it's Harvey. We have you on the speaker phone. I was assured the contract was delivered yesterday. Have you checked your mailbox today?"

"Hi, Harvey, I was wondering where that heavy breathing was coming from. If you hang on, I'll check the mailbox to see if it's there."

Margaret doesn't wait for the gentlemen to reply and walks casually to the mailbox. She finds a "Sorry we missed you" notice with a time and date to pick up the letter at the local UPS store.

Margaret takes her time getting back to the phone, making an important stop to arrange Jack's magazines on the coffee table. She also figures she had better pour herself a nice glass of Pinot.

"Hi, guys. You still there?"

"Yes, Margaret. Harvey and I are still here."

"We missed the delivery but I received a notice, Wilhelm. I'll have to go pick it up tomorrow."

"Well, I am extremely pleased that it's at least in the right country now. Can you please phone Harvey after you have received and reviewed it, dear?"

"Yes, Wilhelm, I can do that. I really need to order our dinner. Was there anything else?"

"No, dear, that is all for now. Please wish Jack a safe journey and we'll talk to him in a few days. Good night, dear."

"Why didn't you ask her, Wilhelm?"

"You heard how she sounded. What am I going to say, Harvey? We would be more comfortable if you joined us as a hostage in Israel while Jack is away, to ensure he carries out the mission? Enough of this nonsense. I'm going to bed, Harvey."

"I know you don't want to hear this again, Wilhelm, but why don't we just kill him? Obviously not now, but give me the word and I'll tell Ian to have Owen do it after the mission."

"Why, Harvey? Why do you find it necessary that we kill Armen? Are you not forgetting we are both going to be in Arlington when Armen captures our Nazi sympathizer?"

"If it wasn't for Jack screwing up in Argentina, none—and I mean none—of this would be happening now. I just don't think we can trust him anymore. Plain and simple, he has to go. I'm just so distraught that you aren't able to grasp it."

"Jack's reasoning was temporarily misplaced, Harvey, that's all. The old Jack is back and he is going to be your boss, so you better start to 'grasp' that."

On his way out of the office the Ambassador is talking under his breath again.

"When this is over, you're right, someone is going to be killed."

"What's that, Sir?"

"Nothing … good night, Harvey, and wake these two idiots and send them to bed."

Back in Orange County…

After putting gas in the GTO, Jack and Owen are pulling up to Jack's storage facility. Jacks back the car up to the door and pulls out the key to open the unit.

"Let's get Roger's shit out of the trunk and put my stuff in."

Jack lifts up a secret panel to reveal Roger's secret wares.

"Look at all this shite. How many jobs does this paddy have?"

"Owen, the man is a friend of mine."

"Sorry, Jack. I meant no disrespect. I have a cousin in Ireland that is also a 'crafty butcher'"—you know, a 'homo' as you say here in America."

"Enough, Owen."

While Jack is grabbing various items for the road, Owen is watching his every move. Every now and then, Jack glances at him as he packs another item and gives Owen a wry smile.

"We're done. Let's go get dinner."

Jack and Owen stop at the Cheesecake Factory to pick up the fish and chips. The guy at the takeout counter hands Jack two large bags.

"Holy shit, do you think they ordered enough."

"Excuse me, Sir, there are two more bags," the cashier tells him.

Jack gets the tab and reaches for his wallet.

"Shit, I forgot my wallet. I never forget my wallet…fuck!"

"No worries, Jack," Owen says, reaching into his pocket and pulling out a small wad of hundreds, which he uses to pay the tab.

On the drive home Jack says, "Is that the money we gave you in Uruguay, Owen?"

"The same. It's not like I had anywhere to spend it."

"Why didn't you get yourself a girl or something, for Christ's sake?"

"That's not who I am, Jack."

"Good boy."

Back at the house, the group gathers around the kitchen table to eat their fish and chips. After they finish, Jack and

Margaret do the dishes, and Marg tells Debra and Owen to go watch some TV in the living room.

"Are you ready for tomorrow, Jack?"

"Yes. Did you want to watch some TV in bed, hon?"

"Are you going to talk?"

"No."

"Can I hold you?"

"Yes."

"Then, I'll meet you in there in ten minutes."

Jack crosses through the living room and sees Owen and Debra watching TV and sitting a little too close for his liking. He wonders to himself just how many people Owen has dispatched in his young life. The man who is now sitting next to his teenage daughter.

"Do you want to watch UFC, Dad? I taped the free card from yesterday," Deb says.

"Who's fighting?"

"Machida vs Rockhold. But I taped it to watch the VanZant-Herrig fight."

"You ever get a chance to watch UFC, Owen?"

"Yes, Sir, I did catch a fight in a pub in Ireland once. The donnybrooks in the pub after the fight were just as good."

"We're Oscar Mike at 0440, Owen. You go to sleep whenever you want. We got a twenty-hour drive, kid, so you make sure you shower before we go. Marg put some clean towels on your bed and there's an alarm clock in your room. I'll get us out of LA, then we'll see about giving you some drive time. Do you have a licence with you, Owen?"

"No."

"So much for that. Good night, kids."

Jack and Margaret spend some time talking in bed, as Jack assures her he only plans on being away a week. And that when he gets back from Arlington, they will have a serious talk about relocating to Israel.

It's now 11:00 p.m. and Margaret has fallen asleep. Jack can no longer hear the living room TV so he decides he'll go do his nightly lockdown ritual.

Jack turns on the house alarm and checks to make sure that all the deadbolts are locked, the coffee pot is filled with water and the timer is set for the right time. He makes sure that the coffee pot is plugged in, the buttons on the stove are all off. The ice maker arm is in the up position. The kitchen garbage can has been emptied. The floor mat in front of the sink is placed in its proper position. The back screen door is locked and secured.

Just then the phone rings, and Jack goes to answer it in the office.

"What the fuck happened down there today, Jack?"

"I was in Vegas, Tom. Why? What happened?"

"I was reading the dailies before heading home from work. There were half a dozen bodies dumped off at a hospital this morning, Jack—two that might not make it. One of the guys was missing a tongue."

"Wow. Were they dropped off at Orange County General?"

"No, someone dumped them at Torrance."

"Well, Tom, that's an hour away in good traffic. And isn't that just out of your jurisdiction?"

"I don't like this, Jack."

"Look, Tom, I'm in bed and I'm heading out for a few weeks early tomorrow. Who knows what happened with those assholes in Torrance, but you do what you gotta do, Tom."

"Well, I can't really do anything, can I, Jack? I'm a fucking captain for Christ's sake, Jack."

"It's all quiet here, Tom. No sign that anything happened here today."

"Okay, Jack. Did you place that bet for me in Vegas?"

"Oh, shit, Tom. See, if you didn't call, I would have forgotten. I dropped a hundred on a thirty-to-one black at the Excalibur and the little fucker hit, Tom. Three thousand clams for you at our next barbecue, big guy."

"Well, that will certainly help dispel our little situation, Jack. Have a safe trip, and you better give my money to Marg to hang on to."

Jack hangs up. On his way back to bed, he rechecks the alarm. He checks to make sure that the locks are all on and the coffee pot is loaded with water and the timer is set for the right time. That the coffee pot is plugged in ...

Jack returns to bed to find Margaret was awakened by the phone call.

"Who was that phoning so late?"

"Tom. He wanted a donation to the Police Benevolent Fund, hon. Good night, Marg."

"Good night, Jack."

As he's dozing off, Jack is running his rudimentary plan through his head one more time. The only thing that he has conclusively decided so far is that there is no way he is swallowing those vials again.

Before bed, Jack managed to grab the three glass vials and he placed them in in a tiny hiding space in the trunk. Roger had bragged to him numerous times about his hiding spot being dog-proof. According to Roger, he sprayed it with a chemical compound he discovered several years ago on a mission in Columbia that apparently won't trigger any of a dog's 5000 sensors.

Jack can only hope that he's right.

At 4:40 a.m., Jack and Owen head off to Arlington as planned.

Back in Arlington…

Having just finished a large room service breakfast, Ian pushes the cart into the hallway. He begins to search his laptop, looking for a nearby boxing club. Just like Jack with his morning fitness regimen, Ian starts to experience mental and physical withdrawal if he isn't punching something a couple of times a week.

Ian's only hesitation is Jack's insistence on no repeated fraternizing with the community. He figures, fuck it. He needs to get out or it's going to be Rick and Carl at the end of his callous-covered oversize fists.

Ian finds a hit on his laptop. Absolute Fitness M.M.A. opens at 5:00 a.m. He figures they should have guys there who just want to spar. Ian starts packing his workout gear when his burner phone rings. He can see it is Harvey calling from Israel.

"Hello, Harvey."

"He's not going to budge on Jack, Ian."

"Then I guess we're both going to have a new boss, Harv."

"We talked about this, Ian. I'm not going to work for that asshole."

"Yes, we did, Harv, and I said I will wait and see how all of this unfolds after the job. Jack is as sharp as they come, and I think he'll pay well. At least we won't be doing any more of these ridiculous time-warp missions."

"We both know this mission and Jack becoming the heir apparent is because of the cancer. The Ambassador is done, Ian. All I hear now is his sentimental shit, legacy this and legacy that. I should have had you put a bullet in his head a year ago."

"I hope for your sake you're talking about Jack, now."

"You know what I mean, Ian."

"I'm not sure I do, Harvey. Should anything happen to that man before I get back, you and I are going to have a real problem."

"Okay, Ian, ask yourself a very simple question. Would you rather work for me, or work for Jack? Why be third, when you could be number two? For fuck's sake, Ian, I have a meeting with a developer today to start designing Jack's palace. That could be your meeting and your palace, Ian. And what's more, I'm tired of living in this bomb-rained fucking shithole. I would move the whole fucking operation to fucking sunny LA."

"Are you done?"

"No, I'm not. I want to know if Owen is still on board with the Jack issue, should it come to that."

"Owen is a soldier—he's not Jack's new pet. He will do as commanded."

"He's going to be in a car with Jack for twenty hours. You know the prick can be charming when he needs to be, Ian."

"I went through all of that with Owen before we picked him and Ivanna up on the Uruguayan dock. The kid has charms of his own, Harv. I trained him myself. If I tell Owen to turn off the switch, Jack's light goes out, Harv. Now if there's nothing else, I've made plans to go hurt somebody."

"At the warehouse?"

"Go have a drink, Harvey."

"I hope you're right about everything, Ian."

Back at the warehouse...

"Rick, have you never owned a dog? You give him the biscuit after he rolls over, not before. It is used a reward for accomplishing a requested task."

"Ah, you don't know shit Sven."

Leon, who has now reached his biscuit limit, walks over and lies down on Mr. Singh's feet, hoping he can get some relief from "training day." Mr. Singh pushes him away with his feet only to have Leon crawl back and resume his favourite spot.

Mr. Singh is sitting at the picnic table. He is reading Sven's collection of the Arlington daily newspapers. He has also been sneaking the occasional glimpse at the dog training activities. He admonishes Rick and Sven for allowing Leon to be in the warehouse in the first place.

"Have you read these articles, Sven?"

"We all have, Mr. Singh, why?"

"I think Mr. Jack is not going to be too pleased about you having a dog in here. Did you forget how he left the compound? I think we have something very bad coming. I just think everyone should start acting a little more professional."

Sven says, "I agree with you entirely, Mr. Singh, but with risk comes reward. We will all make more on this three-to-four week job than we have in the past two years in our chosen fields. I have completed everything on Harvey's list, as I know you have. So why don't we all agree to just wait for Jack and then we'll turn on our serious hats. Okay, Mr. Singh?"

Rick also jumps in. "We're just bored, Mr. Singh. If Leon provides us with a little distraction for a while, so be it. You just need to chill a little, dude."

"Don't call me dude, Rick. I make all of your meals, remember?"

"Sorry, Mr. Singh, I didn't mean any disrespect. Fuck, I just wish Jack would show up. And where the hell is Ian all the time?"

"Ian is a very busy man, Rick. And another thing, when this job is complete, what are you going to do about this dog? Just dump Leon back in the field again?"

"I don't know, man. I was up all night—I'm going to bed. I'll take Leon out to be with Carl if that make you happy. Thanks again for breakfast, Mr. Singh."

"I will take him out, Rick. He needs some water after all of those biscuits."

"Thanks, Mr. Singh."

Mr. Singh walks to the kitchen and without any prompting, Leon follows him. Mr. Singh reaches into the fridge and pulls out a small piece of cooked barbecue beef rib. He looks around to make sure that no one is watching, then he bends down and physically rolls Leon over before handing him the morsel. He then stands back up and says, "Roll over, Leon." Leon rolls over on cue and receives another treat and some water.

As Mr. Singh is walking Leon out to the gatehouse, the warehouse loudspeaker goes off. Sven has it hooked it up to the security headset, so if there's any activity outside, everyone inside will know.

Carl can be heard throughout the warehouse, saying, "We got a car coming, guys, and I don't recognize it."

Somewhere in Arizona…

Jack, wanting to get some serious miles in early, has made it all the way to the Arizona border. He spots a roadside dive, and he decides to pull over and get something to eat and gas up the car.

"Owen, wake up. Time to eat."

"Look at this place, Jack. It's jammers."

"I don't want to wait for an hour, so you hit the head and I'll order us something to go. I want to be back on the road in ten minutes."

Jack orders the quickest thing on the menu and the men are soon back on the road, eating burgers, fries and sipping on vanilla shakes.

"Don't spill anything, kid. If Roger saw us doing this he would kill us."

"What do ya think this car goes for, Jack?"

"Roger said some asshole on the Vegas strip offered him seventy grand on the spot. Obviously, he told him to fuck off."

"So, Jack … Debra probably has a boyfriend, right?"

"Don't take offence to this, kid, but talking about my daughter after you and Ivanna did the deed back in Uruguay… not going to happen."

"You're talking like a Muppet now, Jack. I ain't going to lay with no eejit."

"Look who's the Muppet now, kid. Whatever we say about that woman, there's no denying she was hot."

"Sexy, yes, but how many hats would a guy have to wear to hit that?"

"Did you snog my Debra last night, Owen?"

"No, I did not kiss Debra last night. I never touched her. And the

Irish slang is becoming some dry shite, Jack."

"Yeah, it's getting boring."

"Are we planning on a stopover tonight?"

"If you had a licence I would say no, but I'm going to need a few hours' sleep tonight. I don't want to roll up to Arlington and need a fucking nap as soon as I get there."

"Why are we driving at all, Jack? You really haven't told me anything, you know."

"You just enjoy the ride, kid. All I'll say is that I'm hoping the car is going to be a gift for a friend."

Back at the warehouse …

Carl is still talking on the headset.

"The fucking car stopped, guys. I need someone out here with a gun—I left mine in my room." Carl now screams over the intercom, "Wake the fuck up, Rick, and get out here!"

After a brief moment, Carl relays over the mic, "Everyone can stand down, it's just Bricks and Stryker. They rolled in on a rental car. I wish someone would have fucking told me they were coming. Rick, get the fuck out here and help me deal with this."

Rick, who was abruptly awoken from some serious REM sleep, comes running out in his underwear and is holding a sawed-off shotgun along the side of his leg.

Bricks steps out of the vehicle and stands at the locked front gate. Stryker is still sitting in the passenger seat.

Once Carl see's Rick approach, he tells Leon to stay in the shack and joins Rick at the gate.

As soon as Bricks sees Rick, he starts laughing out loud. So hard that Stryker steps out to see what the fuss is about. Both men are now laughing and can barely contain themselves.

"What the fuck, Rick? Look at your fucking arm, man. We should drive you right to the hospital. Carl, what the fuck is wrong with you, man?"

Carl looks at Rick's arm, and he is now as shocked as Bricks. He had no idea it had swollen up so grotesquely. They actually haven't exchanged punches for the night shift for a couple of days now.

"You two idiots gotta go back to arm wrestling or stop using baseball bats."

"I'm fine. Mind your fucking business. Nobody told us you two assholes were coming. I gotta call Ian before I can let you in, Bricks."

"Fuck that, Rick. Get Jack out here now."

"He's not here."

"Well, where the fuck is he? We were told this was Jack's deal or we wouldn't have come at all."

"Rick, hand me the pig splitter, get some fucking pants on and then get Ian on the line. And make it quick—I don't want to have to shoot these two."

Carl raises the shotgun and aims it directly at Bricks' chest and says, "Until I'm sure you two are supposed to be here, this is where we will all stand. Why were we not told you were coming, Bricks?"

"I don't know, man. We picked up the details on the bulletin board and here we are."

"Who was the postee?"

"Fucking Harvey himself, man. We picked it up three days ago so here we are. So put the fucking shotgun down, Carl, or you and I are going to have a real problem."

Within a couple of minutes, Ian pulls up to the warehouse for the first time today. He was hoping to get in on Mr. Singh's porterhouse steak dinner. Ian spots what's happening off in the distance and is now wishing he had just stayed at the hotel and ordered room service.

Ian slows the vehicle down and takes a long, hard look at the situation unfolding fifty feet ahead of him. Recognizing all of the characters involved and the fact that nobody is lying dead on the ground, he reluctantly decides to drive ahead.

Ian pulls up behind Bricks' car and yells out, "Open the gate, Carl, show them where to park and let's get this fucking street cleared."

The two cars enter the grounds and park at the back.

Mr. Singh is outside manning the grill. He spots Bricks and Stryker and he quickly stops what he is doing. He makes a beeline into the warehouse to the cupboard where he keeps his cleaning supplies.

Mr. Singh grabs his own 9 mm and heads back out as quickly as he came. He leaves the warehouse with his revolver cocked and, with no pretentious false illusion, he aims it squarely at Bricks' head. He is planning to shoot Bricks dead.

With only a half second to spare, Ian steps in front of Bricks and pulls out his own revolver. He aims it at Mr. Singh's head.

"Lower your gun, Mr. Singh. They were invited here."

Ignoring Ian's plea, Mr. Singh moves his body, trying to get a shot at Bricks without hitting Ian. By now Stryker has slipped behind the car and starts yelling, "What the fuck, Cookie? We're not armed. You can't shoot someone if they're unarmed, you asshole."

Mr. Singh then focuses his attention on the hiding Stryker and starts moving toward him. Ian moves in on Mr. Singh and, holding his gun next to Mr. Singh's ear, says, "Enough Mr. Singh. Look, your steaks are burning. You two go inside, now!"

Bricks and Stryker quickly enter the warehouse. Mr. Singh lowers his gun and starts turning the steaks over.

"How long till dinner, Mr. Singh?"

"It's ready now, Ian."

Ian calls Mr. Singh over and puts his arm around him.

"What are they doing here, Mr. Malcolmson? They were going to kill Mr. Jack back in Argentina."

"Relax, Mr. Singh. Jack is the one who requested them for this job. Everything is fine, I promise you. Okay?"

"If you say so Mr. Malcolmson."

"Give me your gun, Mr. Singh. I have a quick call to make. Please feed the guys and I'll catch up. Are we good?"

"If you tell me they are here because Mr. Jack wanted them to be here, then I guess I should not kill them. Unless Mr. Jack changes his mind, then I will kill them both."

"That's right, Mr. Singh. But Jack won't be here until tomorrow. So you will have to wait until tomorrow to ask him. Are we in agreement?"

"No, I'm sorry, Mr. Malcolmson, I'm afraid we are not in agreement. Mr. Jack gave me his private phone number and he said if I ever need anything, I can call him. I think this is the kind of situation that he was thinking about when he gave me his private number. So I am going to call him now and ask him if I can kill Mr. Bricks and Mr. Stryker."

Ian is now frustrated to no end. He is partially amused and angry at the same time.

He is doing his best to refrain from just shooting Cookie in the head and being done with it. But he really likes the dude and not just because of his amazing meals.

"Listen, Mr. Singh. Jack is on his way here and he is driving. You just have to believe me when I say that Jack asked for these two assholes to be here. I don't like them, either. Do you really want to phone Jack while he's driving? What if he crashes the car trying to talk to you?"

"Okay, Mr. Malcomson, but let me tell you something. I may be from India and maybe I'm just a cook here, and maybe I am loyal to a fault ... but they did not start calling me Mr. Singh at seven years old for nothing, do *you* hear me, Sir?"

Ian reaches into his jacket and pulls out his wallet. He flips through a few cards and hands Mr. Singh a blank business card with a single phone number on it.

"Well said, Mr. Singh, well said ... now you have another true friend. Let's go eat together, my call can wait."

Mr. Singh starts loading steak onto plates for dinner.

Bricks and Stryker are sitting at the picnic table, and they are totally fucking pissed off about the two separate, less-than-welcoming greetings they received upon their arrival.

Ian walks over to them.

"Sorry about that, guys."

"That fucking guy is crazy, Ian. Where's Jack's Scotch? I need a drink."

"Sorry again, men. This is another dry operation."

"And I'm sorry too, Ian, but after I enjoy that dick's delicious porterhouse, Mr. Singh is going to sleep."

"Then you can just leave now the same way you came in, Mr. Palmer. Mr. Walker, that goes for you, too, if you don't just relax."

Bricks replies, "We're good, Ian. Just a little startling to have to face that as soon as we get here, don't you think?"

"Can you at least tell us why Jack isn't here yet?"

"All I know is that we are expecting him sometime tomorrow afternoon. Then we can get on with this mission, gentlemen."

The men all sit down to eat. Rick has decided to stay up for dinner and Ian told Carl to come in and eat as well. Carl leaves Leon in the security shack alone on guard duty.

As usual, Mr. Singh is the last to fill his plate. He purposely sits alone at the second picnic table, pretending to read the newspapers in order to have nothing to do with Bricks and Stryker.

Stryker, who still wishes he could shoot the man if he only had a gun with him, is menacingly eyeballing Mr. Singh. As he shovels down his ten-ounce medium rare porterhouse, he says, "The meat is tough, Cookie."

Positive Mr. Singh is going to go get his gun again, Ian quickly jumps up from the table and basically starts pleading for the men to keep it together until Jack arrives. Then and only then, if they all want to kill each other, they can.

The guys in the group all have a modicum of knowledge regarding just who Ian Malcolmson is, and they're feeling a little embarrassed about forcing his plea. More important, they're feeling a bit uneasy about their own mortality. What if Ian should decide he has had enough of this shit and takes matters into his own hands?

Everyone but Mr. Singh, of course.

Right after Ian's admonishment of the men, Mr. Singh pulls Ian's personal business card out of his pocket and slowly raises it to his chin so Stryker can see it. With a wry "What are you going to do now, asshole?" look, he ever so slowly returns it to the top pocket of his shirt, keeping his eyes trained on Stryker the whole time.

Stryker doesn't have a clue as to what any of that fucking means, so he just returns to finishing his meal.

Rick tries to change the mood. "Do you think Jack will let us go to six flags one day?"

Bricks replies, "You need to go to the hospital, Rick. Ian, have you seen this guy's shoulder?"

"Let me see it, please, Rick."

"I'm fine, boss, don't worry about it."

Carl, who is sitting next to Rick, lifts up his friend's shirt to reveal a one-inch-thick blood boil that is about three inches wide and three inches long. It's the colour of a rainbow.

Ian says, "Nobody is going to the hospital, Mr. Walker."

"If you got Ivanna showing up, too, she can take care of it."

Ian ignores Bricks' last comment and says, "Mr. Singh, after everyone helps clean up, boil some water please and I will pop Rick's boil myself. I take it we are fully medically equipped."

Sven speaks up. "Yes, Sir. The containment room is fully equipped."

"Okay, Sven, do you know what we will need?"

"I think I do, yes."

"All right, men, in half an hour we are going to take care of a blood boil."

Sven asks, "Should we do it on the table in the containment room, Sir?"

"I'm not going in there, kid. We'll do it right here on the picnic table. You okay with that, Rick?"

"Fine by me. I'm not going in that room, either."

"Mr. Walker, Mr. Palmer, may I speak to you for a moment please?

I take it you gentlemen came here unarmed and that is why Mr. Singh is still alive to present us with such a lovely meal this evening?"

"Just our clothes, boss."

"Where did you arrive from?"

"Europe, Sir."

"And you saw the bulletin posted by Harvey."

"Yes, Sir."

"Good then, everything you will need is in sleeping pod four. Make up your own kits after you help with dishes. Let's get going, gentlemen."

Ian who has personally dealt with his share of battlefield injuries, preps Rick for his treatment. Once the procedure is complete, he pumps him with antibiotics and sends him to bed.

He looks at Carl. "Now let's see what you've got hiding under that shirt."

Carl lifts up his shirt and, although he's in pretty bad shape, he doesn't require Ian's medical services tonight.

"You and Rick are done with your game. Is that understood, Carl?"

"Yes, Sir, and I'm sorry. I had no idea it got that bad."

Ian calls the group together for the last time tonight.

"All right, gentlemen, come tomorrow, you can knock it off with the 'Sir' and refer to me as Ian or Mr. Malcomson, whatever you're most comfortable with. And unless he has directed you otherwise, you will refer to Jack as Sergeant.

"I should not have to remind any of you that this is a military operation, gentlemen. The Ambassador will be expecting nothing less of each and every one of you. Have I made myself clear?"

With no comments coming forward, Ian finishes. "Good then, we're going to let Rick sleep tonight. Carl, grab some steak pieces for Leon and please take your post. I'm heading back to the hotel. I will see you all in the morning."

Ian stops to talk to Mr. Singh before he leaves.

Mr. Singh is about to put a beef brisket on the grill for Jack's return tomorrow and he wants to let it slow cook for a good fifteen hours.

"Mr. Singh, are you going to be okay tonight?"

"Jack will be here tomorrow. I will be fine, thank you."

"I'm sorry if I sounded disrespectful earlier. That certainly was not my intention. But please listen to me now. Bricks and Stryker are setting up their kits as we speak. They won't be unarmed anymore, do you understand me?"

Mr. Singh takes out Ian's business card and smiles.

"Jack requested my number, too, Mr. Malcolmson. In case *he* ever needs *me*. Maybe when this is over, I will do the same for you."

"I hope you find me worthy, Mr. Singh. Good night."

Back in Israel...

Earlier in the day, Harvey had wrapped up his morning meeting with the Ambassador and Jack's estate developers. He asked the Ambassador for the afternoon off, citing stomach issues, and was granted some personal leave.

Harvey, feeling the weight of the world upon him, is hoping that a drive out to his favourite café in Jerusalem will cheer him up.

One of the most educated lawyers in all of the world is now sitting alone at the Quarter Café in the Jewish Quarter, with a view overlooking the Western Wall.

Harvey is passively sampling his favourite dish, the "*Che Bella Scoporta*," which includes a divine carrot salad, latkes and falafel.

The Quarter Café is a popular lunch-time spot for the elite lawyers of Israel. Harvey is watching all of the top players enacting their unscrupulous meet and greet. They are exchanging business cards and sending bottles of wine to each other's tables.

Harvey thinks to himself, "What a group of pretentious assholes." The reality is Harvey would do anything to be able to go back in time and be a part of their exclusive class. Anywhere else in the world, Harvey would be any company's top lawyer. If he wanted, he could even be one of the most prestigious law professors in the world.

But, regrettably, as a result of working with the Ambassador all of these years, Harvey's extraordinary body of work has gone all but unnoticed by his peers. He works under a constant shroud of secrecy, which is always unscrupulously demanded and assured.

Harvey feels that he has become the chief solicitor of a rudderless dingy. What's worse is he has now been asked to just sit back and watch, as a billion dollar empire is turned over to a US Navy SEAL.

Harvey pays his bill and decides he's going to take a walk toward the Western Wall when his phone rings.

"Hello, Harvey."

"Hi, Ian. How are you doing?"

"I'm okay, Harv…you okay?"

"I'm fine, Ian. I just had lunch in Jerusalem and I was about to go for a walk."

"Find a quiet place to sit down, Harvey, we got a problem."

"Hang on, my car's right here…okay, Ian, what does Jack want now?"

"It's not Jack this time, Harvey. I have a simple question for you and it is imperative that you are completely honest with me right now."

"Just get to it, Ian. Today is not a good day for this shit, all right?"

"I'm sorry to hear that, Harvey, I really am. There could be lives at stake here, so I need you to be completely honest with me."

"I don't know what you're talking about, but you have my undivided attention."

"When Jack requested Mr. Walker and Mr. Palmer for the Arlington job, what did you do?"

"What I always do, Ian. I put out the bulletin to find them and for them to get their asses to Arlington—Oh, fuck…I am so sorry, Ian."

"You didn't delete the post, did you, Harvey?"

"No, I'm so sorry, Ian. With this Jack shit going on, it completely slipped my mind. Please don't tell me that they actually tried to contact you?"

"No, better than that, I just had Mr. Singh's barbecue porterhouse steaks with them right here at the warehouse, Harvey."

There is a drawn-out silence while Harvey now ponders his own mortality. Which is exactly what Ian has been doing since arriving at the warehouse several hours ago—pondering Harvey's mortality.

Harvey is caught up in a moment of miscalculation—that being, Ian is far away in Arlington, Texas, and he is safely in Jerusalem—so he responds, "So what's the problem, Ian? This is perfect. Just kill them there."

"Before I hang up on you, Harvey, answer me one more question. Ivanna. Did you post a bulletin for her, as well?"

"No, Ian, I swear I didn't. Jack said absolutely no Ivanna for this job. And anyway, her family's connection to the mob was confirmed, so were not…."

Ian hangs up the phone while Harvey is in mid-sentence.

Chapter 16

TEXAS FINEST

Approaching El Paso, Texas…

"We'll be pulling over for the night at the next stop, Owen."

"Where 'bouts are we, Jack?"

"We're on the New Mexico-Texas border. We got El Paso, Texas, just ahead. You ever been to Texas, Owen?"

"I've never been to the US before, Jack."

"Well, kid, they say in Texas everything is big."

"Does that include the Shirlies, too, Jack?"

"No, Owen, the women are fine here, but you're just going to have to enjoy them from afar. We'll eat, have a few drinks, then we're back on the road at 0400."

"Good. After this fucking drive I could use a drink, or ten."

Jack and Owen arrive on the outskirts of El Paso and stop at the Mexican Grill and Cantina, a pretty decent border town restaurant.

Jack has a calculable amount of Scotch. Just enough to maintain his wits and assure he'll be able to get some much-needed sleep.

Owen, on the other hand, has his fill of pints. Jack figures Owen should also try some of the local tequila. After a dozen pints and six shots of tequila, Jack figures Owen is ready for bed.

Jack helps Owen into the local Motel 6 and throws him on the bed. He takes off the kid's shoes and pulls a blanket over him.

Jack never calls Margaret while on a job, but had promised her he would, in light of the recent events. It's 9:00 p.m. in Orange County so he dials her up.

"Hello, dear."

"Hi, Jack. Are you safe? Where did you end up at tonight?"

"Everything is good. We're at the Motel 6 on the El Paso border."

"How is Owen?"

"Owen is wasted, hon."

"What is he?"

"He's asleep, hon. He's fine."

"I picked up your contract, Jack. Everything is in there and it's all signed. You're the top dog now, Jack. How do you feel about that?"

"I'm working, hon, and I'm going to sleep now. I'll call you when we get to Arlington and that will be it until the job is done, okay? How's Debra?"

"Your daughter is quite enamored with that young man, Jack. They stayed up and talked all night."

"They must have gotten up again after I went to bed. I was wondering why he slept for eight hours in the car. Gotta go, Marg. Love you."

Jack hangs up the phone and is sitting on the edge of the bed watching Owen sleep. He's thinking about what Marg just said and is now wondering if his whole plan involving Owen was a mistake.

Jack figures he had better turn Owen onto his side in case he starts to puke. He looks over at Owen and says quietly, "You puke, kid, you're cleaning it up."

Jack starts getting ready for bed. He checks that the locks are all secure, makes sure the coffee pot is full and plugged in, and arranges the towels in the bathroom. Then he makes sure the adjacent room door in their room is locked, the drapes are drawn and the alarm is set.

Jack wakes up at 3:50 a.m., showers, dresses and packs. Now he just has to get Owen into the bathroom and then get him strapped down in the backseat.

"Owen, time to get up. Go take a piss and you can go back to sleep in the backseat."

"I'm really tired, Jack. I think I'm still drunk."

"I know, kid, but we gotta get going."

"What the fuck are you wearing, Jack? Where did you get that hat?"

"Don't worry about it, kid, let's go."

Within five minutes, Jack and Owen are back on the road for the last eight-hour leg of their journey.

Two hours into their drive, and just as Jack had planned for, there is a Texas Ranger behind them and the Prowler's lights are flashing.

"Owen, wake up … we got Rangers behind us."

Jack tries a little bit louder this time. "Owen, wake the fuck up!"

"Oh, what … what's that, Jack? What the fuck, Jack … I got fucking handcuffs on … What the fuck, Jack?"

"Shut up, kid, I put them on the front for ya. We got a couple of Rangers about to pull us over. Keep your mouth shut and act like you're a criminal. A criminal. Ain't that funny, kid?"

"I really think I'm gonna puke, Jack."

"Good, go ahead if you have to, but just wait till I stop the damn car."

Jack is watching the Prowler in the rearview mirror and begins to slowly pull over. He spots a side farm road and pulls in a couple of hundred feet. He wants to be out view of any passing highway traffic.

Jack then deliberately slams on the brakes, sending Owen hard into the back of the front seat.

"Oh, fuck, it's coming, Jack."

"Good stuff, kid, right on time. Let's get you outta there."

Jack jumps out of the front seat and with his hands in the air, he gestures to the approaching Prowler that he is going to the backseat. He grabs the handcuffed Owen and carries him to the ditch, where Owen—right on cue—starts puking his guts out.

The Rangers exit the Prowler with their guns drawn and are not happy with what they are seeing. Jack drove far too long before coming to a complete stop, and they are aware they are now out of sight from local traffic and any passing backup. Jack also left the vehicle before being instructed to do so. And now he's got a guy puking in the ditch, wearing handcuffs, no less.

The Rangers are on Jack in seconds and notice he is wearing a US Marshals jacket and US Marshals baseball style cap. Still not impressed, they ask Jack to get away from Owen and raise his hands.

Jack stands away from Owen and starts reaching for his ID inside his weathered nylon jacket. Jack is also wearing a police-issued bulletproof vest which immediately catches the eye of the older, more experienced Ranger, Ranger Lopez.

"I said, get your hands up, Marshal! I'm not going to ask you again. Fields, get his ID. You so much as move a finger, Marshal, I will shoot you dead where you stand."

Jack remains still while the younger officer takes his ID. The officer takes notice of Jack's 9 mm, tucked in his shoulder strap.

"He's got a shoulder strap on, Sergeant."

"Relax guys, we're on the same team. US Marshal Walker at your service."

"Didn't they teach you how to come to a compliance stop in the academy, Mr. Walker?"

"The punk's been puking for two hours now and I didn't want to make a scene by the highway, gentlemen."

"Why is he cuffed at the front, Marshal?"

"You got a problem with your hearing, Sergeant? The punk's a puker and I'm not going to mess up my sweet ride for this scum. Now, if you wouldn't mind, get that fucking gun out of my face before you start to piss me off."

Officer Fields is a Caucasian rookie who has been on the job all of nine months. He works out of a predominantly Hispanic local district and has been waiting for the opportunity to show his sergeant he's got the balls for the job.

"Listen, asshole, until we run you both, my sergeant is going to keep that gun on you."

Owen, having expelled his stomach contents and still feeling a bit drunk, says, "Sheriff Walker, do you know these guys? They got your nickname dead on."

Jack moves over to Owen and says, "Shut the fuck up, you rapist scum, or do you want another kick in the head?"

"Is that right, boy? You a rapist?" Fields asks.

Jack intervenes. "Listen, fellas, I got a 10-16 yesterday to pick up this 261 asshole from Tucson and take him to Dallas."

"Where's your paperwork, Marshal?"

"Let's just run them both, Sarge."

Jack tries one last attempt to not have their IDs run.

"For the last fucking time, all I was told was this was a 10-36, which we all know means confidential. The most I could get out of the kid was that he was diddling some chick back in Dallas and apparently her daddy has some heavy political weight. The kid's been hiding in Tucson and after snatching him up, I'm taking him back. So if you don't mind, I'm getting tired of this shit. I'm going to pick up my prisoner and then I will be on my way."

"After we run you both, Marshal, you'll be free to carry on."

"Fuck this." Jack moves forward to help Owen to his feet and, as he turns, he pulls out his revolver and Owen quickly grabs his .38 from his own ankle holster.

In a split life-or-death decision, Rookie Agent Fields manages to get off two squawks into his hand mic, "Code 2, Code 2," signifying "Officer in need of urgent assistance." Jack now has his 9 mm up against Fields' forehead, as he relieves him of his sidearm.

Owen makes his way over and jams his .38 hard in the back of Sergeant Lopez's head. Lopez, undeterred by Owen's gun, still has his police-issued 9 mm squarely pointed at Jack's head.

Completely unfazed that the sergeant's gun is now pointed at him, Jack quickly checks his watch.

"Officer Fields, in sixty-seven more seconds you are going to call in a Code 4 followed by a 10-15. And if you fail to do so, well, at least it's a beautiful morning…

Code 4 means no further assistance is needed and 10-15 indicates that the prisoner is in custody. These are but a few of the trivial things Jack has read and remembered over the years. For no apparent reason other than self-interest and maybe one day, self-preservation.

Sixty-seven seconds later Officer Fields places the call. "Code 4, I say again, Code 4 … we are 10-15, we are 10-15."

Jack asks the men to turn off their radios. Owen goes ahead and rips off the sergeant's radio. Lopez tells Fields to turn his off, and he complies.

"You know, Marshal, if they call back for a confirmation on the Code 4 and don't get a reply, they're going to be on their way here."

"Sergeant, we both know that they're on their way, regardless, because Officer Fields called in the Code 2. The only thing that can save us now is the clock, gentlemen."

Back in Israel …

The Ambassador is sitting in his office and thinking about taking a late afternoon nap. He's watching Noah and Peter pick up some loose leaves that he just sent them out to clear, when his phone rings.

"Harvey is at the gate, Mr. Ambassador."

"Well, send him in, send him in."

The Ambassador places a call.

"Miss Schuster, Harvey is coming up. Would you please make us an appropriate snack? Thank you, dear."

The Ambassador knocks on his window and waves his leaf pickers back to his office.

"Come in, Harvey. I'm surprised to see you're back so soon. Are you feeling any better?"

"Yes, thank you, Wilhelm."

"You look perplexed."

"I have something for you to read, Wilhelm."

"Certainly, Harvey. I'll just put my glasses on then we will look at it together, shall we?"

Joshua and Peter arrive back at the office and take their seats in the corner.

"Did you wash your hands, gentlemen?"

"No, Sir."

"Go, wash them. Close the door on your way out and you can sit outside when you get back. I should not be too long."

"I'm feeling *al ha'panim* today, Harvey. If you don't mind, I am going to read this on the couch. Come, sit behind my desk."

Harvey hands a sealed letter to the Ambassador. "Would you like me to open it for you, Sir?"

"Thank you, yes."

Harvey opens the letter and turns on a light over the Ambassador's head.

"I believe this is the shortest resignation letter I have ever read, Harvey." The Ambassador reads aloud, "After the American Conference, I regret to inform you that I resign."

"That's all I could bring myself to write, Wilhelm. You are already well aware of my concerns."

Just then there is a quick knock at the door and Miss Schuster brings in a tray of snacks as requested by the Ambassador.

"Thank you, Miss Schuster. And what did you bring us to sample this evening?"

"I have some cold milk for you, Sir, tea for Harvey, if he would like, and some cold blintzes and sable cookies."

"Are those the French butter cookies, Miss Schuster?"

"Yes, Sir."

"Okay, thank you, dear. We will help ourselves."

"Harvey, come, help yourself."

"I'm not hungry or thirsty, Sir."

"Have a blintz, they are delicious cold."

"No, thank you, Sir. In fact, I believe I will let you have your snack in peace and I will be on my way."

"Nonsense, Harvey. You are at least going to give me the opportunity to form a reply to this unexpected letter, are you not?"

The Ambassador loads a small plate with food and begins sampling Miss Schuster's delicacies.

"You know she makes these from scratch, don't you, Harvey."

"Yes, Sir, I do know that. If you could start, please."

"Harvey, please … do we dine like those Palestinian animals now?"

"Are you okay, Sir? In all of our years together you have never spoken of them in those terms."

"That is the issue here, my good friend. And you just said it yourself—all of our years together."

"The reason I do not decry the Palestinian people is because they are just looking for a homeland, the same as our people."

"The bombings, the shootings, the terror they inflict on us on a daily basis … what is that?"

"Misplaced aggression, son."

Harvey has been watching the Ambassador delve into Miss Schuster's snacks. He's had six items already and does not appear to be slowing down.

"Wilhelm, are you okay? Should you really be eating so much?"

Just then the Ambassador starts violently coughing. He expels the remaining food in his mouth and reaches for his hanky, then he begins coughing up large pools of bloody phlegm.

He motions for Harvey to grab him some Kleenex off of his desk.

As he reaches for the Kleenex, Harvey sees that the garbage can next to the Ambassador's desk is full of blood-soaked napkins, monogramed hankies and Kleenex.

"I'm calling your doctor right now, Wilhelm."

"No, he went for a nap an hour ago."

"You need him here, Sir."

"He's upstairs sleeping, Armen."

"I'm Harvey, Sir, Jack is not here."

"Yes, yes, just give me a minute and we will continue."

Harvey steps outside and asks Joshua and Peter to take the Ambassador up to his bed. They get him into bed while Harvey wakes up Dr. Jacobie, the Ambassador's personal physician.

After an hour, the Ambassador is asleep and resting peacefully.

"I gave him something to help him sleep, Harvey. I'll sit with him for a bit."

"Thanks, Doc. Joshua, Peter—I want you two on shifts now. I do not want him left alone, especially at night." Harvey turns to the doctor. "Can I talk to you for a minute, Doc?"

"Three months tops, Harvey. The cancer has spread everywhere. All we can do now is just try to keep him as comfortable as we possibly can."

"He wants to go to Arlington in a few days."

"I know, Harvey, and he will be going and I will be going with him."

"You're a doctor for Christ's sake. How can you let him go?"

"It is his last request in life, Harvey, and I am going to do everything in my power to honour it. He may sleep for some time now, if you want to come back tomorrow."

Harvey heads back down to the Ambassador's office to find Miss Schuster cleaning up the bloody mess.

"Thank you, Miss Schuster. Is Jack's room made up? I think I'll stay here tonight."

"Of course, Sir. I will just turn the blankets for you."

"No, no, please. I will look after it myself. Thank you again."

As Miss Schuster is leaving with her tray cart, Harvey calls her back. "One more minute please, Miss Schuster. I would like to talk to you, if you don't mind?"

"Yes, Mr. Blumberg."

"I know we are not to talk about the Ambassador and, I assure you, anything you tell me will be kept in the strictest of confidence. I would like to know how long he has been coughing up blood like this, and his food intake ... is that normal now?"

"I'm sorry, Sir. You know I can't discuss any of this with you. I will not betray the Ambassador's trust. I will quit and walk out right now before I will say anything. I'm sorry."

"I know, I know. I'm sorry I even put you in that position, Miss Schuster. Please, proceed."

"Thank you, Sir."

Harvey searches for the dusty TV remote and pours himself a tall glass of Scotch. He is left staring at his resignation letter still sitting on the Ambassador's desk.

Back on the I-10 just two hours past El Paso, Texas...

Jack checks his watch and says, "Officer Fields, how far is your shop?"

"Twenty-two minutes from here."

"Okay, at this hour, I expect you two are the only ones out in this district for miles, so we have twenty-two minutes to resolve our little conflict here, gentlemen."

Owen still feeling like shit and wanting Jack to just end this says, "He said all clear, Marshal. What's the issue?"

"Please be quite, Liam. The good sergeant here knows that anytime a Code 2 is sent, regardless of any subsequent messages, they got cruisers rolling right now... Isn't that right, Sergeant?"

"You got twenty-one minutes, Marshal"

"Fuck, Marshal. What are we going to do?"

"Open your mouth again, Liam, and I will shoot you myself."

"That's a good idea, Marshal. Save my guys a couple of bullets when they get here. We both know you're not leaving this ditch alive, *Marshal*."

"Sergeant, if you feel more comfortable, you can keep that gun pointed at my head and Liam is going to move his into Officer Fields' ear. With that said, I have to step back and make a call so that we can all possibly walk away from this today."

"That's going to be one hell of a call...nineteen minutes, Marshal."

"One question first, Sergeant, who is your boss's boss?"

"Captain Velazquez, Marshal."

"Thank you, Sergeant, and if you heard him on my phone, would you be able to recognize his voice?"

"I better, Marshal, he's my fucking brother-in law."

"Okay, gentlemen, if you would all give me a moment, I have a call to make."

Jack places a call to the Ambassador's emergency line, knowing it is monitored twenty-four seven. The problem is, it is still synced to the Ambassador's office, and the now drunk Harvey is sitting back and amusedly watching it ring.

When the call hits ten rings, the number is automatically transferred to Harvey's private line.

Harvey pulls out his cell and puts it on the Ambassador's desk. He listens to it ring another ten times. The call is then transferred back to the Ambassador's desk and allowed to go through yet another ten-ring cycle.

Jack hangs up the phone.

"Sixteen minutes, Marshal."

Jack hangs up and is now thinking about how a Texas jail is going to feel. He doesn't make any eye contact with Owen. He is apprehensive that in Owen's state, any sort of eye signal he makes could be misinterpreted, resulting in a bullet to Officer Fields' head.

Back in the Ambassador's office...

Harvey, feeling quite willfully content, polishes off his Scotch and is deciding if he is going to have a nap, as well. Just then, Joshua enters the room with his gun squarely pointed at Harvey's chest.

"Phone him back now, Harvey! You have one second to start dialing or I will shoot you."

"You've been watching me?"

"Right fucking now, Harvey, please. Do not make me do this."

Peter also enters the room with his gun drawn and says the same thing. "Call him back now, Harvey!"

Having no patience for drunks, Joshua walks over and throttles the butt of his gun against Harvey's forehead. He makes a small gash, and blood is now flowing freely down Harvey's face.

Harvey having being physically altered from his mood of satisfied drunken insurrection, has probably the shortest epiphany known to man. With his cut bleeding quite profusely, he picks up the phone and calls Jack back. Joshua grabs a couple of hankies and starts attending to the wound.

"Jack, sorry there, buddy...I was just away from the phone for a minute. What can I do for you?"

Peter walks over and puts the phone on speaker.

"Harvey, I need you to listen and listen carefully. I'm just outside of El Paso. I'm sitting here at the side of the road with a couple of Texas's finest, and I need a confirmation in eleven minutes, Harvey. Do you understand me?"

"Name, Jack?"

"Captain Velazquez of the Texas Highway Patrol, two hours from El Paso."

"Fuck, Jack, I'll just get the governor to call."

"Listen, asshole, the good sergeant needs to recognize his voice. You got ten minutes, Harvey."

Jack hangs up the phone and looks at his watch. He walks back to the men who are all now covered in sweat. The stress of holding a firearm to someone's head for the last fourteen minutes is taking its physical toll on Owen. Sergeant Lopez still has his gun pointed squarely at Jack's ever-moving head.

"Nine minutes, Marshal Walker."

"The call is coming, Lopez, so maybe you could stow that shit for now. You're not impressing anyone. What are you trying to do, Sergeant, teach the rookie how to die in a fucking ditch with dignity? And there are ten minutes left, asshole."

Jack's anxiety is starting to go through the roof. His primary concern is for Owen, hungover and sweaty and still holding a gun to Sergeant Lopez's head. He quickly comes up with an alternative plan.

"Okay, listen up. Until my call comes in or your guys get here first, why don't we all just lower our guns? We can still keep them in our hands, by our sides. Sergeant,

Liam is going to hand the kid back his gun but not until you start to lower yours. If your guys do roll up early, you don't want to be standing there with no gun, do you, kid?"

"How about it, Sarge? Let's just stand down and see if his call comes. The puker ain't looking so good, and I don't want him to accidentally shoot you, Sir."

Sergeant Lopez takes a hard look at the situation and he can feel Owen's hands are shaking along with the gun being jammed into his ear.

"Okay, Marshal, we will all lower our weapons on the count of two."

"Agreed. Are you ready, Liam?"

Owen and Sergeant Lopez lower their weapons to their sides and Officer Fields grabs his back from Owen's other hand. Jack then places his .38 back in his shoulder holster in hopes of demonstrating some level of conciliation.

"Marshal, do you really think this is a good idea? I don't trust these feckin peelers."

Officer Fields says, "Great. We got an Irish rapist to boot."

"I ain't no rapist, you feckin paddy eejit."

"What did this Irish piece of shit just call me, Sarge?"

"I don't know, kid, but it did not sound very flattering, did it, Marshal?"

"He called Officer Fields a fucking fag who looks like a scabby old woman."

"We gonna take that shit from him, Sarge?"

"Kid … in less than two minutes from now, the Marshal and myself will be involved in something a little more serious than name calling."

Jack's cell phone starts to ring.

"Harvey?"

"Listen up, Jack, and don't say anything. We couldn't locate the captain. I have the governor's assistant on the line with me now. Please hand the phone to the sergeant."

Jack hands his cell to Sergeant Lopez. "Yes, Sir…yes, Sir…I know, Sir…thank you, Sir…you too, Sir."

Sergeant Lopez hands the phone back to Jack. "Fields, put your gun away. We're leaving right now. Jack, my guy wants to talk to you, too."

Jack takes his cell from Sergeant Lopez.

"Yes, Sir…yes, Sir…I know, Sir…thank you, Sir…you too, Sir."

The governor's assistant concludes by saying to Jack, "Thank you for your great service to our country, Marshal. I am going to hang up now. I believe Harvey would like to speak to you, as well. You have yourself a good morning, Sir."

"Jack?"

"Yeah, it's me, Harvey. Hang on for a second, please."

Officer Fields puts his gun back in his holster and, without any provocation, he punches Owen in the jaw, knocking him two feet back into the puke-riddled ditch. He says, "That one's for Texas, bitch."

Sergeant Lopez says, "Fuck! Sorry, Marshal."

Sergeant Lopez and Officer Fields get back in their vehicle and are gone from sight within a minute.

Jack takes a seat on the ground and leans against the side of the car, leaving Owen to his own resolve. Owen promptly starts vomiting again.

"Sorry, Harvey, Owen slipped and fell."

"Uh...okay. Anyway, Jack, I hope you are satisfied."

"You have no idea, Harvey...thank you very much."

"So I guess we can forget about the Thailand incident once and for all?"

"Why, did something happen in Thailand, Harvey?"

"Thank you, Jack. I think you're going to be good now, but you and Owen should probably get out of the area as quick as you can. I've got you clear passage to Arlington—you shouldn't be stopped again. And, Jack? I need you to call me again when you're an hour away from the warehouse. We have a small development in Arlington, but Ian assures me it's nothing to worry about."

"Will do. Thanks again, Harvey."

"Get up, kid. We're leaving."

"Can you at least get these feckin shackles off me, Jack?"

Jack throws Owen the keys to the handcuffs and says, "Listen up, kid. There are some wet wipes and water in the trunk. Toss those clothes and wash up a bit. Put some clean clothes on and hop in the backseat and keep those cuffs next to you."

"What the fuck, Jack? We may have to go through this again?"

"Welcome to Texas, kid."

Back in the Ambassador's office...

"I'll go get the doc, Sir. You're gonna need a couple of stitches."

"Just leave it and get out."

"I can't do that, Sir."

"Who gave you the right to watch me, Joshua? You've been on his team, what, a week? You honestly think you have the right to say anything to me? You should both be out washing my fucking car right now."

"A lot happened while you were away this afternoon, Mr. Blumberg."

"Let me guess…you finally got your first period."

"I know you're upset about the Ambassador, Sir, and you've had a bit to drink. We are Mossad, Mr. Blumberg. We don't wash cars."

"Peter, go get the doc for Mr. Blumberg."

"You are going to need stitches, Sir."

"Fine, Joshua, and when the Ambassador hears that you attacked me for absolutely no reason, you're out…you're both out. You hear that, Peter? Now go get the fucking doc, Pete."

Realizing he's going to be up for a while, Harvey pours himself another double Scotch.

"Okay, Joshua, tell me. What was so important that I missed today?"

"Mr. Malcomson phoned earlier and spoke at length with the Ambassador, Sir."

"And how exactly would that be of any concern to you, Joshua? Your whole training is all about disciplined, discretionary observing and not listening, is that not correct?"

"Yes, Sir, that is correct, but on this occasion the Ambassador called us forward and he insisted we listen in. It was at the conclusion of the conversation between the Ambassador and Mr. MalComson. We were instructed by the Ambassador that, should you return today, we were to monitor your every movement."

"Ah, now I get it … Ian's making a play for the number two spot," "So tell me, Joshua, what was it that I had done to draw such attention to myself?"

"You failed to remove a bulletin, Sir. Mr. Bricks and Mr. Stryker are in Arlington right now and, frankly, the Ambassador needed them for other purposes to appease the Wiesenthal Center."

"I told Ian to just kill them there."

"Well, there it is then. I had some serious doubts as to Mr. Malcomson's claim, but now I have heard it for myself."

Peter and Dr. Jacobie enter the office and the doctor starts in immediately on Harvey's cut.

"How's the Ambo, Doc?"

"He looks better than you, Harvey. Was this really necessary, gentlemen?"

"Just stitch him up please, Dr. Jacobie."

"Peter, can you please go sit with the Ambassador until I'm done? He was starting to move around a bit. I believe he may wake up soon, and I would like someone with him when he does."

"You got it, Doc."

"Okay, Joshua, while the good doc is doing his stitching, you explain to me why it was I was being watched."

"It's simple, Sir. Ian knows you would never forget to remove a bulletin. Therefore he was able to convince the Ambassador that it was your intention to do whatever you could to sabotage the Arlington mission."

"That's preposterous, I would never do anything to prevent that dying, insane man from seeing his—" Harvey starts giggling but he quickly recovers "—misguided seventy-year-old revenge plot against an innocent man and his family come to fruition."

"Just how much have you had to drink, Harvey?"

"I'm just kidding, guys, of course I will do whatever I have to do to help the Ambassador wreak vengeance on the state of Texas."

"Enough, Harvey. We know Jack will be calling back in a couple of hours and you're going to be here when he does. In fact, Sir, make yourself comfortable, because until Jack is actually standing in the warehouse in Arlington, none of us are leaving this office."

Just as the doc finishes his last stitch, Peter and the Ambassador enter the office.

"Who's not going anywhere, Joshua?"

"Sir, should you be up?"

"Yes, yes, I needed to use the washroom and was worried about Jack. Have we heard from him?"

Dr. Jacobie helps the Ambassador to his side chair and covers him in a blanket.

"I spoke to him an hour ago, Sir," Harvey says. "He is six hours out of Arlington and will be calling me in a couple of hours. I just need to advise him about Bricks' and Stryker's arrival, Sir. Aside from that, all is well and on plan."

"Good, good, Harvey. What happened to your head?"

"I had a bit too much to drink, Sir, and I banged it on your curio."

"And the doc fixed you up."

"Yes, Sir, thank you for asking."

"Okay, I think I'll go back to bed. Harvey, please ensure the jet is fueled up and ready for flight at noon tomorrow. I know what Armen said, but I decided we are all going to Arlington tomorrow.

"Peter, can you see if Miss Schuster left out any of those blintzes and bring me up a couple? Oh, and, Harvey, you will not be required to come to Arlington with us. Good night, gentlemen."

The doc looks over to Peter and shakes his head "no" regarding the blintzes. Peter helps the Ambassador back up to bed.

Joshua continues in on Harvey. "Well, there you have it, Harvey. Once our plane is in the air tomorrow, my guess is you are done with this organization, regardless of your so-called resignation letter. And for the record, Harvey, Mr. Malcomson wants out. That was the main reason for his call today. Once Jack arrives in Arlington, Ian asked for—and the Ambassador granted—his request to leave the organization for good.

"So, you can sit there and keep getting drunker if you want, but we are in this room until Jack arrives in Arlington."

Two hours away from Arlington, Texas…

In spite of all the excitement four hours back, Owen was out like a light in the back seat within minutes and is just now waking up.

"Afternoon, kid. How's the head and jaw feeling?"

"You could see I was off balance, Jack. The bitch suckered me and he punches like a pussy, anyway. I can't even feel it"

"We're about two hours from Arlington, kid. We're gonna grab something to eat soon and then I gotta call Harvey back."

"You know he suckered me, right, Jack?"

"Yeah, I know, kid. By the way, the restaurant just ahead makes the best raw pig brain sandwich in Texas. The best part is you get a side bowl of its bile, which is lightly fried in its own blood and smothered in finely diced garlic and fried onions. I'm ordering that for sure."

"Nice try, Jack. I'm Irish, and we don't get hungover… but if you do, go ahead and order that shite. Let's just say Roger may not be too happy with his backseat, though."

"I told ya, kid, this ain't Roger's car no more. It's a gift for a friend."

Jack and Owen are now eyeballing each other through the rearview mirror. Jack is starting to feel the miles of driving behind him. He had his big adrenaline dump a few hours back and is starting to get a little restless with this kid in the backseat that he doesn't even really know.

With Arlington a couple of hours ahead, Jack is looking for some indication of just how much Ian told Owen about his hasty departure in Argentina. Owen only made the scene in Uruguay, and Jack's beginning to wonder just how much he can actually trust the kid.

"You got a friend in Texas, Marshal?"

"You can eighty-six the marshal crap, kid."

"Then lose the fucking cap, Marshal Walker."

"Fuck no, kid. This is a quality cap, Navy SEAL quality."

Owen, sensing Jack's mood has changed and not quite knowing why, tries to innocently change the subject.

"So, Jack, does that Debbie of yours have a boyfriend?"

Jack glares into the rearview mirror toward and is immediately looking for a place to pull over. He slams on the brakes and makes a hard right turn off the highway onto a side farm road.

He stops the car and swings open the back door. As he's reaching in to try and pull Owen out, Owen slides to the far end and hops out of the other door. Owen and Jack are now outside of the car on opposite sides of the back doors. They both start walking around the car.

"Come here, kid. I just want to talk to you."

"What the fuck, Jack? What did I say?"

"You think you're funny, you Irish prick. Come here!"

"Jack, what the fuck … stop … please."

"She's fucking dead, you prick."

"Who's fucking dead?"

"Debbie, you cunt."

"That's impossible, Jack, we just left Debra yesterday."

Jack stops the chase. He puts his hands over his face and slides down the side of the car onto the ground.

Owen walks over and tentatively sits down next to him.

"Jack, please, don't tell me something happened to Debra, please."

Jack puts his hand on Owen's knee and says, "She's fine, kid, just give me a minute."

Jack and Owen are now sitting quietly in the ditch of a farmer's field just two hours out of Arlington Texas.

After a long, unsettling duration of time, Owen starts moving his left leg. He is trying to feel if his gun is in his holster and not somewhere in the back of the car.

In Jack's mind, the long respite has been but a brief flashing moment.

"Jack?"

"Yeah, kid?"

"We gonna get going soon?"

"Yeah, kid."

Another fifteen minutes pass.

"Jack?"

"Yes, Owen?"

"I gotta take a leak."

"Okay, kid."

Owen gets up and relieves himself then returns to stand over Jack. He has managed to reposition his gun from his ankle to behind his waist without Jack's noticing.

"What do you say we hit the road, boss, and we'll get some food in ya. Some real food, that is, and not that shite you were talking about a while ago. What do ya say, big guy?"

"Sit down please, Owen."

Owen takes his seat back on the ground next to Jack, only now it is Owen who is quickly losing his patience.

"I see you moved your piece, Owen. You can pull it out if it will make you feel more comfortable."

"Nah, Jack, I'm good. It was just bothering my leg."

"You and I are going to have a chat, Owen, and if you are not completely honest with me, well ... I'm gonna leave you at the side of this shitty ditch."

Owen has had enough of Jack's dazed and confused bullshit. He stands back up and pulls out his revolver and is now cradling it in his hand.

"The fuck you are. This is no way to treat a friend, Jack, so you either pull your shit together or you'll be the one left in this shitty ditch."

Jack slowly stands up and starts dusting himself off while methodically stretching out his tired joints. He grabs a couple of bottles of water from the trunk and hands one over to Owen.

"Here. It's gotta be ninety degrees already. Drink up."

As both men are drinking their water, Owen notices that a police cruiser has pulled off to the side of the highway and the trooper inside is now staring at the pair.

"Fuck. We got company, Jack."

Jack who is still wearing his US Marshals coat and cap, glances over at the farmhouse about 300 yards away.

"Farmer probably called. Don't worry about it."

Jack leans against the car and gives a wave to the watching trooper. The trooper is on his police mic, most likely calling for backup.

"Should I put my cuffs back on, Jack?"

"Fuck 'em. They can see everything, kid. Don't worry about it."

Jack has his mind set on having what could be a life-or-death discussion with Owen, and no nervous farmers or staring cops are going to deter him from his goal. Owen, on the other hand, is not so relaxed.

"Mr. Malcomson is quite the man, isn't he, Owen?"

"Yeah, sure, Jack, he's a legend, but we already went through this. We both agreed we admire the man, now can we just get going, please?"

"The man gets you out of Ireland, literally saving your life. He assigns you to his own team and at such a young age. He made you one of his soldiers, right, Owen?"

"That's right, Jack."

"You *are* a soldier, are you not, Owen?"

"Sure, Jack, I'm a soldier."

"You are a dedicated, loyal, unquestioning soldier, am I right?"

"Yeah, all that—come on, Jack, just tell me what you want me to say and I'll say it. You're really starting to freak me out right now."

"Do you even know what it is you're rushing to in Arlington, Owen?"

"For fuck's sake, Jack, I'm following you, and I have been since we left Uruguay together. Nothing has changed, man."

"Do you know that once we are in Arlington, Ian and I may have opposing positions on how this mission is completed?"

Just then, the cop sitting by the side of the road toots his horn a couple of times and pulls back onto the road. Jack gives him a courtesy wave.

"Fuck, the Ambo has some real steam down here, Jack."

"He grew up and built his empire here in Texas, Owen. The man knows everyone and has funded every high-level cop and politician in the state."

"Why didn't he just stay in Texas?"

"Eventually Washington called, and the rest is history."

"So what's the deal with everyone still calling him the Ambassador?

Didn't he retire?"

"It's a respect thing, just like our former presidents."

"Before you start up again, Jack, please let me say what I need to say. I know what it is you're asking me—I may be young, but I'm not stupid. Back in Uruguay Ian did ask me for my complete unbridled allegiance. He told me you are an incredibly charming wanker. He asked me if I was given a kill shot order, would I act the soldier and finish the mission, without hesitation or compunction. At the time, I told him I unequivocally could and would."

"And now, Owen?"

"Ian is a great man, Jack. He has done everything you said he did for me and a lot more. I don't want to sound like a complete asshole now, but nobody has treated me like you have in just the last week alone. Like…making me feel like I'm a part of something other than killing people. Not since my own father, Jack."

Owen continues. "I know you had your reason for whatever happened back in Argentina and, to Ian's credit, that's the one thing he did make a point of telling me. He also confided in me that he probably would have done the exact same thing. I know there was a young girl that got hurt back in Argentina, Jack. Is that the girl you thought I was talking about?"

"Yes, Owen, and can you fucking believe it, her name is the same as my own daughter's."

"Is that what this is all about? In some way you're trying to save your own daughter?"

"Okay, kid. Now you're starting to freak me out with this psycho- analysis shit."

Owen presses the issue and says, "I don't think its shit, Jack. Did you love this girl?"

Jack takes a long, hard look into Owen's bloodshot inquiring eyes. Only a few minutes earlier, the young man standing before him was possibly moments away from a quick and decisive exit from this earth. To Jack, the man standing in front of him now is all but an illusion. A mere mirror reflecting back Jack's sudden realization that his two Debras may be two very different women, but they symbolize one unbridled love.

Jack finally answers Owen's question. "I love them both, Owen. The daughter I have and the daughter I tried to save.

"We both learned that in war, there always is and always will be collateral damage, Jack. That is the nature of this shitty line of work we have chosen for ourselves."

"All I'll say, kid, is that I could have prevented this one. Let's get moving, I got a car to deliver to a friend."

Owen decides to stop with his questions. He's not sure how you deliver a car to a dead girl and, quite frankly, with the way the conversation started, he doesn't want to know.

Ian starts to get in the backseat.

"Fuck that, kid, climb up in the front. We'll be good from here on out."

As Jack is getting in the front seat and Owen is doing the same on the other side, Owen mutters just loud enough that Jack may or may not hear him, "Besides, I'm not going to shoot the father of the woman I plan on marrying."

Jack just smiles and says, "Sure, kid." He starts the car and at long last the men are back on the I-10 heading toward a lunch stop and then the last leg to Arlington.

Owen is now shooting quick glances in Jacks direction and he is now thinking to himself, "Fuck, did he hear me? Or, is he just fucking with me again." Owen decides to let the issue drop for now.

"So Jack, can we get some real food up ahead?"

"Yeah, kid, burgers and fries. We'll both wash up and I'll call Harvey after lunch. How's the stomach?"

"It was feeling pretty good until you told me to draw my gun."

"Sorry about that, kid."

Jack and Owen stop at the next roadside burger joint. They have their lunch, top up the car and Jack does a quick check of all the fluids. Jack grabs a couple of waters from the cooler in the back and then drives to the back of the restaurant and parks under a big tree.

"Hand me that cell in the glove box please, Owen?"

"You think you're going to get a signal here?"

"On this phone, you bet."

"What time is it in Israel?"

"It's the evening now, and Harvey better still be there."

Back in the Ambassador's office…

Harvey is passed out on the couch and Joshua is sitting in the Ambassador's chair, waiting for Jack's call. The doc went to bed early and Peter is upstairs asleep in a side chair, presumably watching over the Ambassador.

The Ambassador's private phone line starts to ring.

"Wake up, Mr. Blumberg, you got a call coming in."

"Morning, Jack, this is Joshua. Mr. Blumberg is just walking over now."

"Hiya, Jacko. How's the weather down there in Texas? Hot and sticky is my guess, just like their women. Hey, Jack, if you stop to take a piss on the side of the road make sure no rattlers don't jump up and bite your dick off."

Jack hangs up the phone and passes it back to Owen,

"He's pissed drunk. Do you know how to turn the thing off?"

"Yeah, will do."

"He hung up on me."

"Of course he did, you asshole. I'm gonna call him back, Harvey, and you better hope he answers."

One hour out of Arlington, Texas…

"We got another cruiser behind us, Owen, but he's a fair way back."

Owen turns around and is watching the cruiser, then suddenly exclaims, "Holy shit, Jack. Look at this guy move."

Within twenty seconds the police cruiser is right on Jack's vehicle, only now he's not behind his car, but in the lane next to him. The cruiser pulls real close, right up beside Jack. The cop is in a 2014 Dodge Charger Pursuit. It's one the fastest cruisers in the Texas interceptor vehicle force.

Jack is now driving a respectable fifty-five miles per hour and nods his cap to the staring officer. The lone officer powers down his passenger window and yells loudly toward Jack, "That's an original '68 Mustang, isn't it, Marshal?"

Jack yells back, "Yes, Sir."

"What's it got in it, a 302 V8?"

"No, Sir, 390 four barrel V8 that was bored out to a 500."

"No shit ... hang on a sec, Marshal."

The cruiser slows down and pulls up behind Jack. Jack sees the officer talking to someone on his police mic.

"What the fuck, Jack? Is that shite drunk?"

"I don't know, kid."

The cop pulls back up next to Jack and is again yelling, "I got a 425 Hemi in this thing. What do you say we test it out?"

"We're just trying to make it down the road, Officer."

The officer yells back, "So you're saying your little GTO doesn't have what it takes?"

"I didn't exactly say that, Sir."

"Fuck it, Marshal. You in or not? I'm a busy guy. Say five hundred dollars?"

"Give me a second, Officer."

"It's the fucking car, kid. The Rangers back at El Paso must have put the word out about this car and it went right up the line. That's why that asshole was watching us by the farm—he was looking at the fucking car. I guess they want to test it against their best."

"Fuck that, Jack, just tell him no. This is too strange, even for me."

"Welcome to Texas, kid. How much money you got left?"

"Seven grand."

"Yeah, that's too much for what these guys make. I'll just make it an even grand."

Jack rolls his window back down and shouts to the officer,

"I don't take it out of second gear for less than a thousand."

"You're on, Marshal. Keep it at fifty-five and about a mile ahead we're going to pass a couple of my boys holding up traffic. We go for another mile then you can toss me those bills. And don't make me chase you for them when you lose."

"You got it, Officer. What's your name, by the way?"

"They call me the Interceptor, boy."

Jack just smiles and turns his head to Owen. "What an asshole."

With the vehicles both approaching the cordoned-off mile marker, Jack looks ahead and can see everything looks safe. Jack decides to slow right down and the cruiser next to him follows suit. Both cars are now down to a crawl, maneuvering side by side in their respective lanes.

Jack yells out, "Why don't we make it a real race and start on a line?"

The officer is now looking a little apprehensive about the scene he and his colleagues have set up on the always busy Texas I-10. But he shouts back, "You got it, boy."

The cars come to a complete stop. A fellow officer walks between them and very quickly says, "Go!"

A few minutes later...

"I'll pull into the other lane, Owen. He's going to throw the cash to you."

The officer pulls right up next to Owen's side of the vehicle and throws an elastic-wrapped bundle of one-hundred dollar bills in the car. The men exchange nods and the cruiser jackknifes his brakes and heads off in the opposite direction.

"Quickly count that shit, Owen. I could easily catch him if we need to."

"It's all here, Jack."

"Okay, kid, set your watch to Arlington time. We should be there by two. And tonight you're going to experience the best ribs in Texas, kid."

Chapter 17

A CAR FOR A FRIEND

At the warehouse in Arlington, Texas...

Jack and Owen pull up to the front gate of the warehouse. It takes a moment for Carl to recognize Jack, as he is still wearing his US Marshals jacket and cap.

Carl shouts over the warehouse mic, "The boss is here, motherfuckers. Everyone front and centre." "Come on, Leon, let's go see the boss I've been telling you about."

Carl opens the door to the gate and walks up to the car. "Hi, Jack. It's really good to see you, man. Sweet ride. Howdy, Owen."

"Good to see you too, Carl? "Who's your friend?"

"His name is Leon. Can we keep him, Jack?"

"As long as you can guarantee me that no one is going to come looking for him, I don't see why not, Carl."

"Nah, he's a mutt, Jack, we've had him for a while now. Did you hear that, Leon? Jack said you can stay?"

"You can pull around the back, Jack. Mr. Singh is probably out there right now."

"Thanks, Carl. I'm calling a quick meeting in a bit. I'll have Owen come get you when we're ready. Do you need anything now?"

"No, I'm good, Jack, thanks... It's really good to see you here, Jack."

Carl locks up the gate and plays around with Leon before returning to the security shed. He takes a seat down on his uncomfortable chair and stares blankly out the small window

"We miss out on everything, Leon."

Jack rolls the Mustang around back. He quickly parks and hops out after spotting Mr. Singh at the grill.

Jack walks over to Mr. Singh with a huge smile on his face. The two men exchange a solid embrace of friendship and mutual respect.

"You're a sight for sore eyes, Mr. Singh."

"Very pleased to see you again, Mr. Singer."

Mr. Singh pulls away and his facial expression immediately changes to one of anger, mixed with a bit of contempt.

"What's wrong, Cookie?"

Mr. Singh makes a gesture in Owen's direction, intimating that he would like to speak to Jack in private.

"Owen, would you mind grabbing our bags and heading inside?"

"No problem, Jack. What about your gifts?"

"Leave them there for now. Tell everyone we'll be in in a minute."

"Hi Mr. Singh."

"Hello Owen."

"Okay, Cookie, what's going on?"

"Mr. Walker and Mr. Palmer are what's going on. They eat like pigs, they don't help clean up and they are very dirty men."

Jack takes a brief moment to process what he has just heard and instinctively reaches to see if his .38 is in his shoulder holster. Jack pulls out his gun, flips off the safety, checks the mag and makes sure he's got one in the chamber, ready to go.

"Okay, Cookie. One more time, please. Bricks and Stryker… are here?"

"Yes, Jack, they arrived totally unannounced two days ago. Mr. Malcomson would not allow me to kill them. I have to carry my gun on me now because Mr. Stryker keeps making jokes that he is going to shoot me for making him hide behind the car. If you tell me I can go in now and shoot them both in the head, I will do it, Jack."

"Why was Mr. Palmer hiding behind the car?"

"Because Mr. Malcomson stood in front of Mr. Walker, so I did not have a clear shot."

"I take it they both arrived here unarmed?"

"Yes, but they are fully armed now, Jack."

"Who armed them?"

"Mr. Malcomson told them to set up their kits right after I tried to kill them. Mr. Malcomson also promised that when you get here, if you say I can shoot them, then I can shoot them."

"Cookie, why do you want to shoot Mr. Walker and Mr. Palmer?"

"Because they tried to hurt my friend, Jack."

"Cookie, listen to me carefully. When I left Argentina, Bricks and Stryker were in a perfect position to open up on me with their Kalashnikovs, but they chose to not shoot me and let me drive away. They went against orders from the boss himself and made the decision to not stop me from leaving, do you understand?"

"If you say do not shoot them, then I will not shoot them."

"I invited them here for this mission weeks ago. We just lost track of them for a while. They are extremely disciplined soldiers and will help us complete this mission."

"They can't be that disciplined, Jack."

"Why's that?"

"They disobeyed the bosses order and did not stop you in Argentina."

"Ah, it's good to see you again, Mr. Singh."

Mr. Singh reaches into his barbecue apron and pulls out a small plastic container. He walks ten feet over to a sewer grill and pours the contents into the sewer."

"What did you have in there, Cookie?"

"Poison for Mr. Walker's and Mr. Palmer's dinner tonight."

The back door of the warehouse is partially open and Jack can hear a loud microphone sound coming from inside.

"What the hell is that, Cookie?"

Cookie is happy that Jack is back but is still feeling a little despondent about not being able to poison Mr. Walker and Mr. Palmer. He replies, "Carl just announced that Mr. Malcomson has arrived."

"You could understand that?"

"You get used to it."

Within a minute, Ian pulls around back and parks next to Jack's car.

Ian exits the vehicle and walks over and shakes Jack's hand.

"Welcome home, Jack."

"Thanks, Ian. Where are you coming from?"

"Just got back from the gym. You got Owen with you?"

"He's inside."

"Did you just get here, as well?"

"Yeah, just. I haven't even been inside yet."

"All right, then, let's go inside and say hi to everybody. I have a flight leaving in two hours, Jack, and I have no intention of missing it. We have some important details to discuss before I leave, so if we could get going, I would really appreciate it. What's for dinner, Mr. Singh?"

"For Jack's arrival I have pork ribs, beef ribs and I am slow cooking a brisket so Jack can have sandwiches before bed." Mr. Singh adds, "I'm sorry you are leaving us, Mr. Malcolmson."

"I'm going to miss you, Mr. Singh."

Mr. Singh pulls out a piece of paper from his back pocket. It has a single phone number on it and he hands it to Ian. Ian looks at it, gracefully smiles and puts it in his pocket. He gives Mr. Singh a hearty handshake.

"I'll meet you in the office, Jack."

After Ian heads into the warehouse, Jack looks over at Mr. Singh and gives him a sly look regarding the piece of paper.

"Mind your own business, Mr. Jack."

When Jack walks into the warehouse, he is greeted by all of the crew.

Cognizant and respectful of Ian's desire to leave, he greets each man and tells each of them he will be talking with them one-on-one prior to dinner, in the office.

"Really good to see you, Sarge," Brick says.

"You have no idea, Bricks, my friend, no idea."

Jack walks away from that exchange, smiling, and Bricks, having taken note of Jack's facial expression, is now feeling a little nervous.

Jack goes into the office and Ian is sitting on a metal side chair. He is just finishing the last of a couple of ribs Mr. Singh brought him while he was waiting for Jack.

Jack looks at the chair behind the desk.

"Do you mind?"

"Just sit, Jack. Your humility can be annoying, did you know that, pal?"

Ian finishes his ribs and licks the barbecue sauce off his fingers. Jack looks around the room and spots a roll of paper towels.

Jack hands the roll to Ian, "Here, this might help."

"Man, how did a guy from India learn how to barbecue so damn good?"

"He is a very dedicated man and takes pride in everything he does."

"Okay, Jack, good to see you finally made it. Any problems on the road?"

"No, nothing unusual. We raced a Texas interceptor on the I-10 and won a thousand bucks."

"Ah, Jack, always the asshole. I'm going to miss working with you." Ian checks his watch. He has about a twenty-minute drive to the airport so he calculates he's got about half an hour to conclude his meeting with Jack.

"I know you've been on a long haul, Jack and you're probably ready for a meal and a nap before the big day tomorrow. So if you don't mind, I'm just gonna lay everything out for you. If you can keep the Q & A to a minimum, we can both say our goodbyes and get on with our day."

"Actually, surprisingly I'm not that tired. I'm thinking about going for a run before dinner."

"Yeah? That's great, Jack. Can I start now?"

"Do you run, Hairy? You look like you're in pretty good shape. I know in our line of work it's tough to get out there with any sort of regularity. That's why I always try to get out first thing in the morning. When do you try to get out, Hairy?"

"Are you done, asshole?"

"Uh … let me think … yeah … I … I think I am. No, wait. How is little Maggie doing? Have you talked to her on the phone? You know what I mean, listening to her goo-goo and ga-ga, that sort of thing. Pat's probably getting no sleep. I remember when Debra was born, Marg didn't sleep for six months."

"Maggie has a heart defect, Jack. Patricia brought her to the hospital two days ago."

"Oh shit, I'm sorry, Ian, I really am."

"I know you are."

"If there's anything I can do for you and Patricia, just let me know."

"There is, Jack. You can shut the fuck up for ten minutes so I can debrief you. Then I can get the fuck out of here to catch my flight to be with my family."

"Fuck that. Say good bye to the boys and take off. We'll figure it out from here. Daughters trump missions, Ian."

"Can I start now, please, Jack?"

Jack quickly stands up and walks over to the door. He opens it and shouts out for all to hear, "Anyone knock on this door in the next fifteen minutes, you just bought yourself a fifty per cent pay cut."

"Okay, Ian, the floor is yours. I won't say another word until you're done."

"I am done, Jack, and not just because of Maggie. What I have been witnessing these last several weeks is an organization coming apart at the seams. This mission? Well, I can't see it ending well, Jack. It has already cost Harvey his job, but we'll get back to that.

"Wilhelm, Joshua, Peter and Dr. Jacobie left on his jet at noon, Israeli time. I expect they will be at the warehouse in a few hours.

"As per Wilhelm's instructions, I paid the bill and closed out the rooms at the Hilton. The Ambassador wants to stay here, Jack. He doesn't want to miss a thing.

"When he gets here, have your guys set him up in the containment room—it's got the best bed. I sent Sven out yesterday to get a cot for the doc. He can also sleep in the containment room.

"We have nine sleeping pods, and with Carl and Rick taking turns on security, we have enough room for everyone.

"I had them empty our kit room and put everything in the cabinets.

"Rick's got a bad upper shoulder from their retarded punching game. I put an end to it once and for all.

"Mr. Singh went out yesterday and got as much deli and kosher food as he could locate. I'm worried about Mr. Singh, Jack. Hopefully with you here now he will stop thinking about killing those two assholes.

"The guys adopted a dog. They named him Leon. He's a good dog for security when those idiots invariably fall asleep.

"As per your instructions, no one has made a run out to Karl Zurich's ranch. Sven says it's a forty-seven minute drive from here. He has a map outlining the quickest route with the least probability of being stopped by the cops.

"I got the three zappers you requested, with a box of tranquillizer darts for each. Anything that prevents another Akron is the way to go, Jack, but I suspect you figured that out on your own some time ago."

"Harvey failed to remove the bulletin when you requested Walker and Palmer. They showed up unannounced and oblivious to Wilhelm's decision to have them killed. At this point I do not suspect they know anything."

"Harvey is out, Jack. He was escorted off the Ambassador's property before they left for Texas. Salcom has removed any trace of him from the organization, as if he never existed. A bulletin has been put out about Harvey's exit. I anticipate our colleagues are all aware of it by now. I expect Wilhelm will be pushing you to make the decision for his ultimate demise."

"Your new contact is Gordon Wright. He is staying at the Ambassador's and is awaiting your call."

"And finally, Jack, you know Wilhelm is dying right?"

"What about Ivanna, Ian?"

"She's in the wind, Jack. She's a ghost."

"Did Harvey cancel the contract?"

"Yes, but it was out there for a few days. The family connection to some special Russian people was confirmed by Harvey. I'm not here to give you any advice, Jack, but I guess I'm going to anyway. When I leave, I would shut the door again and give Mr. Wright a call. Wilhelm let me know that it is important that you talk with him as soon as you can."

"Thank you for everything, Ian. If you can spare another moment, what about you? After Maggie is all fixed up, then what?"

"Well, I'm glad you asked, Jack. I'm going to do whatever is necessary to have the contract on Owen lifted back in

Ireland, even if I have to take care of it personally. With that said, can you watch the kid for me?"

"You have my assurance that Owen will be fine. What about after all that, Ian? I'm sure the Ambassador would take you back in light of the things you need to deal with now."

"You still don't get it, do you, Jack? It's that damn humility of yours. There is no Ambassador anymore. You are it now, and our global little community all knows it. If not today, then they will tomorrow."

"You never said a word about the Ambassador's health, Jack."

"I've known for some time, Ian. Again, thank you for everything. Give me a call if you ever want to get back into play."

"Thanks, Jack. I'm gonna talk to Owen for a minute out back then I'll be on my way. Do you want me to close the door?"

Jack stands up and walks Ian to the door and they exchange a friendly handshake.

"I gotta call Marg now, anyway. Safe journey, Ian, and all my best to Patricia and Maggie. You'll let us know how she's doing in a few days?"

"I will. Good bye, Jack."

Jack calls to Owen to come over.

"Ian wants to talk to you outside. When you're done, you can bring in the stuff for the guys."

"Thanks, Jack, I know they could sure use it right now."

Ian leaves the office and says a quick good bye to the group. He grabs Owen and heads out to his vehicle in the back.

"How was the trip, Owen?"

"We raced a fucking peeler car, Ian, and kicked its ass."

"Christ, I thought Jack was just fucking around."

"Listen, Owen, I want you to stick with this guy, all right?"

"No worries, Ian. I'm gonna marry his daughter."

"Does he know? Or I guess the real question is, does she know?"

"We fell in love, Ian. All I need to do is tell Jack."

"Well, congratulations, Owen. I'm going home. I'll see your family and let them know you're in good hands. You're going to be able to go home soon, too, Owen."

"I don't want you to do anything, Ian. You know they won't change their minds if they think you were working with the peelers."

"They'll listen to me. Give me a hug, kid."

"What does Jack want you to get?"

Mr. Singh comes out to check on his brisket and walks over in time to see Owen opening the trunk of the Mustang.

"We made a little stop before the warehouse."

"Okay, guys, I'm outta here, and just in time by the looks of it."

"Can you help me carry all of this in, Mr. Singh?"

"I don't drink, Owen, but yes, I will help you."

Mr. Singh and Owen carry in a half dozen bottles of Scotch, vodka, rum and six 24s of Corona. Owen yells out to the men, "Anyone want to get drunk?"

Back in the closed office, Jack can hear the commotion outside his door with Owen having pulled out the booze. He decides he'll catch up later, and he places his call to Margaret, as promised.

"Hello, Marg."

"Hi, Jack, thanks for calling. How was your trip?"

"Long and uneventful, hon. How's Deb?"

"I'm picking her up from school shortly."

"That's good, hon. Say hi to her for me and that I'll see her in a week or so. How are the new neighbors?"

"They're great. You can't even tell we have neighbors, they're so quiet."

"That's good. You know I have to go now, hon. I won't be calling you again until I'm done here. Anything bad happens there, you give Captain Tom a call."

"Just one more thing, Jack. We got a small problem developing here."

"Debra and Owen? Yeah, I know. We'll deal with it when the job is done. I love you, Margaret Singer."

"I love you, too, Jack Singer."

Jack wants to see his crew, so he puts off calling Gordon Wright until later and steps out to join the party.

Carl has filled one of the kitchen sinks with ice and dumped in a batch of Corona to keep them nice and cold.

With the group all starting to tie one on, Jack goes outside and grabs Carl. After taking a good look at the outside perimeter of the warehouse, he decides Leon can come and join the party, as well.

With all of the noise going on, Rick decides to get up from his nap and go join the party. His morning breakfast is a cold Corona with a Scotch chaser.

Chapter 18

HARVEY AND GORDON

Back in Jerusalem, Israel...

Harvey is sitting at his desk in his palatial multi-million-dollar condominium. It is heavily monitored by one of the most elite private security firms in all of Israel.

Harvey has been on the phone all day, contacting associates, both in the legal field and a few selective corporate executives, all of whom he has collaborated with before on behalf of the Ambassador.

Much to his surprise and relief, his calls have been incredibly well received. Just from his name alone, he was immediately transferred to the private lines of several Forbes 500 companies' top executives.

He no longer has to worry about anonymity.

What Harvey hadn't realized was that on his recent afternoon excursion to the Quarter Café in Jerusalem, it was only out of pure respect that his fellow colleagues didn't think of approaching him—a man of such esteem and dignity.

When Harvey left the café that day, the wine and talk flowed freely well into the afternoon, with every person in the room bragging about that time he or she had worked with the great Harvey Blumberg.

His heart and soul feeling reinvigorated, Harvey polishes off his glass of forty-year-old Scotch. He walks over to his well-stocked bar to crack open a new bottle. Only this time he spots his bottle of Balvenie—a fifty-year-old Scotch he purchased the last time he was in the US for a cool $35,000.

Harvey was saving it for when he took over the empire from the Ambassador.

As he's staring at the bottle, he's ruminating on the idea of running an empire versus being temporarily unemployed.

Harvey finally concedes to his desire and concludes that there's no time like the present. He cracks open the top and pours himself a double.

Harvey walks over to the kitchen with the anticipation that his personal chef has put aside some leftovers from his dinner yesterday. He spots a fresh porterhouse in the meat compartment.

Harvey figures he spent a small fortune on his in-house barbecue grill to go with the commercial flat grill. Maybe he'll give it a shot.

With that, Harvey sets to the task of preparing himself an in-house barbecue. Complete with barbecued red peppers, asparagus spears and some French bread. Just as he drops the porterhouse on the fiery grill, his front doorbell rings.

Harvey's first thought is that the scent of the roasting vegetables is permeating the upstairs flat. He figures it's the wife of the kind, beleaguered man who lives above him. She complains if she thinks he's flushing his toilet too loud. He did try to explain to her one afternoon the concept of gravity.

Harvey grabs his glass of Balvenie Scotch and is determined to politely cut this intrusion short.

Harvey opens the door and standing in front of him is a middle-aged man wearing a long black trench coat and a fedora hat.

"Yes, can I help you?"

The man starts to open his trench coat and, while simultaneously pulling out a double-barreled sawed-off shotgun, he says, "I'm sorry Mr. Blumberg, but you inquired about the wrong gentleman's daughter." The man pumps two blasts square into Harvey's chest. With Harvey on the ground and bleeding profusely, the man says in Russian, "*G-n Zikoski dayet svoi pozhelaniya.*"

Harvey, possessing a functional level of Russian, knows the man's words translate to "Mr. Zikoski gives his regards." It is the last coherent thought he has before he succumbs to his injuries.

Several hours later at the warehouse in Arlington...

"Don't even think about giving that mutt a sip of your beer, Rick."

"Why do you care, Mr. Singh? You don't even like Leon."

"You heard me, Rick, and to the rest of you, *no alcohol* for Leon!"

Mr. Singh walks away from the party area to give his slow-cooking ribs and brisket one final check. As usual, Leon joins him, walking so close to Mr. Singh's feet that the cook gently kicks him away, worried he's going to trip him one of these times when he's carrying a full platter of food.

Several hours earlier, Jack had let the group know that the Ambassador and three guests were on their way. The group agreed that dinner would get in the way of partying, anyway. They took a vote and decided to wait for their company to eat.

Jack is now sitting at the picnic table, slowly sipping a glass of Scotch with his team. Three Scotches ago, he decided against going for a run before dinner. Now he's just listening to Carl babble on, as he has been doing for the last hour, about challenging Jack to an arm-wrestling match.

Jack has finally heard enough. He lifts up Carl's sleeve, revealing his twenty-one-inch biceps and says, "Fuck it, let's do it. Everyone go get your money. Owen, you keep track of the bets. The match is in ten minutes, gentlemen."

"Uh, Jack, can I talk to you for a second?" Owen asks.

"Sure, Owen, what's up?"

"I want to make sure you know what you're doing. I've arm-wrestled and shoulder-punched these guys. They really know what they're doing, Jack."

"Don't worry, kid. It's just a friendly competition, right?"

"Okay… so then you won't have a problem if I bet against you?"

"Oh, I get it now. So that's what this is all about. You go ahead and bet with your heart, kid."

Owen pulls out the rest of the money he got from Jack and Ivanna in Uruguay. He waves it in front of the group, saying he'll give two to one odds against Jack winning.

Jack quickly takes him up on his offer. "I'll take that bet, Owen. Put me down for $500. My half of the winnings we got from the Texas Rangers today."

"Texas Rangers, Sarge?"

"I'll tell you about it later, Bricks. Even you won't believe this one."

Just as Jack is stretching out his arm, his private cell goes off and he doesn't recognize the number.

"Hold off, guys, I'm going in the office to take this."

Jack makes his way to the office, closes the door and takes a seat behind the desk.

"This is Jack."

"Hello, Jack."

"Ivanna?"

"*Ya izvinyayus' raz'yem, no vash karvi besporyadok s nepravil'nym ottsa.*"

"Are you drunk, Ivanna? English please."

"I say to you that I am sorry, Jack, but your Harvey mess with wrong father."

"Well, I'm sorry to hear that, Ivanna, but I should let you know that Harvey no longer works for us."

"Harvey no longer works for anyone, Jack."

"Your people don't waste any time, do they, Ivanna? Now, if there's nothing else, I'm about to enter an arm-wrestling competition."

"I just need to tell you, you will not be touched, my Jack."

"That's very nice of you, Ivanna, but if what you are telling me is actually true, you had better just stay a ghost."

"But your Mr. Ambassador… he will not be so lucky as you."

"Good bye, Ivanna, wonderful hearing from you again." Jack hangs up the phone.

He leaves the office and walks toward the men who are eagerly anticipating the arm-wrestling competition.

Bricks can tell the difference between the Jack that went into the office and the Jack that exited it. He knows something bad has just occurred.

Anticipating what is about to happen, he yells, "Shut the fuck up, everyone. The Sarge has something to say."

"Thank you, Bricks. Okay, gentlemen, something has come up. Everyone, finish the drink you have then put the booze away for another day.

"Sven, go on the Net and find out if anything happened to Harvey Blumberg in Israel. And Sven, hit the dark Net if you have to."

"Is there any other way, Jack?"

"Owen, you and Carl head out to the shack and bring your kits." He pauses. "And take what's-his-face with you."

"Leon?"

"Yeah, Leon."

"Rick and Stryker, get this place cleaned up, the Ambassador will be here in the next hour. I want both of you to go through everyone's kits, make sure everyone has enough ammo.

"Mr. Singh, lay out the dinner on the table now, please. Everyone go ahead and eat when you can. I'll be in the office making a call. Bricks, you're with me.

"Thank you, gentlemen, and everyone hold on to your bets, we're not done with that competition."

With Jack's last comment, the group swings into action, confident that Jack has everything under control.

Stryker says, "About fucking time something happened around here."

Jack and Bricks enter the office and Jack leaves the door open so he can keep an eye on what's going on outside.

"Can I ask you what just happened, Sarge?"

"Ivanna just called me, Bricks. She told me Harvey Blumberg was executed today."

"No shit, who by?"

"Well, that's what's so fucked up. Harvey inadvertently brought this upon himself. I called you in here to tell you something, Bricks, and you're not going to like it. But then you're going to have to excuse me, pal, while I make a call that's outta your pay group."

"I'm a soldier, Sarge, just like you. You and I don't have the stomach for the kind of decisions the Ambo and Harvey make on a daily basis."

"You have no idea."

"Okay, asshole, that's twice you've said that to me today."

411

"I guess there's no other way than to just tell you flat out, Bricks.

The Wiesenthal Center contacted the Ambo last week about the Akron Eight. Harvey came up with the plan to pin it on Ivanna, Stryker, and I'm sorry to say, you, too, Bricks. And the Ambassador agreed with the plan. They wanted to make it look like a simple robbery gone bad."

"Are you forgetting you were in Akron, as well, Sarge?"

"No, Bricks, I have not forgotten that evening. Anyway, a couple days prior to the Wiesenthal meeting between Harvey and the Ambo, I was in Israel to pick the team for the Arlington mission. I requested you and Stryker. I made it clear to the Ambassador that I did not want Ivanna back under any conditions.

"Harvey sent out the Request for Services bulletin for you and Stryker to take notice. Evidently you picked it up and that is why you are both here today. In the interim, Harvey also initiated a disposal team for you, Stryker and Ivanna."

"And that Jew bastard forgot to clean the first bulletin. Jesus Christ, Jack, are we still a target?"

"No, Bricks, I had our best geek send out the cancel order. Everyone who needs to know, now knows."

"What do you mean, you had it done?"

"Well, there's the rub, pal. You're looking at the guy who makes the decisions now."

Just then Mr. Singh walks quietly into the room carrying two platters of food. He places Jack's plate in front of him. It includes a half rack of slow roasted pork ribs, a half rack of beef ribs, a couple slices of garlic loaf, a large salad and a large portion of barbecued Texas potatoes.

He drops Bricks' plate on his lap. It has three small ribs on it, a slice of unbuttered bread, a small salad and one potato.

Mr. Singh says, "You need to eat, Jack." And he quietly leaves the room.

Bricks is looking at the two portions and says, "I should have just killed you in Argentina."

Jack stands up and trades plates with Bricks. "I'm not hungry, anyway, Bricks, and I'll talk to Singh, again."

"So, why didn't you just shoot me, Bricks?"

"Well, you killed Stevens and he surely would have killed you. I pushed Stryker's gun down when you were leaving on that Jeep and he surely would have killed you, as well. But me, watching you drive away on a hope and a prayer, all just trying to save a girl—well, when I kill you, Sarge, you will be standing right in front of me, not running away.

"I believe we left off with you now being the boss. What you haven't explained yet was your involvement in the hit squad."

"I hope you believe me, Bricks, but it happened very quickly and without my knowledge and I was already back in the States."

"If you say so, Sarge. So what am I supposed to do about Stryker? If I tell him the Ambo is dead upon arrival—"

"I'm hoping you won't, Bricks," Jack interrupts. "And as stupid as you may think this sounds coming from me, I want you to remain with the company after the Arlington job."

"I'll follow you anywhere, Sarge, you know that. What I won't do is abandon Stryker."

"Keeping Stryker would be counterproductive to what I hope to set up once this job is done, Bricks. The Akron fiasco will never happen again, not on my watch."

"Well, listen to you, Sarge … or should I call you Mr. Singer from now on? I'll let you make your call and go help the guys."

Bricks angrily leaves the office, dropping his full platter into the garbage can on his way out.

Jack doesn't have the time to be too concerned about Bricks' comments or his attitude. He'll make an attempt later to mollify his friend.

Sven is next to show up at the door. He gives a quick knock and Jack waves him in.

"What do you got there, Sven?"

"A pile of newspapers I've been collecting for you. I think you may want to look at them later."

"Thanks, just leave them there, please. What did you find out?"

"Mr. Blumberg is definitely dead. Killed at the front door of his condo."

"Any word on the shooter?"

"No, sorry, Jack, that was all I could get. I've been running a quick theory for you, would you like it now?"

"Go ahead."

"With a killing in such a prominent, highly secured building, there should have been more chatter on police and private sites. It is conspicuously quiet. Therefore,

I believe the Ambassador is aware of the shooting and has managed to cloak the scene with the help of Salcom, no doubt."

"Thanks, Sven, my next call will determine if your theory is right or not. I'll let you know." "What's with the papers again?"

Sven grabs a paper lower in the stack and holds up the front headline for Jack to see.

Arlington Lays to Rest One of Its Best and Brightest

"Thanks, Sven, I'll read them later. Please close the door."

With the Ambassador due to arrive at any time, Jack has to push aside his immediate interest in the newspaper as he places a call to Gordon Wright.

"Sorry for calling so late, Gordon. I was going to wait until tomorrow but you're obviously up, and I'm also guessing you've heard?"

"Yes, Jack, but before we continue, I must tell you that Harvey was a friend and a mentor to me. I am extremely fucking pissed about this, Jack, and I am a man who never swears."

"Why is that, Gordon?"

"That I'm mad about Harvey?"

"No, that you never swear. Is it a religious thing like the Ambassador?"

"Are you kidding me, right now?"

"No, Gordon. What makes a man decide he does not like to swear?"

"I think if a man is intelligent enough he can get through a conversation without the need for profanity."

"I swear all the time, Gordon. Are you saying I'm not intelligent?"

"On the contrary, Jack, your intellect is well noted. In your case, I believe it is due to the line of work you're in as well as your years in service."

"So are you saying that we who serve are too stupid to communicate without profanity?"

"Is this really what we want to be focusing on now, Jack?"

"What if I told you George Washington was a prolific swearer?"

"I would ask what proof you have."

"I'm quoting now, Gordon, 'I just don't want the federal government making laws about swearing.'"

"That doesn't prove anything, Jack."

"It proves to me that one of our country's founders, a highly intelligent man was also a prolific fucking swearer, Gordo."

"I guess we'll agree to disagree, Jack."

"Do you want me to quote Mark Twain, as well?"

"No, Jack, I'm familiar with Mark Twain's opinion on the subject."

"Okay, how about Captain Yardley?"

"I don't know even who that is, Jack. Can we please move forward? There are several important items we really need to address."

"Are you sorry for saying that our fine men and women in uniform swear because they are not intelligent enough?"

"Well, actually, I never said that, but fine, I apologize, Jack."

"Don't you want to know why I think very bright people swear?"

"If it will let us get on with the business at hand, then yes, Jack, please enlighten me."

"Atta boy, Gordo. Some of the brightest people I have met over the years are prolific swearers. These people are men and women of confidence. That is the key here, Gordon, people with confidence. Forbes 500 executives, neuroscientists, police, firefighters, doctors, teachers—they are always dealing with the prophetic mundane, stymied by society's so-called moral compass. When they let their hair down and want to relax with friends and colleagues, what better release than the nonconformist word 'fuck.'"

"I got a police captain friend of mine with a 145 IQ who is stymied all day long dealing with the public. But I tell ya, Gordo, when he is with his good friend, Jack, relaxing over a cocktail, every second word out of his mouth is fuck."

"So what it's all about, Gordo, is a release. Therefore, never trust a man who does not have the intelligence, the confidence or even the self-discipline to know when to unleash his release."

"And those who don't, well, they're the hard-ons in our society that we would all be better without."

"I take it you've put some thought into this, Jack."

"Nah, it just came to me. Okay, what do ya got, Gordo?"

"Well, to start, my fucking God given name is Gordon, you overbearing pretentious fucking asshole. Hang on a second, Jack, it's my cell. It's coming from the U.S."

Jack sits back in his chair and with a huge grin on his face starts to work on the three ribs Mr. Singh put on Bricks' plate. After one bite he quickly spits it into the garbage can. He's thinking, "Shit, who knows what he did to them?"

"Jack?"

"I'm still here, Gordon."

"It's the Ambassador. He landed an hour ago and Dr. Jacobie wants to take him straight to Arlington General. I guess he's been spitting up more blood than usual. They're all going to stay there until his release, possibly not till morning."

"Thanks, Gordon. Would you give me a moment, please? I just want to let my team know."

Jack walks over to the door and calls over Bricks.

"Ambo won't be here till probably the morning. Tell the guys they can pull out the booze again, but I want everyone to remain Alert Ready. I'll be out in ten minutes."

"Uh, Sarge, what's the Alert Ready for?"

"You trust the Russians?"

Jack closes the door and once again has Bricks walking away confused and thinking, "What fucking Russians?"

"Sorry, Gordon, I'm back. Look, my guys are getting antsy. They're waiting for an arm-wrestling match, so can we speed this up?"

If Gordon Wright had a gun in his hand and if Jack was standing right in front of him, the man who abhors violence would blow Jack's fucking head off right now.

"Thank you, Jack, my thought exactly."

"Your arm-wrestling match notwithstanding, I think we need to touch on some business issues before we delve into Harvey's murder. I'm only stressing it now because, if I am correct, you go into full-operational mode tomorrow."

"Yes, Gordon, we do, but can't this wait until next week? The Ambassador is now here and you are at the helm there. Why don't we just let me do what it is I do, and then you and the Ambassador can do your thing."

"Because the situation with the Ambassador is graver than you think, Jack. At this time we have an entire organization to think of. We have what I call our 'paper board members' to appease. We have an employee base that needs a leader and direction, Jack.

"The signed completed and notarized contract I have in front of me, right at this moment, lists you as the president and CEO. The Ambassador's role has been reduced to that of a transitional consultant, Jack, and that is what Wilhelm wanted." Gordon pauses a moment and says, "You really should have read all of this already, Jack."

"I was busy racing a Texas State Trooper on the I-10 when it finally arrived at my home, Gordon."

"I'm sorry, Jack, but you are now it—not tomorrow, not next week, and not when the mission is complete, but today, now."

"If anything, Jack, you need to think about your family. This is their future, too, and it is happening whether you like it or not."

"Gordon, as the Ambassador would say, 'Yes, yes.' So if I'm already the guy, what's the fucking issue?"

"I guess the issue from my standpoint is whether or not I remain as your primary lead counsel after the mission is complete. The Ambassador has a team of lawyers from all over the world that would jump at the opportunity to fill Harvey's shoes."

"You don't want the job, Gordon?"

"Do you remember me, Jack?"

"Yes, yes, I do, Gordon. If my memory serves me correctly, you described yourself as a colleague of Harvey's and you needed me to get Harvey out of that Thailand predicament. The noteworthy aspect was that I was already out on a level one assignment for the Ambassador. And it was *you* who called me to interrupt said assignment. And further, you assured me that I could retrieve Harvey and be back in a day with no one the wiser.

"It didn't quite work out that way, did it, Gordo?"

"Do you like black people, Jack?"

"I love black people, Gordo. I hate blood-sucking fucking lawyers."

"Do you remember what you said to me when the Ambassador secured your release three days later?"

"Yes, I believe it was something along the lines of, 'If we ever meet, Gordon, I'm going to kill you.' Does that sound about right?"

"Yes, but it was the comment you made just before that. You made a remark about the two men who tortured you for three days."

"Yes, once again, I believe it was something along the lines of, 'If I ever see those two fucking niggers again, I'm going to fucking skin them alive.'"

"Is that what you're looking for, Gordo? Let me guess, now you're going to tell me what I already know, that you are a man of colour."

"Very good, Jack. So I guess my question for you is, with the nature of our work, you need counsel that you can unequivocally trust. Someone who will spend the rest of his career—his life, in fact—assuring that you, and you alone, are 100 per cent protected from any and all transgressors.

"And that man, whom you will be instilling so much faith and trust in, is all but a lowly, 'nigger.'"

"You shouldn't be so hard on yourself, Gordon."

"Really, Jack, is that all you got? Harvey pained himself to tell me you were one of the brightest assholes he had ever met."

"What do you want me to say, Gordon? That the two black men who took great delight in stripping me of my fingernails did not deserve to have a disgusting racial epitaph levelled against them in the heat of the moment? Hang on a second, Gordo."

Jack walks to the door and calls for Bricks.

"Bricks, can I borrow you for a minute please?"

Bricks appears and Jack says, "Thanks, man. Can you tell this asshole on the phone that I don't have a problem with black people? He's our new lawyer, Bricks, and as much as we don't need this shit right now, we do need him, at least for now."

"Are you kidding me, Sarge? You hate my beautiful people of colour."

"Stop fucking around, Bricks. The quicker you tell this guy the truth, the quicker we can get back to drinking and that arm-wrestling match."

"Yesses, Massa. Hands me the phone, please, Sir."

"My fellow brother, how is you doing this fine evenin'? I hear you is questioning Massa Jack's volition."

"I take it this is Mr. Walker."

"Make it quick, my nigger, we got better things we could all be doing."

"I am sorry to bother you, my brother. Jack called you over, it wasn't my idea. So, if you could please just hand the phone back to Jack, I will tell him I get his point."

"No, I don't think you do, brother. I watched this man put himself between a live grenade and our people of colour. So what I am going to do is tell my true 'brother' that whoever the fuck you are, you are the racist and Jack should just fire your ass."

Bricks hands the phone back to Jack and says, "Seeing as how you're keeping everyone waiting with this bullshit call, you and I need to talk before lights out tonight, Jack. You kind of glossed over your involvement in Harvey's plan on the Akron Eight solution."

"We'll talk tonight, Bricks. You have my word on it."

Jack grabs the phone and says loudly into the phone, so Bricks can also hear him before he leaves the office, "And, boy, what did I tell you about keeping my Scotch glass topped up? Get a move on, it's running low."

"Hello, Gordon. You know all that stuff you mentioned about unequivocal trust? The organization, my family, protecting me from all transgressors? The Ambassador had Harvey—they were both of the Jewish faith. But what Mr. Walker has me thinking now is how am I going to be able to put my life in the hands of a racist, Gordon?"

"You really aren't as cute as you think you are, Jack. That bullshit may have worked on the Ambassador but it doesn't work on me."

"Okay, Gordon, you tell me. Are you staying or not?"

"I'm committed to the end of this mission, Jack. When you are back in Israel then we can meet in person and, ultimately, the decision will be yours."

"Excellent, thank you, Gordon. You have a good night."

"Uh, Jack?"

"Yes, Gordon."

"We've spent the last ten minutes talking about your view on profanity and racism. We have not spent a single minute on what it is we should be discussing."

"The racism bullshit was all on you, Gordon. I've just come off of one of the most surreal twenty-hour road trips you could possibly imagine."

"I'll admit, I've had a few Scotch. I would just like to unwind, have some of Mr. Singh's amazing ribs then brief my team before our mission begins tomorrow. I'm committed to arm-wrestling a dude with twenty-one-inch arms and I'm probably going to get my ass handed to me. But what pisses me off the most right now, is that you leveled a charge against the wrong guy, asshole."

"Five hundred dollars."

"Five hundred dollars, what?"

"Put me down for five hundred on you winning. And Jack, I apologize for the accusation."

"Okay, Gordon, the floor is yours."

"Thank you, Jack. The Ambassador had a contact already instilled at Harvey's building. Our man was able to breach the scene immediately and he was able to remove all of Harvey's personal files and was out before police arrived."

"Was he spotted?"

"Some old Jewish lady was yelling down from the top floor about the noise but our guy says he was not physically seen by anyone."

"You know I'm Jewish, don't you Gordon?"

"Yes, I know that, Jack."

"Well, I'm just saying that kinda smacked with a bit of that racism thing. You're gonna need to work on that, Gordo."

"Yes, Jack, I will work on that. Again, I apologize."

"Okay, Gordo, what about any security tapes?"

"Yes, it would appear Harvey was quite paranoid. We were able to retrieve a disk that contains footage of the inside of his suite."

"Are you sure you got everything?"

"Our guy is our top cleaner and has been situated in place for some time now."

"Okay, next."

"It would appear Harvey had drawn up legal documents to have your contract voided due to the Ambassador's diminished mental capacity. He also had a notarized statement from an independent psychiatrist, but neither document had yet been filed with the courts."

"What did Harvey hope to gain from that?"

"Harvey was a member of the 'paper board.' I believe he was waiting for the Ambassador to deteriorate further before filing. His goal was to take over the company, Jack."

"Here's what we do, Gordon. You start the process of eliminating the board and we will replace them all after the mission. Harvey could not have done this alone. There must be a few members on the board that were in cahoots with him."

"Very good, Jack. I'll start on that right away. I will add, Jack, that I have in front of me a partial contract that the Ambassador had drawn up eighteen months ago. It has you assuming the leadership role, as well. This was initiated by the Ambassador before any signs of illness. It was in Harvey's possession and likely would have never been disclosed. I'm surprised Harvey did not just go ahead and destroy it."

"Then we have nothing to worry about."

"Also, Jack, if you would have had the chance to read your contract, you would have known that the following needs to occur at the completion of the mission. You are to return promptly to Israel and assume your leadership role. You and your family will reside in the Saviorey Ramat estate in Tel Aviv for a period of not less than one year. At the end of that year, you can relocate the organization's head office anywhere in the world you choose.

"If you do choose to move, it is the wish of the Ambassador that you always keep the home in Israel. This is not a legal requirement, Jack, just his hope that you will."

Not having heard a peep from Jack's end of the phone, Gordon asks, "Can I continue, Jack?"

"Sure thing, Gordo."

"Salcom is continuing to monitor the traffic at the Wiesenthal Center. If we are we still going to pursue the 'simple robbery' angle regarding the Akron Eight, we will still need some scapegoats, Jack."

"I believe we now have that covered with Harvey's shooting, Gordo. A Russian friend of mine called me earlier. Tell Salcom to find everything he can on the Zikoski family. When I'm back in Israel, we'll make the final decision then."

"You want to mess with the Russians, Jack?"

"They fucked with the wrong kike, Gordon. Contrary to what Harvey thought of me running the organization—and I suspect these last few weeks he was pushing for my own demise—I had a genuine respect for the man with regard to his competence and reliability. He kept the Ambassador anonymous and insulated for a whole lot of years, Gordo."

"Exactly what I will be able to provide for you, Jack."

"So you're thinking of hanging around after the mission, Gordon?"

"That will be your call, Jack."

"Where are you from, Gordon?"

"My family roots are in Mississippi, Jack."

"Ouch!"

"We can discuss my life another time, Jack. I have nothing else to discuss and I know the guys are waiting for your arm-wrestling competition, so make sure you put me down for five hundred on you to win. Make sure you find someone to take that bet."

"My guess is all of them will, with maybe the exception of one. So your money will be covered. You should probably get some sleep, Gordon, we may need you tomorrow."

"There is one final thing, Jack, but I'm not sure how to tell you."

"Straight out always works for me, Gordon."

"Dr. Jacobie told me that the Ambassador packed some very personal and religious items for his trip. I think he believes he will not be returning to Israel, Jack."

"We'll take good care of him here, Gordon. Good night."

"Goodnight, motherfucker."

Jack hangs up the phone with a light chuckle. He takes a look at the stack of newspapers but decides they will have to wait. He leaves the office with one task in mind, and that is to refill his glass of Scotch.

Sven, Bricks and Stryker are sitting at one picnic table and Mr. Singh is sitting at the other reading the *Arlington Times* that Sven picked up that morning.

All the men have eaten and helped clear and wash the dishes.

"Who's ready for some arm-wrestling?"

The group is now fully lubricated and salivating for some entertainment.

"Do you want me to go get the guys, Sarge?"

"Thanks, Bricks, but I'll get them, I haven't seen the shack yet. Top up your glasses, men. Come tomorrow we're a dry operation."

Jack walks out to the shack. Owen and Carl are playing blackjack with about a dozen empty bottles of Corona at their feet. Leon is out checking the perimeter.

"You guys didn't waste any time, did you? I hope you at least ate something."

"Mr. Singh brought us out a shitload of ribs."

"Where's what's-his-name?"

"I told Leon to go do a security check."

"So, in other words, Leon is out taking a crap."

"Yeah...uh...Jack, if you want, why don't I just tell the guys that my shoulder is too sore, like Rick's."

"Is, your shoulder too sore like Rick's, Carl?"

"No, it actually feels pretty good."

"Then why would we tell the guys that it is?"

"Come on Jack, you're the man here. I don't want the guys to hate me when I take down the man."

"Who is everyone betting on, Owen?"

"I'm holding three grand against you Jack and twenty bucks for you to win."

"Who's the guy so confident in me winning?"

"Mr. Singh."

"Okay, guys, let's go inside. Leave what's-his-name outside to watch the grounds."

"His name is Leon, Jack."

Jack gathers all of the men around the picnic tables and says, "Before we start the competition, gentlemen, we have to cover some boring issues regarding why we are all here."

"You chickening out, Jack?"

Bricks stands up and addresses the group.

"I told you assholes already, when Jack gets here you will address him as Sarge or Sergeant. You got too much wax in your ears, Rick?"

Mr. Singh looks over at Bricks and clears his throat.

"Right, except for you, Mr. Singh. Any of you other fuck wads will deal with me. Go ahead, Sarge."

"Uh, thank you, Bricks."

"Tomorrow morning, we are Operation Go, gentlemen. The Ambassador will be here in the morning. He will be with the doc and two security men.

"Sven, when you go for your morning coffee and paper, I want you to take Owen with you. I want you to take a look at the containment room and figure out what it needs to make the Ambassador and the doc as comfortable as they can possibly be. If that means more blankets, pillows, duvets, whatever. You're the shopping expert, Owen, so you take care of it."

The group of men are now hooting and hollering about Owen being a shopping expert.

"Shut the fuck up!"

"Thank you, Bricks."

"Mr. Singh, please check the fridge and make sure you have enough kosher food to last up to three days, max."

"As usual, gentlemen, all cash. Mr. Singh has the lockbox."

"Uh, Sarge?"

"Yes, Carl."

"We were told this was a four-week job and we've only been here for what, a week? What's up?"

"Thank you, Carl. There has been a change of plans, guys. You will all be receiving your full contractual pay. There have been some developments outside of our little world here that have dictated we accelerate our timeline. I have all of the logistics in place and it is a doable job in two or three days. You will be receiving your daily objectives from me.

"Bricks and Stryker, when we're done with the competition, I want one guy outside and one guy inside. We have way too much visible light coming out from the windows. I want blackout conditions, gentlemen.

"Sven, after the competition I want you to join me in the office to go over the target's property schematics. Can I take it you already have that done?"

"I have everything on that property down to a needle in a haystack, Sarge."

"Bricks, as discussed, we will meet later as well. Tomorrow morning, I am going for a run at 0500. Mr. Singh, if you could have breakfast ready for 0630, we will have our first meeting during breakfast, gentlemen."

"Carl, is what's-his-name potty trained?"

"Yes, Jack, Leon is potty trained."

"Good, he will be the only one coming with me on my first run out to the property. I'm going right after breakfast."

When Jack finishes speaking, an angry Bricks stands up and walks over to Rick. He was the one who replied to the Leon question instead of Carl, and he also said "Jack" instead of Sarge.

Bricks pulls him out of his seat and is ready to punch him in the arm.

"No, Bricks, the other arm."

"Right, thank you, Carl."

Bricks slams Rick in his left shoulder, knocking him back three feet.

"The next guy that forgets operational discipline is going to get it in the face."

Mr. Singh looks at Bricks and does a light cough.

"Right, except you, Mr. Singh."

Rick sits back down and says, "Sorry, Sarge."

"Final thing, guys, Ambo you will be seeing tomorrow is not a well man. If you are not doing anything related to the operation, I want you to ask the doc or Joshua or Peter if there is anything the man may need. If he just wants peace and quiet, then that is what we will give him.

"This is the man that brought us all here, gentlemen, and he is paying us very well to complete this job. So let's not let him down. And now, let's get this fucking competition started. Are all bets in, Owen?"

"Yes, Sarge."

"Oh, shit. Sorry, guys. I got five hundred dollars from our new lawyer on me to win. Do we have any takers to cover the man's bet?"

A small argument ensues as all of the men want to take the full bet. Anything to take money from a lawyer for a change.

Bricks yells out to stop the fighting. "Okay, shut the fuck up. There are six of us not counting Mr. Singh, who is betting on Jack. The fairest thing is for each of us to drop seventy-five dollars, agreed?"

All the men agree and hand their money over to Owen.

"Uh, Sarge?"

"Yes, Owen?"

"I need three grand from you to cover all the bets and another five hundred to cover your lawyer's bet."

Jack reaches into his pocket and hands Owen a very large stack of hundreds.

"Take it out of that, Owen. We all good, gentlemen?"

Jack and Carl take their positions. Bricks has been chosen to be the hand setter and referee.

"Okay, guys, you get two attempts to get it right. If you keep pulling apart, we'll bind your hands together."

Jack replies, "We'll only need one go at it, Bricks. Oh, sorry, guys. Just let me take this shirt off, I don't want to get it all sweaty."

Jack stands up and removes his shirt, revealing a six pack and an upper body that looks like it is chiseled out of stone. Jack flexes his right bicep in preparation for the match and reveals a fully flexed eighteen-inch bicep.

Stryker chimes in. "Have you been feeding this guy spinach, Mr. Singh? He looks like fucking Popeye."

Rick adds, "Sarge, when this operation is over, your new nickname is Popeye."

Bricks is ready for the match and says, "Okay, enough of this shit. Men, take your positions. Get your hands locked in, and we start as soon as I release your hands."

Jack and Carl spend a couple of minutes fighting for best grip. Bricks releases his grip, starting the match.

Carl immediately goes for the "over the top" position and Jack quickly adjusts by sliding his grip up and moves into the "top roll" position, creating a leverage advantage that counters brute strength. Jack smiles at Carl, and then slams his hand down for the three second win.

Bricks walks over and raises Jack's hand. "We have our winner, gentlemen."

The men are all bellowing and moaning about losing their money and berating Carl.

"Two out of three, Sarge?"

"No, thanks, Carl. I'm not sure I would win again. My money, please, Owen."

Owen hands the money over to Jack. Rick and Carl walk despondently over to a corner, while Rick is asking his friend what the hell went wrong.

"He's done this before, Rick. He knew how to counter the over-the-top move," Carl says.

Jack's sitting at the table and counting his money. He says to the group, "Everyone grab a drink. Cookie's got brisket sandwiches coming, so we'll have a few more drinks. And for those of you that I did not assign a task this evening, when you're done you can help Cookie clean up."

The men all sit down to sandwiches and a few more beverages.

Bricks and Stryker then begin to work on blacking out the warehouse and Sven approaches Jack about their meeting.

"I'll meet you in there, Sven. I just got to talk to Owen for a minute."

"Owen, here's the wad. I'm keeping a thousand from our Rangers' race to give to the lawyer. I want you to give the guys all of their money back, just place it under their pillows. And make sure you got the right bunk and the right amount. Give this Forty to Singh, the only guy with true faith, brother."

"How'd you do it, Sarge?"

"He let me win, kid. I could feel it in his arm."

Jack goes into the office and shuts the door.

"All right, Sven, show me what you got." Jack smiles to himself. "That's what she said."

"Funny, Sarge... not."

Sven clears a bunch of stuff off the desk and unfolds a three-foot by three-foot collage of four-inch by eight-inch pieces of paper taped together.

"I got this off of Google Earth. It shows the complete Zurich ranch or estate or whatever you call something this massive."

"Holy shit, Sven. How many acres does this guy own?"

"Looks like half of Texas, doesn't it?"

"Anyway, Sarge, there is only one public road that brings you right to the front gate. As you can see on the map, there are many other ways out around the perimeter but they are all within the target's property boundaries."

"What are all those dots?"

"Cattle, a ton of them."

"I thought this guy was just an oil baron."

"I guess he branched out, Sarge."

Just then, Owen and Carl come knocking at the door and Jack waves them in.

"Just wanted to say good night, Sarge. Rick's on watch tonight, so I'm going to hit the rack."

"Good night, Carl, and good match, champ. Owen?"

"I took care of what we discussed. I'm heading out to sit with Rick. If his shoulder starts to bother him, I'll take over his shift."

"Thanks again, guys."

Owen and Carl look around and, not seeing Bricks anywhere, say, "Good night, Popeye" and quickly close the door.

"Jack called you champ, more like feckin chump," Owen says to Carl.

"What's your problem, you Irish prick?"

"Jack told me you threw the match. He had me put everyone's money back under their pillows."

"What do the Irish call a fool, Owen?"

"A Muppet, why?"

"Because if you think I threw that match then you are a fucking Muppet, kid. I wanted to beat him and I wanted to beat him bad. I put it all in. Plain and simple, Jack kicked my ass. I'm going to bed, keep an eye on Leon and check his water dish, will ya?"

"He's sleeping in the kitchen now. Mr. Singh is making biscuits for tomorrow's breakfast. I'll get him later."

Back in the warehouse office...

"So as you can see, here are the front gates," Sven says. "About 500 feet down, you have the main house, you got the pool in the back, all of these other buildings I'm assuming are guest houses, stables, barns, workshops...you got a six-car garage here, etc., etc."

"And these buildings way back here?" Jack asks.

"Same thing, I suspect—crew houses, stables, barns, who knows?"

"You got me a travel map?"

"Right here. As I said, it's about a forty to fifty-minute drive, depending on the time of day and trains. It's a good route, you're on the outskirts of any major traffic and the chance of seeing a cop is slim to none."

"So tell me if I'm wrong, Sven, but judging by your map here, if I was to pull right up to the front gate, I'd have a vantage point of the front door of the main house, correct?"

"If you bring your binoculars you should have no problem. Anyone looking out from the house should not be able to identify a particular individual, if that's an issue for you."

"And what did you find out about any security systems?"

"You were dead on, Sarge. With a little constructive hacking, I found they already had a pretty good security system in place. But they just received a shipment on a shitload of new gear. We got the usual monitors, cameras, perimeter sensors, but I had to look this one up. It looks like sensors you would install under the road somehow, setting off an alert of any incoming vehicular motion. No way to tell if it's been installed or not, sorry, Sarge."

"This is all good work, Sven. Thank you. Okay, what do you have for me on the Clement property?"

Sven unfolds another map and lays it on Jack's desk. This one is only two feet by two feet.

"It's about a tenth of the Zurich ranch but still a pretty good chunk of land. As you can see on Google Maps, the owners must have spotted the drone in the air. You got this asshole pointing a shotgun, those three are flipping the bird and some flat-chested broad is flashing her tits. Also, you can see they are loaded with cattle, as well."

"Those aren't cattle, Sven, those are feral hogs. I was told that by a friend. Do you have the last item I requested?"

"Here you go, one 'Lost Dog' poster. A five-hundred-dollar reward offered by the Clement family and a pretty good picture of Leon, wouldn't you say?"

"Any of the guys see you take it?"

"Just Mr. Singh, but he didn't seem to care what I was doing."

"All right then, thanks again, Sven. Good work. I'll walk you out. I got to talk to Bricks before hitting the rack myself."

Jack looks around the warehouse and finds a bottle of Scotch and a couple of glasses. He finds Bricks sitting alone, watching the late-night news.

"Mind if I sit down?"

"It's your kingdom, Sarge. Do as you please."

"Scotch?"

"No I'm good, it just makes me piss all night long."

"You getting old on me, Warren?"

"You're older than I am, 'Armen'. So what the fuck, Jack? You really need to tell me your involvement in my kill order, man."

"Bricks, my friend, I found out that they had already set up Ian's team to do the job, against my wishes. Ian can be messy, so I insisted the dispatching be quick. I immediately and quietly reached out to Ian, and it was not hard to convince him to not follow through with the kill order. The best thing we could come up on such short notice was to take your and Stryker's trigger fingers as proof of death for the Ambo. He was then going to give you enough cash to disappear. Ian said they could always put you to work in Ireland.

"Any ways there it is, Bricks. It was a crazy week, and as I said, I got to Ian before anything would have been carried out."

"What's keeping me from just leaving now, Jack?"

"Nothing Bricks. I don't need you or Stryker. Plans have changed, the mission has changed and the expected outcome has changed. As far as I'm concerned, this is down to a one-man job come tomorrow. And that one man is me, and maybe Owen. I haven't decided that part yet."

"What's keeping me from waking up Stryker right now? I tell him your shit story and then you'll see what's up."

"My thirty-eight, Bricks."

"Fuck you, Jack. I'm going to bed."

"If my door opens tonight, Bricks, you better come in shooting."

"I'm not a chicken shit like you, Jack. I'll do it to your face and when you're awake."

Jack turns off the TV and takes a look around the warehouse. The guys cleaned it up good enough for the Ambassador, so he heads outside to say good night.

Carl and Owen are still playing cards and there's no sign of Leon. The warehouse is also blacked out properly, as Jack requested.

"Just popped in to say good night, guys. Where's what's-his-face?"

"Probably still with Mr. Singh. Good night, Sarge."

"You guys are armed, right?"

"As you requested, Sarge. We expecting anyone?"

"I hope not, Owen. Good match, Carl. You got one hell of an arm, soldier."

"Thanks, Sarge. You, too."

Jack heads back into the warehouse and makes his way to the kitchen. Mr. Singh is sitting, reading the paper, and Leon is asleep on his feet.

"Cookie, you going to hit the rack soon?"

"I'm just making the Ambassador some soup for tomorrow. Fifteen more minutes and then I'll lock up for the night, Jack."

"You're the only one I'm telling right now, Cookie, but the Ambassador has been battling cancer for over a year now. We will make him as comfortable as we can tomorrow. Can I rely on you to watch the man when I'm out?"

"Yes, you can. What I'm making should not increase his phlegm production or bother his digestive tract."

"Maybe you could clear his menu with the doc as far as what he can and can't eat."

"By now, the Ambassador will be expelling the contents of his stomach and coughing up bloody pools of phlegm after each meal. I know more than that doctor about how to keep him nourished and as comfortable as possible, under these most dire circumstances, Jack."

"You ever going to tell me what it is you do or where you go after your missions for the Ambassador, Cookie?"

"Mr. Singh leads a very boring life, Jack."

"Okay, Cookie, another time then. I'm going to bed. I'll probably see you before I go for my run."

"I'm sleeping in tomorrow."

"That's good. Then I'll see you at breakfast."

"What are we going to do about this dog, Jack?"

"I don't know, Cookie. The truth is I never really gave it any thought."

"Do we just put him back in the field where they found him when the mission is complete?"

"Uh, did you want to take him when we go?"

"Mr. Singh doesn't like dogs."

"I don't know, Cookie. Maybe Rick or Carl will take him."

"Back to Israel? I don't think so, Jack."

"Well, how about Sven?"

"His apartment doesn't allow dogs."

"Well, Bricks and Stryker are out and Owen doesn't even have a home yet, so I guess it will be back to the field, Cookie."

"Maybe Mr. Singh is not feeling well, Jack, I may sleep through breakfast tomorrow. There is some cereal you can make for yourself tomorrow. You allow the guys to take in a stray mutt, he helps with security and then we throw him back into the street."

"Well, I just don't know, Cookie. I guess I could think about taking him with me."

"Thank you, Jack. I will tell Leon when he wakes up that he has a home now after the mission. See you at breakfast. Good night, Jack."

"Uh...okay...good night, Cookie."

Jack leaves a relieved-looking Mr. Singh to his soup, grabs the newspapers from the office and heads for his rack do to a little reading before bed. Nestled in bed, Jack reads the first headline again.

Arlington Lays to Rest One of Its Best and Brightest

Jack flips through a few more papers and also sees,

Record Attendance for One of Arlington's Own

Jack reads several subheads and scans the newspapers to see if there are any pictures of the funeral.

The subheads are:

Debbie Zurich Passes Away of Congenital Heart Defect
Family Requested Closed Casket
Family and Friends Memorial Held at Beacon Centre

Jack stands up and is now opening up all of the papers on his bed. There is one thing he is looking for that he does not find.

There are no pictures of any events at the Zurich ranch. Jack remembers Rafael's stories back at the dig in Argentina—how he said that the Zurichs were always opening up the ranch to host one social events or another.

Jack goes to bed wondering, "Why was Debbie's wake not held at the ranch?"

Chapter 19

THE MISSION

Even after only a few hours' sleep, Jack is still up at four-thirty. Knowing he has a busy day ahead of him, he decides to skip his morning crunches and gets dressed for his run. He has a couple of important tasks to complete before he heads out, however.

Jack makes a fresh pot of coffee and takes a seat in the office. Then he places a call to Gordon Wright in Israel.

At the conclusion of his twenty-minute conversation, Jack grabs his .38, a small flashlight, a handful of poker chips from the picnic table and heads to Bricks' sleeping pod.

Jack carefully opens Bricks' door and steps inside. With his flashlight on, he sits down on a chair next to Bricks' bed.

Jack carefully reaches under Bricks' pillow and pulls out his .45.

He then starts dropping poker chips, one at a time, on Bricks' face. Bricks, who is a heavy sleeper, swats away each consecutive chip that lands on his face. After about a half dozen chips or so, Jack begins to wonder, "What is it going to take to wake this fucking guy up?"

Jack now shines the flashlight directly into Bricks' sleeping eyes. After some more instinctive swatting, the big man finally starts to come to.

Bricks wakes up and, with the flashlight still aimed at his eyes, begins to frantically search under his pillow for his .45. While he is searching for his gun, Jack walks over to the door and turns on the pod light.

Now recognizing who is in his room, Bricks angrily wipes off a couple of chips still stuck to the drool on his face.

"What the fuck, Jack? Is this how you're going to do me? What time is it, asshole?"

"It's 4:55 a.m., Bricks. I want to get to my run in, so listen up."

Jack, still with his .38 in his hand, walks back over to the chair and sits down.

"Are you sober now, Bricks? Can I put my gun down?"

"Fuck you, man. Nothing's changed."

"Should I give you your forty-five back then, and we just shoot it out right here, right now?"

"Yeah, give me my forty-five and back the fuck up, brother."

Jack hands Bricks his .45 and backs up to the door.

"Whenever you're ready, Bricks."

Bricks checks his gun, takes off the safety and can see there is one in the chamber. He raises his .45, pointing it directly at Jack's chest. Jack has his .38 pointed squarely at Bricks' chest.

Bricks is now nervously trying to measure Jack's emotionless face. After a brief moment, he comes to the realization that the next move and his very own mortality lies solely in his hands. Bricks decides to set his gun down on the chair.

"It's too early for this shit, Jack. What? You didn't have your morning coffee yet, asshole?"

"Do you know why you didn't shoot me in Argentina, Bricks?"

"Believe me, Jack, I wish I had now."

"I don't believe that, Warren. Stevens, Stryker, Ivanna, they are emotionless assassins. Do you know what we have that they never will, Warren?"

Bricks nods his head, intimating that he isn't interested in playing guessing games.

"Honour, Warren. Honour."

"What honour is there in putting me on your hit list, Sarge?"

Jack reaches into his pocket and throws Bricks a set of car keys.

"You and Stryker are out. I want you to wake him up now and leave quickly and quietly before the other guys get up."

"There's a little issue about our pay, brother."

"I just got off the phone with the lawyer. You and Stryker were just wired double your quoted fee to your accounts."

"And why should I believe you?"

Bricks is now staring at a visually emotionless Jack again.

"Okay, okay," he acquiesces. "Just please don't tell me this is all about a dead girl, Jack."

"When this is over, you and I will talk. What I need to do now, I need to do alone."

"Was our 'finger displacement' really going to happen, Jack?"

"Oh, it was going to happen, Bricks."

"What do I tell Stryker?"

"You tell him whatever gets you out of here in the next ten minutes. What I will say again is there is no room for the likes of Stryker in our new organization."

"You said 'our.'"

"If you're out of here in ten minutes without a fuss, I will contact you when this is all over."

"Consider us gone, Sarge, and good luck with whatever the fuck it is you got planned, brother."

"Quickly and quietly, please, Bricks."

Jack heads out of the warehouse and stops by the security shack. Carl and Leon are sound asleep on the floor. Owen is dozing in and out, listening to some early talk show on the radio.

Not wanting to wake Carl, Jack asks Owen to come outside to talk.

"After breakfast, I want you to get a good sleep. I may need you with me tonight, I haven't decided yet."

"Okay, Jack, will do."

"Also, keep an eye out for the Ambassador. I have no idea when he'll show up. And Owen … Bricks and Stryker will be leaving in one of the rentals in about nine minutes. Let them out, please."

Jack heads out for his run.

He returns in an hour and twenty minutes. He's able to squeeze through an opening in the back, and takes note that one of the rental cars is now gone. He mentally checks off one item from his to-do list.

"Morning, Mr. Singh. How did what's-his-name get in here?"

"Leon smells Mr. Singh's food, and he sneaks in the back door."

"What's he eating?"

"Bacon."

"Going to shower up, Cookie. Make sure he doesn't eat it all."

"A car is missing, Jack."

"Bricks and Stryker left early this morning, Cookie, and they won't be back. I take it you were still asleep when they left."

"No, I was waking up and I watched them pack and leave from a crack in my door. I had my gun next to me just in case."

"That's good, Cookie. I know you can take care of yourself."

"That's right, Jack. I can."

Jack gets out of the shower just as the remaining men are bringing their food to the picnic tables.

With the men all feeling the effects of last night's drinking, they sit down for a quiet morning breakfast of pancakes, bacon, eggs and toast.

Jack is a little surprised that no one mentions Bricks' and Stryker's absence at the breakfast table. Each man has his own reasons to be relieved they are gone. Jack finally breaks the ice at the end of breakfast to let the group know they will not be back. Proclaiming a simple and straightforward, "We don't need 'em."

After clearing the dishes, Sven and Mr. Singh head out on their morning shopping assignments. Carl and Owen are watching morning cartoons before they hit the rack, and Rick is back in the shack with Leon.

Jack is feeling like a kid on Christmas morning as he gears up for his first trip out to the Zurich ranch. His mind is racing with curiosity as to what he might find there.

All this time, energy and planning. The murder of an associate. Jack's own surreptitious betrayal of a friend. It's all now finally coming to a much anticipated but still uncharted conclusion.

Jack looks at his watch and calculates that in less than an hour, all of his optimistic uncertainty will finally be confirmed or expunged. And he can't wait to get the hell out of the warehouse.

The office phone starts ringing and reverberating over the warehouse speakers.

Jack sees Owen still watching cartoons and says, "Oh, can I get that for you, Owen?"

"We all know it's for you, anyway, Jack."

As Jack is walking to get the phone, he mumbles just loud enough so that Owen can hear him, "Lazy bastard wants to date my daughter. Good luck with that, pal."

Owen jumps out of his chair like a racehorse out of the gate.

"Wait, Jack, I'll get it."

A race to the phone ensues, with Jack winning by a nose.

Jack snatches the old phone off the receiver. Owen is now wearing a look of indignant resignation and wistful sadness. He is looking for some sort of emotional reprieve from Jack.

Having some fun, Jack purses his lips and shakes his head back and forth, indicating, "No fucking way, kid. You just blew it all."

While watching Owen sullenly walk out of the office, Jack happily puts the phone to his face and says, "Good morning. This is Jack."

"Jack? Everything okay?"

"Yeah, everything's fine here, Doc. I'm just on my way out. You guys coming or not?"

"It's Wilhelm, Jack. He's not doing so well and the hospital administrator is objecting to us removing him."

"I'm on a tight schedule today, Doc. As quickly as you can, tell me what the issue is."

"They put Wilhelm on a morphine drip last night to lessen his pain."

"Was he on morphine in Israel?"

"He would never take it, Jack. He always said it made him feel too tired."

"As you requested, Doc, we have it here, as well. So if it's a comfort issue, we have that covered. You're his personal physician so we both know that you can legally have him released. Is there something you're not telling me?"

"It's you, Jack. Wilhelm was talking all night about you finally ending his pain. Is there something you would like to tell me?"

"Listen, asshole. I believe your fingers are important for the job you do so get him discharged and get it done now. The Ambo was talking about the conclusion of the fucking mission, for which you have now put me behind schedule."

"If you're not all here in an hour, my next call will be to Gordon Wright. Do you understand the implication of that phone call, Doc?"

Jack hangs up the phone before Dr. Jacobie can reply. He grabs his kit, says good bye to Owen and Mr. Singh and is on his way out to the car. Jack pulls up to the gate, rolls down the passenger side window and honks the horn for Carl to come out.

"Has he pissed lately?"

"He just went."

"Good stuff, let him in and open the gate, please, Carl."

"You look after him, Jack."

"No worries, Carl. Me and what's-his-name are just going out for a fun car ride."

Jack revs the engine and races off in the '68 Mustang, missing Carl's plea, "His name is Leon, asshole." That last word was said under Carl's breath.

Having put the road map to memory, Jack quickly clears the commercial district and is tearing up the road. He wants to make up for the four minutes he lost conversing with the doc.

"So, Leon," he says. "Tell me a bit about yourself. Are you Jewish?"

Jack reaches into his pocket and pulls out a baggie filled with pieces of bacon he got from Mr. Singh.

"Here you go, Leon. Have a snack, and listen up. When we get to the ranch, you got to look sad. Like you're missing your pretend Clement asshole owners. You think you can handle that, Leon?"

Within twenty minutes Jack is on the only road that goes towards the Clement and Zurich properties. To Jack's surprise, what he expected to be a gravel road is paved the entire way. No doubt Karl Zurich paid private contractors to do it for his own personal comfort.

Jack puts the 'Stang's bored-out 500 cc engine to the test, and he makes up for lost time.

"Okay, Leon, get your shit together. We're approaching the Clement property."

Jack slows down to a crawl and is faced with a shithole far worse than anything Rafael described to him back in Argentina.

"My God, Leon. I can't believe this is where you live. Are you sure you want to go back there?"

With no time to waste and disappointed that no one is outside, Jack slides into fifth gear for the remainder of the drive.

"Okay, Leon, we're going to stop up here and take a look down the road. If you gotta go, I suggest you go now."

Jack stops the car and he and Leon take a piss at the side of the road. Jack pulls out his Navy SEAL binoculars from the trunk and can see the front gate of the Zurich estate.

"I can see company at the gate, Private Leon. So get your shit together cause were Oscar Mike in two minutes."

Jack grabs a cowboy hat from the trunk and puts on some mirrored sunglasses. He places the missing dog poster on his dashboard and tells Leon to hang the fuck on.

Jack races up to the front gate fast enough that when he slams on the brakes, he leaves a twenty-foot-long skid mark. The screeching tires make a loud enough noise to draw the crowd he is hoping for.

Jack observes that the two men who are standing watch at the front gate were distracted enough to make a significant backward jump. But neither makes any sign of reaching into their knee-length leather coats for the side arms he knows are there. A good first sign, Jack figures.

One of the men approaches Jack's side of the 'Stang while the other looks down the road to make sure that it is just a single vehicle that has approached. He then starts peering into all of the windows of the vehicle.

Just as Jack is rolling down his window, he spots two more men hastily leaving a side bunkhouse. As they are sprinting toward his vehicle, they are trying to put their long coats on, as well. Jack is able to see that they are both wearing shoulder straps with the accompanying weaponry.

One of the men is now at Jack's window.

"What the fuck you doing, boy?"

"I'm sorry for startling you, Sir. I'm just so distraught. I have this lost dog and I'm looking for the Clement property."

"You passed it fifteen minutes ago, boy. Maybe if you weren't driving so fucking fast you would have noticed it."

"Again, I'm sorry, I'm just not from around these parts."

The other man takes notice of Jack's licence plate.

"He's from Nevada, Cliff."

"What's a Nevada shit kicker doing in Texas, boy?"

Jack hops out of the car with the lost dog flyer. He lowers his cowboy hat in an attempt to shield his full face from any peering eyes that may be watching from the house.

He walks around to the front of the car. As he is showing the flyer to the men, he is eyeing the layout of the property through his mirrored sunglasses.

"I'm not sure you want to return that dog to the Clements, fella."

"Why not, Sir?"

"Well, let's just they aren't the most reliable folk."

"Yeah, and good luck on getting that five-hundred-dollar reward."

"Oh, I'm not doing it for the reward, Sir. I'm a dog lover and I just want to get this little guy back to his rightful home, that's all, guys."

"Well, as I said, boy, the Clement property is about fifteen minutes back the way you came. But the way you drive, you should be there in ten."

Jack having seen everything he needs, starts walking back to the front seat.

"Well, thanks again, fellas. Again, sorry for coming up so fast. Sometimes the accelerator sticks."

Jack jumps into the driver's seat while one man walks over to his window. He's not completely satisfied with the early morning visitor's explanation.

"Hold on for a minute, fella. What brings a Nevada boy way out to these parts for a missing dog? We're a long way out here. Where'd you say you found that dog again?"

"I was eating at a Taco Bell with my family yesterday and my daughter noticed this little guy wandering on the street. We picked it up and kept it for the night. We went back the next day and found this flyer on a light post."

"Where you staying while you're visiting the great state of Texas?"

"We're at the Arlington Hilton, Sir."

"There is a Taco Bell down that way, Cliff."

"Why isn't your daughter returning the dog with you?"

"I got up early. I just feel so bad that that poor family's missing a beloved family member and I wanted to return him as quickly as I could."

"Okay, Sir, you better get on your way now. I hope your little driving stunt didn't wake up the family at the house. Final piece of advice. You look like a pretty decent guy—just keep the dog, fella. I think he would be better off with you and your daughter. Now off with ya."

"Oh, I couldn't do that to the Clements, Sir. You gentlemen have a good morning, now."

Jack pulls away slowly at first, then lets it rip like he's doing a zero to sixty road test.

"What do you think, Cliff? Should we let Karl know about this little visit?"

"Nah, he looks too dense to be a threat. Just some Nevada asshole."

Jack drives down the road a ways and stops right in front of the Clement property. He lets Leon out for a bit and puts his hat and glasses back in the trunk.

Leon sits down next to Jack who is leaning against the car staring at the Clements' front door.

"So what do you think, Leon?"

"No, not about the Clements, about the Zurichs. Do you think the mission is doable? Yeah, me, too. I think they're just cowboys with guns, they're not pros."

Jack reaches into his pocket and gives Leon the rest of the bacon. He also bends down and pours some water into his mouth from his water bottle.

Leon quickly moves onto the grass to take care of his morning constitution.

As Leon is squatting, a scantily clad woman comes running out of the front door of the Clement house and just makes it to a tree where she squats down to take a leak. She looks around and notices Jack standing there and then spots Leon just finishing his business.

She yells out to Jack, "You gonna pick up that shit, mister?"

Jack yells back, "Good morning. I'm sorry, but I don't have a bag with me."

The woman yells out, "Stu, Jeffrey, you better get out here."

Jack can hear yelling from the house. "Fuck off, Tammy. We're just going to bed."

"We got some asshole letting his dog shit on our grass."

"What the fuck you say? You keep that bastard there. Do not let him leave, Tammy."

The Clement boys come flying out of the house in various stages of undress.

Tammy wipes herself with some leaves and stands up to join the men now walking toward Jack.

"Don't you run, mister, or we gonna be on ya."

The Clement boys are still thirty feet back and are flexing their muscles and making gestures as if there's going to be a fight. When they get within ten feet of Jack, they see this is not the wimpy looking dude they were hoping for.

"Good morning, gentlemen," Jack says.

"What you doing way out here, boy?"

"I just paid a visit to the Zurich family and my little dog Leon here had to use your facilities."

"Did you see a sign that says, 'Let your dog shit here', asshole?"

"Well, judging by your front yard, I didn't think anyone would mind."

"Well, that's our dog's shit and we can do with it as we please. We don't have to deal with your dog's shit, so pick it up and be on your way before I change my mind."

"Change your mind about what, Sir?"

"About letting you walk away with all your teeth, asshole."

"Well, that wouldn't be pleasant. I kind of like how my teeth are. And I'm not sure that your cursing is really necessary on such a fine, early morning, Sir."

"Look at this fella, Jeffrey. He kinda purdy looking."

"Hee, hee, hee. Yeah, Stu, he really purdy."

"What do you think, Tammy? Would you fuck this guy?"

Tammy, who is missing three or four front teeth and whose face and arms are covered with meth scratches and lesions, slowly staggers closer to Jack. She gives him a once-over from head to toe, lingering on his groin area.

"Yeah, I might take him for a spin, but I don't think he could handle all of this."

"What ya say, fella? Fifty bucks and you can take Tammy into the bushes there for a quick howdy-do."

"No, thank you, fellas, Tammy. I'm a happily married man."

"Well, you just pick up your mutt's shit, and then you better be on your way before I change my mind."

"You already said that, Stu."

"Said what?"

"You know, leave or my teeth thing."

"Huh?"

"You told me I had better leave or you were going to damage my teeth."

"Yeah, that's right. So get going."

"Well, what about the dog poop?"

"Huh?"

"You want me to take the dog poop?"

"I think this guy is fucking with you, Stu."

"Shut the fuck up, Tammy. I'm handling this."

"What exactly are you handling, Stu, Jack says?"

Tammy, Stu and Jeffrey are now confused as hell and back up a bit to discuss their next move amongst themselves.

"Look, mister, just pick up your dog's shit or I'm going to go in the house and get my shotgun."

"Well, I have a gun, too, Stu." While Stu ponders how to respond to that, Jack says, "Okay, fellas and madam, it was nice talking to you but I really should be on my way. I do have a question for you before I leave, though. It was real shame what happened to your neighbor, Debbie Zurich. You must have attended her funeral, huh, fellas?"

The Clements' mood quickly changes with the mention of Debbie.

"Oh yeah, we was there. Sad, really sad what happened to that poor girl."

"You know she stole my dog a few years back."

"Shut the fuck up, Tammy."

Jeffrey adds, "You know I used to date her not so long ago."

"So you fellas must have been invited up to the ranch for the wake."

"The what?"

"The wake, you know, where family and friends gather to eat and drink and talk about how much they loved Debbie."

"No, they never had one of those. They had everything in the city."

"All right, then, fellas. It was nice talking to you this morning but I really should be on my way."

"Well, you, too, now, fella. Have a good rest of the day. We're all just going to bed now…up a little late, know what I mean."

Jack and Leon hop in the car and are off to the warehouse.

"That was a nice fella, huh, Jeffrey?"

"Sure was, Stu."

"Tammy, pick up that shit."

"Fuck you."

Jack arrives back at the warehouse by nine-thirty and Carl meets him at the gate.

"Did the Ambassador get here?"

"About thirty minutes ago. They drove up in a stretch limo, one of the security guys was driving it."

"How about Sven and Cookie, did they get their shopping done?"

"They got back an hour ago."

"And Owen?"

"Bed after you left."

"All right, thanks Carl. How's the arm feeling?"

"Feels good, Jack."

"Yeah, mine, too. All right, lock her up tight. You need anything?"

"No, I'm good, thanks. Probably use the washroom in a bit. Leon will take over when I do."

Jack parks and enters the warehouse from the back. He stops to talk to Mr. Singh, who is reading today's paper that Sven picked up.

Just as Jack is about to take a seat next to Mr. Singh, Leon comes flying in through the back door and climbs onto Mr. Singh's feet to start his nap.

"You want me to kick him out?"

"I don't care what you do with him, he's your dog. Maybe just let him rest for now."

"What are our new arrivals doing, Cookie?"

"The Ambassador and those two other fellows are all sleeping. Dr. Jacobie is in your office. I authorized him to use your phone."

"Thank you. The two security guys are Peter and Joshua. Their primary function is to stick to the Ambassador like glue."

"Mr. Singh is not concerned with their names or what they do, thank you very much. But they are both sleeping in Bricks' and Stryker's beds. Not quite like glue, are they?"

"I'm sure they were up all night at the Ambassador's bedside. You okay, Cookie?"

"The Ambassador did not look very well."

"He has stomach cancer, Cookie, but maybe they can do something for him? I don't really know."

"No, Jack. It has metastasized and spread through the rest of his body, and it is too late for a gastrectomy."

"What's that?"

"Surgery to remove the cancerous sections of his stomach."

"Were you talking to the doc?"

"No."

"I'm sorry if you lost someone close to you with the same illness, Cookie."

"Mr. Singh did not lose anybody to cancer."

Jack is getting restless and starting to feel a little creeped out and, quite frankly, a little mentally inferior to Mr. Singh. He stands up and starts fiddling around with some of Mr. Singh's cooking gadgets.

"What does this thing do?"

"It's called an egg beater, Jack."

"Uh, yeah, that would come in handy."

"Yes, Jack."

With Mr. Singh not allowing himself to be distracted from finishing the morning paper, Jack continues to fumble around the kitchen. He's thinking of something clever to say to counter Mr. Singh's medical diagnosis of the Ambassador.

He spots a little black book in the corner of a shelf and opens it up. He can see it is in Mr. Singh's handwriting, and it contains a couple hundred phone numbers.

Jack turns his back to Mr. Singh and quickly flips through the book. He spots a name and number written inside in feminine script. After a second and third glance, he realizes it is the name of a young Hollywood starlet. Jack quickly puts the book back and is thinking, "Must be someone with the same name."

"Hey, Cookie? How do you get a blonde to kill herself?"

"I would think you would give her a gun and tell her it's a hair dryer, Jack."

"Uh, yeah, that's right. Heh, heh … funny."

Jack has been hoping to have a serious conversation with Mr. Singh about life after the mission. But he is not feeling quite so articulate right now, so he excuses himself.

"Okay, Cookie, talk to you later. I'm going to see what the doc is up to."

Jack walks toward the office and convinces himself that his diminished IQ this morning is a result of too much Scotch last night.

"Morning, Doc. Glad you could make it."

"Oh, sorry, Jack. Come, take your seat."

"No, no, relax, Doc., I'll sit right here."

"I'm sorry about the call last night, Jack. I've known the Ambassador for what would seem like a lifetime. It's just so hard to watch him deteriorate so quickly."

"I understand that, Doc, but this is what he wanted and this is where he wants to be. Texas is, his second home, remember."

"Yes, you're right, he's been talking about this trip for some time now. And as I said, he was talking on the whole flight here and at the hospital about being with you at his end, Jack. The man really does admire you."

"So what can we expect over the next couple days?"

"He'll need to be watched constantly. I have Sven with him now. With the morphine drip, there is a risk he could start vomiting and ultimately choke on it. He is in a state of extreme fatigue, nausea, bloating after meals, severe stomach pain and on it goes.

"With the movement and trauma of the flight here and the excessive amount of blood he is coughing up, there is a very real possibility the Ambassador won't live through the night."

"Okay, Doc, so based on what you just told me—and please tell me if I'm wrong—the Ambassador's cancer has metastasized and has now spread through the rest of his body, and, sadly, it is too late for any type of a surgical solution such as a gastrectomy, right?"

"Very good, Jack. That is exactly what I described to Mr. Singh not more than an hour ago."

"Yes! I fucking knew it."

"Excuse me?"

"Sorry, Doc, just a private joke."

"I don't think the Ambassador's condition is anything to joke about."

"Of course not. We should just move his bed to the security shack. That way we will be sure he is watched twenty-four seven."

"I hope you're joking now."

"Uh-huh, anyway, why don't you go find a bunk and get a few hours' rest? I'll relieve Sven and keep an eye on the Ambassador for a while."

"I better not wake up and find him in the shack."

"Of course not, Doc. The Ambassador has always had a morbid sense of humour, so it's not time for us to lose ours."

"Well I do know he is certainly dying to see you, Jack."

"Good one. Good night, Doc. I'll wake you at dinner."

Jack walks over to the containment room and is very pleased to see how Sven has set it up.

"Morning, Sven. Excellent job on the room. Thank you."

"Thanks, Sarge."

"Bricks ain't here, Sven. You can just go back to 'Jack.' Everyone else has. I got some things for you to look up and I need it done ASAP. On your way out, go wake one of the security guys to watch the Ambassador. I don't care which one you choose."

"All right, what do you need?"

"I want you to find anything you can on purchases the Zurichs have made recently. More specifically, anything related to the handicapped."

"What exactly are we looking for?"

"Wheelchairs, access ramps, bathroom modifications and the like. On that dated Google map we were looking at of the property, do you recall seeing any wheelchair ramps out front?"

"No, I don't recall, but we weren't specifically looking for them. I'll bring the maps when I come back and we can take a closer look."

"Thanks, has he been up?"

"No, but there's been a lot of belching and farting."

"All right. Would you also find out what Mr. Singh has planned for dinner? He didn't seem to be doing anything about lunch, which is like an hour from now."

"You got it, Popeye."

Feeling as if the day is running away from him, Jack takes a seat next to the Ambassador's bed. He starts rolling up the pneumatic bed in an attempt to try and wake him.

The Ambassador starts to open his eyes and Jack raises the bed to a comfortable sitting position. Jack grabs a towel and rinses it in some water. He wipes down the Ambassador's face and puts on his glasses for him.

Upon recognizing Jack, the Ambassador valiantly attempts to come across as anything other than the dying man that he is.

"Armen, we don't hug anymore," he says.

Jack stands up and gives the Ambassador a warm but soft hug and sits back down with the Ambassador's hand in his.

"It's good to see you, Sir. Would you like a sip of water?"

"No, thank you, Armen, but you can stop that little bag from dripping please."

"Are you sure Sir, you're not in pain?"

"I would rather talk to you with some level of lucidity, Armen."

Jack stands up and turns the morphine drip down to its lowest level.

"Look at this room, wonderful Armen. Not exactly the room I had envisioned for our special guest, is it?"

"No, Sir. The men did a great job making it comfortable for you."

"There is no comfort for a dying man, Armen."

"I guess not."

"Are you ready for tonight?"

"Yes, Sir."

"Are you ready for what you must do after, Armen?"

"Yes, Sir, I am."

"Good boy."

"If you're feeling up to it, Sir, I would like to ask you a few questions. I have decided to continue your legacy and I will be assuming your role in Israel."

"That is wonderful news, Armen. What better news could a dying man possibly receive? Please tell me that Margaret and Debra will be joining you."

"They're at home packing now, Sir."

"Wonderful, just wonderful."

"You have some questions for me?"

"The team you picked for the compound in Argentina."

"Ah, Rick and Carl?"

"Yes, Sir, and Mr. Singh."

"Yes, yes, our people have always picked the best and the brightest, just like yourself, Armen. Several years ago, along with the rest of the world, I was watching the late night news. At the time, a young Israeli officer was killed by a large rock thrown by Palestinian teenagers from the West bank."

"As you know, it was a daily occurrence back then. But in retaliation, our temporarily misguided government felt it necessary to set an example for all future behavior of that nature."

"Teams of Israeli soldiers were enacted to breach the groups and isolate certain rock throwers. And with the world's cameras watching, the soldiers' orders were to beat the youths and, for the lack of a better term, displace their bones."

"I do remember seeing that myself, Sir."

"You and the world, Armen. I will continue. About a week into the nightly carnage, I was watching two young soldiers who were systematically—and unsuccessfully, I might add—trying to break a young man's arm. What caught my attention was how sickened the soldiers looked at having to follow their commander's orders."

"Rick and Carl?"

"Within a couple of days, I was able to secure their release to me and they have been with me ever since. Now the only people they hurt are themselves."

"Thank you, I will keep them on in Israel."

"Do you need anything, Sir?"

"No. Remind me, Armen. What was your next question?"

"Mr. Singh, Sir. Do you know where he goes after each mission?"

"I don't know, Armen. Harvey always contacted him and he would always arrive a day early and ready to go."

"About Harvey, Sir, I'm very sorry. Despite our differences I did like the man."

"Harvey was an incredibly gifted man. But wealth and, of course, power became Harvey's master. In the beginning it was your role as second-in-command that Harvey coveted. Then I became aware that even that was no longer going to appease his desires. He had undertaken measures to have me declared incompetent.

"Now the man is dead. *Baruch dayan emet,*" he says, which translates to "Blessed is the true judge."

"Gordon and Salcom are already working on using the Russians as our solution for the Akron Eight, and for your vengeance, Sir."

"Yes, yes, we have a hundred dedicated soldiers to their one, Armen."

"We have that many, Sir?"

"You have no idea what I was able to amass in my lifetime, Armen, but you will. Don't piss Gordon off. Right now he is your key to the kingdom."

Jack is recalling his last conversation with Gordon and thinking, "Too late on that front."

"Let me get you some water."

"I asked Peter to bring some of Miss Schuster's delicious blintzes for the trip. Can you please see if we have any left?"

"If it's okay with you, I'll look as soon as we are done, Sir. If we don't have any left, I'll send Sven to find some in Arlington."

"If I recall, Armen, there was an amazing Jewish bakery on Arkansas Street. I believe it was called Baklava Bakery."

"We will get you whatever you want, Sir."

"Yes, sable cookies, fresh bread and baklava, Armen."

"Are you hungry now?"

"No, thank you. I had some of Mr. Singh's matzo soup when I arrived. Did you try it, Armen?"

"Not yet, no. So back to Mr. Singh."

"Oh, Armen, when you talk to Harvey today make sure he is having Salcom monitor the Wiesenthal e-mail traffic."

"Gordon, Sir?"

"Yes, yes, have Gordon cover that instead."

"Yes, Sir. Sir, when I return to Israel I would like your thoughts on the discontinuation of our organization actively pursuing any remaining war criminals."

"I anticipated you would take that path, Armen. Harvey has a contact for you at the Wiesenthal Center, he is a very good, long-time friend of mine. You will still fund their searches, though, right Armen?"

"Yes, Sir, until the last one. I will make reaching out to your friend is one of my top priorities upon my return to Israel. Harvey is gone, Sir."

"Yes, yes, horrible. *Baruch dayan emet.*"

"I am thinking of asking Mr. Singh to join us in Israel, on a full-time basis. I'm just concerned with how to approach him on the subject. Whenever you think you are going to sit down with the man and ask him about his life, he quickly directs the discussion to that of your own life and family."

"Have you considered he may have a happy, full life outside of our missions, Armen?"

"I really hope he does, but I can't help but think he does not. Can I ask you about Sven, Sir?"

"Sven likes Texas, Armen. He is a six-foot-five handsome, blond former chopper pilot. The most difficult part of our missions for Sven is being away from his girlfriends. We have Salcom in Israel. Sven will be fine without us."

"Yeah, I guess so."

"How about Peter and Joshua?"

"Good men. They have not been with me long, so you decide their fate."

"How much does the doctor know?"

"He knows nothing about our business. It would be advantageous for you to keep him on for you and your family. He really is a good, decent man."

"I have a question for you, Armen."

Jack, anticipating what the Ambassador wants to know, saves him the trouble of speaking.

"I will only stay for the one year in Israel, Sir. I will then relocate the Company to the US. Israel is just too dangerous and I have to think of my family, Sir."

"I will, however, keep your estate for ever, Sir. All of your staff will keep their roles. I was going to ask if Gordon would like to live there when we move after the one year. Along with Mr. Singh, should he accept."

"Thank you, Armen, but what I was going to ask you is, are you prepared for what you must do tonight?"

"Yes, I am, Sir. Are you ready, Sir?"

"Yes, I am, Armen."

"Thank you for talking with me, Sir. Would you like me to turn up your IV a bit?"

"Yes, and put the bed down, please. I will rest before dinner and I am eagerly awaiting my desserts."

"I'll have Sven get on that right away. Have a pleasant rest, Sir."

As Jack is walking back to the office, Sven is just approaching with the Zurich searches.

Sven had woken up Peter and he passes the men on his way to the containment room.

"He just started a nap, Peter. You keep awake and make sure he doesn't puke in his sleep."

"All right, Jack."

"Okay, Sven, what do you got?"

"The Google picture is dated eight months ago. No sign of any handicap ramps, Jack."

"So the ramp I saw today is obviously new. What about any purchases?"

"I got a recent delivery to the Zurich ranch for an Orion Explorer Magellan power wheelchair. I looked it up and the fucker retails for seven grand."

"How is that comparable with what else they offer?"

"There are a lot of models in the three to five range, so this is the Cadillac of power wheelchairs, boss."

"Did you manage to grab a picture?"

"I knew you were going to ask, so yes, I did, and here it is. I did a little research as well. What makes this model so unique and expensive is that it is designed for those unfortunate bastards that are paralysed from the neck down. They call it quadriplegia."

"It has a breath-activated device that controls the pertinent features of the chair, such as movement. And if you're really fucked, it has one on the other side that can hook up to a speech computer."

"Quadriplegics are most likely ventilator-dependent, boss."

"Like Stephen Hawkins?"

"Exactly, but my guess is Mr. Hawking's chair cost a slight more than seven grand."

"As far as the ramps go, there was a large order received from a company called Texas Ramp. I couldn't find anything specific as to house or bathroom modifications. But they could buy all that shit just from Lowes."

"Thank you, Sven. Good job. I'd like to ask you what your plans are for after the mission."

"Just return to my IT job and wait for the next mission, I guess."

"So, Sven, I see no ring on your finger. You must have a ton of girlfriends, I'm guessing."

"Uh, Jack … I'm gay."

"Oh … okay. My best friend is former military and he's gay, too. Maybe you know him? His name is Roger."

"No, Jack, we don't have a gay directory for former military members."

"I'm just fuckin with ya, kid." Jack has now lost his train of thought and finds himself staring at Sven, and he says, "Gay, huh?"

"You're too old for me, Jack."

"I'm not that old, kid. I could give you a run for your money."

"Catching or throwing?"

"Okay, now I'm gonna puke, no offence, kid."

"None taken. It's an acquired taste."

"Now I'm really gonna puke."

Jack's private cell starts to ring.

"Holy shit, Sven, it's fucking Roger. Talk about serendipitous."

"Roger, boy, how you doing?"

"I'm sitting here in your kitchen having a beer with Margaret. Uh, Jack, where's my fucking Mustang?"

"Yeah, how about that, Roger... I thought you were in Asia."

"No, Jack. I'm in Orange County, California, in your kitchen with Margaret, here to pick up my car."

"Hey Rog, you won't believe this, I'm sitting in an office with a guy named Sven. He's a six-foot-five handsome, blond former chopper pilot and guess what Roger? He's gay like you, too."

"Does he know where my car is, Jack?"

"Hang on a sec, Rog."

Jack writes down the name of the bakery and the approximate address on a piece of paper and tells Sven to go now.

"And Sven," he calls after him. "Get two of everything that sounds Jewish. Mr. Singh will give you the money."

"I'm back, Roger boy. Can you please put Margaret on the phone for me?"

"I'm so sorry, Jack. He just showed up without calling first or anything."

"Yeah, he does that, doesn't he? He's a weird fucking guy sometimes."

"Jack, language please."

"Mission mode, hon. Anyway, I'll be home in a day or two. I love you and tell Debra that I love her, too. Now if you could please hand the phone back to our visitor."

"Love you, too. Be safe."

"My car, Jack?"

"Roger, walk into my office for a minute. Just tell Marg I'm about to tear you a new verbal asshole."

Roger walks to Jack's office and closes the door.

"I had to go, Jack!"

"You leave my family alone in Vegas under the charge of a backstabbing cunt, Roger? No offence, by the way."

"None taken, asshole. He told me what you did to him. That was actually quite fucking hilarious. Thanks for not costing him his job, though. He really did appreciate that part of it, and I think he's really changed, Jack. How about that Debra and her role in all of it? She's really turning into quite the young lady."

"She's her mother's daughter, no doubt about that, Rog."

"My car."

"I'm giving it to a friend in Arlington. My truck's in the garage so you can take that home and we'll just call it even."

"And the sixty grand difference?"

"We'll chalk that up to bad judgment on your part, Rog."

"All right, Jack, I know there is no talking to you when you are in your mission mode. We can discuss terms later. See you soon."

As soon as Jack hangs up with Roger, he grabs the office phone and places a call to Gordon in Israel.

"Gordon, how are we this evening?"

"Fine, thank you, Jack. And you?"

"I'm good, thanks. Unless there is something critical that can't wait for a day or two, I just need you to listen."

"Go ahead."

"Where's the jet?"

"On a hangar at Arlington Municipal."

"Where's the pilot?"

"At the Hilton."

"Good, get it fueled and ready to go. Call the pilot and make sure he's sober and get him to the plane."

"He was advised to stay on call and that he may be leaving in a hurry. The pilot will be sober, Jack."

"Good stuff, Gordon. I got a party of five, maybe six, that will be there in the next two, possibly three hours. Their destination is Israel."

"Can I take it that the Ambassador is not included in the five or six?"

"You know how this ends, Gordon."

"Yes, I do, Jack. It is the Ambassador's dying wish."

"Jack, I want to assure you that there will be no legal repercussions at our end. The Ambassador went to great lengths to formulate his own planned demise with no circumspect level of suspicion."

"I will have the jet immediately return to Arlington upon its arrival in Israel. I cannot emphasize enough Jack, that you must return to Israel immediately following the conclusion of the mission."

"That's my plan, Gordon, but hold the plane in Israel until I give you the US destination for pickup."

"Good night, Gordon, and thank you for everything you have done. I will give the Ambassador your regards."

"Thank you, Jack, I would really appreciate that. I will stay by the phone until I hear from you again. Good night."

Jack hangs up the phone and makes his way toward the kitchen. He wants to see what the deal with lunch is and to try and finally have that meaningful conversation with Mr. Singh.

On his way there, Jack stops and thinks, "Fuck it. Let's just get this over with." He changes direction and heads out to talk to Carl in the security shack.

"Afternoon, Carl. Where's what's-his-name?"

"Probably sitting on Mr. Singh's feet, where else?"

"I want you to listen carefully, son. Wait thirty minutes, then wake up Dr. Jacobie, Joshua and Rick and tell them all to wait for me at the picnic tables. I want you to let Owen sleep. Sven should be back soon and he will take over watching the Ambassador from Peter."

"I want you at the meeting, as well, so make sure Leon is watching the yard and that he doesn't come around and sneak in the backdoor."

"Aha, Jack, I knew it. You never had me fooled."

"What?"

"Leon. You knew his name." Carl started to sing, "Jack likes Leon, Jack likes Leon."

"What's not to like, kid? Twenty-nine minutes and then do your thing."

Jack walks back into the warehouse and heads for the kitchen.

"Don't your feet fall asleep with him laying on them?"

"Oh, I never really noticed. Is he down there again?"

"I need some kind of a tin container with a lid on it, Cookie, about four inches long."

"Cupboard above the sink. It's my empty mint container. You can have it."

"So, is Mr. Singh on strike? Because I have not seen Cookie making anything for lunch or dinner."

"We're having leftovers for lunch. I have two dozen fresh rib sandwiches made, along with fresh garden leaf salad, potato salad my homemade coleslaw and an assortment of kosher pickles. Satisfied, Mr. Jack?"

"And dinner?"

"There is no dinner tonight. I made enough sandwiches for you, Sven and Owen for this evening. Mr. Singh is already packed and ready to go home."

Jack stopped shaking his head some time ago when it comes to Mr. Singh's remarkable intuitiveness and he just carries on with the conversation.

"About that, Mr. Singh. If you don't mind me asking, where exactly is home?"

"Mr. Singh has many friends and family and many places to stay."

"You have no home of your own, Cookie?"

"I did not realize that Mr. Jack was such an obtrusive man as to peer into the lives of others, especially when it comes to his friend, Mr. Singh."

"That's why I'm asking, Mr. Singh, because you are my friend. But if we are to be truthful with each other right now, you are the one not treating me like a friend."

"What was the question?"

"Do you have a home to go to after the mission?"

"No, I do not."

"Well, I respect our friendship enough to stop there."

"Thank you."

"As you have somehow miraculously already figured out, the mission for everyone, but myself, Owen and Sven concludes this afternoon."

"They will all be taking the Ambassador's jet back to Israel."

"I am here to ask you if you would like to join them and return to Israel."

"Mr. Singh does not abide any form of charity. I will make my own travel arrangements, thank you."

"To where?"

"As I see it, once the contract is completed—and as you have so informed me, that will be this afternoon—Mr. Singh will be in charge of his own comings and goings. Both of which are determined solely by Mr. Singh."

"Jesus Christ, man, I'm trying to offer you a fucking job and a home in Israel. And if you say no, I'm going to take Leon out to the woods right now and put a fucking bullet in his head so he doesn't have to scrounge for food for the rest of his life."

"Is Leon going on the jet to Israel this afternoon?"

"If that is what it will take to get you to go, then, yes, Leon is going on the jet to Israel this afternoon."

"Mr. Singh accepts your offer of employment and residency. I suspect we will discuss remuneration at a later date."

"Just tell me what you want and you got it."

"Is that how you intend to do all of your employee negotiations? You will have the Ambassador's company bankrupt in a year."

"When I get to Israel, we will have an official meeting and sit down and decide what we both think is fair. Is that all right with you?"

"Mr. Singh can't wait … cough … cough."

"What? What's up with the fake coughing?"

"It's nothing. You clearly saw Mr. Singh had run out of mints. I will now prepare for lunch and Sven just pulled up. Should I put everything out on the picnic tables so they can eat during your meeting?"

"Yeah, that will work. Oh, and Mr. Singh? I spoke with Dr. Jacobie. That was an amazing diagnosis of the Ambassador you came up with. You were dead on."

"If you are to converse with Dr. Jacobie again, please ask him who precipitated the discussion and who agreed with whom."

"Yeah, that's right there at the top of my list of things I got to do today."

"And Jack—"

"Yes, Mr. Singh?"

"May I anticipate that our contract negotiation in Israel will not include any further vulgarity?"

"Well, that would be darn right inappropriate, Mr. Singh. I can hear the guys are up. I'll help you take the plates out to the tables."

Jack slides Mr. Singh's mint container into his pocket and the two men carry out the lunch trays to the picnic tables.

Sven is in the containment room, watching over the Ambassador.

Dr. Jacobie, Joshua, Peter, Rick and Carl are now enjoying Mr. Singh's delicious lunch.

Owen is sleeping soundly, unaware of the going away gathering.

Jack is sitting anxiously and, growing irritable, he excuses himself from the men. He goes and checks the equipment he will be bringing tonight—it's the fourth time he's double-checked today.

Satisfied he finally has everything in order, Jack returns to join the group for the mission's final meal. Jack is just too amped to sit down, so he grabs a plate and a few sandwiches and some of Mr. Singh's delicious homemade coleslaw. Once his plate is full, he begins to address the men while standing.

"I hope everyone is enjoying Mr. Singh's lunch. As I will be seeing you all back in Israel in the coming days, I'll make this quick."

"After lunch, I want everyone packed and in the limo within an hour. The Ambassador's plane is fuelled and ready to take you all home."

Mr. Singh interrupts, "And Leon."

"Yes, Mr. Singh, Leon, too."

"I'm going to eat in my bunk and then take a nap. Thank you gentlemen for everything you have done. If you have any questions, Joshua or Peter, you can ask the doc when you're in the air."

"Any questions?"

The men are all quiet and a little disconcerted, but remain silent.

"Thank you, and have a good flight."

Jack enters his pod and gently closes the door behind him.

Chapter 20

THEY ALWAYS CHOOSE THE GUN

Jack managed to get a few hours' sleep. Over the hum of the generators, Jack was not able to hear the crew pack up and leave.

His only concerns when he went to bed were Joshua and Peter. Men who had pledged to stay with the Ambassador at all costs.

If it had been Mohammed and Noa here instead, Jack would have had to come up with another strategy to get the group to leave.

Jack determined his final comments to be austere and maybe a little hard hearted. But it was imperative that his group of friends were out of Arlington and beyond reproach when the final die was cast this evening.

Jack gets dressed and leaves his pod.

Owen woke up an hour earlier and, having made himself breakfast already, is now watching TV.

"Morning, Owen."

"Hi, Jack. I see everyone has left."

"Just us and Sven left, kid."

"And the Ambassador, Jack."

"Right. How is he? Did you check on him?"

"When I got up, I checked everywhere. I thought you were all playing some daft game of hide and seek."

"The Ambassador?"

"Sven gave him too much bakery shit. He's got a bucket full of puke and blood beside him, but he did manage to fall asleep."

"So, Jack, do you think we might have a chance to talk for a minute?"

"Don't worry, kid, we'll go over everything in a couple hours. You will be joining me tonight. I have all of our gear set and ready to go."

"That's good, Jack, thanks for including me. But, what I wanted to talk to you about is of a more personal nature."

"Are you up for what needs to be done tonight, Owen?"

"I'm with you 100 per cent, Jack."

"Good, then we can start right now by checking the warehouse. If Sven and Ian did their job right, when this place implodes, all that will remain is an empty lot of dust. Can I take it you're familiar with military ordinance?"

"I've helped rig a few bombs, yeah, Jack."

"Not like the shit Sven has rigged up. You check the outside, I'll check in here. You're looking for continuation in the prima cord flow, all right?"

"I got it, Jack."

Jack and Owen spend the next hour inspecting Sven's work.

"Well, how did it look?"

"Impressive, Jack. The IRA should borrow Sven for a month."

"I thought you're done with that shit, kid."

"I am Jack, I'm just thinking about Ian."

"If I ever had confidence in a man Owen, it's Ian."

"It's just that when he left, he made a vow to me that he would have that shite 'peeler' tag dropped back in Ireland."

"You never did tell me what happened with that. Maybe someday?"

"I was seeing a girl and her da was a member of the real IRA and he just didn't like me. Next thing I hear, I'm being falsely accused of working with the peelers, end of story."

"Did you love her?"

"That's the shite of it. She just liked to fuck and a lot of us. I just happened to be the unlucky bastard the old man chose to use as an example."

"That sucks, kid. Did you ever have a real girl-friend there?"

"There was one girl I really fancied, but I was always too afraid to ask her out. When I saw your Debra for the first time on your front doorstep, well, I guess she made me think of home."

"Well, that's too bad, Owen. All right, I want you to take everything out of Roger's car and put it into the back of the rental van. And, kid, don't touch the vials."

"You got it, Jack."

Jack walks over to check on Sven and the Ambassador.

"How long has he been sleeping, Sven?"

"He's been out a couple of hours."

"Here you go, Sven."

"Keys?"

"Last rental car here, kid, and your ride home."

"What about the Ambassador?"

"He'll be fine, Sven. Owen and I will watch him."

"Can I ask you something, Jack?"

"No, kid, just go pack. The gate is unlocked so if you could be gone in fifteen, I would appreciate it."

"I was gonna ask if I could take the rest of Mr. Singh's sandwiches."

"Ha, ha, always the soldier, Sven. Have at it, just leave me and Owen one each—it's going to be a long night."

"Sven, I have a place for you in Israel, if you ever change your mind."

"Sorry, Sarge, too far away from my family"

"How about LA in a year?"

"Will Roger be there?"

"Fuck, I hope not."

"See ya, Jack."

Sven leaves the containment room and is packed and off of the site in fifteen minutes. Jack, Owen, and the Ambassador are all that remains of the crew.

Jack leaves the Ambassador alone and walks outside to check on Owen's progress.

"The van looks good," he says. "Arlington's own Atmos Energy."

"Your uniform is in the back, Jack. What do ya think of mine?"

"You're a natural, kid. Did you switch the plates?"

"Done. What do I do with the rental plate?"

"Just leave it in the back. We'll put it back on after the job."

"Aren't we gonna blow the van?"

"If we leave the car at the ranch, that's our only ride home, kid. We want Arlington's finest here all night, not putting out a van on fire somewhere else."

"Makes sense. What if we do end up diching the van? Shouldn't we bring some shit to blow it up? And what about the rental contract? Are we going to be okay on that?"

"You got a lot of questions, Owen. You getting nervous?"

"I'm fine, Jack. I just got something else on my mind."

"Well, clear your fucking head, kid. I can easily make this a one-man job. Harvey didn't put the van in my fucking name for Christ's sake. Are you satisfied now?"

"I'm fine, Jack. Fuck. I think the question is are you the one getting nervous? That's the fucking question."

"Yes, I am Owen. I'm nervous about what you want to fucking talk to me about. Now grab whatever sandwiches and water bottles are left and put them in the van. Then come and help me pack the gear."

"I loaded everything as soon as I got up. It's all there, take a look."

Jack opens the back of the van and everything is in place and packed into two separate piles. The items are even packed in order of Owen's estimated timed usage for tonight. Jack looks at all the equipment laid out and is thinking that is exactly how he would have arranged it himself.

"I got a question for you, Owen."

"Shoot."

"Do you ever, you know, check things more than once, even after you've already checked a couple times?"

"Are we talking about your OCD?"

"OCD, fuck you!"

"I was awake back at your house listening to you lock the front deadbolt. What was it? Seven times you clicked it open and closed."

"It was only four, asshole."

"As long as it doesn't affect you tonight, Jack, I'm good with it. As long as when we penetrate the house you don't ask for a few do-overs until you get it right. I'm thinking the Zurichs won't have any patience for that."

"You're hilarious, kid. I gotta hit the head."

As Jack is walking away, he once again mutters loud enough for Owen to hear him, "Date my daughter, like that's ever gonna happen."

This time Owen is not too upset. He's thinking he just may be wearing the old man down.

When Jack returns to the kitchen, Owen is leaning against the counter, browsing the *Texas Observer* newspaper.

"Are you ready, Owen?"

"Let's do it, Jack."

"Give me about twenty minutes, and then drive the van to the front of the warehouse and keep the gate wide open. When I'm done in here, I'll drive the car around to meet you. You got the map?"

"Yes."

"But you're not going to fall behind, right?"

"As long as you don't put the 'Stang into third gear, I'll keep up."

"You charge the headsets?"

"Done."

"Okay, see you outside in twenty."

Owen leaves for the van and Jack makes his last walk to the containment room. Upon entering the room, Jack can see that the Ambassador is awake. He has managed to put his glasses on and has raised the bed by himself.

"Is it time, Armen?"

"Yes, Sir, it is. Are you sure this is what you want, Sir?"

"Do it now, Armen, please."

Jack leans forward and gently pulls down the Ambassador's covers, then unbuttons the top four buttons of his pyjama top.

He removes Mr. Singh's mint container from his pocket and places it on the table next to him. He opens the container and pulls out one of the glass vials and places it into the Ambassador's hand.

The Ambassador quickly crushes the vial, cutting both his thumb and forefinger in the process. Jack quickly wipes up the broken shards of glass and hands the Ambassador a tissue for his fingers.

Jack covers the Ambassador back up with his blanket and both men are watching each other intently.

Within a moment, the already heavily medicated Ambassador displays a minor reaction to the bite and subsequent penetration.

"How long now, Armen?"

"The neurotoxin will have you paralysed in about fifteen to twenty minutes, Sir."

Jack stands up and walks over to the morphine drip. He turns it up to its highest level of release.

"Do you have any final words, Sir?"

"I always thought I would die in Israel, but I think it is fitting that, as I was reborn in Texas so many, many years ago, this be my final resting place. What do you think, Armen?"

"I think it's a hell of a way to go, Sir." Jack pauses and asks, "Do you have any regrets, Sir?"

"My only regret, Armen, is what I put you through with that young lady. I would die a peaceful man if you told me she was all right."

"I'll know for sure in a couple of hours, Sir, but I think she may still be alive."

"Thank you for that, son ..."

The Ambassador loses the ability to keep communicating with Jack. His final thoughts slowly take him back to the narrow farmhouse pathway in the Ukraine. He is back there again, standing alone in front of everybody as an eight-year-old child.

His mind has him again surrounded by Nazi soldiers, complicit Ukrainian farmers and the long-forgotten victims of the day.

Wilhelm, resembling any other small Ukrainian child is spotted by a German soldier and, with a smile on his face, the soldier waves at Wilhelm and shouts in German, *"Kommen, kommen bei der party."*

The young girl that had been transfixed in Wilhelm's mind for the last seventy years was in fact an illusion, created by Willhelm's own mind as a coping mechanism. It was Wilhelm himself who had been chosen to join the killing party, and it was Wilhelm himself who was picked up and carried forward in front of the group. And it was Wilhelm himself who was left to choose the next man to be tortured and killed.

Wilhelm was forced to stay for the remainder of the executions and quietly slipped away at the end

It was one day of many. A day of demonstrative horror and inconceivable violence. A crime against the very fabric of human dignity.

These were the Ambassador's final thoughts as he passed away.

Jack leans in to check his vitals and gives the Ambassador a final kiss on the forehead and says, *"Baruch Dayan emet."*

He then walks over to Sven's timer and sets it for six minutes. Within four minutes, he and Owen are two blocks away and are waiting for the explosion.

Jack steps out of the Mustang and both he and Owen go stand behind the van.

Jack checks his watch against the setting sun. *Boom.* Right on time.

"Let's go, kid. It's going to get busy around here real soon."

Jack and Owen climb back into their respective vehicles and in twenty minutes, they are on the single-lane road leading to the Zurich estate.

"Ya got me, Owen?"

"Loud and clear, Jack."

"This is a single-lane road the rest of the way, buddy. We'll stop two miles before the Zurich entrance and get geared up."

"You got it, Jack."

Another ten minutes down the road, Jack and Owen are just approaching the Clement property.

"Hey, Owen?"

"Yeah, Jack."

"We'll slow down a bit as we pass this next property. They're new buddies of mine. There's a girl named Tammy that lives there, maybe you could ask her out. Holy shit… hang on, kid… don't rear-end me."

Jack slams in the Mustang's clutch and shifts down to first gear. Owen was able to hit the brakes and stop within inches of Jack's bumper, sending everything in the back of the van flying to the front.

As Jack is talking to Owen, Stu Clement comes racing onto the street, chased by his brother, Jeffrey. Jeffrey is running with three Budweisers still held together in their plastic six-pack casing. Just as Stu reaches the street, Jeffrey throws a full can of Bud and hits Stu squarely in the back of the head. It knocks him out cold and he's now lying in the middle of the road, bleeding.

"You okay back there, Owen?"

"I'm fine, but our gear is all fucked up. What the fuck just happened, Jack?"

"Fuck, we don't need this right now. Hop on out and we'll get Stu off the road."

"Who?"

Jack and Owen get out of their vehicles and help the now semi-conscious Stu get to his feet.

"What the fuck, Jeffrey? Are you trying to kill him?"

"Who the fuck are you? And get away from my brother, ya piece of shit."

"We met yesterday, Jeffrey. Remember the guy with the dog shitting on your lawn? Stu asked if I wanted to take Tammy for a spin for fifty dollars."

"Oh yeah, I remember you now. I knew you'd be back. Tammy, get your ass over here, girl, we got a paying customer."

"Coming, Jeffrey."

"So what the fuck, Jeffrey? Why are you trying to kill your brother?"

"He took my last piece of jerky, that's why."

"You okay, Stu?"

"Yeah, I'm fine. Don't hurt but a little."

"Okay, mister, show me the fifty bucks and you can lean me against that tree right there," says Tammy.

"Owen, get in the van and pull up 100 yards, now, please," Jack says into his headset.

"So Stu, Jeffrey, Tammy, I'm gonna have to take a rain check on that offer, but I'm gonna stop by on my way back, I promise."

"What's a rain check, shit-fuck?"

"It means I'll be back later, Jeffrey. Now help Stu get some ice on his head, and Tammy?"

"What?"

"Some of those dogs look like they could use some water."

"Rain gives them all the water they need, asshole."

"Okay, folks, see you in a bit."

Just then, Jack spots a bunch of headlights coming toward them, and fast.

"Uh, Jeffrey, are you expecting company tonight?"

"Yeah, we're having a party tonight. You can stop by if you want."

"Oh, don't worry about that, Jeffrey. We'll be back. Save me a hit of meth, will ya?"

"Fuck you, man,. You got to bring your own or you gotta pay."

Jack and Owen are back on the road and stop two miles before the Zurich estate entrance.

"Nice friends, Jack. Remind me of some mates from back home."

"Let's get geared up, Owen."

"You want to get all sweaty in the van for four or five hours?"

"Fuck that. We're going in now, kid."

"Do you normally run missions by the seat of your pants, Jack?"

"Nothing's normal about this job, kid. Anyway, I want to get back in time before they're all too wasted to make it a fair fight."

"Fuck me… I'm done trying to figure this day out. Whatever you say, Jack."

Jack and Owen get geared up and Jack finally tells Owen the plan.

"Best as I could tell on my trip up here yesterday, they haven't installed the road sensors yet. So, we are going to drive right up to the front gate. We'll take out whoever pops their head out and walk right in through the front door.

"The darts we're using will penetrate their leather coats and knock 'em out for a good four hours. You see any giant motherfucker, you shoot him twice."

"Here's a picture of Karl Zurich—you do *not* shoot him. Him, I need to talk to. Do you understand me, Owen? You shoot him and we're waiting here for four hours."

"What about the alarm system?"

"I got that covered, and we'll take care of that right now."

Jack pulls out his cell and places a call to Gordon in Israel.

"Hello, Jack."

"Hi, Gordon. Is he on the line?"

"It's me, Sir."

"Okay, Salcom, do your thing."

Jack looks over at Owen and gives him a wink.

"It's done, Sir. Their system is down."

"For how long, Salcom?"

"Uh, until they buy a new one."

"Thanks gentlemen, gotta run."

"Okay, Owen, keep your window down and we'll just tap whoever pops out all the way to the front door. You then check all of the structures and tag anyone you see."

"What if they're kids?"

"That's what the plastic cuffs are for. Just strap them to something and we'll let them go on our way out."

"When you're done outside, I want you to just sit on the front deck and have a cool lemonade."

"How do you know they have lemonade?"

"Have you not being paying attention, Owen? We're going to a ranch in Texas—they've gotta have lemonade.

"And Owen, in spite of how we are breaching, we're going in real quiet, so stay off the comms unless it's an emergency. Once I clear the house, I need thirty minutes. Then we're going to a party."

"What if someone gets a shot off?"

"These are cowboys, Owen. If you let anyone get a shot off then you can say goodbye to that 'talk' you want to have with me."

Jack and Owen start their vehicles and make their way into the ranch.

Seven minutes later, Owen is sitting on the front deck drinking some cool lemonade.

Owen has company—a teenage niece and nephew of the family who happened to be sitting on the front deck at the time of the breach. As the incident was unfolding before them, they thought it was best to just remain seated during the ordeal.

Owen felt it wasn't necessary to tie them up after assuring them that nobody was, or would be, hurt. So they are all sitting quietly enjoying their drinks.

Jack has made his way through the main floor of the house and is now sitting in Karl Zurich's office. Karl Zurich is sitting behind his desk.

As soon as Jack entered the office, he checked the desk and the immediate area for any hidden weapons. He found a loaded .44 Magnum in the right-side desk drawer.

"You were smart for not going for that gun, Mr. Zurich," Jack says. "Who's upstairs?"

"No one."

"Who's upstairs, Karl?"

"Debbie and her caretaker."

"Do you know who I am?"

"The asshole who is here to finish off my daughter, I expect."

"And how is Debbie?"

"She's paralysed from the neck down."

Jack reaches into his pocket and pulls out Mr. Singh's mint container. He places it on the desk in front of Karl.

"Open it."

Karl opens the container and finds the two remaining glass vials inside.

"What is this supposed to be?"

"The dead-looking little bastards inside are regenerated with simple fresh oxygen. One of these things bit Debbie on her chest in Argentina. I have to apologize, but I really don't know much more about them, other than don't break the glass."

"What I do know is that, with your financial resources, maybe you could have them analysed and use them to come up with some sort of an antidote for your daughter."

"Why are you doing this?"

"I'm writing the wrongs of a very dear but misplaced man. He's dead now, so no further harm will come to you or your family."

"Why should I believe you?"

"'Cause you're not dead. I am, however, going to have to knock you out for a few hours because it is very important to me that I speak with your daughter."

"Just promise me you won't hurt her."

"I promise you on my own daughter's life, Karl."

"Stand up. I hear the thigh is the least painful place to get it."

Jack unceremoniously pops one into Karl's thigh and makes his way upstairs.

Jack can see a light illuminating from under a door as he walks down the hall. Jack reaches the closed door and says, "I'm coming in, Rafael. Don't do anything stupid."

"I got a shotgun trained at the door, Jack. That door opens, you're dead, asshole."

Jack opens the door and walks right in.

"Hi, Rafael, good to see you again."

"You really are crazy, aren't you, Jack?"

"Put the gun down please, Rafael."

"As you have probably seen out the window, my friend is sitting drinking lemonade on the porch with some well-behaved young people. I would appreciate it if you would join them. I need to speak with Debbie for a few minutes and then we will be on our way."

As Jack entered the room he avoided making direct eye contact with Debbie. She, in turn, has remained silent.

Rafael puts the shotgun on the ground and starts to leave the room.

Jack's recollection of the unconscious beating he took aboard the Miranda at the hands of Rafael comes to the forefront. As the big man passes him he says aloud, "Ah, fuck it," and he pops a dart into Bear's ass.

Jack slowly looks around the room. The upper floor has been modified for Debbie and he can now see her Cadillac of wheel chairs, as well as a plethora of medical devices scattered around the room.

Jack approaches Debbie tentatively, with no preconceived notions about how he is going to be received.

"Look at my tits. With no muscle tone they sit here and flop on my bed. I've been waiting for you, Jack. What took you so long? Nice car, by the way, and that cowboy look … wow.

"I guess you thought you would just come here and sweep me off my feet. Well, here I am, handsome, pick me up and let's go."

"Deb, stop, please."

"What do you want, Jack? Why the fuck are you here and what did you do to my family?"

"I promise you, Debbie, your family will be fine. I gave your dad two of the bugs that bit you in Argentina. With your dad's wealth and contacts he can have them analysed and try to reverse whatever it is that happened to you."

"You happened to me, asshole. You."

"I have to go now, Debbie. I just had to let you know, outside of my own mother, you are the most impressive woman I have ever met. The thought that I would never see you again has been killing me."

"I'm leaving you a Mustang. My dream is that one day you will be behind the wheel."

"Once I'm downstairs, I'll send the kids up. Everyone else will be up in about four hours. Please tell Karl to concentrate on your cure and not on us. We are simply too big and powerful, Debbie. For the sake of you and your family, please understand that."

Debbie looks up at Jack and asks him to raise her bed.

Jack raises Debbie's bed and helps her into a comfortable seated position. Debbie has only one final thing to say to Jack.

"I want you to kiss me goodbye, Jack, and promise me—promise me with your heart and soul—that I will never see you again."

Jack leans forward and goes to give Debbie a kiss on her cheek. At the last second, Debbie moves her lips an inch, connecting her lips with Jack's. They exchange a long, loving kiss.

"Goodbye, Jack."

"Goodbye, Debbie."

Jack starts to speak on his headset to Owen.

"Send the kids upstairs, Owen. We're leaving the 'Stang. Get ready to roll, kid."

Jack and Owen leave the Zurich property, each preoccupied with his own thoughts.

Still at the Zurich ranch...

As soon as Jack and Owen drive off the property, Debbie's niece and nephew come running upstairs to check on Debbie.

"Are you okay, Debbie? Did he hurt you?"

"No, I'm fine. Listen to me—phone your mother and tell her to get here as quick as she can. I want you to go check on everyone. And one more thing, do not phone the police. Do you understand me?"

"We know, Debbie, no one is to know you're still alive."

"Well that's gonna change, kids, but for now, just do as I say."

The kids leave the room, leaving Debbie alone.

Debbie, whose thoughts are racing a mile a minute, has never felt as helpless as she does right now. She can't stop thinking about seeing Jack again. She is looking down at her toes when the blanket moves above her right foot. Remarkably... Debbie felt it.

In front of the Clement property...

"We're here, kid."

"Fuck, are you kidding, Jack? I don't want to party with these assholes."

"I only have one request, Owen. If you leave this van for any reason—and I mean, *any* reason—you and I will never have that 'talk' you've been pressing me so hard for."

"All right, Jack, are you at least going to tell me what the fuck it is that we're doing here?"

"Saving the world, kid."

Jack exits the van in front of the Clement property. As he is stretching his body, he is recalling all of the shit he has had to endure since his Argentinian "vacation."

Owen, who is just now figuring it out, rolls down the window.

"You know there are half a dozen dudes there, don't you, Jack?"

Jack looks back at Owen and just smiles as he walks toward the party...

Scott Mowbrey in his garage 'writing office'
babysitting Mark Mowbrey's dog 'Rocky.'

CPSIA information can be obtained
at www.ICGtesting.com
Printed in the USA
LVOW08s0752150217
524270LV00002BA/3/P